CL

RULES OF THE GAME

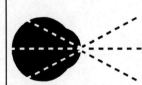

This Large Print Book carries the
Seal of Approval of N.A.V.H.

RULES OF THE GAME

LORI WILDE

THORNDIKE PRESS

A part of Gale, Cengage Learning

GALE
CENGAGE Learning·

Farmington Hills, Mich • San Francisco • New York • Waterville, Maine
Meriden, Conn • Mason, Ohio • Chicago

GALE
CENGAGE Learning

LIBRARY OF CONGRESS CATALOGING-IN-PUBLICATION DATA

Names: Wilde, Lori, author.
Title: Rules of the game : a Stardust, Texas novel / by Lori Wilde.
Description: Large print edition. | Waterville, Maine : Thorndike Press, 2016. | © 2015 | Series: Thorndike Press large print romance
Identifiers: LCCN 2015047574| ISBN 9781410488572 (hardcover) | ISBN 1410488578 (hardcover)
Subjects: LCSH: Large type books. | GSAFD: Love stories.
Classification: LCC PS3623.I536 R85 2016 | DDC 813/.6—dc23
LC record available at http://lccn.loc.gov/2015047574

Published in 2016 by arrangement with Avon, an imprint of HarperCollins Publishers

Printed in Mexico
1 2 3 4 5 6 7 20 19 18 17 16

JODI CARLYLE'S WEDDING CRASHER RULES

Rule #1: Look the Part

Rule #2: Never Use Your Real Name

Rule #3: Fight the Urge to Tell the Truth

Rule #4: What Happens at the Wedding Stays at the Wedding

Rule #5: Do Not Have Sex in the Coat Closet

Rule #6: You Can't Save the Wedding Cake and Eat It Too

Rule #7: Go for the Gusto

Rule #8: You're from Out of Town . . . Always

Rule #9: Have an Exit Plan

Rule #10: For God's Sake Don't Fall in Love

*To Christie Craig. I'm so grateful
for your friendship.
You inspire me!*

CHAPTER 1

Jodi Carlyle's Wedding Crasher Rules:
Look the part.

A year to the day after she'd been dumped at the altar, and two days after her thirtieth birthday, Jodi Carlyle followed the advice of her cognitive behavioral therapist and crashed a wedding.

"You need to do this," Dr. Jeanna had said. "Not only to break free from the shame cycle you can't seem to snap out of, but also to stop being such a rule follower. Good girls finish last."

"You think?" she had asked, trying not to sound snarky. Whenever she snarked, Dr. Jeanna scribbled wildly in her notebook.

"You're not enjoying life." Dr. Jeanna steepled her fingers. "It's time for a change."

Jodi knew that. It was the main reason she'd started seeing a counselor.

That and the fact she was still having

dreams of cheerfully strangling Ryan with a blue garter. He'd left her stranded in front of three hundred wedding guests, wearing a white dress and glass slippers like some deranged Cinderella, while he caught a plane to the Cayman Islands with a knock-kneed stripper named Chrysanthemum Greene and several million dollars embezzled from the Stardust Savings and Loan.

The glass slippers had been Ryan's idea. He'd wanted to drink champagne from one at the reception. He was showy like that.

Hammering the shoes into smithereens on the back steps of the wedding chapel hadn't made her feel any better, so she'd picked up her I'll-show-you-attitude that Mom sometimes called stubbornness and turned those wedding day lemons into lemonade. She'd marched back into the church to announce she'd been jilted and that she was turning the reception into an impromptu fund-raiser for Dallas Children's Hospital. She'd then gotten on social media to ask people who'd sent gifts, but were unable to attend, if she could liquidate them for charity and received an overwhelmingly positive response. In the end, what could have been a pity party turned into a celebration of life, and she'd raised seven thousand dollars for the hospital.

Take that, Ryan Amos.

But even though she was proud of her in-the-moment triumph, whenever she heard the word "wedding," or came across anything bridal-related, her knees would lock up and her stomach would quake to the point where she had to brew herself some ginger tea.

Believing it would soothe her wounds, well-meaning friends and relatives couldn't resist the mantra, *It's better to have loved and lost than never to have loved at all,* but if one more person said that to her, Jodi swore she was going to lose it.

And that bothered her.

A lot.

She hated being controlled by fear. Hated that by doing so she effectively allowed Ryan to win.

It wasn't until her younger sister Bree-anne asked Jodi to be the maid of honor at her Valentine's Day wedding that Jodi knew she had to do something.

Flooding technique, Dr. Jeanna called it. Exposure therapy.

The doctor had started small, asking Jodi to hold wedding-related items — garters, invitations, Jordan almonds — until she could do it without breaking into a cold sweat. Slowly, Dr. Jeanna exposed her to

11

more and more stimuli until she declared Jodi ready for the coup de grâce.

Which meant attending . . . *ahem* . . . crashing a wedding.

In retrospect, if she'd been smarter, she wouldn't have chosen one of the most high-profile weddings in Texas. But when it came to New Year's Day weddings the pickings were kind of slim. And she'd always wanted to see inside the Grand Texan Hotel when it was decked out for the holidays. Unfortunately, she failed to fully consider the consequences of intruding upon the union of the lieutenant governor's son to the daughter of Betsy Houston, one of the new owners of the Dallas Gunslingers baseball team.

Hindsight was most definitely an ironic bitch.

At noon on January first, her last guest of the season checked out of Boxcars and Breakfast, her unique B&B made from old boxcars that she'd renovated herself. And she'd closed the business until the following Monday. Early January was her slowest time of year and she didn't have a single booking for the upcoming weekend.

She had four whole days all to herself for the first time since she'd opened the B&B a decade ago.

She waved her only employee, and best friend in the whole world, handyman Hamilton Gee, off on his annual ski trip that she gifted him with as a Christmas bonus. She packed up her suitcase, and told a little white lie to her close-knit family about where she was going — a white lie she promptly felt guilty about — and drove from her hometown of Stardust two and a half hours west to Dallas.

Jodi checked into a Motel 6, just down the road from the Grand Texan, and spent an hour doing her makeup. She dressed in a slinky emerald ball gown she'd gotten for seventy percent off at Neiman Marcus's online post-Christmas sale. Even on deep discount it was the most expensive, and the most elegant, garment she'd ever owned, including her own wedding gown. May it rest in shreds.

Yes, buying the dress meant spending two weeks' revenue, but if she was going to pull this off, she had to look the part. Which entailed, besides the dress and a sleek new hairstyle, arriving in a limousine. Although, to save money, she planned to grab a taxi back to the Motel 6 when the wedding was over.

And everything was trucking along according to plan.

The limo pulled up outside the Grand Texan at six-forty, twenty minutes before the ceremony was set to begin. The valet who helped her from the car cast approving glances her way. When she pressed a twenty-dollar bill into his palm, his smile widened.

A million white twinkle lights turned the hotel into a fairy-tale castle. The hum of voices, the rustle of skirts, the whistle of the bell captain buzzed the air with festivity. A modicum of slush from the New Year's Eve snow flurry dampened the ground, the dropping night temperature threatening to freeze it to ice.

Jodi drew her coat tighter around her shoulders, clutched the silver beaded evening bag she'd surreptitiously borrowed from her parents' antique store, Timeless Treasures, and jockeyed for position in the middle of the well-heeled crowd streaming toward the front entrance.

The hotel itself was as impressive as she imagined it would be — Texas elegance in all its swaggering, staggering glory. She tried not to stare as she moved along with the throng. If she hoped to pull this off she could not look like what she was, a small-town girl in over her head.

She could do this. She *would* do this. Hell. High water. Whatever. She'd been stuck in neutral for far too long. Time to fully shake off Ryan's betrayal.

Up ahead lay the pavilion where the ceremony was being held. A columned altar had been set up beneath the domed ceiling decorated in golden angels, white poinsettias, and silver bows. Security guards funneled guests over stone footbridges wreathed with more twinkle lights, and flanked by sparkling fountains.

One of the security guards met her gaze, and narrowed his eyes.

She heard the thundering of her heart, felt it slamming against her chest. Oh no! Had he seen right through her? Had she made some kind of serious country-bumpkin faux pas? Darn it, busted before she ever got started.

The guard stepped toward her.

She broke out in a cold sweat.

Stay calm.

Jodi moved behind a tall man, shrank her shoulders, and willed herself to sink down until she was invisible. The way she used to do when she was four years old and her mother, Vivian, left her home alone and someone would come to the front door. She'd slip behind the couch and pretend she was something tiny. Vivian had a bad habit of disappearing for days at a time, leaving Jodi with big boxes of Cheerios on the kitchen table, orange juice in the fridge, and the terrifying threat that mean people would take her away if she dared open the door.

Until the day she ran out of cereal and risked opening the door when a knock came. People did indeed take her away, but Vivian had been wrong. They weren't mean. They bought her a hamburger and ice cream, a Barbie and new clothes, and took her to live in a clean place with people who smiled a lot and never hit her or left her alone.

And Jodi never saw her mother again.

In the crowd beside her, a young woman was yammering on the cell phone. Jodi heard the sharp snap of the guard's shoes as he stalked across the floor, and her stomach rolled over.

"Miss," he called. "Miss."

This was it. Busted.

"Miss." The guard's raised voice was insistent and he was so close she could feel his body heat. Why had she picked this wedding of all weddings to crash? Her palms went hot and sticky.

Failure.

She imagined being hauled out of the building, everyone staring and pointing.

Humiliated.

She deserved it. Crashing a wedding was not an above-board thing to do. She might as well throw her hands in the air and surrender. Guilty as charged. Cringing, she turned to face the security guard, and confess.

But he touched the shoulder of cell phone girl. "Miss, could you please turn off your cell phone and put it away?"

Not her. He hadn't been talking to her. Jodi exhaled forcefully, lungs aching from holding her breath, her knees bobbling.

Safe. She was safe.

Whew.

On the other side of the footbridges, the crowd spread out, fanning toward the entrance to a smaller pavilion. Eight bulky men in cowboy hats and dark suits, dark sunglasses, holster bulges underneath their jackets, microphones nestled in their ears, stood sentinel, Arnold Schwarzenegger arms positioned imposingly over broad chests.

Octuplet cowboy Terminators.

Not out of the woods. Not by a long shot. These guys were Texas State security detail.

Jodi slowed. Not at the sight of the bodyguards. She'd expected them.

No, what snatched her breath from her lungs was her first unobstructed view of the

17

altar. It was a heart-shaped archway twined with stargazer lilies opened in full bloom. Stargazer lilies. Ryan's favorite flowers. The damn altar was almost identical to the one she'd stood under a year ago on this same date. The panic she'd come here to squash snaked around her spine, strangled her. She felt so stupid. So foolish.

What were the odds the bride would choose stargazer lilies?

Memories pelted her. Ryan kissing her for the first time beneath the mimosa tree at Boxcars and Breakfast, between the caboose that served as a dining room for the guests and the royal blue Santa Fe Pacific railway car where he'd been staying while he looked for a house to rent in Stardust. The way he'd proposed to her at the best restaurant in town over less-than-stellar bananas Foster. The thrill she'd felt as they planned the wedding, Ryan weighing in on everything — which at the time she'd thought was romantic — but now she understood it was all about control.

Honestly, she found the scent of stargazer lilies nauseating. She'd learned her lesson. No more idealizing love.

Jodi stopped short, giving serious thought to throwing in the towel and going back home, when someone smacked into her.

The impact knocked her off balance, and she stumbled in unaccustomed high heels, fell to her hands and knees with a loud *clop* that echoed off the high domed ceiling. Her purse spun across the polished marble, skidding to a halt at the toes of one of the burly cowboy bodyguards and spilling the contents — lipstick, a hairbrush, pepper spray, condoms. The condoms were a last-minute addition. She hadn't even known why she'd put them in there.

She grabbed for the condoms, anxious to get them out of sight, when a big hand reached from behind her and closed over the packets at the same time a strong, manly arm clamped around her waist and hauled her to her feet.

Her cheeks stung as smartly as her knees.

Wobbling, she snatched the condoms from the anonymous fingers. Heard a soft masculine chuckle. Smoothly, the owner of those fingers retrieved her purse and her remaining belongings. She grabbed at those too, stuffing everything into the purse and out of sight.

Except for the metal skeleton key with the heart-shaped head resting in his big palm. He shifted the key from his palm to his fingers, extended the key toward her.

"Not mine," she said, and finally had the

courage to take a quick peek at his face.

Tall, dark, and handsome, well built, easily topping six feet. Gorgeous. A bone-melting smile. Pearly whites. But of course he had perfect teeth.

Oh crap. She was a sucker for tall, dark, and dashing.

But despite the dapper tuxedo and debonair bow tie, he managed to look rugged and ultra-masculine.

It was probably the beard. Normally, she wasn't a fan, but his beard was thick, full, and neatly trimmed. He looked to be one of those guys who sprouted facial hair easily, each follicle steeped in testosterone. His eyes were sharp as needles too, the luxe color of roasted cocoa beans. He carried himself with the bold air of someone accustomed to both being in charge, and getting his way. Something about him seemed vaguely familiar, but she was certain they'd never met before.

"The key fell out of your purse," he said in a deep voice that sent her knees into a *Pride and Prejudice* swoon.

Okay, she'd borrowed the purse from Timeless Treasures. Maybe the key had been inside it.

Last summer, her sister had given her an antique hope chest with skeleton key locks, but no key that fit. Ever since then, Jodi had been looking for a key that would open the trunk. Maybe this one would do the trick. She wrapped her fingers around the key. The metal was still warm from his body heat.

Knock it off! She was supposed to be getting over Mr. Tall, Dark, and Wrong, not falling for another one.

"You really should look into taillights," he murmured. "Or at the very least, a backup beeper." He paused, his smile deepening into a grin that would have given Cary Grant a run for his money. "Not that I'm complaining. Knocking into you is the most excitement I've had all week."

"Maybe *you* shouldn't have been tailgating." She dropped the key into her purse. She'd been on the verge of apologizing when he'd made that crack.

"Come on, you can't seriously expect any red-blooded male not to tailgate a caboose like that." He craned his head around for a better look at her backside.

Train metaphors. She could so love a man who used train metaphors. Reason enough to get the heck away from him.

"Excuse me." Jodi spun from his reach, more because his comment aroused her than offended her, and she couldn't figure out what *that* was all about.

"I'm sorry. That was a douchy thing to say, but you do have a great caboose," he called after her.

In a desperate bid to quell the blush blooming at the base of her throat, Jodi envisioned stepping into an icicle shower. That cooled her off momentarily until she paused and turned back for another look at the sexy hunk of man. Why was she encouraging him?

"I'm guessing most women fall all over lines like that," she said dryly.

"Most women, yeah." He canted his head, narrowed his eyes, and kicked up the charge on his smile. "But you're not most women, are you?"

Dammit, why did he have to make that sound like such a good thing? Pulse thumping far too erratically, she ducked her head and breezed past the bodyguard, who reached out and snagged her by the elbow on her way past.

"Whoa there, ma'am. Hang on a sec."

She stopped, her heart sliding to her toes.

The bodyguard extended a shovel-sized palm. "Invitation."

Jodi opened her purse to take out the invitation originally meant for her sister Breeanne and brother-in-law to be, Rowdy

Blanton, a manager for the Dallas Gunslingers. She'd fished the invitation out of her sister's trashcan after Breeanne had RSVP'd that she and Rowdy had a prior commitment and were unable to attend the wedding. Jodi's plan had been to try to pass herself off as her sister and hope for the best. But it dawned on her that the invitation had not been her purse when the contents spilled out. Oh no. She must have left it back at the motel.

"Invitation," he repeated.

"I . . . I . . . I . . ." she stammered, still so dazzled by Mr. Tall, Dark, and Smart Aleck she couldn't think of a quick response.

"If you can't produce an invitation, I'm going to have to ask you to turn and head the opposite direction," the cowboy bodyguard said. His tone was pleasant but his eyes said, *Don't even think about bullshitting me.*

"It's . . . um . . ." *Say something.* Why couldn't she think? Why was her brain mushy?

"She's with me." Mr. TDSA handed an invitation to the bodyguard.

The bodyguard waved it away. "Go right on in, Jake."

In a proprietary manner that rubbed her the wrong way, *Jake* took hold of her arm and escorted her toward the pavilion.

Jodi tried to shake him off, but Jake held on tight. "You're on a first-name basis with the security detail?"

"I'm on a first-name basis with a lot of people," he replied.

"Hello, Mr. Popularity." Her tone could have frosted the wedding cake. "How *do* you do it?"

"It's called being nice," he said. "You might look into it."

"I *am* a nice person," she said.

"Sure you are."

"I am. You just rub me the wrong way." *Rub.* In context with this virile guy, it was a perilous word.

"Uh-huh."

"I'm extremely nice, ask anyone."

"Because wedding crashers are known for their highly moral behavior?"

"I'm not a wedding crash—"

"Watch it." He raised a finger. "Nice people don't lie."

She snorted. "Let go of my arm."

He ignored that. His touch sent her body temperature soaring, and she felt both freaked out and intrigued.

"You're welcome, by the way," he said.

She drew her head back so she could glare down her nose at him. "For what?"

"Saving your bacon."

"Thank you," she said. "Now will you please let go?"

"Not until you answer one question."

"What's that?"

"Bride or groom?"

"I don't see —"

"Wrong answer."

"You didn't give me a chance to —"

"If you were bona fide, you would have immediately said either bride or groom without hesitating."

"Fine, bride."

"Too late. You're impersonating a guest."

"How did you know?" she whispered, and glanced over her shoulder. People were staring at them.

"You're gorgeous and alone and you show up at a wedding dressed to kill without an invitation. A first grader could put it together."

"I have an invitation. You intervened before I had a chance to produce one."

"*Do* you really have an invitation?"

"I did. I must have misplaced it."

"Sure you did."

"Okay, I did have an invitation, but it wasn't mine," she admitted.

"A wedding crasher and a thief. Two for two."

"You caught me on a bad day."

"What's your name?" he asked.

"I don't see how that's relevant."

"It would make things easier."

"For what?"

"You know . . ." His everyone-loves-me shrug matched his smile. "Since we're going to be spending the night together."

Her mind called up images of the two of them in tangled sheets, hot, sweaty, sated. Alarmed, she said, "We are not spending the night together!"

That came out louder than she intended and the soft conversation rippling through the crowd instantly stopped as curious gazes swung their way.

"*I* was referring to the wedding reception. Because you're my plus one," he murmured with a wicked gleam in his eyes. "But if you'd like to —"

"No." She yanked against his grip, and finally, thankfully, he let her go.

Cradling her elbow, still warm and tingly from his touch, she dipped her head and rushed to find a seat. He'd gotten her inside the venue, but that didn't mean she had to sit with him.

An usher intercepted her. "Bride or groom?"

"Groom," she said without hesitating, and

the usher seated her.

Jodi plunked down and took a deep breath. Her gaze strayed to the altar. She had dreaded walking into the wedding venue alone with the ghost of her failed wedding a year ago. But somehow, she'd managed to walk into the venue with her head held high and her stomach settled. Thanks to Mr. TDSA distracting her.

She didn't coat check her coat because she had a tendency to get cold, so she slipped it off, draped the coat across her knees, ran a hand over the skirt of her dress to smooth it out, straightened her shoulders, and lifted her chin. So far, so good.

Someone settled into the empty chair beside her. She glanced over to smile at the new arrival and say hello, but saw *him.*

Jake. His name was Jake.

The contrary part of her wanted to resist the attraction, but another part of her — the part that had been in deep freeze for the past year — unfurled, yawned, stretched, and muttered, *Why the hell not?*

"We meet again." The scent of peppermint and pine wafted off him.

"Oh, like you didn't intentionally sit next to me."

"Don't let it go to your head. This was the only seat left on the groom's side," he said.

"I thought you were a friend of the bride."

She shot him a glance. Really, they were still playing that game?

He looked amused. "You never did tell me your name."

She didn't want to tell him that, but neither did she want to compound her sins by lying, so she said, "Hush, the wedding is starting."

Music swelled, the first bridesmaid started down the aisle, the audience turned to watch the spectacle unfold. Love was in the air.

And the infuriating man beside her stretched his arm across the back of her chair like it belonged there.

She glared at him.

Unapologetically, he drew his arm back and gave her an it-was-worth-a-shot grin. "Let me guess. Your name is Jessica."

"Shh."

"I hope it's not Jessica because I dated a Jessica in high school and she left me with a nasty taste in my mouth for the name."

"You're being rude to the bride and groom. And no, it's not Jessica."

"I'm rude? You're the wedding crasher."

She pressed her foot against his toe, meaning that he should shut up, but he must have thought she was trying to play footsie because he angled closer to whisper into her ear. "Is it Jennifer? Nice name, but a little too common."

Snorting, she moved her foot away. Fast.

"Ashley?"

She scowled and pressed an index finger against her pursed lips.

A gray-haired, muscular woman dressed in a tuxedo, who Jodi assumed must be Betsy Houston, escorted the bride down the aisle to the beat of the wedding march. The bride carried a bouquet of stargazer lilies and baby's breath, just like the bouquet Jodi had carried. It was obviously a popular winter bouquet.

Jodi could taste the bride's fear. Feel the panic building in her chest.

Not the bride. *Her.* A year ago, pacing the back of the church, two pairs of Spanx cutting off her circulation, her shoes chafing blisters into her toes, sweat soaking the armpit of her puffy-sleeved, fairy-tale princess dress. Her father trying to comfort her, volunteering to hunt down Ryan and punch him into next year.

How time flew. "Next year" was now.

She took a deep breath, shook out her hands. No worries. No sweat. Ryan was out of her life. She'd gone through hell and back with the federal investigation that followed

29

her ex-fiancé's departure until the authorities were thoroughly satisfied she was as much a victim as the Stardust Savings and Loan.

After the bride passed them, Jake took out his cell phone, tapped something into a text box, and then showed Jodi the screen.

U MARRIED GWENDOLYN?

Gwendolyn.

He was teasing her. How long had it been since a man had teased her like this? Certainly not Ryan, he'd been so serious, all about making money and climbing the corporate ladder. Which at the time she thought was a hopeful indication of their future. She'd thought he was responsible, hardworking just like she was, but it turned out he was a lying, cheating, thieving louse.

She met Jake's dark eyes full of lively adventure, and realized just how anesthetized she'd become. Living in the same small town she was raised in, never stepping outside her comfort zone. That is, until Ryan had pulled what he pulled, making her question not only her taste in men and her ability to read people, but also her entire faith in love. She felt duped, hoodwinked, betrayed, gullible, and irrevocably stupid.

How could she have missed the warning signs? She had been with Ryan for two years and not once had she questioned his moral character.

Why not?

What was wrong with *her*?

Jake nudged her with his knee, tapped the screen of his phone.

U MARRIED GWENDOLYN?

A prudent woman would have lied and said yes, and that would have been the end of it, but damn her, instead of nodding, she shook her head.

Briskly, he rubbed his palms together in a hot-dog gesture.

She should have been annoyed, but she wasn't. In fact, he entertained her. Which was not good.

He held up a bare ring finger.

She shrugged, signaling that she didn't give a rat's patootie about his marital status, but her heart rate quickened.

He typed into the text message box on his phone,

SIT 2GETHER @ RECEPTION?

She gave him a chiding look, and inclined

31

her head toward the altar as the groom took the bride's hand. *Shh.* But she couldn't contain her smile. He was keeping her from thinking about last year. She reached for his phone, and accidentally brushed her knuckles against his muscled thigh.

Immediate sparks burst through her hand. *Holy crap.*

His handsome head jerked up, his eyes so startled that she knew he'd felt it too. Lust, unlike anything she'd ever experienced before, blazed through her body, a crackling forest fire of desire that raced down her nerve endings to lodge brilliantly at the eager spot between her legs.

He chuckled.

Terrific.

He probably thought she'd touched him on purpose. Determined not to let him see how much he affected her, she laser-beamed her gaze on the phone, still nice and warm from his hand, and tapped in,

I'M YOUR +1 WHERE ELSE WOULD I SIT?

CHAPTER 2

Jodi Carlyle's Wedding Crasher Rules:
Never use your real name.

The Dallas Gunslingers' newest cleanup hitter, Jake Coronado, wasn't a psychologist, but he was fairly certain the instant attraction he felt for the gorgeous redhead sitting beside him had a whole lot to do with the fact that she resembled his dead wife.

Reason enough to make his excuses and leave the reception.

She even sounded a bit like Maura, the same low, throaty voice that made him think about things like rich Swiss chocolate, midnight mood music, fine oaken whiskey, and darkened bedrooms.

But unlike his quiet Maura, who never in a million years would have crashed a wedding, this woman was daring, and he was surprised by how much that appealed to him.

Jake rubbed the tip of his thumb along the back of his bare ring finger. Three years since he'd lost her, and while he'd managed to put the bulk of his grief behind him, the joy of being married to the right person was still strong enough to make him want to try again.

But neither could he go falling for the first redhead with cinnamon freckles sprinkled over the bridge of her nose, nor could he devalue Maura's memory by dating a look-alike.

Still, there was nothing wrong with taking in the stunning scenery for an evening.

When he studied her up close, she didn't look as much like Maura as he'd first thought. Sure, they were both natural redheads with incandescent skin, lively blue-gray eyes, and wide, generous mouths. Maura had been slightly taller at five-seven, possessed a strong jaw, oval face, and regal nose. Gwendolyn here had a soft chin, heart-shaped face, and button nose.

She'd refused to give him her real name, telling him Gwendolyn worked just fine for the night, and while he had an urge to badger her for the truth, he quelled it.

He found their seats and was relieved to discover their table was on the fringes of the upper-crust affair near the exit. He wondered why he hadn't been seated with other members of the team, but honestly he didn't care. This was better. He could have Gwendolyn all to himself.

But before they even sat down, Gwendolyn excused herself to the ladies' room. Jake visited with the group of mostly older couples who welcomed him warmly, commented on his addition to the Gunslingers' lineup and then returned to their personal conversations about grandchildren, vacation plans, and retirement portfolios.

After several minutes, Jake got antsy. Gwendolyn had been gone a long time. He checked his watch. Had she ditched him?

Tuxedoed waiters moved through the crowd, serving filet mignon for the carnivores, mushroom ravioli for the herbivores. A live band tuned up for the dance. Nosegays in crystal bowls served as centerpieces. A serpentine line snaked around the tables, destination: open bar.

He waved at a couple of people he knew. Teammates. Their wives. Nodded. Smiled.

After making it big as a major league hitter, Jake had learned to be comfortable in this world of wealth and privilege, even though he'd come from a lower-middle-class home life. His parents had divorced when he was seven, but they'd done their best to keep things civil and had provided him and his two older sisters with a stable upbringing. He prided himself on his ability to navigate any gathering and find a way to fit.

Mom said his talent for blending in stemmed from a need to be adored. Maura, bless her, said it was because he had a natural affinity for people. Truth be told, they were probably both right. Which was why it killed his soul every time he struck out at the plate. He hated disappointing fans.

Gwendolyn — it was starting to bug him now that he didn't know her real name — returned from the bathroom. At the sight of her, happiness pooled in his stomach, spread warmth through his blood like champagne. She'd come back. Perplexed at his excitement, Jake hopped to his feet to pull out her chair.

"What a gentleman," one of the older women at the table muttered to her husband. "Why don't you pull out my chair for me?"

" 'Cause you'd expect it every time," the husband replied. "I don't want to set a precedent."

Hell, pulling out a chair was so easy to do, and if it made a woman feel special, why not do it?

Gwendolyn scooped the back of her dress smooth with her palms as she sat, a half smile touching her lips. She laid her purse on the floor, reached for her linen napkin, and spread it over her lap.

Jake stepped back, and took the opportunity to study her. The green dress fit her as if it had been tailor-made, and maybe it had. No doubt it set her back a nice chunk of change. Whatever she'd spent had been worth it. The dress pushed her breasts up into cleavage that made him want to drool and it nipped her in at the waist, showing off how curvy she was in all the right places.

Her gaze flicked to the bow tie he'd loosened while she was in the ladies' room. "Are you going to stand there ogling all night?"

If she'd let him, yeah, but clearly, she wasn't gung-ho on the idea. Grinning, he took his seat.

The wedding party assembled at the long table at the front of the room. And once they were seated, the food started to flow, interspersed with speeches and toasts. It irritated him that he didn't get a chance to strike up a real conversation with her during the meal. He was determined to get her name and phone number before the evening was over.

While the servers cleared dinner plates, the bandleader took the microphone and announced the first dance. Everyone watched as the bride and groom waltzed for the first time as Mr. and Mrs.

Well, not everyone, *he* was watching Gwendolyn.

Her auburn hair was pinned back at her temples in an elegant upsweep, while the back of her hair curled halfway between her jawline and her shoulders in a half-up/half-down hairstyle that promised refinement on the one hand, untamed passion on the other. A seductive promise that he longed to explore.

But he wasn't going to pursue that line of thinking. He'd had his fill of casual hookups. Once he'd passed the deepest depths of despair following Maura's death, he'd gone through a crazy, anything-goes phase. Over the last three years, he'd traveled from monkish celibacy, to sex-addled, back to celibate again. Now he was ready for a real relationship. And for that, he shouldn't be looking to beautiful wedding crashers who refused to surrender their names.

Why had she crashed the wedding? Was *she* looking for a casual hookup? Considering the condoms in her purse, maybe so.

Maybe she was some nutter who loved weddings and had bouquet-catching dreams of being the next bride. Maybe she wanted to photo bomb a celebrity wedding for Facebook bragging rights. Or maybe she was just a groupie who wanted access to a roomful of baseball players.

Except he wasn't getting any of those vibes from her, and he'd fought off his share of groupies. Other than the wedding-crashing thing, Gwendolyn seemed quite normal.

The music changed from a waltz to a jazzier beat.

Gwendolyn extended her hand. "Dance with me."

He hesitated for a fraction of a second, momentarily surprised by her invitation. He'd thought she was on the verge of bolting. "How do you know I can dance?"

She eyed him up and down. "You look athletic."

"Just because I'm in shape doesn't mean I can dance." Actually, he'd taken ballroom dancing classes with Maura so he could dance at their wedding, but Maura was the only woman he'd ever danced with.

Miss Wedding Crasher just stood there, one hand cocked on her shapely hip, the other palm held out for him to accept, a challenging quirk raising one perfectly arched eyebrow, her long eyelashes lowering seductively.

"I'll dance with you," said one of the older men, the spot on the linen tablecloth surrounding his empty plate dusted with yeast roll crumbs. His glaring wife poked him in the ribs.

Jake settled his napkin on the table. "I got this."

Gwendolyn's soft laughter sounded like snow landing on angel wings.

Jake took her hand and got to his feet in one fluid movement, pushing his chair back with a bump of his knees. He couldn't help noticing the sensuous curve of her breasts beneath the silky fabric of her V-neck dress. She smelled as enticing as she looked, a girl-next-door combination of vanilla and cream that contrasted with the glossy sophistication of her appearance.

It was surreal, the force of instant attraction. Oddly, he found himself resenting her for stirring his desires. He didn't like feeling out of control. He didn't have to dance with her. Or pretend to be her date. He could just walk away.

That was the thing. He did not want to walk away.

Bottom line? He wanted her. His desire

tasted smoky and loamy, lingering more real than the taste of the champagne he'd been drinking. He wanted to taste her. Crush those glossy red lips with his. Take possession of them. One sip of sin and the daydream kindled, burning into his mind the image of long summer nights and sweaty flesh pressed hotly together.

She walked backward, swishing her hips, leading him out onto the dance floor.

Reluctant to draw her too near him for fear she'd steal his heart away, and feeling awkward dancing with someone other than Maura, Jake draped one arm around her shoulder instead of her waist.

The packed dance floor caused her to wriggle closer, forcing him to drop his hand from her shoulder to the middle of her back. He could feel the outline of her bra, and his body hardened. He was in over his head.

"I was right," she murmured, looking up at him through a fringe of auburn hair.

"About what?"

"You're a good dancer."

"I'm out of practice," he said.

"Why is that?"

He didn't want to get into the reason. Especially not with someone he would never see again. "Are you ready to tell me your name?"

"You don't want to tell me why you're out of practice, huh?"

"Not particularly."

"Then I'm not going to answer your question."

"Fine," he said. *Gwendolyn.*

"You've got a stubborn streak."

"Ditto." He glided her around an amorous couple groping each other. She was light on her feet, more graceful than Maura. He quickly squelched that disloyal thought.

"I've got a question for you," she said.

"What's that?"

"Why did you rescue me?"

"My friends say I have a damsel-in-distress complex."

"Do you?"

He shook his head, not so much as an answer, but denying the idea she was a defenseless flower. This woman had grit. "You weren't in distress."

"You're right. If I hadn't gotten into the wedding, what was the worst that would have happened?"

"You tell me."

"I would have been embarrassed."

Now he was doubly intrigued. If she didn't really care whether she'd gotten into the wedding or not, why *was* she here? "Your skin looks pretty thick to me."

And soft, very soft. The only thing that stood between his palm and the bare skin at the small of her back was the silky material of her dress.

He felt sweat gather on his brow and prayed she didn't notice.

She canted her head, her eyes bright, inquisitive. "How come a guy like you isn't married?"

"I'm picky," he said. "How about you?"

Distress flickered across her face for half a second, and she quickly dropped her gaze. "Like you. Picky," she said, but he could tell from the way her lashes fluttered that she wasn't being totally honest.

He leaned down to her ear. "What's his name?"

She stiffened. "Who?"

"The guy who put you off men?"

"I don't want to talk about him."

Ah, so there was a guy. "Whoever he is, the man's a dumbass for letting a woman like you get away."

A faint smile played at the corners of her mouth. He'd pleased her. He hadn't been trying to please her. He was just being honest, and he meant every word.

The band eased into a slower tune, "Kiss You," and more people drifted onto the dance floor, pushing them even closer together.

Their hips touched.

Jake heard her sudden, sharp intake of breath. The trumpet player tugged a mournful note from his instrument and the sound slid right down Jake's spine to lodge in the center of his chest. The resonant vibrations throbbed through him, pounding rhythmically with each squeeze of his heart.

The fruity taste of champagne mixed with the earthiness of his desire. It tasted as right as this felt. His eyes fixed on her raspberry-colored mouth and he found himself wondering what she tasted like. Fruity bubbles no doubt, but beyond that he was certain she would also taste of mystery, spice, and adventure.

A light sheen of perspiration dewed her forehead, matching his heated skin.

He had a snapshot image of her tangled in his bedsheets, her head cradled on his pillow, hair spread out like an auburn fan as she gazed up at him. He imagined her lips puckered in a playful pout, her shapely legs drawn up beneath his long-sleeved white dress shirt, the pink of her perky nipples peeping at him above the open collar.

He shook his head to dispel the vision, but it didn't want to leave, clung sticky like cobwebs.

"Please tell me your name." Yeah, he was begging now, but the suspense was killing him.

"Shh." She pressed an index finger against her lips. "No talking. Just dance."

Frustrated, he propelled her across the floor, the movement carrying her away from him, but he tugged her back, her hair flying out gracefully behind her. They moved as one unit, as if they'd been dancing together all their lives, gliding and swaying, sliding and whirling.

Christ, she was hot.

And that mouth. So close. So kissable.

He'd sworn off one-night stands. Promised himself no more. He was ready for a real relationship and he wasn't going to have that with a woman who wouldn't even tell him her name.

Junk food. She was like junk food. It sounded delicious until you scarfed it up, and got caught in the logy hangover of fat, salt, and sugar.

But dancing with her made him feel alive again in a way he hadn't felt since Maura.

She leaned her head against his shoulder and his heart jumped right up into his mouth. He made a strangled noise, half groan, half sigh. She tilted her chin, angling her head in order to slide him a sideways glance. The movement, languid and curious, was identical to the one Maura used to give him when she was in a romantic mood.

Jake's gut twisted into knots.

A strand of hair fell loose from the pin at her temple and wilted over her face. She reached up to tuck it behind one perfectly shaped ear studded with an emerald earring that matched her dress. Whenever he looked at her, inhaled her vanilla and cream scent, all he could think about was forbidden secrets and starlit nights.

The music shifted into a song with a tempo so slow they were barely moving. He tightened his hand around her waist, breathed in her smell, heard the sound of blood pounding against his eardrums.

He peered into her eyes and caught a glimpse of naked vulnerability that gutted him, and he understood why she was here. She was getting over a broken romance, a love affair gone sour, and this was her version of whistling in the dark.

The woman was hurting . . . and she'd crashed a wedding to blunt her pain and loneliness. Hell, he understood terrible loneliness. Felt it when he was swinging at home plate in a stadium filled with thousands of fans. Felt it when his friends dragged him out of the house to go clubbing or play poker. Felt it when he was by himself in that king-sized bed late at night.

His damsel-in-distress-rescuer instincts kicked into hyper-drive. He wanted to tell her everything would be all right. That she wasn't alone. That he was here and no one would ever hurt her again.

Then just as quickly as it had fallen, she zipped her guard back up, locking herself inside her ivory tower, hiding her emotions beneath those long, thick eyelashes. What would it take to breach that wall?

"I'm thirsty," she said matter-of-factly, stepping away from him so quickly that she almost collided with another couple.

"Whoa." He took her elbow and guided her off the dance floor. Her muscles tensed beneath his fingers and she twisted from his grip.

"I'll get you some water," he offered.

"I can get it myself."

He met her eyes. "Did I do something wrong?"

"No, it was a nice dance. Thank you." She smiled but sounded sad, like there was a rain cloud hanging over her Sunday picnic.

"Am I being dismissed?" he asked.

Her shoulders sagged, and she hoisted a

half-hearted smile. "I'm just tired of dancing."

"Is there something else you'd like to do
instead?" He didn't mean it suggestively,
but he heard the innuendo. He thought
about clarifying, but figured that would
make things worse.

"I'm calling it a night," she said.

"What? You're leaving before the chicken
dance?" Desperate. He was desperate to
keep her here a little bit longer. "Everyone
knows it's bad luck to leave before the
chicken dance."

As if wired into his desperation, the band
launched into the chicken dance polka.

She smiled for real this time. "You set that
up."

"No, but I'll take credit for it if it will get
you to stay." He motioned her toward him.
"C'mon . . ."

Everyone was on the dance floor now,
even little kids.

Jake held out his hand to her. "Please."

She cut her eyes at him, shook her head,
but in good-natured defeat slipped her palm
into his. He edged her back onto the dance
floor. They joined the flock doing the silly
dance. Elbows flew as people misstepped,
laughed, bumped into each other.

When the chicken dance melted into a

slow waltz, their gazes met again. She did not walk away with a chunk of the crowd that left the dance floor. She was intrigued, and unless he missed his guess, she was as stumped by their chemistry as he was.

He spun her around the room. The chandeliers shifted colors, darkening to midnight blue against white side lighting. Jake glanced up and for the first time saw the mistletoe hanging from the ceiling.

Mistletoe.

How could he pass up mistletoe?

He wanted her. That's why he used the mistletoe as an excuse, a pretense to explain his motives instead of what they really were — lust. Plain and simple. Okay, maybe not so plain, because his desire was rocking off the charts. And maybe it wasn't so simple either, because he'd sworn off this kind of impulsive behavior, yet here he was, going for it.

Back on track. He had to get his life back on track. But . . .

He.

Wanted.

Her.

Jake pressed his lips to her forehead. Felt feverish heat. Was it his heat or hers? Both? He tracked his mouth to the slight dip between her eyebrows and the top of her nose.

She tilted her face up to him and he kissed his way down the bridge, her hair brushing against the back of his hand as he cradled her cheek. Kissed the sweet tip. Heard the soft hum of her breath. Smiled. Pressed his lips in the cozy indentation between her nose and her upper lip. Inhaled her feminine fragrance. Felt her tremble.

"Jake," she whispered, and curled her hand into a fist.

To protest? Resist? He didn't give her a chance.

He closed his mouth over hers.

She reached up and knotted her hands at the back of his neck, tugging his head down. He tasted champagne on her lips. He kissed her sweetly, softly, as if it was the first kiss either of them had ever received.

She parted her teeth and a quiet gasp slipped out. He swallowed that gasp. Tasted heaven. Smiled wider.

Gwendolyn.

God, he wished he knew her name.

If he knew her name this could be real. Could be something more. The strangest feeling came over him. There was an undeniable mind-body connection between them. A synergy of energy.

He raised his head, looked down into her eyes.

The waltz came to an end. The band took a break. Microphone in hand, the wedding planner announced the cutting of the cake.

She stepped back from him. "It's been real, Jake, and it's been fun. But like Cinderella at midnight, I've really got to run."

CHAPTER 3

Jodi Carlyle's Wedding Crasher Rules:
Fight the urge to tell the truth.

Her heart was a gun chamber, her blood bullets. Each pump shot a fresh stream of hot fluid circling throughout her body. Jodi snatched up her coat from the back of her chair, grabbed her purse from underneath the table where she'd left it and darted out the nearest exit.

Hurried footsteps pounded behind her. She feared that if she turned, she'd see Prince Charming back there trotting after her with a glass slipper.

No way. No more glass slippers. She wasn't falling for that fairy-tale stuff again. Fool me once, shame on you. Fool me twice . . .

Hurry! Get to the coach before it turns into a pumpkin.

"Wait!"

His urgent voice blinded her. She walked as fast as she dared in high heels. Saw nothing but a blur of walls. She felt dazed, and light-headed — remembering his kiss, that devastating, mind-warping, incomparable kiss that clipped every thread of her self-confidence.

The footsteps slowed but they were still behind her. She picked up her own pace through the lobby, felt rather than saw heads turn as she flew by. She zoomed past the front desk, the concierge, the bell captain, and tumbled, gasping, out of the building near the valet stand.

She trembled there a second, trying to remember where she was, who she was, and what the hell she was doing.

"Taxi?" asked the valet. "Or do you have a car?"

She shook her head.

"Gwendolyn, wait."

She turned and there he was behind her. One half of him hidden in night shadow, the manicured beard cloaking the bottom part of his face, leaving her only a quarter for assessment. He looked at her as if he knew her inside and out, his brandy-brown eye pensive, the black pupil swelling big as a marble. And his powerful mouth — how it tormented and vexed her!

Her lungs emptied. The man shoved every carnal instinct she possessed — and until she met him she hadn't realized she had a lot — into overdrive.

He took a deep breath, inhaled her spent air, and, it seemed, inhaled her.

Her mind was a tumbler, and she was whirling, spinning, fumbling. Unable to find the right combination that would crack open her brain and unlock his spell.

She stepped back. He stepped forward.

"Hey, maybe I've been painting it on a little thick, but please don't let me chase you off. I had fun tonight and it's been a long time since . . ." He waved a hand. "You don't want to hear my backstory. Upshot? I like you. From the minute I spotted you headed into the wedding I wanted to know more about you."

"That's . . . um, nice." This felt way too much like a grand gesture for her comfort, and her heart pounded harder.

"Would you like to go get a cup of coffee and just talk?" He looked like a seven-year-old with one present left to open on Christmas morning, and he hadn't yet gotten what he'd asked for.

"I appreciate the offer." She shook her head. "But I don't think so."

"We didn't have a chance to eat cake, and

I have it on good authority the diner across the street makes the best German chocolate cake in town. Can't end a wedding without cake, right?"

She did love cake, and she couldn't resist the plea on his face. Normally, she would have scuttled out of there, but tonight was special. She'd faced her fear, and not only survived but thrived. As long as she kept this in perspective, she'd be okay.

It was only nine-thirty, but it felt as if the clock was striking midnight. If she stayed she risked losing her mysterious, wedding-crashing, Gwendolyn mystique. But if she left, she'd be turning back into plain old, boring, rule-following, good-girl Jodi.

This evening had been delightful. She wanted to end it on an up note. Wanted to cup the flame of happiness in her hands so that the winds of time didn't blow it out.

For better or worse, instead of telling the valet that yes she did need a taxi, Jodi nodded at Jake.

He slipped his arm through hers and spirited her along to the diner on the opposite side of the road. "Open 24 Hours" buzzed in blue neon. Big, sparse flakes of wet snow spiraled from the night sky, drifting down and landing like sprinkles of kosher salt in his beard.

They exhaled at the same time, their breaths puffing out billowy and white. In unintentional unison, they hunched their shoulders forward against the cold, and he slipped his hand from around her arm to encircle her waist.

Maybe she should have been put off by the proprietary gesture, and she was certainly not going to romanticize this. For sure. Ryan had made her cynical, but as she turned her head and caught the sunshine smile spreading across his face, she felt an amazing surge of hope. Then again, maybe it was just champagne making her loose and malleable.

Either way, it felt *terrific.*

He pushed open the glass door, ushered her inside. A sign instructed them to seat themselves. It was too early for the bar crowd, too late for the bulk of dinner diners. He found them a booth in a far corner near a window away from most of the customers, but a place where they could watch the snowfall. He took her coat, shrugged out of his own, and hung them both on a nearby coatrack.

She sat down, wondering why she was doing this. She did not pick up random men at weddings she'd crashed. Or for that matter, weddings she hadn't crashed. She'd never done anything like this in her life.

A fortyish waitress, with rainbow-colored hair pulled back in long fishtail braid, sidled up to their table. She wore half-inch ear gauges and a mother's ring with three rubies on her right hand as if all her kids had July birthdays. Who knew? Maybe she'd given birth to triplets. Her name tag said Fiona.

"What'll ya have?" Fiona asked.

"Two cups of coffee," Jake ordered. "And a big slice of your German chocolate cake with a couple of forks."

"We're fresh out of German chocolate."

"Dang," Jake said. "We were looking forward to it."

"Honestly" — Fiona leaned forward and lowered her voice as if sharing a state secret — "our pecan pie is even better than the German chocolate. No kiddin'."

Jake met Jodi's eye. "Pie?"

Jodi shivered. They were seated near the window and she told herself that's why she was shivering. That it had nothing to do with the hungry look in Jake's eyes. Nor did the fact that her heart seemed determined to knock a hole in the middle of her chest.

Jake smiled at her as if he knew exactly what trouble her heart was giving her and he was proud of himself for it.

"Sure," she said. "Pie's fine."

Fiona tapped her chin with an index finger, and her cuff bracelet slid down, revealing a tattoo on the back of her wrist of a heart entwined with a rose, one thorn stabbing through the heart and a drop of blood leaking out.

The tattoo stirred memories of her biological mother. Vivian had had a black rose tattooed on her wrist. When Jodi was a child, Vivian would get stoned, and if she were in a nice mood, she'd call Jodi "Freckles" and tell her stories about how she got her tattoos. Jodi liked those times when Vivian would cuddle with her on the couch and there were none of *those* men around. But if Vivian was in a mean mood, she'd poke fun at Jodi. *You look like a carrot and a beet went at it in the backseat of a 1976 Impala. You've got a mouth like a bass. No man is ever gonna wanna marry a neat freak like you. Lighten up. Loosen up. Get that stick out of your butt.*

After Vivian would come down off whatever drug she was on, she would be sweet and apologetic and put strawberry Pop Tarts in the toaster and give Jodi a big hug and say, "There's nothing wrong with being who you are. I'm glad you stack your clothes in neat piles and line your toys up on the windowsill just so. You make me feel normal."

"Are you disappointed about the cake?" Jake asked. "You look disappointed."

"No, not disappointed," she said, and shook off the mood. Why was Vivian haunting her now?

"We could go somewhere else."

The thought of getting into a car with this gorgeous stranger and driving off to parts unknown had her fighting off another shiver of ominous pleasure. Walking across the street to a diner with him was one thing, but leaving with him was another.

"The pie is fine," she said. "I don't normally eat sweets, but tonight I'm feeling —"

"Sinful?" he finished, his eyelids drooping to sexy half-mast.

That wasn't what she was going to say at all, but it was the truth. Taken aback Jodi stared at him. Over the Formica tabletop, the man's disquieting chestnut eyes held hers and the sultry look pushed heat up underneath her skin.

"Why would you think that?" she asked.

"You're a rule breaker."

She laughed at that. If he only knew how far off the mark he was.

"So crashing a wedding is out of character?"

"First time." She toyed with a sugar packet, turning it around and around in her hands to keep from looking at him, felt the sugar shift from one side of the packet to the other.

"Do you intend on making a habit of it?"

"Only if I keep meeting men like you," she teased.

"You're making me jealous," he said, too smooth for her own good. "I don't want you to crash weddings with anyone else but me."

She combed her gaze over him, got an electric thrill. "You've got nothing to worry about. My career as a wedding crasher is over. Besides, why be jealous, you could have any woman you wanted."

"Except for the one sitting in front of me?"

"You don't want me. Not really."

"Why's that?"

"You're attracted to the rule breaker you fancy me to be, but I'm the furthest thing in the world from that."

"Not tonight you're not."

"Tonight was an exception."

"What's got you testing boundaries? Tired of being the good girl?"

"Something along those lines."

"Don't let the jerk who treated you badly cause you to do something you don't really want to do," Jake said.

Sideswiped by his insight, Jodi swallowed, and smiled as if she was unruffled. Was she that transparent? Or was he that perceptive?

"Tonight was for me." She notched up her chin. "Not him."

"Good for you."

Fiona appeared at their table with two cups of steaming coffee and a thick slice of pecan pie topped with a scoop of vanilla ice cream, and oozing sweet goo onto a blue china plate.

"What would you have done if I hadn't claimed you as my plus one?" he asked once Fiona left.

"I don't give away my secrets." She coyly lowered her eyelids. Truth was, she hadn't had a backup plan.

"There's nothing I can do to convince you to tell me your real name?" He sank his fork into the pie, spearing it through the layers of packed pecans to the flaky homemade crust.

"No." She concentrated on doctoring her coffee with a packet of Stevia and a dollop of creamer and avoiding his dark-eyed gaze.

"Why not?"

"Because it doesn't matter."

"We really can't get to know each other if I don't know your name."

"Exactly."

"So this is . . ." He looked hopeful.

"Coffee and pie."

"Pie and coffee." He waited, for what she didn't know, his fork poised over the plate centered on the table between them, a sensual expression smoothing out his handsome features.

Truthfully, she could go gaga over a good-looking man just as easily as the next girl. But she'd learned the hard way that sexy was only skin-deep. What really mattered were honor, loyalty, and kindness. She'd take those qualities over good looks and charm any day of the week. Kindness touched her the most because the trait arose from suffering and the ability to learn from that pain. Kindness developed from getting knocked down and dragging yourself back up again. It sprang from rejection and loss and disappointment. Kindness created a universal bond with others. It was kindness that understood and forgave human frailties. When she saw kindness in a man it triggered something inside her — an ache to be a better person, a longing to learn from the hard lessons of her mistakes, a desire to bask in the glow of a man who cast such a bright light.

She saw it in Jake — in the depth of his dark brown eyes fringed with thick black lashes. Looking into those magnetic eyes she wanted to tell him everything, confess her sins, and find absolution in his embrace. But she'd lost the ability to trust her own judgment, much less a gorgeous man.

Who was she kidding? She didn't know a thing.

Disturbed by her thoughts, Jodi dug into the dessert, using a spoon, making sure she got a bite of ice cream along with every bite of pie.

He sat watching her.

"What?"

"It's fun watching you eat. I noticed how you divvied things up when we were eating at the reception."

She felt the need to explain. "I like things to come out even."

He raised an eyebrow. "Even?"

"Whenever I eat I want a bite of everything on the plate in one mouthful."

"Amuse-bouche?"

"Yes." She smiled because he knew the term. "The perfect bite."

"A lot of people are quirky about food."

"I have a sister who eats everything separately. She'll eat all her meat, and then she'll move on to the potatoes, then the beans. Drives me crazy."

"Why?"

"Too one-dimensional."

"You like symmetry."

"I suppose." She wrinkled her nose, considering that. "I like things I can count on."

"What do you do when a meal comes in courses and you can't even out the bites?"

"I hold on to the first course until the second course arrives."

"What happens if one helping of food is smaller than another and you run out of one helping first?"

"I never run out because I plan ahead, and I divide the smaller serving item into smaller pieces."

"What if there's a big gap in proportions and you can't stretch the serving of one food to match the others?"

"I stop eating."

He leaned back in the seat. "Fascinating. I never analyzed how I ate."

"You're haphazard," she said.

"That sounds bad."

"Actually, it's good. Means you're not OCD about food."

"You're OCD?"

"No. Maybe. Not bad. A little. About food." She lifted one shoulder, to show she wasn't loony, but simultaneously fiddled with the necklace at her throat. "Also about locks. I recheck locks a lot."

"With that skill you could be a prison guard." He took a sip of coffee, and a scalawag grin claimed his face. "Are you a prison guard, Gwendolyn?"

"It's a career path I never considered, but now that you bring it up . . ." she teased.

"What *do* you do for a living?" he asked.

"Shh. I'll never tell."

"I'm —"

She cupped her palms over her ears. "Please, I don't want to know."

"How can I get to know more about you if we don't swap stories?"

"I just told you my weird fixation about making food come out even and that I rechecked locks. What more do you want?"

"It's not enough," he said, staunch-eyed.

"I could just get up and walk out. Leave you with half a pie to eat," she threatened, but didn't mean it.

He reached out a hand to cover hers. "Don't go."

His touch shoveled heat through her bloodstream like coal into a furnace and he held her gaze a few seconds too long, a clear sexual signal. She could hang on to it, or bounce her gaze away, deflecting the invitation in his eyes.

She hung on. Uh-oh.

The snow and the wind, the cold whispering against the windowpane, the wink of Christmas lights on their last hurrah of the season, the pecan pie, Blue Bell ice cream, hot coffee, his handsome face cast the diner in a Hallmark-moment-greeting-card-snow-globe-Hummel-figurine perfection.

"Give me one good reason to stay."

"You can't resist my magnetic charm?" he asked, lifting hopeful eyebrows, his smile turning over easy.

Too true, but she wasn't about to admit it. No doubt that grin got him laid left and right, and she refused to add another layer to his ego.

He ran a thumb over her knuckles. Jodi felt the now familiar heart surge again and sank her teeth into her bottom lip, but she didn't move her hand.

Someone put a song on the Wurlitzer. Alycia Miles sang in a smoky bedroom voice.

"This song is too sexy," she said, her hand growing so warm she could have used it as a cookstove. "A diner should play songs like 'Rock Around the Clock.' "

"I like this song."

She did too. Just not in this context when she was already feeling susceptible. "You like R&B?"

"Love it. I go to the Sweet Note a couple of times a month," Jake said, referring to a downtown rooftop nightclub that was one of Dallas's best-kept secrets. Jodi had only heard of it because her youngest sister, Suki, frequented Dallas hotspots. "I go with friends and we sit in the back listening to up and coming artists, taking in the night skyline and drinking aged scotch —"

"And going home with some pretty young thing on your arm."

His eyes darkened and his smile vanished. "Not anymore. New rule. These days, I always go home alone."

"Always?" Jodi couldn't believe she'd asked.

"Lately. But for you, Gwendolyn . . ." He swept a stare over her that singed her from the inside out. "I'd break the rules."

Quickly, she glanced out the window toward the Grand Texan, and forced herself to breathe slowly and deeply. The man sure knew how to charge a woman up.

From the side entrance of the hotel, she saw the bride and groom dash out, guests lined up on either side of the walkway throwing rice or birdseed, it was hard to tell in the dark. The groom had a tight hold on the bride's hand and she was smiling like all her dreams had come true.

Jodi shut her eyes. Emotions coursed through her body, pounding against her temple, broadcasting along her nerve endings. Somewhere, a coffee cup rattled and settled. She opened her eyes.

Jake was watching her, measured and assessing.

He'd completely undone his bow tie. He'd raked a hand through his hair, mussing it. His eyes were more complicated than straight brown, she realized, a dark yellow tint hidden in the depths that she hadn't noticed before. Murky amber.

She should go.

"What do you do for fun when you're not crashing weddings?" he said as if he was planning a future date.

"I don't have much free time," she said quite honestly.

"Ah," he said. "A workaholic."

"You're fishing," she said. "I'm not telling you what I do for a living."

"Guilty." He chuckled and held up both hands. "The truth is, *Gwendolyn,* I like you and I want to see you again."

She was flattered, but she wasn't at a place in her life to encourage him. It was time for her to find out who she was alone. "Another time, another place . . ."

He looked confused. She imagined women did not often turn him down. "That's it? No chance?"

"I don't want to give you false hope," she said kindly, ignoring the thrust of her heartbeat as it sped up.

He changed the subject and they talked for a while about safe things, movies, books, hobbies, favorite vacation spots, and favorite cuisines. She was surprised to discover they had a lot in common. Neither one of them cared for New Orleans, fried pickles, August, politics, sand in their shoes, garden gnomes, sun-dried tomatoes, or aluminum siding. They both loved caramel popcorn, waterskiing, October, farmers' markets, Tex-Mex, scary movies, Craftsman-style homes, and John Steinbeck.

The conversation lagged, but Jodi didn't try to stir it. Strangely enough, the silence between them didn't feel awkward. It felt nice. Natural.

Fiona came back, a carafe of coffee cocked in her hand. "Refills?"

Jodi placed her hand over her cup. "None for me, thanks." To Jake, she said, "I've got to go."

He nodded at Fiona. "Check please."

The waitress pulled the check from her pocket and presented it to him with a flourish. He opened his wallet, peeled out a twenty and a ten for a healthy thirty percent tip. Did Jake always tip so lavishly or was he just trying to impress her?

"This is too much," Fiona said.

"Keep it," Jake said. "My mom worked as a waitress when we were growing up. I know how tough the job is."

"Thank you," Fiona said. "I appreciate it. You two make a cute couple by the way."

"We're not a couple," Jodi said.

"Oh, you were so easy together I just assumed." She looked embarrassed, and scurried away.

"That was nice of you," Jodi told him. "Leaving such a big tip."

He shrugged. "She looked like she'd been on her feet all day."

There it was, his kindness for others. She felt something twist loose inside her chest. "Thank you for the coffee and pie."

"You're welcome."

Simultaneously, they got up. Jodi clutched her purse in front of her, a paltry shield against the strength of her feelings.

"Well," he said.

"Well," she echoed.

An awkward end-of-the-evening moment hung in the air, weird and quivering. They weren't dating. They'd never see each other again. What was there to say?

Jake insisted on helping her on with her coat. She started to protest, but didn't want to be rude, and then wondered why she cared. She'd never see him again. His fingertips brushed the back of her neck and she felt his touch to the marrow of her bones.

She tried to shake off the yearning that his touch stirred insider her, but it lingered stubbornly, tingling her nerve endings provocatively. When he opened the door for her, she got another whiff of his scent. She liked the way he smelled — appealing, male, distinctly *him.*

They stepped out into the cold. The snow was falling faster now, liberally salting the ground. Across the street at the Grand Texan, the last cab at the taxi stand pulled away, red taillights disappearing into the glassy murk of snowy night. The elaborately gabled roof of the Grand Texan glistened in the light from the neon sign above the diner, silvery gothic slants cracked by diagonal black angles. It was both romantic and slightly spooky, like a fairy-tale castle.

He took her arm to help her cross the street through the mirrory darkness, and she did not resist. But neither was she falling for his gentlemanly gestures. Ryan had opened doors and helped her on with her coat and took her arm when the footing was treacherous. The gestures were showy, but ultimately meant nothing. Although Ryan never left big tips, in fact, Jodi always had to slip back to put extra money onto the table when he wasn't looking. It should have been a clue to his real character. Why hadn't she seen it before?

"Let me give you a ride home," Jake said when they reached the door of the hotel.

She canted her head, eyed him, felt the charge of blue-hot electricity jump between them. "How do you know I'm not staying here?"

"I saw you arrive in the limo."

"Maybe my limo is coming back."

"Is it?"

"No," she admitted. "I planned on catching a cab back to —" She stopped before she said, "Motel 6."

"It's no trouble to give you a ride."

She tucked her clutch purse underneath her left arm and held out her right hand. "Thank you for coming to my rescue and playing Prince Charming. I had a lovely evening."

A so-did-I smile plucked up the corners of his mouth. She supposed a handshake was ridiculous when they'd shared such a passionate kiss, but it was all she was prepared to offer. He took her hand, held it for too long, stared deeply into her eyes.

She felt so many things at once — nervousness, attraction, sexual frustration — and he was the cause of it all.

The impulsive part of her she'd kept strapped inside a straitjacket for thirty years wanted nothing more than to grab him by the collar, lead him off to some darkened recess, and jump his beautiful bones right then and there. Jodi felt her entire body grow warm. She felt as if she was sliding, melting, losing her grip. She yearned for what his lips promised — sex and lots of it.

But she was afraid of it too. Afraid of what his passion might unleash in her. Afraid that if she got a real taste of him she'd become addicted and couldn't live without him.

His skin was flushed and there was a languidness to him that she found engaging. Jodi realized that even though he didn't show it, he was nervous about this attraction too. And she liked that. His nervousness made him more approachable and it meant he wasn't stuck on himself.

Every cell in her body ached. She met his eyes, mentally begging him to kiss her again.

He read her thoughts perfectly, and pulled her into his arms. A little forcefully, but in a good way, and crushed his mouth against hers. It seemed he knew exactly what she wanted.

Her pulse fluttered as he deepened the kiss, and their surroundings were forgotten as she got swept up in his taste.

She felt the sharp poke of his erection pressing hard against her thigh, and a thrust of dizziness nearly crumpled her knees out from under her. He was long, thick, and hard. She thought of their naked limbs entwined. Imagined him inside her, filling her up, making her whole.

Ridiculous. Romantic rubbish. One person could not complete another. They were people, not jigsaw puzzles. But secretly, she wanted to believe.

Her fingers curled around his biceps and she clung to him, afraid if she let go she would topple over.

He was at once both oddly volatile and incredibly steady. His lips were wild but his inner core unshakable. She could feel his solidity in the calm way his hands held hers. But his mouth! That astounding mouth was a furnace, hot, hazardous, and unquenchable.

The wind kicked up, blew a frosty chill and a flurry of snow over them. She remembered how he'd held her on the dance floor. And how she didn't want to say good-bye, and catch a cab back to her lonely room at the Motel 6. She swayed, unsteady on her feet from too much possibility and too much pie, wobbly on her high heels and fears.

Jake's palm was still clasped against hers, his fingers locked around her wrist, his eyes hot on her face.

How easy it would be to give him her name and phone number and tell him to call her, to start a relationship with him. But she was far from ready for that. So she said nothing. Held her tongue. Kept Gwendolyn and her desires tucked into a tidy corner of her mind that had nothing to do with real life.

Finally, he dropped her hand and stepped away.

She fingered her branded lips. "Well." She straightened. "Good-bye."

He hesitated as if he was going to argue, but then he nodded and turned to go inside the hotel.

"You're staying at the Grand Texan?" she asked.

He paused, looked over his shoulder at her. "I am."

For some reason that answer stirred up the goose bumps again. Cold. It was because she was cold, not because she was imagining just how daring it would be to follow him upstairs to his hotel room.

A long moment of silence passed.

"Good night again," she said.

"Good night." He didn't move.

She could smell the faint hint of his cologne, something woodsy and masculine. If she swung her hand at her side, her fingertips would graze his outer thigh. Her heart jumped. Missed opportunity, two ships passing in the night, blah, blah.

He shifted toward her and she was sucked straight into his aura, both fiery and cool. Everything about him was fresh and exciting. He was wholly exotic, a sophisticated visitor who intrigued her like an intricate renovation project.

"Good-bye, Gwendolyn," he murmured. "Have a nice life."

CHAPTER 4

Jodi Carlyle's Wedding Crasher Rules:
Don't linger too long.

Jake disappeared into the building.

Jodi exhaled.

Whew. Close one. Crisis averted. All he had to do was ask her to come upstairs and she would have gone. That's how fragile — and let's face it, sex-starved — she was.

Good job.

She'd done what she'd set out to do. She'd successfully crashed a wedding, danced with Mr. Tall, Dark, and Smart Aleck. Faced her wedding phobia so she could move on after Ryan and be the best maid of honor she could possibly be to Breeanne. And she'd managed to do it all while still hanging on — albeit by a thread — to her self-control.

Hunching her shoulders deeper into her coat, she huddled on the sidewalk, glanced up and down the snow-slick streets. No cabs in sight. When she'd planned to catch a cab back to her motel, she hadn't expected to be out this late, or for the snow to be coming down so steadily. But surely one would be along in a minute.

No sign of the valet either.

She paced to the end of the hotel's expansive driveway, feeling like a target in her wedding finery and high heels. This was dumb. She should wait in the lobby. And risk running into Jake again? No thank you. She shivered. Where was a taxi when you needed one?

"Come on, come on," she muttered, pulled out her cell phone to check the time, and was surprised to see it was nearly midnight. No wonder the place was dead. She was just about to call the cab company when footsteps sounded behind her.

Her heart leaped into her throat. How stupid of her not to have waited inside. She fumbled in her purse for pepper spray. Found it, and with the canister in her palm, finger on the nozzle, she whirled, growled, "Back off!"

Jake raised both arms. "Don't shoot."

"Oh," she said, and let out a breath. "It's you."

For a moment, they stood like statues, gazes locked.

"You know how to protect yourself," he said, approval in his eyes.

She dropped the pepper spray back inside her handbag. She hated to admit it, but she was glad to see him. "You came back."

"What kind of guy would let you stand out here alone?" He gestured vaguely at the sky. The wind blew harder, sending the snow falling at a sharp angle. "Let's get in out of the weather."

The combination of his handsome smile, his delicious masculine smell, and the increasing cold dismantled her. She nodded. He hooked her elbow again and guided her inside. They waited together in the lobby, not speaking, staring out the window at the snow coming down. Behind them, a crackling fire in the fireplace warmed their backs.

She glanced over at him. "Really, I'm good. You don't have to wait with me."

"I don't mind." His shrug was casual as a river, long and slow. The earnestness in his eyes unnerved her. Why did he have to be so nice?

A Christmas tree still stood in the lobby, the star at the top almost touching the ceiling. The multicolored lights winked merrily, throwing soft colors of the rainbow around the room, making everything seemed translucent, and transformed.

His eyes were dark and mysterious. He spread his palms wide and pressed them against his outer thighs as if to keep from touching her. He leaned toward her, and she found herself helplessly leaning in toward him. All it would take was another kiss from those rugged lips and she'd dissolve like sugar in hot coffee.

And judging from the look he was giving her, he knew it.

The air around them snapped with sexual energy. His gaze hung on her mouth and he angled his head lower.

Was he going to kiss her again? Right here in the lobby with the desk clerk watching them from behind the polished marble registration desk?

She saw invitation in his eyes but he wasn't crossing any boundaries. She flicked her tongue out to moisten her lips.

"A taxi just pulled up." He nodded toward the street.

"Did it?"

"Which is a damn lucky thing, because I was just about to ask you up to my room."

"You were?"

"I was."

Jodi knew a crossroads when she saw one, and she had always chosen the well-traveled path. She wasn't a gambler. Taking unnecessary risks wasn't smart. But his eyes promised the pleasure of great sex, and she longed to take him up on the offer.

Did she dare?

Shocking herself, she wrapped a hand around his forearm, gazed up at him with earnest eyes. "So ask."

He blew out his breath, cupped her chin in his palm, and tipped her face up to his.

Jodi's heart was a battering ram slamming against her chest. She could do this. She could have a one-night fling. Put a delightful affair in a box inside her mind, and label it "Jodi's One Wild Night." If she could do that, she would be safe. Tidy. Organized. Controlled. Just like always.

Jake brushed his lips over hers. Not so much a kiss as the promise of one. Then he pressed his mouth to the pulse beating at her throat. Heat shot through her body, pooling low in her abdomen. Her natural impulse was to push him away, to deny the powerful pull. His kiss scared her that much.

Her voice came out strangled. "Jake."

His lips were back on hers in a feather-soft kiss. She had to have more. Against all common sense, she curved her body against his and opened up her jaw. Hungrily, he devoured her.

She liked it. She liked it a lot.

He possessed her.

Daring Gwendolyn could not resist temptation. *She* wasn't about to wrench her mouth from his. Not for a million dollars.

Dreamy heat swirled through her body. Would it be so wrong to have just one night with him? They were both mature, consenting adults, they were both unattached, and attracted to each other. What could possibly be the harm in letting nature take its course?

He bit her gently and she almost yelped. Not because he'd hurt her, but because his boldness took her by surprise. Had she ever in her life been this turned on?

If she had, she couldn't remember when.

His mouth was alive, kissing, nibbling, suckling her in a way only a devoted lover could. He wanted her. That much was clear.

A shiver shook her spine. He tasted so delicious and he was so damn sexy.

How had she gotten here, in this unreal fantasy? In the lobby kissing a strong, gorgeous stranger who could so easily ruin her. And why did that thought make her so hot?

He pulled back and looked into her eyes. The unspoken question hung there. He was waiting for her to answer it. *Come upstairs with me.*

She unfastened her caution, flung it into

the wind. "Take me to bed, Jake. Take me there now."

Standing in the hallway with Gwendolyn cradled in the crook of his arm, Jake tried to slip the electronic key through the card reader while still kissing her. He was so nervous, wanted her so badly that his thumbs wouldn't function properly.

He had one thought and one thought only. Make this a night to remember.

Because women like Gwendolyn didn't come along every day. Smart. Strong. Funny. He'd take whatever she was willing to give him.

He wanted her. That's why he'd gone back outside. Yes, he'd wanted to make sure she was safe, but he could have watched over her from the shadows. He'd gone back to her because he enjoyed looking at her, holding her, smelling her, feeling her.

And now, here she was, in his arms, and by all indications, he was going to have her.

After three failed attempts, and a few choice words, he finally got the door open and they tumbled inside. She giggled and fell against him.

The door slammed closed behind them. A statement. They were doing this. He yanked off his tuxedo jacket, tossed it across a chair.

She carefully set her purse on the desk, went to the closet for a coat hanger, and moved to hang up his coat.

"What are you doing?" he growled.

"I like things tidy," she said.

"That OCD thing?"

She shrugged.

"Screw the coat." He lightly bit her neck. "Screw tidy."

"I —"

"You're killing the mood." He took the coat from her hand, flung it across the room. "Come here."

She laughed, and sank into his arms. He branded her with another scorching kiss. She tasted so damn good. Honeyed heaven. Devilishly, she tickled the roof of his mouth with the tip of her tongue.

Jake groaned. He was gone. Blitzed as a frat boy at his first kegger.

Her mouth was on his and her arms were twined around his neck. He could feel her heart thumping, jackrabbit fast. Was she scared? He hoped she wasn't scared. He didn't want to scare her.

Excited was good, scared, not so much.

"It's okay," he murmured against her lips. "It's gonna be fine. Relax."

He realized then that his own heart had picked up her frantic rhythm and he was breathing as hard and fast as she was. Or maybe she'd picked up his.

Take your own advice, Coronado. Get a grip on yourself.

Hell, how could he relax when her lips were so soft, and warm, and willing? He felt ambushed, but that was dumb because he was the one who'd started this.

Christ, he'd only met her six hours ago and she had him so crazy he could hammer nails with his dick.

She lifted her chin and closed her eyes. Her face turned up to him, so trusting and defenseless. He studied her features, memorized them, and tucked them away in the back of his brain, a memento of this night — the taste of sweet, minty moistness, her mouth burning against his, her fingers interlaced around his back as they waltzed dizzily across the room, Gwendolyn softly humming one of the songs from the wedding, "Kiss You."

Struggling for self-control, he attempted to change the pace and kiss her gently, but the kiss came off much rougher than he intended. She was so eager, so pliable, so damn tasty that he couldn't slow down if his life depended on it.

She rattled him to the bone. Rattled the pane right out of his window. Had he ever been so perturbed? He cast his mind back, trying to remember his first time with Maura, but he couldn't recall a damn thing.

That scared and sobered him, and he was about to stop kissing her and reorient himself, but he'd triggered something inside her and Gwendolyn wasn't backing off. She tangled her fingers in his hair, letting him know that she wanted him as much as he wanted her.

Good. Fine. He didn't want to back off. He pulled her hips against his, but her weight shifted and he lost his balance and they ended up sprawled on the bed together, laughing.

Jake was on his back and she was astride him.

Ferociously, she tugged his shirt from his suit pants and plowed her hands, small and hot, underneath the shirt to skate her palms over his bare belly. Then she lowered her head and planted hot kisses around his navel.

Oh shit. He was in deep water.

She stroked his chest with a fingernail.

His body burst into flames. His blood burned and his groin throbbed. He hadn't been with a woman in almost a year. That's why he was so hard. So blindsided. Hell, he was lusty as a pirate and all he could think of was stealing himself some booty.

A soft moan of pleasure slid from her throat. He cupped her face between his palms and ignored the part of him that warned things were moving way too fast. He knew that. He didn't care.

Her body promised sweet delight. Her skin was so sensitive, her mouth so full and ripe. Dreamily, he caressed her, enchanted, entranced.

She traced her thumbs over his nipples and Jake groaned aloud. The breath left his lungs along with the sound. He grabbed her hips and pressed her flush against his pelvis, letting her see exactly what she was doing to him and what he ached to do to her.

"Ooh." Her eyes widened.

The bedsprings creaked beneath their weight, but he didn't care how noisy it got. He had to have her.

He flipped her over, pinning her to the pillow-top mattress, and speared his fingers through her lush auburn hair, held her in place while he savaged her with kisses.

She wrapped a come-here-big-boy leg around his waist, simultaneously opening her mouth and letting his tongue slip deeper. She tasted incredible — rich and robust and rocking hot.

"I want you, Jake. I want to feel you inside

of me," she murmured.

"We've got all night. Let's take our time." He said it as much to convince himself as her. What he wanted to do was hike up the skirt of her dress, strip off her panties, and plunge into her hard and fast.

Disoriented by how out of control he felt, he paused and lifted his head. Noticed snowflakes dancing prettily outside the window. Christmas lights on the roof reflected a soft yellow-white glow into the room. She turned her head to see what he was looking at.

"It's beautiful," she murmured.

"You're beautiful," he said. "I feel like Santa left my Christmas gift a week late."

Her smile turned wicked as she dropped her shoulders back to the mattress and stared up at him, her lips glistening from his kiss.

She felt so damn good against him, her body molded to his, feminine and strong. He reached for the zipper of her dress, but she planted a palm against the flat of his chest and pushed him away.

"What is it?" he rasped huskily.

"Wait."

"What's wrong?"

"Sit down," she commanded, and patted the mattress with her hand.

Jake obeyed, swinging his legs off the bed and sitting upright. She stood. Where was she going? A pill of disappointment wedged against his tongue. Had she changed her mind? Was she leaving?

No, babe, don't go!

She stepped away from him and in the dim, misty light from the window, slowly began to disrobe, sliding down the zipper of her dress inch by inch in excruciating slow motion, glancing up now and again to shoot him provocative looks over her shoulder.

A striptease? Yes, please.

She eased the material off one shoulder, blew him a Marilyn Monroe Happy-Birthday-Mr.-President kiss, and then raised the material coyly back up again.

Jake groaned. "You're driving me crazy."

"That's the general idea." She giggled and then wriggled her butt in a shy but seductive bump and grind. She kept alternately moving the dress up and down her shoulders, teasing, testing his self-control, but he could tell she was feeling a bit insecure about her performance. No need to worry. He was blown away.

He gulped, clenched his jaw. What a show! "Take it off, Gwendolyn," he encouraged.

A bashful blush bloomed on her face as she turned back, blew him another kiss, and finally dropped the material from both shoulders and let the dress float down her body to pool at her feet. In black lace panties and a matching bra molded to her high, sumptuous breasts, she stepped from the circle of the dress ringing her feet, like Venus emerging from the stars.

His hands tingled with the need to touch her, to fill his palms with the weight of her breasts. He wanted to run his tongue over her skin, taste her rich, womanly flavor. He yearned for her in the most primal way.

It felt as if he'd spent the last three years holding his breath, just waiting for her to appear. She was his salvation when he hadn't even realized he needed saving.

His gaze tracked from her chest to the smooth curve of her belly to her black satin thong panties, clinging so provocatively to her sweet, luscious ass. Her skin was smooth and creamy, her belly flat, waist narrow, her breasts the perfect size of full, ripe peaches.

"Do you have any earthly idea how sexy you are?" he asked.

Emboldened by his approval, she smiled and moved toward him as if she owned the world — lithe, supple, latching on to a self-confidence she seemed surprised to find buried inside her.

Slowly, she raised her leg, her stilettoed

foot floating above his thigh. He waited. She lowered the thin spike of a heel onto his thigh, dug in lightly.

"Unbuckle me," she said.

Holy shit!

He fumbled with the delicate buckle at her slender ankle, his fingers feeling big as sausages. *Smooth, Coronado, real smooth.*

Her breathing grew quicker, shallower.

The buckle was stubborn. Refusing to yield. Or maybe his mad haste was the problem.

In irritation, Jake slipped the strap under her heel and peeled the shoe off her foot, leaving the buckle still fastened. He flung the stiletto over his shoulder, and it landed with a plop on the other side of the room.

He waved at her other foot. "Gimme."

She propped her heel in his outstretched palm. He latched his fingers around her ankle, cradled the delicate bone that merged into the polished patent leather of her shoe, ran his other hand up the back of her leg.

The sensuous curve of her calf stirred dark, primal urges in the base of his spine. He felt the color red fill every cell. Fond fright. Grim jollity. Jittery calm. His body stretched, grew, swelled, ached.

For her.

She gifted him with a small smile that was

part modesty, part pity, part lusty desire. Those earnest blue-gray eyes, combined with the flick of her pink tongue over raspberry lips, unspooled him.

She stole his breath. Burgled it right from his lungs, a dazzling sneak thief.

He wanted to tell her to give it back. Look what a mess he was in. Breathless. Helpless. Caught.

What could he say? How should he feel about this? Would she even care what he was feeling if he could find the words?

In the course of one short evening she'd taken his story and changed it all around with her smile. The grieving widower tale used to read all right, but now it didn't fit. It was getting harder to wear the old identity. Impossible to keep playing the old roles. He was ready to let go, make a fresh start.

She leaned forward, wearing nothing but those black panties and bra, giving him a sweet view of her cleavage. She stole his breath away, left him stunned and stumbling. She smiled, smug in her larceny. What a sweet combination. Shy on one hand, poised on the other. She was the sun. The moon. The stars. The galaxy. She was his silver lining. His hope for the future. She knocked his lights out. Babe Ruth in the ballpark on his best day couldn't equal her.

And the amazing thing was, she didn't seem to recognize the sway of her power.

He blinked, trying to turn the lights back on again, but he could no longer see where he was going. Couldn't tell where he'd been. It had been a curveball kind of day. It felt like he'd lost his bat, and was swinging empty-handed.

Inhale, fool.

He managed to drag in a thin whistle of air, but it wasn't enough. Solved nothing. He had to have her.

Now.

He dispensed with the second shoe, then wrapped his hand around her delicious calf and lay back against the mattress, pulling her along with him.

She made a soft noise of half surprise, half pleasure. She was atop him again and his hands spanned her waist. Her breasts were pressed against his chest and her head was cocked to one side so she could study him.

His fingers went for the clasp of her bra.

She reached back and closed a hand over his fingers. "Not so fast. It's your turn to remove an article of clothing."

He didn't need any more encouragement than that. Quickly he sat up, toed off his shoes, and pulled his shirt over his head without bothering to unbutton it. Her fingers plucked at the waistband of his pants, working the snap and zipper almost simultaneously.

Making an "attack" noise, she shucked the pants down the length of his legs. Jake lifted his hips to help. His slacks quickly joined her dress on the floor and they were left in their underwear staring into each other's eyes and breathing hard.

"Don't even think about folding those clothes and putting them away neatly," he warned.

She chuffed out a short laugh. "How did you know that's what was running through my head?"

"I can read you like a roadmap, Gwendolyn."

Normally, he was more at ease naked than clothed. He knew his strength. He was an athlete. Women went crazy over his six-pack and his biceps. But he didn't care what other women liked. All he cared about was what she thought.

A lock of hair fell across her face and she reached up to tuck it behind one perfect ear. His gaze slid down and he caught himself staring at the smooth hollow underneath her raised arm. The sight of her armpit shouldn't have been sexy as hell but it was.

His self-control was unraveling like a greenhorn hitter his first day at the plate in the major leagues.

He was in over his head, a drowning man. She kissed him back, tentative at first, but her confidence quickly picked up strength and tempo. Instinct took over and he crushed her lips with his. Surprise flashed across her face and she stared him directly in the eyes.

Yep, babe, I'm as freaked out about this as you are.

Just horny, he told himself. But Jake was afraid that wasn't the whole truth. She resembled Maura. Was that the primary reason he was feeling these things? Trying to recapture the love he'd lost so tragically.

That pulled him up short.

But before he had time to fully examine the thought, she kissed him again, increasing the pressure, upping the pace. Her lips blasted him into another realm of awareness, making him forget everything except her intoxicating taste.

Her lips were velvety soft and so damn feminine. Her teeth parted, letting him in. He kissed her passionately, fiercely.

Too fast. Too fast.

He was plunging ahead too quickly but he did not know how to slow down. His body was filled with the pressure that had been steadily building from the moment he helped her up off the marble floor.

Sweet Christ, she had no mercy. Her short fingernails dug into the back of his head. A deep flush of arousal painted her face, spread down her neck to her perky bosom. The flick of her tongue over his teeth was lazy, seductive, teasing him by degrees — slowly at first, but then with steadily building intensity.

She was small. Her waist so narrow that his spread hands could almost span her. God, he itched to touch every inch of her, to explore all the pleasures her body had to offer.

"Jake," she moaned softly and the way she breathed in his name on a shivery sigh drove him insane. His head spun, his heart pounded. He couldn't even remember where they were or how they'd come to be here together. None of that mattered.

She was all that mattered and he had to have more of her.

He slipped his hand down to cup her tight, round bottom. His shaft strained against her thigh. Flexing, he curled his fingers into the soft, willing flesh of her buttocks. Heard her quick intake of breath.

"You okay?" he asked, worried that in his

eagerness he'd hurt her.

"Fine," she whispered. "Just fine."

He couldn't stop kissing her, or touching her. So tasty. Her mouth was hot and moist and so was his. Beneath his palm, her bottom was warm and growing hotter with each passing second. He kneaded her skin where the curve of her butt met her upper thigh and instantly she trembled against him.

"You like that?"

"Uh-huh." She nodded.

He kneaded the sensitive spot, drawing another soft groan and quiver from her. The discovery of an erogenous area pleased him and he couldn't stop grinning.

Note to self. Don't forget this spot.

But she'd made it clear enough this was nothing more than a one-time thing, but God, he was trying to figure out a way to change her mind.

She broke from his mouth and began kissing a path down his chest. Every sensation was amplified, exaggerated — the weight of her body against his, the feel of her fingers tickling his anklebones, the rhythm of her breathing, the perfect shape of her head as he stroked his fingers through her hair.

She slid down his body, stopped at his navel, lifted her head for a long look at him, a wild glow of excitement in her eyes. The contour of her lips changed. Loosened. Her fingers slipping lower to wrap around his shaft.

The air vibrated between them, rich and hot, as rich and hot as the testosterone stampeding through his veins. Her wily grin weakened his defenses and cut right to the root of his sexual longings. It was as if she knew everything that was in his heart and in his mind.

Scary.

Especially since she looked so much like Maura.

She studied him in that coy way she had, and he knew if he were smart he'd get up, put on his clothes, and walk right out that door.

But he wasn't smart. In fact, he must be as dumb as a pumpkin because all he wanted to do was sit here and soak up her glow.

She was velvet. He was steel.

Jake flinched at the first touch of her mouth on his skin. It was startling, but the sensation was achingly sweet and so inti-mate, he had to lace his fingers through her hair to keep from pulling her back up to him.

He was a lucky bastard. No doubt about

it. He looked down at her and his heart stuttered.

The push of her rose-petal lips, the heat of her breath disoriented him. The form and curve of her mouth; the delightful swell of her lower lip, the sculpted bow of the upper, the edge where the textured velvet of her mouth gave way to the deeper mystery of her inner self.

At long last, she pulled away and peered at him, her eyes rounded wide with excitement.

She spread her hands underneath his buttocks to tilt his hips upward. And then her mouth latched on to him with suction so strong that Jake's eyes rolled back in his head.

She tickled the back of his thigh with one hand, gently stroked him with the other. The feeling was so incredible, he almost yelped.

Systemically, she dismantled him with her mouth.

Jake groaned as the heat drenched him. Her rhythm picked up. Her hands were magic. His chest expanded, tightened.

She moved her head back and forth, her tongue doing maliciously wonderful things to him, her hair a silky glide beneath his fingers.

"Yes," he hissed. "Yes, yes, yes."

She worked magic with those fingers and her tongue, leading him far past temptation, guiding him to paradise.

Her warm, wet mouth, the sweet taste of her on his tongue, and the heavenly smell of her feminine sex tangled up in his nose. She was beyond beautiful. She was pure life, pure joy. Her mouth moved over him without caution or fear. She pushed him past his knowledge of himself. He had never before been so consumed. She was an earthquake, rocking his world. The walls of the hotel room seemed to ripple and sway.

"Let go," she murmured. "Release it all."

How had she discerned the mental shift in him? His acceptance. Letting her be in charge if that was what she needed.

A deep humming started inside his brain, vibrating with energy. He shook his head but the humming intensified, growing louder and stronger the deeper she took him. He was about to come. He stiffened, suddenly nervous about the whole thing.

"Gwendolyn?" he asked, wishing like hell he knew her real name.

"Shh," she whispered against his shaft. "Shh."

He stiffened and almost told her to stop but he couldn't speak. His knees were elastic and he was as loaded and hot as any man could ever be. He'd shot far beyond coherent thought, his brain vibrating, humming, buzzing.

Relentlessly, she pushed him. He was aching, gushing, throbbing. He threw back his head and let out a primal cry, pleading for release from her exquisite torture.

Tingling. Pounding. Rushing.

Soon. Please, please let him come soon. If he didn't come soon, he would drop dead from need.

She moved her head down, then up, in firm, stroking motions, finishing him off.

Jake broke, jerking and trembling. Lost. He was lost.

Through a mist of unbelievable sensation, he peered down, blinked. He could barely see. She was sitting up, a diffident smile tipping her glistening lips.

Jake collapsed against the pillow, lay there sweating, shuddering, panting for breath, trying to wrap his mind around what had just happened. He pulled her to his chest, tucked her against him, and curled them into a fetal position together. For a long while they lay there together, not speaking, just breathing.

When at last he could speak, Jake turned

Chapter 5

Jodi Carlyle's Wedding Crasher Rules:
Be gone by sunrise.

The bed moved as Jake flipped her over onto her back. She did not resist. This was why she'd come here, for an adventure, to boost her self-confidence, to show there was life after betrayal, to prove she was brave.

"I want you," he murmured, miraculously growing hard again.

"It's not me you want. I'm —"

He pressed his mouth to hers, cutting off her protests. When he finished kissing her thoroughly, he said, "I want *you.*"

How could he want *her*? He didn't even know her name. He wanted her body. That was all and that was fine. That's all she wanted him to want.

He nuzzled her neck, planting a kiss under her chin, running his tongue over the hollow of her throat, sucking, nibbling, licking,

103

trailing down to her breasts.

His mouth felt so good. She switched off her mind, and let herself drift on a current of sensation. He teased her nipples, first one and then the other, his tongue swirling over her. Jodi's toes curled and she fisted the sheets, arching her back up off the mattress.

Fully ensnared by him, she moaned softly, and squeezed her eyes shut. He tracked down to her belly, ran his tongue around her navel. She squirmed against the tickly sensation. Joyous agony. Her nipples pebbled against his calloused palms.

Anticipation jerked her up a mountain of expectation, hauling her to the top of an overwhelming ledge. How hard would she fall?

She traced her fingertips over Jake's masculine muscles. The man was a work of art.

For a moment he paused, and she forced her eyes open. A myriad of sensations pelted her — the sound of his ragged breathing, the heat of his flesh, the soft scratch of his beard as he claimed her mouth in a scorching kiss. A maelstrom of wicked delight swept her away, a rushing river of passion surging high, swelling. He tasted robust and piquant, like the roasted coffee brew they

104

had shared at the diner. She was thirsty for more.

Their tongues played.

Gliding in and around and over each other. The tender slide of his palms underneath her breasts a hungry hunt to increase her pleasure.

The burning urge to stroke him, to travel the tempting terrain of his body possessed her. She ran her fingertips over his belly, exalting in the way his taut stomach muscles quivered at her touch. His low groan of pleasure lit her up inside. She tracked her hand lower, finding her way through the coarse curls to glide her palm up the long, hard length of him.

Excitement stirred her blood. A murmured whisper of delight slipped past her lips at the sexy feel of him pulsating in her palm.

Her body clenched, anxious to have him inside her, filling her up. But she didn't want to rush things. She wanted to savor this moment, savor him. It took all the strength of will she possessed, but Jodi forced herself to hold back. He was worth the wait.

He eased her hand from his shaft and pulled his mouth from hers. "You keep doing that and I won't last two minutes."

Jake kissed his way down her neck to her swollen and achy breasts. His mouth settled over one straining nipple, sending a coil of heat firing like an inferno into her blood.

Her body grew heavier, more languorous. He nibbled her nipples and then made idle circles around her breasts with an index finger.

She writhed against him.

He circled back.

This time she moaned through clenched teeth when he reached her nipples and rolled them between his rough fingers. Her breath came out in low, episodic gasps and her entire body felt swollen and achy. His lips tugged on her earlobe, suckled on her flesh and the emerald stud nestled in her lobe. She shuddered at the wetness of his tongue, the heat of his mouth.

He spread his legs, nudging her knees wider apart with his. His hand slid down her hip and across her inner thigh. His other hand gently massaged her buttocks. Her breathing quickened and her heart thumped.

"I'm going to kiss you here," he promised. Not asking her permission, simply telling her what he was going to do.

Flashes of pleasure bombed her and she let out a desperate purr, letting him know she approved of the path he was following with his wicked mouth, dancing his tongue down her belly. She felt his hands at the waistband of her panties, his fingertips taunting her.

He fueled her arousal to fever pitch. His heated breath against her bare belly was driving her insane. His fingertips shifted through her moist curls, headed for the area she most wanted him to touch.

In response, she arched her back.

Come on. Come on.

If she didn't feel the warmth of his hot, wet tongue against her soon she was going to lose her mind.

Jake slipped her panties over her hips, slid them down her thighs, past her knees. She kicked them off.

"You smell so good." He inhaled and then placed a smattering of kisses down the area below her navel.

She felt every quiver of his body, every ragged breath.

With excruciating slowness, Jake moved his hand to cover the triangle of hair between her legs.

Jodi moaned her pleasure as his hand cupped her, and she allowed her legs to drop open, giving him full access to her body. He lay on his belly between her knees and lightly brushed his lips over her.

He hissed in air. "You are so wet."

Her heart skipped a beat at the sound of wonder in his voice. Desire for him seared her nerve endings as she surrendered to him completely.

It wasn't easy for her. Jodi wasn't used to exposing herself like this, neither out of bed nor in it, but urge forced her to relinquish the reins to Jake's tender tongue. She wasn't sure she liked it.

The air was thick, weighted with tension and strange meaning. The sheets smelled slightly scorched. Her breath crawled sluggishly through her lungs, filling her with lazy heat. Her limbs were made of granite, heavy and smooth.

Then everything vanished from her mind except the erotic moisture of his lips against her throbbing sex. And when his mouth formed a gentle suction over her clit, she came unraveled.

Gently, he inserted one thick finger inside her. She lost all sense of herself, all sense of time. The world tumbled, an easy fall into ecstasy.

The pressure mounting inside her womb was sublime torment. At that point, nothing else mattered to her except Jake making love to her with his mouth and his fingers.

He teased her, nipping lightly with his teeth.

All the air left her body and she felt reborn. Her pulse pounded in her ears, rushing heated blood through her engorged veins.

Jake tried desperately to fight off the need biting into him, but it was almost impossible. The soft sounds of her sexy cries of pleasure, the way she threaded her fingers through his hair.

She wanted him to be inside her. He had to get inside her now. "Please," she whispered. "Please take me."

"Not yet."

Cruel, sweet torment. He kept at her. Licking and teasing until she was quivering from head to toe and oh so wet.

He paused long enough to retrieve a condom in his wallet and slip it on. Bracing his body over hers, he looked down into her eyes, and just like that, he slipped inside.

He peered down into her.

She stared up at him.

He pulled her hips flush against his and held her there for a hundred heartbeats, not moving inside her, just being there.

They hung on the prongs of an epic mind-body connection, the cosmic merging of physical form with dynamic spirit. A hypnotic string of energy stretched from him to her and back again as he slowly began moving inside her. She watched his pupils widen, heard his breath quicken.

"You're shaking," he said. "Scared?"

She nodded silently.

"Why?" His voice was a sliver of glass, high and brittle as if all the oxygen had been sucked from his lungs.

She couldn't find the words to describe what she was feeling.

"Do you want to stop?"

"No!" she said, alarmed, and wrapped her arms around his waist. "Don't stop."

"Then tell me what's wrong."

"Nothing's wrong," she said. "It feels . . . I feel . . ."

"Yes?" His voice sounded anxious, like a man waiting on a verdict. What was going on here? What was happening between them? She felt like a stranger who'd stumbled into a foreign land, only to discover it was her long-forgotten home.

His eyes, dark and mysterious, pried deep inside her, as if trying to excavate all her secrets and put them on display. "What is it?" he whispered. "You can tell me."

"I'm afraid." She whimpered.

"Of what?" he prompted when she didn't go on, his voice as tender as a newborn baby's skin. So tender and filled with concern that the purity of it blinded her.

"I don't know," she admitted, unable to give voice to her fears.

"Are you absolutely certain you want to do this?" His naked belly was placed flat against hers and she could feel him inside her, big and warm.

"Yes. God, yes." She clasped the cheeks of his butt with both palms, pulled him deeper inside, held him snugly in place. Tears misted her eyelashes. "I'm afraid I'll never be the same again."

"You won't," he said huskily. "Nor will I."

They moved together in mindless wonderment. Their bodies in tune on a level so primal it leveraged their souls.

Jodi whimpered gratefully.

Her body enveloped him. She met each of his thrusts with corresponding movement of her hips, arching her back up to meet him. Urging him to quicken his pace.

Instinct took over.

She could no longer think. Could only feel. Her focus was attuned to one thing and one thing only, the merging of their bodies. His energy swirled up through her until her whole universe spun dizzily. His stark reaction was such a powerful thing to behold. Jodi felt both awed and blown away by his power.

His hands trembled as he held her. He thrust into her again and again. Her entire being seemed to pull him deeper and deeper into her until she simply could not differentiate where his body stopped and hers began.

He cried out one last time and shoved himself as deep as he would go into her warmth, the walls of her body sucked at him — gripping, kneading, pulling.

Then Jake's body shuddered as he poured into her.

He collapsed onto her breasts, with his arms wrapped around her. She clung to him. Bent her head and kissed the top of his. He stayed inside her and she held him close. Memorizing every minute of it.

The one time in her life she'd had head-banging sex — wild, casual, beautiful sex with a gorgeous stranger.

And she looked up at the ceiling and smiled.

Jodi woke in a panic. Oh God, it was dawn.

She hadn't intended to stay all night. Her plan had been to slip out as soon as he was asleep and head back to the Motel 6 a changed woman. No longer the good-girl rule follower who got dumped on her wedding day, but someone new and strong and bold. A sassy woman who could have a one-night stand and not get hung up about it.

But by the light of day, a one-night stand could look a little seedy. She wondered how she was supposed to handle this casual new way of being. Didn't know if it was freedom or rock bottom.

Why had she allowed herself to fall asleep?

Softly blowing out her breath, she cast a wary glance to the other side of the bed. Jake was lying on his side, turned toward her, hands stacked under his cheek, looking way too adorable. Thankfully, he was still asleep.

Yay!

Maybe he was a sound sleeper. Maybe she could ease off the mattress without waking him. Get dressed and get out of here. Except that she had to pee something fierce.

Pee later. Lobby bathroom. Get out while the getting is good.

Carefully, she pushed back the covers. Waited a second. He didn't move.

Running her tongue over her lips, she touched one foot to the floor, and then the other, and glanced over her shoulder at him.

What a gorgeous profile. Then again, everything about him was irritatingly gorgeous. His nose was the perfect size. Not

113

too big, not too little. Straight and sure. Not broad, not thin. Jodi reached up to finger the slight bump at the bridge of her own nose.

Get a move on.

Yeah, okay. But she indulgently let her gaze caress his biceps. Last night, those magnificent arms had been holding her tight. Mmm. She went dreamy remembering. What if she leaned over and . . .

Snap out of it. That was last night. This was today. Her parents were expecting her for dinner.

She stood up, winced when the bed creaked, waited a minute, then looked over her shoulder at him again. Still sleeping.

Moving as quietly as she could, she tiptoed around the room, gathering up her things. She found her purse, her shoes, and her evening dress. Now where were her bra and panties?

She searched the room. *Nada.* Gosh, but she had to pee.

Forget peeing. Find your underwear.

On it. She pulled the dress over her head, dropped quietly to her hands and knees, and raised the bed skirt. Nothing under there, not even dust bunnies. Kudos to the diligent housekeeping staff at the Grand Texan, but boo to the fact that meant there was only one place her underthings could be.

The bed.

Ugh.

Carefully, she inched over and lifted the top sheet. Jake's breathing stayed slow and deep. Gotta love a one-night stand who was a sound sleeper.

Aha! There her panties were nestled at the foot of the bed. She ran her hand down the sheet, snagged her panties, and wriggled into them as stealthily as she could.

Now where was her bra?

Forget the bra. Just get out of here.

And go jiggling out of the hotel dressed in last night's rumpled dress and call-girl stilettos?

Yes, that might be embarrassing, but she simply had to get away from the naked man on the mattress and the smell of their lovemaking and that weird sensation knotting up her stomach.

Besides, she seriously had to pee.

Bra be damned, she was out of here. She plunked down in the chair parked at the desk just long enough to slip on her shoes. She grabbed her purse, lifted her head, and froze.

He was sitting up.

His hair was adorably tousled and his eyes

were half closed, but he was awake and eyeing her like she was his favorite dish of ice cream. She could almost feel his gaze reach across the room and stroke her. Luckily, he had the sheet draped over his waist.

Inwardly she groaned and dipped her head, unable to hold his direct gaze.

"Running out on me?" His tone was light, but his eyes were disappointed.

She couldn't help feeling guilty. Guilt. The good-girl default mode. Dr. Jeanna had asked her why she thought she had to fulfill everyone's expectations but her own, and she hadn't been able to give her an answer.

"Hmm, no, not at all," she lied. "I've got a really busy day ahead."

"Such as?"

"I really have to go." She headed for the door.

Um, said her bladder. *Now that he's awake, you might as well pee.*

Okay, fine. She darted into the bathroom and took care of business. When she came out, he was still lounging in the bed looking way sexier than any man had the right to look. Good grief, where did he get those amazing genetics?

"Sure you don't want to grab some breakfast? And by breakfast I mean sex." He wriggled his eyebrows.

116

She tried not to smile. She didn't want to encourage him.

His mouth curled into a you-don't-know-what-you're-missing grin. "C'mon." He swept a hand at his bare chest. "How can you turn down this buffet?"

"I'm not greedy," she said. "I'll leave some for the next wedding crasher."

His grin softened, humbled. "Then breakfast for real? I know this great little diner and it's the most important meal of the day —"

"Propaganda from the breakfast food industry."

"You've got a gorgeous butt. Did I tell you that last night?"

"I'm not coming back to bed with you."

"Ouch. Cock-blocked."

This time she couldn't stop the smile.

"Ha!" He pumped a fist in the air. "You *do* like me."

"I like cake too, doesn't mean I binge eat." Gosh, it would be so easy to get sucked into that smile.

"Hey, you like me, I like you —"

"Not happening." Gingerly, she took two steps backward toward the door.

He made an imaginary phone with his thumb and pinky finger, held it to his ear. "I'll call you."

"You don't have my number."

"Then you call me."

"I don't have your number."

"It's 555 —"

"I don't want to know it." She covered her ears.

He snapped his fingers. "Curses, foiled again."

"Charm away. I'm not giving you my name or number."

"I feel so cheap."

Jodi rolled her eyes. "Gotta go."

"Really? This is good-bye?"

"Good-bye, *hasta la vista, ciao, au revoir, daag, sayonara . . .* you get the picture."

He held his arms out, faux beseeching, his eyes laughing. "Parting is such sweet sorrow."

"Seriously, keep that up, Romeo, and I *will* hurl." Why did he have to be so much fun? Determined to make her escape, she headed for the door.

"Wait."

She stifled a sigh and turned back. "Yes?"

"Aren't you forgetting something?"

"No. I'm good."

He held up her bra, the thin strap of material dangling from the tip of his big masculine finger.

Jodi's nipples got hard. Jake's gaze

dropped to her breasts. She folded her arms over her chest, and stalked back across the floor. "Give me that."

She snatched for it.

He pulled his hand away, dangled the bra just out of her reach.

She lunged and lost her balance on the stilettos, ended up with her face planted in the mattress. She glanced up. Jake looked down.

Wham!

In his eyes lurked a mixture of longing, regret, and sadness so deep she felt it straight to her soul. The look disappeared, quickly replaced by stark sexual hunger and that knowing smirk.

Curiosity urged her to grab him and just go at it again, but that was exactly why she had to get out of here. She wasn't ready for this. Wasn't ready for him. She was still gluing back the pieces of life. Last night had been about facing her fears, asserting her independence, and having some fun. That's all she wanted. All she needed. All she had room for.

She scrambled to her feet, or at least that was the intention.

But before she could get there, Jake handcuffed his hand around her wrist. "I'd like to see you again."

"Impossible."

"Impossible?" His touch burned her skin, sent heat flaring up her arm. "Such a negative thinker."

Jodi sucked in her breath. She might be a lot of things but she was no coward. She'd been cornered. She'd tell him the truth.

"Look, Jake . . ." she began, and tried to tug away from him, but he wasn't letting go.

"I'm listening."

"Last night was great. We met each other's needs, and I thank you for being there when I needed someone. It's just that —"

"In the light of day you're ashamed of me?"

"No, no." She shook her head. "That's not it."

"What then?"

He had a way of looking at her that made her feel both guilty and empowered. It was a bizarre combination. She cleared her throat. "Look, I don't normally do things like this. Crash a wedding, spend the night with someone I don't know."

"And you think I do?" His hand was a bear trap, holding her fast.

"You don't?"

He shook his head. "Not in a long time. This was . . . you were . . . special." He looked so earnest that she believed him, and that made her feel worse.

"I'm still getting my footing after a bad romance," she said.

"I could help you with that," he said hopefully.

"Another relationship is not the solution."

"We could just be friends."

"No we couldn't. You're not a friend-zone kind of guy."

He cocked his head, considering that for a moment. "True."

She shrugged. "Impasse."

"Screw friendship then. We don't have to label it. Let's just spend some time together."

It was so tempting. Too damn tempting. "Look, I don't even live in Dallas."

"Where are you from? I don't mind driving."

"I'd rather just have this one great night and let it go at that."

"You sure?"

She nodded. He scared her. Not because he was so big and imposing. Not because he was so damn hot. Not even because his self-control barely masked a powder keg of sexually potent emotions. What really frightened her was this impulse to jump headlong into a relationship with a stranger. Which was why she absolutely, positively could not do it.

His smoldering eyes took her in and she felt as if she was not wearing a stitch of clothing. Jodi trembled as violently as if he had just cupped her bare breasts in his calloused palms. She held his gaze and they were joined as surely as if he had just slid his hard, angular body into hers.

He said nothing.

Neither did she.

Abruptly, he let go of her wrist, and Jodi, who'd been steadily tugging against his grip, stumbled backward at the sudden release. She had to get out of here before she crawled back up in bed beside him and begged him to make love to her again.

"Take care of yourself, Jake," she said, grabbed up her purse and coat, and ran out the door.

"Yo, Gwendolyn," he said.

With her hand on the doorknob, she turned back one last time. "Yes?"

He looked so wistful it hurt her chest. "Don't crash any weddings without me."

CHAPTER 6

Jodi Carlyle's Wedding Crasher Rules:
Smile! You're having the time of your life.

After her night with Jake, Jodi couldn't stop smiling. Whenever she thought of that evening — which was a lot — a helpless grin stole across her face.

Memories of the wedding, the diner, that swanky hotel room, swamped over her at the most unexpected time — while checking in guests, having dinner at her parents' house, during phone calls to Breeanne's bridesmaids to confirm they'd made it to their fittings. She'd hum or laugh or blush for no reason. Her glee was a little annoying because *everybody* noticed. Had she really been that much of a Debbie Downer since Ryan stood her up at the altar?

Well, no more. She'd set herself free, or at least Jake had. That mouth. That tongue. Those hands.

She still couldn't believe how quickly she'd hopped into bed with him. Or how liberated she'd felt after sex. No strings. No bonds to nurture. No need to worry when he'd call or if she'd ever see him again. She wouldn't see him again and she was good with that, and although she wouldn't have minded a few more nights in his bed, she'd segmented that part of her life into a neat compartment. A fun memory no one else would ever know about.

Thinking about him got her all hot and wet and bothered again. The orgasms he gave her — volcanic.

She fanned herself. Whew.

On Sunday a week after the wedding, her sisters Suki and Kasha dropped by the B&B to discuss plans for Breeanne's upcoming bridal shower and bachelorette party. They were seated on the floor around a coffee table in the converted train engine that served as her business office, with their tablet computers, and printouts of wedding planning spreadsheets laid out in front of them.

Breeanne and Rowdy had asked for a couples' shower. Personally, Jodi wasn't a fan of couples' showers. Men at showers tended to stand around at loose ends, jiggling their car keys in their pockets, checking cell phones, and saying things like, "How 'bout them Cowboys?"

But she didn't want to disappoint Breeanne, so she came up with the idea of hosting the shower during the Super Bowl. The guys could happily yell at the TV screen over buffalo wings, while the majority of the women oohed and aahed over shower gifts and finger sandwiches. Win-win.

Because Rowdy had the largest house and the biggest TV, they were holding the shower/Super Bowl party at his place. She'd thought about having it at the B&B, but the boxcar concept didn't lend itself to large group gatherings. And they had more than fifty guests coming to the shower.

As for the venue for the bachelorette party, the pickings were slim in Stardust. Unless they wanted to drive two hours to Dallas and stay overnight in a hotel, the options were the Swimmin' Hole, a fun but divey bar on the outskirts of town; tea at the Honeysuckle Café, which was located in her parents' antique store; or a spa weekend at the Lodge, a rustic but elegant resort that was part four-star spa, part hunting lodge.

Weird combo, spa and hunting lodge, but that was Texas for you.

"The Lodge is the obvious choice," Kasha said, swinging a curtain of long black hair over her shoulder and revealing a caramel-colored ear studded with four gold earrings. Everything about Kasha was regal. From the way she moved, to the sound of her voice, to the flowy fabrics she wore. She worked at Stardust General Hospital as a physical therapist and she was a yoga devotee. Kasha reached for a celery stick on the crudités tray in the middle of the table, and dipped it lightly in Jodi's homemade low-calorie buttermilk dressing. "This is a special day."

"Obviously the Lodge wins," Suki replied, piling a small paper plate high with potato chips and French onion dip. Her hair was even darker than Kasha's, glossy and blue-black in an intriguing asymmetrical style that complemented her Asian features. She was dressed in stylish clothes and wore rings on every finger, and multiple necklaces hung around her throat.

All four of the Carlyle sisters were adopted. Dan and Maggie Carlyle had taken in Jodi and Kasha when their untenable home lives fell apart. Breeanne and Suki had been adopted as infants.

"Although," Suki went on, pausing to crunch a dip-laden chip. A dollop of dip landed on her chin. She laughed, wiped it off with a napkin. "The Swimmin' Hole does have some rockin' awesome karaoke on Saturday nights. Just saying. And we could hire a male stripper if we had it at the Hole."

"We're not having it at the Hole," Jodi said. As the oldest, she was accustomed to issuing edicts, especially to Suki, who could go off on wild tangents if she wasn't reined in.

Suki pushed out her bottom lip and shot her a look that said, *You're no fun.* "So no strippers?"

"No strippers." Jodi put metal in her voice. "Spoilsport."

"Breeanne isn't the stripper type," Kasha soothed. "Can you imagine? She would blush nine hundred shades of red."

"But that would be the point," Suki said. "To embarrass the fire out of her."

"We're *not* embarrassing Breeanne. This is her big day. She deserves the best life has to offer. Remember how many times we almost lost her?" Jodi asked.

Breeanne had been born with a heart condition, and she'd been a sickly kid. Many times, their parents had awakened Jodi in the middle of the night telling her to mind the babysitter and help watch over Suki and Kasha while they took another late-night ambulance run to Dallas Chil-

dren's Hospital with Breeanne. Remembering those scary nights, she wrapped her
hand around her glass of iced tea and took
a long drink. She was happy that Breeanne
had found her Mr. Right.

"Jo?" Kasha said.

Jodi blinked. "Huh?"

"Where'd you go?"

Jodi straightened her shoulders, cleared
her throat. "Okay, the Lodge. It's settled."

"Still lost in your wild weekend?" Suki
winked, noshing on a carrot and looking
chic in black leggings and plaid miniskirt,
her blue-black hair shining in the lamplight.

Jodi felt warmth bloom on her cheeks. "I
don't know what you're talking about."

"C'mon." Suki playfully poked her in the
ribs with her elbow. "You can tell us. We
won't judge. What's his name?"

Jodi shook her head. "There is no guy."

"Uh-huh," Kasha said in a you-are-so-
lying-your-ass-off tone.

"There's not," Jodi insisted, feeling the
flush spread down her neck and up across
her forehead. "Concentrate, we've got work
to do."

"Let's review the evidence," Suki said,
completely ignoring her. "You were gone
overnight to Dallas without giving a reason
why, and when you came home you couldn't

stop grinning, and, oh yeah, you had a big hickey on your neck."

"I did not." Jodi slapped a hand to her neck and realized as she did it that she'd effectively confirmed Suki's suspicions.

"Gotcha." Suki wagged an index finger back and forth like a metronome. "Don't bother denying it. I know the signs. You got laid."

"I . . . I . . ." *Great. Stutter. That'll throw 'em off the scent.*

"Good for you." Kasha clapped her on the shoulder. "It's past time you moved on after Ryan and got a new boyfriend."

"Shh, don't even mention that douche-bag," Suki said.

"There is no boyfriend," Jodi insisted.

"Sure there's not." Suki looked as pleased with herself as the family cat, Callie, whenever she brought in a dead mouse.

"I'm not moving on. Well, yes, I am, I'm so over Ryan. But it's not what you think. I don't have a boyfriend, I —"

Suki's eyes widened and she slapped a palm over her mouth. "Omigod! You had a one-night stand!"

Jodi wanted to deny it, but she had such a hard time lying that she merely nodded and inwardly cringed.

"High five!" Suki raised her palm.

Sheepishly, Jodi slapped her sister's up-raised palm. She wasn't especially proud of her one-night stand, but neither was she ashamed. It had liberated her in a way she hadn't expected, but she wanted the incident to remain isolated. A single event she would never repeat. She'd needed this for her development. Like a snake shedding its skin, a watershed moment symbolizing out with the old and in with the new. Reborn. A dividing line between the old Jodi who put everyone's needs before her own, and the new Jodi who wasn't afraid to ask for what she needed.

"Tell us all about it." Kasha rested her arms on the table, sank her chin in her upturned palms, and leaned forward inquisitively.

"Not much to tell." She shrugged, not wanting to dilute the memory by rehashing it with her sisters.

"How did you meet him?" Suki ate a cracker, and when she was finished, ate a square of white cheddar.

Jodi reached over, picked up a small sesame cracker, topped it with cheese, and ate it in one bite.

"She's feeling backed into a corner," Kasha said. "She had to fix the way you ate your cheese and crackers by eating one her way."

"What? I did not," Jodi denied.

"Yes, you did. It makes you nervous when things don't come out even." Kasha nodded knowingly. "Why are you nervous?"

"Did the one-night stand go badly?" Suki lowered her voice, her eyes turning sympathetic.

"No. It was great." That helpless smile overtook her face. "Best sex ever."

"So why are you nervous?" Kasha asked.

"I crashed a wedding," Jodi confided.

"What!" Suki squealed, as gleeful as a mouse that stumbled onto a giant wheel of cheese. "No way."

"It was Dr. Jeanna's idea."

"You have the coolest therapist." Suki bobbed her head. "If anyone ever stands me up at the altar, I'm calling her."

"Whose wedding did you crash?" Kasha asked.

"The one Breeanne and Rowdy got invited to and couldn't attend because they were committed to another event," Jodi said.

"The son of the lieutenant governor and Betsy Houston's daughter?"

"That'd be the one." Jodi helped herself to another cracker and cheese.

"No kidding." Suki laughed. "This is way

too juicy, my rule-following big sissy crashing a high-profile wedding? Love it."

"I had to do something." Jodi dusted cracker crumbs from her fingers onto a paper napkin. "Following the rules landed me with a guy like Ryan. On paper he seemed so perfect. In reality, what a dud!"

"Dud, hell. He was a criminal," Suki said.

"Which goes to show how clueless I was." No more. Her eyes were wide open now. She'd never trust so easily again.

Kasha rubbed her hands together. "So dish the dirt on the guy you picked up at the wedding."

Jodi shrugged, as if it was no big deal, but an image of Jake as he looked laid out across the bed, studying her with those hot, sexy eyes, popped into her head. "Not much to tell. Chemistry. Sparks. Sex. End of story."

"So just how hot was the sex?"

Jodi grinned and ducked her head.

"That good, huh?" Kasha poked her gently.

Pressing three fingers to her mouth in a useless attempt to quell the heat burning her cheeks, she whispered, "Fab-u-lous."

"And you're not going to see him again?" Suki sounded disappointed.

"No."

"Why not?" Kasha asked.

"Because a one-night stand is for *one* night," Jodi said. "That's why they call it a one-night stand."

"Hey, that's another arbitrary rule," Suki pointed out. "Feel free to break it."

"I don't want to break it." Jodi ironed her lips flat, making sure she wasn't smiling. Damn Jake. Whenever she thought of him her mouth had a mind of its own. "This was about asserting my freedom. Other women can go off and have casual affairs. Why can't I?"

"Um," Kasha said, "because you're not built that way."

"Kash is right." Suki plucked a grape off the tray and popped it into her mouth. "You're a long-term kind of woman."

"Yeah, well, look where that got me."

"Yes, okay, Ryan was a monumental tool, but you can't let him sour you on love. If you do that, he wins."

"I'm not writing off relationships forever," Jodi explained. "Just for right now. I need to explore. Meet all kinds of men. Ryan is only the second guy I ever slept with. How pathetic am I?"

"Hey, now you've got three notches on the bedpost." Suki held up three fingers, and the numerous wire bracelets on her wrist jangled as they knocked together.

"I'm thirty and single. I should have a few more notches than that."

"You're not pathetic," Kasha soothed. "You're just not adventuresome. You like your routines and there's nothing wrong with that."

But there *was* something wrong with that, wasn't there? In her attempt to find the safety and security she'd never had in her early childhood before the Carlyles adopted her, she stuck to the rules, toed the line. She was the good girl who struggled to make sure she always did the right thing. The same girl who didn't open the door to strangers until she ran out of cereal and survival forced her into it.

And because of that she'd become staid and boring. Honestly, Ryan's criminal behavior aside, was it any wonder that he had run out on her? She was the proverbial stick-in-the-mud.

Until her night with Jake.

Jodi grinned again. *For Pete's sake, stop smiling.* But she couldn't. She'd walked away from the Grand Texan feeling like a phoenix rising from the ashes. From now on her new leaf was staying turned. No more woulda, coulda, shoulda.

"Oh, before I forget." Jodi hopped up to retrieve the antique beaded purse from the desk where she'd stowed it when she'd come home after her rendezvous with Jake. "Return this to Timeless Treasures for me, will you, Suk?"

Suki still lived at home with their parents, and she ran the Internet side of the family antique business. She also had a side business of her own, making jewelry and selling it on Etsy.

"Will do." Suki accepted the purse. "Hey, something's in here." She opened the snap and pulled out the skeleton key. "Where did this come from?"

"I'm assuming the store." Jodi shrugged. "It was in the purse when I borrowed it."

"Can I have it?" Suki asked, curling her palm around the key. "My skeleton key necklaces are selling like mad. In fact, I'm out of inventory."

"It's not my key. Ask Mom."

"Did you try the key on the hope chest?" Kasha asked, unfurling her long legs and getting to her feet to stretch out her lean body. She struck Tree Pose, balancing perfectly.

Last summer, Breeanne had found an antique hope chest at an estate sale. It was an unusual trunk, possessing five locks instead of the customary one. Five individual compartments contained inside one wooden box. Carved into the lid was the inscription:

Treasures are housed within, heart's desires granted, but be careful where wishes are cast, for reckless dreams dared dreamed in the heat of passion will surely come to pass.

The old woman who sold Breeanne the chest told her that if she made a wish before she unlocked the compartments, her wish would surely come true. She also cautioned Breeanne to be certain of her desire, because once made, the wish could not be undone.

Romantic, head-in-the-clouds Breeanne had instantly fallen in love with the crazy myth. The old woman had no keys for the trunk, but hoping that any skeleton key should work on a skeleton lock, and captivated by the tale, Breeanne had bought the hope chest.

They'd gone through every skeleton key they could find in Timeless Treasures — which was when Suki hit upon the idea of making skeleton key necklaces and selling them in her online store — but none of the keys they'd found had opened any of the five locks on the trunk.

Mysteriously, neither could either of the

two locksmiths in Stardust open the trunk without drilling into the locks, nor could they adequately explain why they couldn't unlock it.

The hope chest sat unopened for several days after Breeanne bought it, until Suki used up all the skeleton keys they'd had in the store and she put a sign in the window offering to buy skeleton keys for a dollar. A customer brought one in that had fit the lock on the fifth compartment at the bottom of the trunk.

As Breeanne turned the key, she wished for a boost in her writing career. Right after that, she'd gotten a call from the agent who'd snubbed her for over a year, telling her local sports hero Rowdy Blanton was looking for a ghostwriter from their area.

Inside the compartment, Breeanne had found a smaller box with another cryptic saying etched into that lid and when she opened the smaller box, Breeanne found a cheetah scarf that felt soft only to her and Rowdy. To everyone else, the scarf was rough and scratchy. Breeanne took it as a sign that she and Rowdy were meant to be, even though they had something of a bumpy road to their romance.

Romantic myth aside, Jodi had to admit Breeanne and Rowdy were a perfect fit and made for each other.

After Breeanne and Rowdy got engaged, her sister passed the hope chest on to Jodi and told her not to give up on love. Because Jodi loved her sister so much, she'd gracefully accepted the trunk, but that didn't mean she believed it had the power to grant wishes. In fact, the hope chest had sat untouched in the corner for months, gathering dust.

"I have no interest in the trunk," Jodi said. In fact, the only reason she hadn't asked her mother to sell it in the antique store was that she didn't want to hurt Breeanne's feelings.

"Let's try the key on it." Suki's eyes sparkled. "Where is the hope chest?"

"By the bookcase." She waved at the far corner of the room.

Suki pressed the key into Jodi's palm. "Open it."

Kasha had moved into Warrior One and was busy staring fixedly at the wall.

"Hey, yogini," Suki said. "Give it a rest. We're opening the trunk."

Kasha ignored her.

"Sure, go ahead, be steady as steel, strong as stone." Suki gave Kasha a little push to tip her off balance.

Kasha barely swayed. "It's strong as steel,

138

steady as stone."

"Whatever. Move it. We're cracking open trunks."

"Slim odds the key will fit," Jodi said. "Leave Kasha to her yoga."

"What's it gonna hurt to try?" Suki challenged. "Nothing ventured, nothing gained."

Mainly because Suki was standing there with her hands on her hips, looking like she wasn't going to let up until she complied, Jodi walked over to the trunk and sank to her knees in front of it.

She stuck the key in the first lock.

"Wait." Suki knelt beside Jodi, put a restraining hand on her arm. "You've got to make a wish first."

"I don't *have* to make a wish," Jodi argued. "Besides, the saying on the lid seems to suggest a wrongly made wish could backfire."

"You can't do it in retrospect," Suki warned. "No do-overs. What if the lock opens? You will have missed your opportunity to find true love."

"Suki, this trunk can't grant wishes. It's an inanimate object. Besides, if I made a wish, it wouldn't be for true love. I'm not interested in a relationship. At least not right now."

"True love knows nothing about timing,"

139

Suki said. "When it's right, it's right."

"What are you going to wish for?" Kasha asked, coming to stand behind them. "If you could have your heart's desire, what would it be?"

It was a good question. What did she want for her future? She'd been in a holding pattern for a year just trying to survive the fallout from Ryan's betrayal.

"It's not that hard of a question," Suki prodded. "What do you want more than anything in the entire world?"

What indeed?

She had her own business, a roof over her head, a family who loved her, lots of friends she could depend on. The only thing missing in her life was a love relationship, and she did not want one of those. Not for a long time. She needed space to heal and grow. In any romantic relationship, no matter how good or how strong, you had to lop off parts of yourself in order to fit with the other person, and she was done pruning. She wanted to see what she would look like grown wild and bushy. Where would her interests take her? She had no idea.

"I wish for adventure," she announced, and tried to turn the key.

It did not yield.

Suki sighed. "Rats. I was so sure it was

going to work. If anyone needs a miracle it's Jodi."

"Hey," Jodi protested. "What does that mean?"

"You just had wonderful sex with a hot guy and you didn't want to keep seeing him after he expressed an interest in seeing you? Something's wrong with you. You need help."

"Keep going," Kasha said. "There are three more locks to try."

To humor her sisters, Jodi wished again for adventure and tried the key in the second lock. Nothing.

"Dammit." Suki nibbled a thumbnail.

"You are too optimistic," Jodi said. "You set yourself up for a letdown."

"It's better than always expecting the worst." Suki sniffed.

"I'd rather be prepared for the worst than always expect the best, and get bitch-slapped by life," Jodi said, but if she were being honest, she was disappointed too.

"Chicken counting," Kasha said. "They haven't hatched yet. Two more locks to go."

Jodi sank the key into the third lock, made the wish, same negative results. "This is silly. Take this and make jewelry." She handed the key to Suki.

"One more left," Kasha said. "Might as

well keep going."

"It's not going to open," Jodi predicted.

"Stop being such a Negative Nelly." Suki planted a hand on Jodi's shoulder. "Or I swear I'm going to pinch you."

"You're right," Jodi said. "I am being negative." Enough of that. She squared her shoulders. This was a brand-new year. Brand-new future. Brand-new life.

Into the lock she stuck the key.

"I wish for a grand adventure," she said, but silently she amended, a grand *sexual* adventure. Jake had stirred something new and different inside her. Something she wanted more of. She turned the key.

The lock clicked.

Surprised, Jodi drew back. "Whoa, what was that?"

"It opened!" Suki crowed and hopped to her feet. "It worked. I told you it was going to work. Why doesn't anyone ever listen to me?"

"Because you chatter nonstop," Kasha said kindly. "No one listens to jabber."

Suki stuck out her tongue.

"And you are how old?" Kasha shook her head as if she was the wisest pine tree in the East Texas forest. "And you wonder why no one listens to you?"

"At least I'm fun." Suki tossed her head

and the long side of her asymmetrical cut brushed her left shoulder.

"Granted," Kasha said.

"Well?" Suki nudged Jodi with her toe. "Open the damn trunk already."

Jodi lifted the lid and it unhinged to reveal the contents of the fourth compartment. Inside she found a square wooden box, three inches wide, three inches deep, and three inches tall. It was identical to the box Breeanne had found when she opened the fifth compartment. Taking the smaller box from the hope chest, she noticed an inscription.

"What's it say?" Suki breathed down the back of Jodi's neck.

Jodi traced her fingers over the engraved words, surprised to find her fingers trembled slightly.

A scent to love; a smell above all others, only two can know that the fragrance of deep passion belongs exclusively to mates of the soul.

Jodi stared at the box for a long moment, feeling strangely sluggish and at the same time, oddly magnetized.

"I hate this cryptic stuff," Suki said. "What does it mean?"

"Breeanne's box had something to do with the sense of touch," Kasha said. "From the inscription, my guess is that whatever is in the box has something to do with the sense of smell."

"Ooh," Suki said. "You are so smart."

Kasha smiled an inarguable smile.

Jodi opened the box and bingo, Kasha was right. Nestled on a black velvet cloth was an antique, rose-colored perfume bottle and atomizer. Around the neck of the bottle, tied with a thin white string, was a small piece of yellowed paper labeled with the words: "SMELL ME."

Jodi glanced up to meet the curious gazes of her sisters. "What do I do?"

"Give yourself a spritz," Suki said.

"What if it's not perfume in the bottle?" Jodi asked. "What if it's something toxic?"

"Oh for hell's sake. You are such a worry-wart. Give it." Suki leaned over and snatched the perfume bottle from the box, spritzed some on her wrist.

The liquid puffed droplets on Suki's golden skin and filled the air with the most enticing aroma of lavender fields, white linen, summer raindrops, and Madagascar vanilla. If angels had a scent it would most surely be this.

Jodi's nostrils twitched. It was the most

arousing, and at the same time, comforting thing she'd ever smelled. It smelled like her past and future rolled into one big perfect now. She wished she could wrap the scent around her like a blanket, an aromatic shield against the world's ills.

Suki brought her wrist to her nose, took a long whiff. "Eh, it must have lost its oomph after years in that trunk. I don't smell a thing." She stuck her wrist under Kasha's nose. "You?"

"Nada."

"Very funny," Jodi said, and claimed the perfume bottle from Suki, sprayed the heavenly fragrance at the pulse point at her neck.

Suki wrinkled her nose. "Do you smell anything?"

"We should have expected it," Kasha said. "After Breeanne."

Suki took another long whiff of her wrist. "All I smell is me."

Kasha took Suki's wrist and brought it up to her nose. "Yep, all I'm getting is eau de Suki."

"What does it smell like to you?" Suki asked, sticking her wrist under Jodi's nose.

Jodi inhaled deeply, smiled as her head lightened. "Like purple sunshine ice cream."

"Very psychedelic," Kasha said. "Maybe it

is toxic."

"Purple, huh?" Suki said. "Like grapes?"

It was too hard to explain the delightful aroma creeping through her nose, seeping into her brain, making her heart beat illogically faster.

"You know, I've heard that perfume smells differently on different people," Kasha said. "Depending on your body chemistry."

Suki leaned over to smell Jodi's neck. "Naw, not getting anything."

Nostrils flaring, Kasha sniffed at her too.

Jodi raised her shoulders to her ears, muscling them off. "You guys sound like Skeeter," she said, referring to her neighbor's Great Dane, who couldn't seem to get enough of sniffing her trashcans. "Stop smelling me."

"Oh wow." Suki tapped Kasha's arm. "This *is* just like Breeanne and the cheetah scarf. We all thought it felt like burlap, but she thought it felt like silk."

"And Rowdy thought it was so soft too," Kasha reminded her.

"You know what that means, Jodi." Suki angled her head, and the short side of her haircut fell over her rounded chin.

"What's that?"

"The guy who can smell your invisible perfume is your soul mate."

146

"That's silly."

"Too bad you didn't have this perfume when you slept with one-night-stand guy. He might have been The One."

Jodi rolled her eyes, but part of her thought, *Yeah, too bad.*

"Ooh." Kasha shivered. "I just got goose bumps for you, Jo. Your soul mate is just a sniff away."

"Stop being woo-woo," Jodi said. "I know you're a bit New Age, granola-bar crunchy, but it's all just coincidence. Most likely the perfume has lost some of its potency and I simply have a stronger sense of smell than you guys do."

"Fine. Let's go test your theory and find someone else to sniff you," Suki said. "Where's Ham?"

"Give the perfume to me," Kasha suggested. "I'll take it to the hospital and have my friend in the lab test it."

"Don't be silly," Jodi said, holding the bottle out of their reach, feeling oddly possessive of the perfume and not wanting to let it out of her sight.

"I think she doth protest too much," Suki said to Kasha. "I think she believes."

"I do not," Jodi denied, but she couldn't help wondering, if she'd had this perfume

147

to wear when she crashed the wedding, would Jake have been able to smell it too?

CHAPTER 7

Jodi Carlyle's Wedding Crasher Rules:
What happens at the wedding stays at
the wedding.

While Jodi was smelling lavender heaven, Jake spent the day at the batting cage with ten-year-old LeShaun Aimes, assigned to him through the Big Brothers Big Sisters organization.

The Dallas Gunslingers' new field manager, Rowdy Blanton, had gotten Jake involved in the program. He'd been doing it for only a couple of months, but he enjoyed spending every other Sunday afternoon with the kid.

"Battin' two hundred today," LeShaun said, and pinched his nose. "You stink."

Yeah. He deserved that. No matter how hard he tried, Jake couldn't seem to shake Gwendolyn from his mind. He wondered where she was and what she was doing.

"What's your score?" he asked.

"Two forty," LeShaun said proudly. "I'm beatin' the pants off you." The boy did an I'm-a-badass dance.

"Gotta hand it to you, you're good, kid." Jake thumped the bill of LeShaun's blue and green Dallas Gunslingers cap and sent it flying backward off the boy's head.

"Hey," agile LeShaun said, catching the cap before it hit the ground. "Sore loser."

"Gloaty winner."

They grinned at each other. Jake had grown up with two older sisters and he had to admit that it was kind of nice having a little brother. He could only hope LeShaun was getting as much out of this relationship as he was.

He took LeShaun home, but when he got to his condo, it felt so quiet and empty after spending the day with the lively kid that he circled back to a popular sports bar near Gunslinger Stadium for a beer.

Overall he wasn't much of a bar guy, preferring to spend his free time at the gym, playing sports, or hanging out with friends. But he needed something to take his mind off the beautiful wedding crasher he couldn't seem to forget. He kept conjuring up images of long, lovely calves encased in those screaming hot stilettos, kept hearing her soft sighs of pleasures, kept tasting her on his tongue.

What was up with that? He'd never had trouble letting a casual fling stay casual. Was it because she looked like Maura?

It didn't take a PhD in psychology to put two and two together and figure out he was displacing his feelings for his Maura onto Gwendolyn. It wasn't Gwendolyn that he was attracted to, he rationalized. He didn't even know her.

That thought bothered him more than he wanted to admit. He told himself he had moved on when he'd gone through Maura's personal effects last year — keeping only her wedding rings and their wedding photos. He'd given the rest of her things to her parents, and what they didn't want he'd donated to charity. The only thing he had left to deal with from their short-lived, ill-fated marriage was the house in Jefferson they'd bought together. The place where they'd sat on the back porch and planned the life they were going to have. He hadn't been back there since she died.

He paid a landscaping company to keep up the yard for appearances, and had a handyman to keep an eye out for any needed repairs, but he still hadn't dredged up the courage to put the house on the market.

Maybe he was afraid that disposing of the house would close the last door.

He needed to get a move on if he hoped to sell it this year. Spring training started in late February. He had less than two months to get the house in shape. If he waited any longer, it would be October before he would have another crack at it.

After Gwendolyn had left him at the Grand Texan, he'd been uncharacteristically bummed out, and he called his mom in San Antonio. They had a nice conversation about his visit at Christmas, but when she asked him how he'd spent his New Year's, he hadn't been about to tell her, *I met a girl I really like, but she looks so much like Maura it scares the hell out of me.*

He was damn grateful now that Gwendolyn had refused to give her name or number. If she had, he would have called. And how could he build an honest relationship with her if he was subconsciously looking to replace what he'd lost?

He took a sip of his beer, swallowing past the lump clogging his throat. "I'm sorry, Maura," he whispered. "I'm so damn sorry for everything."

"What didja say?" asked the bartender.

"I'll have another." Jake nodded at his beer that had warmed while he brooded.

"Sure thing." The bartender turned to get him a drink.

Jake felt someone settle onto the bar stool beside him. Praying it wasn't a woman he'd have to fend off, he swung his gaze to his left and was relieved to see Rowdy.

"Hey." Jake grinned.

"You're a hard guy to track down. Do you ever answer your text messages?" Rowdy asked.

"Sorry," he said. Truthfully, he wondered if he was the only guy on the planet under forty who hated how the world demanded 24/7 access to his time. "I turn my phone off whenever I'm with LeShaun and I forgot to turn it back on."

"How's that going?"

"Good." Jake nodded. "I really like the kid. I hope he's getting as much out of it as I am."

"Glad to hear that. I hoped the program would be a nice fit for you."

"What's up?"

Rowdy ordered a beer, picked up a cardboard coaster, toyed with it. "I've got a big favor to ask of you."

"Yeah?" Jake shifted toward him. "What's that?"

"Please don't feel obligated to say yes, but . . . well, you were the first person I thought of."

"In regard to what?" Jake would do anything for his friend. They'd played for the Cardinals together when they were both starting out and Rowdy had saved Jake's bacon on more than one occasion when they were both young and punch-drunk with success at a sport they both loved.

And then later, after Maura, Rowdy was one of the people who managed to get through to him when he hit rock bottom.

"My wedding," Rowdy said.

"I got my invite last week. Sorry I haven't RSVP'd yet. I am planning on coming."

"I'm glad because Warwick's backed out of being my best man." Rowdy rotated his left shoulder. A little over a year ago Rowdy had been assaulted by a baseball bat–wielding attacker outside a Dallas nightclub. The attack had left him unable to pitch in the major leagues.

Jake shifted on his stool. "Is Warwick all right? What happened?"

"Stage fright."

"Warwick? He's scared of something?"

"He finally confessed that the thought of giving the best man speech made him want to vomit and the closer it got to the wedding, the more he started freaking out about it."

"Seriously? I can't imagine Warwick being scared of anything."

"He only agreed to do it in the first place because we've been friends since the dawn of time. He said he'd still do it, but he had to let me know how he was feeling. The big guy was sweating bullets just talking about it. He's my best friend and I want him there, but I can't torture him like that."

Jake laughed. "So you want to torture me instead?"

"C'mon, you love being in front of a crowd. And you're great at giving speeches. I still don't know how you were able to give such a touching eulogy for Maura. If it was Breeanne —" He broke off, shuddered. "You're a stronger man than I am."

"No." Jake pressed his lips together, fighting off the ache that pushed against his chest at the memory of that terrible time. "I was shattered, and I don't even know how I managed to pull it together. But I was saying goodbye to the woman I loved most in the world. I did it to honor Maura. You would do the same for Breeanne."

Rowdy squeezed Jake's shoulder, gulped, and damn if there wasn't a glimmer of moisture in his eyes. They said nothing for a long moment, just sat sipping beer. The pain slid away quickly and Jake let out a relieved breath. It took less and less time for him to recover from those flashes of grief. He'd made it through the worst. He was going to be okay. And in the course of his healing, he'd learned the best way to handle his grief was to do things for others. Keep his mind busy and off himself.

"I hate to ask. I know it's an imposition on short notice," Rowdy said. "The wedding is only five weeks away. Warwick has already planned the bachelor party, so you don't have to worry about that —"

"Rowdy," he said. "It's no problem. It would be my privilege to serve as your best man, but shouldn't you pick someone you're closer to?"

"For one thing, I respect the hell out of you, Jake. And although we haven't kept in touch over the last couple of years, I consider you a good friend."

"And I can fit into Warwick's tux."

"True enough." Rowdy laughed, but something in his tone said there was more behind the request than that.

Jake pressed. "You have a lot of good friends. Why me?"

Rowdy rubbed a thumbnail over the label on his beer bottle, peeled it back, but didn't meet Jake's gaze. "I heard you hadn't sold the house in Jefferson."

Ah. Meddling. Rowdy was sticking his nose in Jake's business.

Jake turned to face forward, studying the myriad liquor bottles lining the wall behind the bar. Tequila. Vodka. Whiskey. Rum. He'd tried them all when he went in a tailspin after the trial. Making sure he put away Maura's killer had given him purpose, and it was only after the murderer had gotten a life sentence that it had sunk in on Jake that Maura was truly gone.

Rowdy was the one who got through to him before his drinking got completely out of control. Thank God. He owed his friend. Owed him big-time. If it weren't for Rowdy, he might be dead by now.

But thanks to his friend, he had gotten it together. And he was proud of himself. He was ready — no, he was *eager* to find love again.

He thought again of Gwendolyn. Smiled. Wished he'd gotten her real name and number, even as he knew it was probably best he hadn't.

"I heard you still haven't put the house in Jefferson on the market," Rowdy said.

Past. Gone. Poof. Over.

Jake turned to face Rowdy again. "What of it?"

Jefferson was a quaint town thirty miles

northeast of Stardust, where Rowdy had grown up. Rowdy still owned a house there, even though he also had a residence in Dallas, just as Jake did.

"Since the wedding is being held in Stardust," Rowdy said, "you could stay at the house in Jefferson during the activities. It would give you a reason to go back and figure out what it needs to be put on the market."

"So you're asking me to be your best man because you think being that close to Jefferson will light a fire under me?"

"Couldn't hurt."

"You're sticking your nose in my business," Jake said amicably.

"As I recall, you didn't appreciate me sticking my nose in your business three years ago, but where would you be if I hadn't?" Rowdy countered.

"You saved me," Jake said. "I owe you for life."

"I'm not using that as a trump card. If you don't want to be my best man, I understand. But do yourself a favor and put the house on the market. I care about you, Jake. It's time."

Caught by an updraft of emotions he didn't want to feel, Jake rolled his eyes. "If you go all touchy-feely on me, Blanton, I'm gonna buy you a box of tampons for a wedding gift."

Rowdy laughed. "Fair enough. So you'll fill in for Warwick?"

Part of him wanted to say no, but he owed Rowdy so much and his friend was right. It *was* time to unload the house. The last letting go. He needed to put the past to rest before he could fully step forward into the future.

"Sure," he said easily. "I'll be your best man. Whatever you need."

"Wow, thanks." Rowdy thrust out his hand for a shake. "Just FYI, Breeanne has a big family and they're pretty traditional."

Jake arched an eyebrow. "Meaning?"

"Her folks are hosting us an engagement party."

"You're having a Valentine's Day wedding. Shouldn't you have already had an engagement party?"

"We would have, but things were in such a turmoil after that mess with Dugan Potts, we didn't have a chance to squeeze it in."

Last year, Rowdy had been instrumental in exposing the former general manager of the Dallas Gunslingers, Dugan Potts, for his role in a massive steroid doping scandal that had rocked baseball to its core. It happened about the same time that Rowdy and

Breeanne had gotten engaged. The Gun-slingers were just now shaking off the stigma under completely new management.

"I get that," Jake said, even though the scandal had occurred before he joined the team. "Last year was crazy for you. I can see why you postponed the engagement party."

"Anyway, the party is next Saturday in Stardust. Can you make it?"

Jake blew out his breath and tried not to look pained. He hadn't really braced himself for heading back to East Texas this soon, entering the empty house that he hadn't been in for three years.

He didn't know if was ready for that quite yet. Maybe he could just grab a motel room in Stardust for one night. Then make a decision about going on to Jefferson or coming back to Dallas the following day.

"No sweat," Jake assured him. "I'll be there."

It had been two weeks since Jodi crashed the wedding. Two weeks since she'd had sex with a stranger. Two weeks since she'd taken a walk on the wild side and loved every second of it.

She had reported back to Dr. Jeanna, skipping the part about having a one-night stand, but she'd been totally honest about how liberated she felt. Rather than scheduling a follow-up appointment, Dr. Jeanna said she was encouraged by the strides Jodi had made and suggested that she return only if she felt a need.

And it had been a week since she found the odd perfume bottle in the hope chest. No one had been able to smell the sweet, evocative scent that so captivated her, and she'd begun to think it was all in her head. Maybe so, but that didn't stop her from spritzing herself with the delicate fragrance that morning. It was the most perfect scent she'd ever owned.

After clearing away the breakfast buffet she'd put out for the guests, Jodi set about cleaning the boxcars. Starting with the blue Southern Pacific railcar that was located nearest the renovated train engine that was the guest services office.

Old Blue was the first boxcar that she'd ever owned. She bought it for two thousand dollars when she was nineteen and, with Ham's help, had renovated it in eight months' time. They'd perfected the renovation process since then, and now they could overhaul a boxcar in eight weeks. Of course, she also had more money now too, which helped speed things up.

Last spring, they'd finished the latest addition to her B&B, a Texas Northeastern railcar they'd painted TCU purple, bringing the number of guest rooms up to nine. She and Ham renovated a new boxcar every year, and she envisioned a full dozen of them eventually. The cars were ringed in a circle on property abutting Stardust State Park on the west and a fingerling tributary of Stardust Lake to the south. She'd inherited the land from her biological maternal grandmother on her eighteenth birthday.

The minute she saw the undeveloped property, she'd instantly known what she was going to do with it. She had a passion for customer service that she'd honed while working at Timeless Treasures as a teen, and her natural talent for order and organization had served her well in the hospitality industry. She loved making sure guests were well fed, comfortable, and entertained.

For Jodi, running a B&B was a calling as much as a livelihood. She couldn't imagine herself doing anything else, even though her job was a sixty- to seventy-hour-a-week commitment, and cut deep into a social life. Unlike many of the men she'd dated, Ryan had understood her devotion to the B&B. Which was one of the things that appealed to her about him. In retrospect, his understanding probably stemmed from the fact that he had not been so devoted to her.

She should have listened to Ham, who had not liked Ryan from the moment he clapped eyes on him.

"What's with the oily, slicked-back hair?" he'd asked her the first time Ryan came to pick her up at the B&B. "He looks like Robert Mitchum in *Night of the Hunter.*"

Ham was a movie buff and he'd been the one to suggest they make a theater boxcar. The theater car also served as a library. One half stocked with books, the other half containing seating for sixteen, rescued from the demolition of the old Stardust Theater. Besides the nightly showings for guests, every other Friday night, they ran old movies for free to the community, along with complimentary popcorn and soda. Most everyone who attended put more money into the donations jar than what the refreshments cost, showcasing the generous spirit of Stardustians.

Thirty years ago, she and Ham had been born the same week, at the same hospital, and they'd lived next door to each other in the same sad-ass part of town where Breeanne's fiancé, Rowdy, had grown up. Rowdy was three years older than they were and she hadn't known him when she lived in that neighborhood. From the time she and Ham could walk, they were best friends, close as brother and sister.

Jodi had lived in that house with Vivian until cops and social workers had shown up at their door on that fateful day. Later, she learned that Ham's mother had been the one who called CPS, and even later still, she'd learned the reason his mother had not come home was that she'd been found dead of an overdose in the home of a known heroin dealer.

There'd been no one else to care for Jodi. Jodi's maternal grandfather was dead, her maternal grandmother in an Alzheimer's care facility. She'd ended up in foster care system. Thankfully, it had been with Maggie and Dan Carlyle. Her biological mother had been an only child, and because of Vivian's lifestyle, there had been a revolving door of men in and out of the house, and no one knew who Jodi's biological father was.

Over the years, she'd tried to search for him with her adoptive parents' help, but Jodi had never been successful. In the end, she figured it was all for the best. What if he was a druggie like her mother? Or in prison or dead? She had a family who loved her deeply and as the years went by, she cared less and less, until she rarely thought about it.

When she'd first gone to live with Mom and Dad, they had just adopted Breeanne, who was a premature newborn with special health needs. Jodi watched over the baby as if she was her own and she loved Breeanne with all her heart. Jodi did her best to fit in with the family, kept her room clean, and did as she was told without complaint. She knew what a wonderful thing she had going and didn't want to mess up. Her good behavior paid off and the following year, Maggie and Dan adopted her too, and she'd felt like the luckiest girl in the entire world. Still did.

But through it all, she never forgot Ham.

Stardust had only one high school, and it was during her freshman year that she met up with Ham again. The minute they saw each other it was as if they'd never been apart. They struggled through history class together, but both aced geometry. They studied together, spent Saturdays at the movies, shared secrets and hopes and dreams. Jodi would never tell her adopted family this, but Ham was the only one with whom she could fully be herself. At home, she was the caretaker, the responsible one, the older practical sister who did her best not to step out of line. It was a role she perfected to keep her darkest fear at bay — that if she failed to measure up, she'd be sent away and end up like Vivian.

She finished cleaning Old Blue and picked up the used linen to take to the hamper. For no good reason at all, she thought of Jake, and that sent her daydreaming. He'd been on her mind every single day since their hookup.

And she was smiling again.

Jodi hoisted the laundry in her arms, locked the door behind her, and started across the decorative railroad tracks to the canvas laundry hamper parked on the sidewalk.

That's when she saw him getting out of the red Corvette as it pulled up to the office.

Jake.

As if by thinking of him, she'd conjured him up.

She went both hot and cold at the same time as it fully hit her. Oh shit! He'd tracked her down. But how? She'd been so careful. She hadn't told him anything personal about herself. Maybe he'd gone into her wallet while she was sleeping. Damn him. That had to be it. How else had he located her?

Great. The last thing she wanted was to have a conversation with him.

He hadn't seen her yet, but if she didn't do something quickly, he would spot her.

For a half second, she stood frozen in the January morning, the air crisp with a bite of cold. The nearest boxcar was ten yards away. She could streak behind it, but he would see her and then he'd know she was intentionally hiding from her.

What to do? What to do?

The canvas wheeled laundry cart was right in front of her. Empty because Old Blue was the first room she'd cleaned.

He hadn't seen her yet. His gaze was fixed on the office door. He walked up the steps leading to the front door of the engine car, and opened the door. As soon as he discovered the office was empty, he would come back out.

Quick! Quick! Do something.

Spurred by thoughts of humiliation and embarrassment, she flung the sheets on the ground and jumped into the laundry cart.

CHAPTER 8

Jodi Carlyle's Wedding Crasher Rules:
If you get caught, play dumb.

Gwendolyn?

Jake stood on the steps of what had once been a Hondo Railway engine, lovingly restored. He cocked his head to stare curiously at the wheeled canvas laundry hamper parked at the top of a slope several yards away.

From the corner of his eye, he'd seen a woman climb into the hamper, and he could have sworn it was Gwendolyn.

You're seeing things. You just want it to be her.

True enough. He couldn't seem to stop thinking about her. But the odds that she was the woman in the hamper were three hundred million to one.

And if by some strange quirk of fate she *was* the woman in the hamper, obviously she jumped in there because she didn't want to see him.

She told you to buzz off. Respect that.

He started to head toward the hamper, but thought better of it. She couldn't stay in there forever and he was a patient man. He'd wait. Jake sank down on the top step and watched curiously as she thrashed around inside the hamper. It couldn't be comfortable in there.

Amused, he glanced at his cell phone. Ten-fifteen. He'd time her.

While he sat waiting, a huge brindle Great Dane sauntered around the side of the engine.

"Hey, fella," Jake called, and the dog loped over.

The Great Dane plunked down in front of him, rested a massive paw on Jake's blue-jeaned knee, and gazed up with huge milk chocolate eyes.

"You are such an attention hound." Jake leaned forward to scratch the big beast behind his years. The Great Dane thumped his tail against the metal steps — *whang, whang, whang.*

A minute passed.

And then another.

Inside the laundry cart, the woman wriggled. And the cart moved. If she wasn't careful, she was going to send the cart rolling down the incline and end up taking a nasty spill on the cement.

Jodi lay curled up in the canvas cart feeling like a tuna caught in a net, listening to her heart pounding, trying to stay still so that she didn't look like what she was — a nutty woman hiding out in a laundry hamper from her one-night stand.

Jeez. Why had Jake come after her when she'd made it perfectly clear that she did not want to see him again? Couldn't the dude take no for an answer?

Maybe he was a stalker. That would be her luck. She finally did something out of left field, let go of her good-girl ways for half a second and simply acted on her feelings, and look what happened. A stalker. See? Right there. This was why she did not do impulsive things.

She wadded herself up tight, held her breath. How long would it take for him to leave?

Hiding had not been a brilliant solution. Bad idea. If he was intent on talking to her — and clearly, since he'd bothered to track her down all the way to Stardust, she had assumed that he was intent on talking to her — the man was not going to give up easily.

Craptastic.

Why had she jumped into the laundry hamper? She should have just dealt with him. Now she was stuck waiting for him to leave.

Why hadn't he gone already? Ham was out running errands. There was no one else here for him to talk to. What if he was snooping around the office? Going through her things?

Damn. Damn. Damn.

Straining her ears, she listened for the sound of a car door closing, or a car engine starting. Any indication that he'd gone on his merry way.

No such luck.

All she heard was the call of a grackle. Wait. What was that? Rhythmic clicking. Like dog toenails on cement.

Skeeter.

Oh no. Not Skeeter. A sniffy nose nudged the outside of the laundry cart.

"Go away, Skeeter," she muttered. "Go home."

The nose, overjoyed at having discovered her, bumped at Jodi through the canvas that formed a sling around her butt.

"Beat it, Skeeter," she hissed.

The Great Dane whimpered joyously and bumped the cart again. The huge dog was little more than a puppy and wanted to play.

She felt the wheels of the cart move. *Please let Jake be gone.* If she had to look like an utter fool, please don't let anyone see her.

Another bump from Skeeter and the laundry cart took off down the sidewalk. Seriously? Talk about bad luck. Her only hope was that Jake had already driven away.

But she hadn't heard the car door shut or the engine start. He was still on the property and she didn't know how to get out of this gracefully.

Forget dignity. You're about to bust your ass.

The cart picked up speed on the downhill slope. Feeling like a goofy cartoon character, she tried to figure out how she was going to keep the cart from steering off the sidewalk and into the stream that fed into Stardust Lake. Why had she built her B&B so close to the water? Uh, because normally the tributary was a good thing, a nice draw for customers who liked to fish or canoe, but right now, she hated that damn stream.

Don't blame the stream. Blame the dumbass who climbed into a laundry cart when it was parked at the top of a hill.

Forget blame. Forget being embarrassed.

How was she going to get out of here without getting skinned knees and elbows?

The cart was flying now, bumping along the sidewalk. If she flung herself sideways, she could seriously hurt herself on the concrete. So what was the alternative? She had to stop the laundry cart or end up in the stream.

She could hear Skeeter trotting along beside the laundry cart, panting with glee as if to say, *Mobile hide-and-seek, what fun!*

Maybe the cart would stop on its own. When the sidewalk ran out, it could just topple over into the dirt instead of pitch forward into the water. That could happen, right? Except the cart showed no sign of slowing or stopping. It kept rolling, gathering speed, zooming toward an unhappy destiny.

Skeeter let out a deep-throated bark of canine warning. She startled. The cart jerked, the wheels catching on something. Jodi pitched forward, felt the cart leave the sidewalk, tilt, tip. Momentum shot her from the downed cart. Her plan was to somersault forward, plant her feet, stand up. Ta-da. Unhurt. Unfazed.

Except it didn't turn out that way.

Gravity claimed her somersault, sent her tumbling feet-over-head into the stream.

She tried to brace herself, to cushion for the fall, but she ended up splayed facedown in the cold, muddy water.

Brr!

Her teeth chattered and she was shivering so hard, it took a second to orient herself. Before she could push up to take stock of her injuries, a strong masculine arm reached down for her.

It was the same masculine arm that had picked her up when she'd fallen at the Grand Texan. She knew without looking up that it belonged to Jake. If she lived to be a hundred, she would never forget the feel of those particular biceps. He must think she was the clumsiest person on the face of the earth.

"Are you all right?" His warm voice brushed against her ear.

Oh Lord.

She closed her eyes. Struggled against her desire to melt into his embrace, raise the white flag, give up, tell him he was hot as a firecracker and all she wanted was to screw his brains into next week.

But she couldn't do that. He was supposed to have been nothing more than a sweet fling, an exciting adventure to help her put the memory of Ryan and her wedding day humiliation behind her. She had closed him up in a mental box and he was supposed to stay there, dammit. Nothing more than a lovely fantasy she pulled out along with her vibrator from time to time.

Why on earth was he here? Did she really want to get involved with someone so persistent that he'd tracked her down even after she'd told him she never wanted to see him again?

Um, yes.

"Gwendolyn?" His hands were so gentle, so kind, and that was odd because he was so big, so strong, so rugged. "Speak to me."

She opened her eyes and finally looked at him. One glance into those dark brown eyes and the same emotions seized her — hunger, desire, need. One night had not been nearly enough. Jodi gulped, shivered, her teeth bumping together so fiercely she couldn't speak.

"You're freezing wet," he exclaimed.

Yeah, okay, her body was kind of numb. She took a step away from him, ankle-deep in mud. Well, at least that was the intention. Her body moved, but her right foot stayed mired in the muck. She went down again, falling on her knees in the stream.

Dammit! She hated appearing weak. Especially in front of him. She was the oldest. The strong one. The one who took care of everybody. The mother hen. And yes, okay, according to her sisters, the bossy one.

But right now, she couldn't even boss her own body around.

In fact — *horrors* — her frustration threatened to turn to tears. She was frustrated with her body for betraying her so completely. Frustrated with Jake for showing up here when she'd told him she did not want to see him again. Frustrated with herself for being so glad to see him.

Jake picked her up from the mud, scooped her into his arms, and started carrying her. Where was he taking her?

"Put me down," she protested.

He did not. He marched — all alpha he-man — up the sidewalk, his black cowboy boots striding across the cement. Jodi's heart thumped and her breath was short and shaky. *Demand he put you down. Struggle! Put up a fight. Do something!*

But she'd been fighting for so long. From the time she was a small girl. Fighting to survive with a drug-addicted mother. Fighting to prove she deserved to be a Carlyle. Fighting to hold her adopted family together when Breeanne was so sick. Fighting to build her business from the ground up. Fighting to live down Ryan's felonious betrayal.

Dammit, dammit, dammit. Why was she having a meltdown now? Why did she want this man?

He climbed the steps to the office, paused to jiggle open the door with one hand while transferring the bulk of her weight to his other arm. She was shivering uncontrollably. The cold January wind was blowing through her soaking wet sweater. She wasn't even wearing a coat because it was too bulky to wear when cleaning the boxcars and too inconvenient to keep taking on and off between coming and going from the rooms.

The door to the office swung open and he carried her inside. Skeeter trotted in behind them like he lived there. Her fault. She snuck him meat scraps. The black potbelly stove in the corner exuded heat. He kicked the door closed, and finally, thankfully, set her on her feet. She lost her balance, swayed into him.

"Whoa there." He put out a restraining hand, steadied her.

"I'm fine," she said, her voice coming out soft and weak. Alarmed, she starched her voice, lowered her tone, moved away from him. "I'm good."

She crossed her arms over her chest, her nipples hard as rocks beneath her wet sweater. Skeeter loped over to lick the back of her hand.

Jake's eyes flicked to her chest, and a knowing smile lit up his eyes.

She felt the color rise to her cheeks, burn pink. "Down boy," she said to the dog, but she was really talking to Jake.

"Sit," he commanded, pulling out a chair near the potbelly stove.

Immediately, Skeeter sat.

"Your dog is well trained."

"Skeeter's not my dog. He belongs to a neighbor, but he loves hanging around. Probably because I feed him."

"Explains why he obeys better than you do. Sit," Jake told her pointedly.

Skeeter looked up at him with baleful eyes as if to say, *But I* am *sitting.*

Jodi shook her head, not liking his bossy tone, but her knees were kind of wobbly, so she sat anyway. She blinked, trying to orient herself. How had she gotten into this situation? Oh yeah, she'd stupidly climbed into a laundry cart. It was nobody's fault but hers.

Jake whipped off his jacket and wrapped it around her shoulders. The front of it was damp and smeared with mud from carrying her. He swore under his breath, muttered, "Need something warmer," glanced around the room, grabbed the lap blanket from the sofa, and tucked it around her shoulders.

178

She shivered, more from his nearness than the cold, although she was pretty darn cold. She lowered her lashes so he couldn't see that she was studying him. Oh man, but he was hot. Really, really hot. The man was utterly edible.

He wore blue jeans and a red flannel shirt that hugged broad shoulders. Red was his color. It complemented his tanned complexion and dark head of hair. Although he'd looked debonair in a tuxedo, he was even hotter in flannel and jeans. A regular guy's guy. Macho. Rugged. Like the dude on the Brawny paper towel commercial. This was more his true self. While he'd worn the tuxedo with ease, it was not a natural fit. His mouth was full, but not too wide, and seriously, she should not be thinking about his mouth because that made her think of kissing him, and kissing him made her think of — Well, never mind what kissing him made her think of.

A scowl creased his forehead, but his lips lifted in an unexpectedly sweet smile. That kindness thing again. Clearly a man of action, he trod across the room to the coffee machine she kept for guests, grabbed the carafe, poured coffee in a Styrofoam cup, and brought it back to her.

"Drink," he commanded.

The man was bossier than she was. She sat with the steaming cup in her hand, stubbornness latching on to her.

"Drink." He glowered.

She balked.

"Please don't make me force-feed you."

"It's drink, not food."

"You know what I mean."

Just to get him off her back, she took a sip. The warm liquid slid down her throat, braced her. Felt really good. She kept drinking, and slowly the shivers racking her body ebbed.

"Good girl," he said, sounding self-satisfied.

"Don't patronize me." She glowered. "I'm thirty years old. I haven't been a girl in twelve years."

"Good woman," he amended. An amused smile plucked his angular mouth. She remembered what those lips tasted like — heat and peppermint and *Jake*.

"I'm good because I obeyed you? If I hadn't, would I have been bad?"

"You're a disagreeable cuss."

"Is that a problem?"

His grin spread. "Not at all. I like a good argument."

So did she, but she wasn't about to say that.

He knelt in front of her.

"What are you doing?"

He didn't answer, just untied her sneaker.

She curled her feet underneath the chair rung.

"Give me your foot."

"I can take off my own shoes."

"I know that." He reached for her right ankle, slowly untangled her foot from the chair rung, and settled it on his knee. The sight of her foot on his leg sent a memory rushing over her and she recalled his big fingers working the buckle on her high heels. A fresh shudder ran through her.

He slipped off her sneaker and her soaking wet pink Hello Kitty sock. "Love the socks," he said.

"Yeah, well, sometimes I feel frivolous." Actually, the socks had been a Christmas gift from Hannah, the seven-year-old girl for whom she served as a court-appointed special advocate volunteer.

"I'll keep that in mind."

"No," she said. "Don't keep it in mind. You have no need to know that I wear Hello Kitty socks upon occasion."

"But I already do know." He smirked and reached for her other foot.

Jodi rolled her eyes, caught a glimpse of herself in the glass of the potbelly stove.

Eeek! Her hair was matted to her head, face bare of makeup, a smear of mud over her left cheek. She tried to fluff her damp hair and scrubbed at her face, knocked flecks of mud into her lap. What a mess. Good grief, what was wrong with the man that he wanted her enough to hunt her down?

Now that he had both her bare feet propped up on his knees, he started vigorously rubbing first one freezing pale foot, and then the other. Instantly, her skin tingled at his touch, toes pinking.

"That feels good," she admitted.

"Next time don't be so stubborn."

Next time. What did that mean?

"The color is back in your cheeks too," he said. "A few minutes ago you were white as a corpse."

"Wow. That's a wildly romantic simile," Jodi said, and cringed the second the words were out of her mouth. Why had she said "romantic"?

"I wasn't trying to be romantic."

Good. She dropped her gaze back to her coffee cup. It was almost empty.

He got another lap blanket from the sofa — this one she'd knitted — and wrapped her feet in it, and then he moved to lean his gorgeous butt against the desk, pressing big hands to his upper thighs, and sent one eyebrow jutting up on his forehead. Skeeter trotted over to join him, aligning himself with the stranger against her. *Et tu, Skeeter?*

"Why were you in the laundry cart?" he asked.

"Why are you here?" she countered. She did not owe him an explanation, if she wanted to go jumping into laundry carts that was completely her business.

"You were hiding from me." A teasing tone crept into his voice. He sounded victorious that he'd driven her to rash action.

"Who wouldn't hide from a stalker?" she countered, raising her chin.

That caused him to look alarmed. "You think I'm a stalker?"

"Well, you did show up after I explicitly told you to leave me alone."

"I wasn't stalking you."

"No?" She sprinkled a dusting of Death Valley dry into her voice. "Then what are you doing here?"

"I came to rent a room. I've got business in Stardust. I didn't know you'd be here. How would I know you'd be here? Are you a guest? Or do you work here?"

"I own the place."

He looked surprised and impressed. "No kidding."

"You expect me to believe you just showed up out of the blue to rent a room in the small town where your one-night stand runs a B&B?"

"Believe what you want," he said. "It's the truth."

She wanted to believe him. "Big coincidence."

"Maybe, but it's the truth. I'm here for one night and then I'm gone," he said, his eyes lit up with a hopeful here's-your-chance-to-get-more-of-what-happened-at-the-Grand-Texan gleam.

Well, he could hope all he wanted. She was not going to take him up on the unspoken offer.

"The laundry cart," he pressed. "Why'd you dive in?"

"Why do you think? Because I didn't want to see you."

"And you couldn't just tell me that?"

She shrugged. "I wanted to avoid . . ." She waved a hand between them. "This."

He winced, and then chuckled like her words hurt. "Was I that bad that you'd rather risk life and limb in a runaway laundry cart than talk to me?"

No, he was that damn good. "I told you I didn't want a relationship."

"I know. I completely respect that." He

raised both arms, surrendering. "I swear I did not come here to romance you."

Well, that was disappointing. Even if she didn't want him to romance her, she liked thinking that he *wanted* to. "I thought you came here looking for me."

"Didn't." He raised one palm, but the other was down as if taking a Bible oath. "Promise."

"So you need a room?" She should tell him no vacancy, but she wasn't big on lying.

"Don't get up." He pushed a palm downward.

"No trouble." She dropped the lap blanket, but wrapped his coat more securely around her, acutely aware of Jake's brazen gaze on her body. She hopped to her feet, kicking off that blanket too, folded both neatly, and put them back on the couch. When she finished, she hustled over to the desk, giving him a wide berth, and plunked down in the chair. She felt safer behind the desk here in her domain.

Business mode. When in doubt, fall back on what worked.

Work.

"Boxcar #3 is vacant. Lucky for you it's my slow season. It's the orange Boot Hill and Western." She fished a key off the

185

pegboard behind her.

Was she making a mistake by giving him a room? What if he was stalking her? The chances of him stumbling into her B&B by coincidence were too astronomical to be believed.

She looked into his face, didn't see anything to cause alarm. In fact, his eyes were so warm and friendly, she felt flattered that he'd made the effort to find her, if indeed he had. But what the hell did she know? She'd dated Ryan for two years without a clue he was a lying, embezzling cheat. While her instincts might tell her Jake was trustworthy, how could she trust her own judgment?

"You're uncomfortable." He read her mind. "I'm making you uncomfortable."

She wasn't about to admit that. Instead, she held his gaze, raised her chin. "Not at all."

"You sure? I could go to the Best Western on the highway." He gestured over his shoulder in the direction of the interstate.

Yes, say yes. Tell him that would be a great idea. "Just one night?" she said.

"Just one night," he echoed.

She pushed the key toward him. "Enjoy your stay in Stardust. I won't be around this evening. I have a family function. If you

186

need anything, my assistant, Hamilton Gee, will be on duty."

"Okay." His big tanned hand closed around the key and she couldn't help staring at his long, tapered fingers. Couldn't help remembering what it had felt like to be caressed by that hand.

She gulped down her lust, shoved it to the bottom of her stomach. Realized she was still wearing his jacket. Gave it back to him.

He smiled. It was a genuine smile that started somewhere deep inside him, as if he was overjoyed at seeing her again. Thank heavens she would be at Breeanne and Rowdy's engagement party tonight.

Otherwise . . .

She might do something irrevocably stupid like knock on the door of the orange boxcar and ask him to make it a two-night stand.

No, no. That's not how it went. If a woman was looking for a casual hookup she did not extend it. Not if she was trying to keep her heart intact. "Do you need me to show you to your room?"

"Don't you want to see a credit card?" he asked.

"Oh yes, yes." What was wrong with her? The man scrambled her brains. All the more reason not to spend any more time with him.

He pulled out his wallet. Extracted an American Express black card. Okay, so he was rich as hell.

The name on the credit card said Jake Coronado. Hmm. Why did that name sound familiar? She had a feeling she should know the name, but she couldn't place it. She could ask, but she didn't want to give him a reason to hang around the office chitchatting.

"All set." She forced a smile and handed his credit card back to him.

He reached for the card, his fingers brushing lightly against hers.

Zap.

That same sizzle.

No. Not the same. This was stronger than before. Disconcerting. Powerful.

Her smile wobbled, but she propped it back up, determined not to let him know how much he knocked her off kilter. Yeah, as if the laundry cart incident hadn't been a dead giveaway.

"Enjoy your family event," he said, and then disappeared out the door.

Jodi blew out her breath through puffed cheeks, slumped back in the chair. Yep, just her luck. She'd had a one-night stand and it had come back to bite her in the ass.

Now what?

CHAPTER 9

Jodi Carlyle's Wedding Crasher Rules:
When challenged, keep your cool.

Vincente's, the Italian restaurant where
Rowdy's engagement party was being held,
was hopping by the time Jake arrived at
seven p.m. His face was tingling from the
cold. In concession to his new role as best
man, he'd gone ahead and shaved his face
after checking into the B&B, losing his
winter beard a month earlier than he usually did.

He felt exposed. Raw. Open. But in a good
way, if that made sense. Ready for new
beginnings. He rubbed a hand over his chin,
surprised at the smoothness of his skin.

"OMG!" squealed the cute blond hostess.
"You're Jake Coronado!"

"Yeah," he admitted sheepishly. "I'm here
for the Blanton engagement party."

"Of course you are. You are my absolute

favorite baseball player in the whole world," the young woman enthused. "Well, except for Rowdy. He's our hometown hero, but you're second on the list."

"Thanks," he mumbled, and jammed his hands in his pockets. He'd never felt comfortable with fame. Some people courted it, but Jake found it ill fitting. He played ball because he was good at it. It was the only thing he knew how to do. He loved the sport. Wanted to see how many records he could break. Wanted to leave a legacy.

But his lofty dreams had cost him a lot. Maura. The ba—

He shut that thought down quick, winced. If he hadn't been so hell-bent on breaking records and reaching the pinnacle of success he would not have lost Maura. She wouldn't have been . . . Jake clenched his jaw. Willed away her memory. Maura was gone. He couldn't change the past.

In fact, tomorrow morning, he'd decided he was going to Jefferson to start fixing up the house and talk to a realtor about putting it on the market. This was it, his final letting go. He was ready, eager even, to move forward.

The hostess batted her eyes. "Could I trouble you for an autograph? It would mean so much to me."

"Of course." He dug around and found the remnants of a real smile, pushed it into his eyes. He was done suffering. He'd punished himself enough. It felt good to admit that.

And Gwendolyn was the reason he was finally ready. He'd realized it that morning when he'd fished her out of the stream.

His mouth twitched and he puffed out a breath. He probably should have gone to Jefferson instead of renting a room at Gwendolyn's B&B, but it was easier to stay in Stardust for the evening. He didn't know how long the party would last and didn't want to be on the road late at night. At least that was the excuse he gave himself.

Truthfully, he hadn't been quite ready to walk into that lonely, dark house. Not yet. Not today. Not until he got past the engagement party.

He couldn't believe Gwendolyn owned the B&B — dammit, he still hadn't gotten her real name — and that he'd come across her so unexpectedly. The chance meeting felt fated somehow, and that unnerved him.

It unnerved her too. He could tell that he made her uneasy. Hell, she made him uneasy.

He'd thought he would never see her again, and now she was here.

192

Two memories sparked in Jake's brain. One was of Gwendolyn as she sank her stilettoed heel against his thigh, standing in front of him wearing nothing but lacy black lingerie, looking queenly and in control. The other was of her shivering in his arms as he carried her to the train engine, her cheek smeared with mud, her nipples beaded hard beneath her sweater as she nibbled her bottom lip, looking embarrassed and vulnerable. The first memory fired his lust. The second stoked his shielding instincts. He wanted to both make love to her and protect her.

After the hostess pocketed the autograph he signed for her, she led him through the public dining area down a long corridor toward a banquet room. Heads turned as they walked past and he heard murmurs of "That's Jake Coronado."

How was it that he could impress most anyone by simply walking into a room, except the woman he most wanted to impress? Just his luck. The first woman who'd interested him in three years wanted nothing more from him than a one-night stand.

"Would you like to check your coat?" the hostess asked, stopping in the corridor to open the door of a walk-in closet full of coats.

Jake shrugged out of his jacket, waited for the hostess to hang it up, and then followed her into the banquet room with exposed redbrick walls, rustic beamed ceilings, hand-scraped oak floors, and a long rack of artfully displayed wine bottles. White linen cloths adorned tables, topped by the ubiquitous Chianti-bottle candleholders.

Warwick — no one seemed to know what the guy's first name was — Rowdy's childhood chum, bodyguard, and former best man, stood at the front of the room, arms crossed over his chest. He and Jake were the tallest guys in the place, both over six-foot-three. Warwick caught his eye, nodded. He wasn't much of one for words, but Jake got his message. *Thanks for stepping in.*

Jake telegraphed him a no-sweat smile and that was all the communication they needed to understand each other.

A hand slapped Jake on the back and he looked over his shoulder to see Axel Talbot grinning like a loon. Talbot batted third in the Gunslingers' lineup and he had the second best batting average on the team. Dubbed T-bone by the press for his meaty physique, he was a good four inches shorter than Jake, five years younger, ten pounds stockier.

"Yo, Coronado. Best man, huh?" Talbot

grinned, showing a mouthful of ultra white teeth.

"Hey, Talbot."

"Can't believe Blanton of all people is biting the bullet and getting married."

"We all grow up sometime."

Talbot, the perpetual Peter Pan, looked horrified. "Not all of us."

"You're the exception of course," Jake soothed.

"We gotta throw the guy a blowout bachelor party. I've got some ideas —"

"We're not going to Mexico."

Talbot's face fell. "C'mon, just think about it. You, me, the guys, a bus, pretty senoritas . . ."

"I have no interest in ending up in a Mexican jail."

Talbot thought this over, nodded, and raised a hopeful eyebrow. "Vegas?"

"Warwick already made the arrangements for the bachelor party and we're sticking to it."

Talbot shot a glance over at Warwick. "Him? Aww hell, it's gonna be dullsville."

"It won't be if you're there."

That brightened him. "Truer words were never spoken. I'll figure out something . . ."

Jake spied Rowdy at the same time his buddy raised his hand and motioned him over. Rowdy was talking to an older couple, a petite Asian woman, and a tall exotic-looking woman. Rowdy had his arm around the waist of a sweet-faced blonde in her mid-twenties and he was staring at her as if she had waved her little finger and created the sun and the moon and the stars. Smitten. Yeah. He knew how that felt. Missed it. This must be Rowdy's bride-to-be, Breeanne.

"Duty calls," Jake told Talbot. "Catch you later, T-bone."

"Two words for you, Coronado," Talbot called after him. "Busty strippers."

Jake waved at him over his shoulder, and headed toward Rowdy.

When Jake got closer, Rowdy reached out, gripped his elbow, and steered him into the small group. "Breeanne, this is Jake. Jake . . . meet my bride-to-be, Breeanne. And these are her parents, Maggie and Dan Carlyle, her sisters Suki and Kasha."

Sisters, huh? He glanced at the Carlyles, who didn't look a thing like any of their daughters. Some if not all of the Carlyle sisters had to be adopted.

Both women grinned at him as women usually did.

He shook hands with everyone. Smiled. Made small talk. Did what he needed to do to make sure his buddy had a great evening.

"Rowdy's told me so much about you," Breeanne said.

"Uh-oh," Jake said. "And you're still letting him have me as his best man?"

Breeanne's smile was so radiant that Jake immediately understood why Rowdy was crazy about her. "Well, you're not *completely* vetted yet. You've still got to pass muster with the maid of honor, my oldest sister, Jodi."

"Better be on your best behavior," Rowdy said. "Jodi's no-nonsense."

He must have looked startled because Breeanne chuckled lightly. "Don't worry," she said. "Yes, Jodi can be a tough nut to crack, but you're in as best man. She doesn't really have to like you. Rowdy likes you and I like you and that's good enough for us."

"But it would be nice if you and Jodi got along," Rowdy added, looking a little anxious. "You'll be seeing a lot of each other over the next month."

"I'll be sure to pour on the charm." Jake winked.

Maggie Carlyle wrinkled her nose and shook her head good-naturedly. "That might backfire on you with Jodi. Slick doesn't impress her. Not since —" She broke off as if she'd said too much. "Just be yourself, Jake."

Wow, this Jodi person sounded like a pain in the ass. He'd do his best not to butt heads with her. For Rowdy's sake.

"Speaking of Jodi, here she is right now." Petite Breeanne went up on tiptoes, struggling to see over the shoulders of the men. "I'll go get her."

Bracing himself, Jake turned to get a good look at prune-lipped, tough, no-nonsense Jodi.

Auburn hair.

Blue-gray eyes.

Extremely kissable lips.

Oh shit.

It was Gwendolyn.

Jodi froze in mid-step.

Seriously?

The beard was gone, but it was he. Jake Coronado. Nah. Couldn't be. He could not be here. Not twice in one day.

But there was no mistaking the guy.

What was he doing at Breeanne and Rowdy's engagement party? It couldn't be coincidence. There had to be a connection.

She wanted to turn and run.

Too slow. Out of luck. Breeanne took her arm and dragged her to the corner of the room where Jake stood with her parents and her sisters, his eyes rounding in surprise. He hadn't expected to see her any more than she expected to see him.

He'd changed clothes from this morning, wearing chinos and a long-sleeved black polo shirt.

"Jodi, this is Jake. Jake, this is my older sister, Jodi. She's my maid of honor." Breeanne turned to Jodi. "Jake is Rowdy's best man."

Jodi swallowed, not sure what to say or do. "I thought Warwick was Rowdy's best man."

"He chickened out," Breeanne explained. "Fear of public speaking, so Jake volunteered to pinch-hit."

Craptacular. Just her luck she'd be stuck with him as best man.

"Hello, *Jodi,*" Jake said, humor tugging up the corner of his lips and lighting his eyes. "Nice to meet you."

"So that's why you're in town," Jodi blurted.

Breeanne looked perplexed. "You've met?"

Jodi wasn't about to get into the details of their sexcapades at the Grand Texan. She said, "Jake just rented a room at Boxcars. Why didn't you tell me you were Rowdy's best man? Your lodging is on the house."

At the same time she was talking, Jake said, "I didn't know you were Breeanne's sister."

"Why would you? We never met before this morning." She sent him a don't-you-dare-contradict-me warning frown.

"Let me get you both a drink," Breeanne offered. "Wine? Beer?"

"Sure. Whatever," Jodi said.

Anything. She needed something to do with her hands. Needed something to take the edge off the tension knotting up her muscles as it fully sank in what this meant. Jake wasn't a stalker, he was Rowdy's new best man. Which meant she'd be seeing a lot more of him. Oh super, terrific joy.

But even as she grumbled inwardly, her heart fluttered with excitement, and that worried her.

"There's Aunt Liz and Uncle Marty," Breeanne said. "We better go say hello." She held her hand out to Rowdy. "Honey."

Rowdy sank his hand in hers and Breeanne led him over to greet the relatives. Their parents, Kasha, and Suki all followed Rowdy and Breeanne, leaving Jodi alone with Jake.

Would it look too obvious if she sprinted to the opposite side of the room?

"Guess I need to fend for my own drink,"

she muttered.

"Don't worry," Jake said, his voice dipping deep in a conspiratorial tone as he leaned in closer. "You don't have to run away or get soused. Your secret is safe with me."

"I don't know what you mean," Jodi tossed her head in desperate denial of the anxiety. She had to do something to put up roadblocks. *Stop. Don't Walk. No Outlet. Caution: Dangerous Curve Ahead.* If she gave an inch, she'd fall a hundred miles. He was that compelling.

"We can't let it get out that straitlaced, no-nonsense Jodi is secretly wild and sexy Gwendolyn the Wedding Crasher."

"My word against yours," she replied tartly.

He smirked, switched on his cell phone, thumbed through his camera roll, and showed a picture of her doing the chicken dance at the wedding, an out-of-control smile on her face. "I present to you exhibit A."

"You didn't!" A sick feeling sloshed against the sides of her stomach.

"I did. Wanna see exhibit B?"

"No!"

"C? D?"

"Put that away right now."

His smirk widened and he switched off the phone. "Just so you know. I could blackmail you."

"I changed my mind. Let me see your phone." She held out her palm.

"No way, you'll delete the pictures."

"Damn skippy."

"Can't let that happen." He shook his head in slow, sexy movements that lit up her nerve endings.

"Don't make me wrestle it out of your hand," she threatened, feeling vaguely dizzy at the idea of getting that close to him again.

"You do realize that the thought of wrestling you is not a deterrent." He lowered his voice. "In fact, quite the opposite."

"Grrr. You are a frustrating man."

"I can't let you delete cherished memories."

She snorted. "Cherished. Good one."

"I'm not kidding," he said, his voice so full of sincerity that she almost believed him. "It was one of the best nights I've ever had."

She studied his face but he looked completely serious. A trickle of perspiration slid down her breastbone. "What do you want from me?"

"Nothing more than polite conversation, *Gwendolyn*."

"Please don't call me that."

"You liked it on New Year's Day."

"Shh."

"Jodi . . ." He canted his head. "I like the name Jodi. It fits you. Girl next door."

"You didn't think I was the girl next door when you met me."

"You're right," he said. "It wasn't until this morning when you jumped into the laundry hamper to avoid seeing me that I realized Gwendolyn the femme fatale was all an act."

"Femme fatale? Me?" She laughed, not just because the image didn't fit with who she was, but also because it tickled her to think she'd managed to pull off the vamp thing, at least for one night. "Hardly."

"Oh very *hard*ly," he put emphasis on "hard," wriggled his eyebrows, and leaned in closer.

"Stop it," she hissed. "Someone might hear you."

"My God, but you smell good. What *is* that scent?" He was so close now that he was almost sniffing her neck.

She stepped back. "You can smell it?"

"Smell it? Hell, it's invading me."

She put two fingers to the pulse point at her neck where she'd daubed the perfume she'd found in the hope chest, just seconds before she'd walked out the door. "What does it smell like?"

"Heaven." He breathed. "It makes me want to lick you from head to toe."

She thought about the prophecy on the hope chest, the warning to be careful what you wished for because you *would* get it. Her pulse galloped. This was silly.

"I thought you smelled good the night of the wedding, but this . . . wow . . . Whatever that perfume is you're wearing, it's something extra special on you."

He could smell it, the perfume that no one else could smell. She remembered the inscription on the box the perfume had been in.

A scent to love; a smell above all others, only two can know that the fragrance of deep passion belongs exclusively to mates of the soul.

Soul mates.

Oh, that was so stupid. Dumb. Fanciful. She didn't believe in fairy tales. Not anymore.

"Whatever that perfume is, it makes me want to strip your clothes right off your body and do what we did after the reception —"

She held up a palm, uselessly trying to deflect the heat waves coming off his body and squashing her steamroller-style. "Can we stop talking about that night? Let's just forget it happened. Can we please do that?"

Yes, she sounded desperate, because she was. If he kept talking like that, she was toast. Burnt. Crispy. Gone.

"I can't forget. That night is forever etched in my brain." His sultry eyes caressed her.

"Then please stop being charming." *Begging now, Jodi? Really?*

"Why?"

"Because I don't want to like you."

"So you do like me?" A pleased grin twitched his lips.

"I'm on the fence," she lied, and crossed her fingers behind her back to make up for it. He couldn't handle the truth. Scratch that, she wasn't the one who couldn't handle him knowing the truth. That would make her too vulnerable, and after Ryan, she'd sworn never to go to that place again. "I could go either way." She pointed a finger at him. "So watch yourself."

"I'll try," he said, and his grin turned so wicked she knew he had absolutely no intention of trying.

"So you're a ballplayer too?" she asked, desperately scanning the room in search of rescue, silently willing Breeanne and Rowdy to come back. "That's why you looked vaguely familiar to me. I don't follow sports, but my dad and Breeanne are baseball fanatics. Can't help but absorb some of it by osmosis."

"Yep." Jake leaned in toward her. "Cleanup hitter. The Gunslingers just traded for me."

Now everything was starting to make sense. It explained why he'd been at the wedding she'd crashed.

"I was happy to come home to Texas," he said.

"You're a native Texan?" Jodi pulled her shoulders back.

"Born in San Antonio, but I lived in Jefferson for a while."

"Wow, small world."

"How long have you known Rowdy?" Maybe if she made normal conversation she could slow her leaping pulse, quell the quivering cells in her body that whispered mischievously at her to jump his ever-loving bones.

"Ten years. We were in the minor leagues together."

Hmm, well that topic of conversation had run its course. What she knew about base-ball she could fit into a hummingbird's beak. "Well, I better go say hello to my aunt and uncle."

"Introduce me to them," he said.

"No."

"Why not?"

"I don't want to."

"Why not?"

"Let's get something straight," she said, her tone coming out pricklier than she intended. But if she cut this guy slack, she had a feeling he'd hogtie her with it. "I don't want to get to know you. We have to be around each other because you're the best man and I'm the maid of honor, but that's it. We're not going to do anything to mess up Breeanne and Rowdy's wedding. You hear me?"

"Mess up? Like what for instance?"

"We will not be repeating what happened at the Grand Texan on New Year's Day."

He lowered his voice, and took on a let's-knife-Julius-Caesar-in-the-back conspiratorial tone. "Not even if we make sure no one finds out?"

"No." Damn her fluttery heart. "This is a small town. Someone *always* finds out."

"You've got a stubborn streak."

"So I've been told."

"Is that your biggest flaw?"

"If you consider being strong-willed a flaw."

"Depends."

"On what?"

"If that strong will keeps you from having an open mind."

"What's *your* big flaw, smart guy?" she asked, turning the tables.

"Who says I have one?" He gave her that I'm-so-likable-how-can-you-possibly-resist-me grin that had backed her into this corner in the first place.

"Everyone has a flaw," she said. "You especially."

He stroked his clean-shaven chin with his thumb and index finger, and dammit, she couldn't stop staring at his chiseled jaw. Why would he ever cover such a magnificent jaw with a beard? "Let me think on that."

"I know what your flaw is," she volunteered.

"Yeah?" His eyes narrowed to beads of amusement. "What's that?"

"Arrogance."

He tilted that gorgeous chin to the side, studied her so long she started to squirm. "I prefer to think of it as self-confidence."

"You've got it in spades."

"Why, thank you."

"I meant it as a complaint, not a compliment."

"You are so cute when you're riled."

"I'm not riled. Being riled means I care. I don't care."

"Uh-huh."

"I don't."

"If you don't care, why did you jump into the laundry cart?"

"Stop talking about the laundry cart."

"If I can't talk about the wedding you crashed or our night together or the laundry cart, what can I talk about?"

"Breeanne and Rowdy and their wedding day. It's why we're here."

"Fine. Let's talk about their wedding. So Valentine's Day. They're getting married on V-Day. What's with that?"

"They're soppy in love, but from a practical standpoint, they wanted to get married and have their honeymoon over with before spring training starts. February fourteenth won out."

"Let me guess, their colors are red and white."

"And pink."

"Ugh."

"You can say that twice."

"Ugh, ugh."

"I didn't mean to literally say it twice."

"Does this mean I'll have to wear something pink?"

She nodded, enjoyed herself. "Pink bow tie."

He groaned. "Please say it ain't so."

"I would feel sorry for you, but I have to wear pink from head to toe. Consider yourself lucky. Despite the Molly Ringwald *Pretty in Pink* mythology, pink is not the best color for a redhead."

"I know," he whispered. "It's emerald green. I'll never be able to look at emerald green again without thinking about how you looked in that dress —"

"Do you ever do anything you're told?"

"I try not to."

Jodi blew out her breath through clenched teeth. "It's gonna be a looong month."

Someone cranked up the volume on the music that had been trickling through the sound system, unleashing the strains of "Kiss You." The same song they'd waltzed to at the wedding. What lousy freaking timing.

Their song.

His eyes met hers. He was thinking the same thing.

No. It wasn't their song. They didn't have a song. Two people could not have song if they weren't dating.

"I have an urge to dance," he said.

"Tuck those urges away."

"I miss Gwendolyn." He shook his head in mock woefulness. "She was so much fun."

"Gwendolyn isn't real."

"She felt pretty real to me."

"Some dreams are like that."

Thankfully, the music cut off midway through while Rowdy asked everyone to be seated at the banquet table so they could start the food service.

Yes! This was her chance to escape him.

Except there were place cards on each table, and she was seated beside Jake.

Breeanne sat across from her, Suki to her left. Jodi did her best to stir conversation with her sisters, but Breeanne's face was perpetually turned toward Rowdy. Suki struck up a flirtation with one of the groomsmen, another batter for the Dallas Gunslingers named Axel Talbot.

Finally, she peeked over to gauge what was going on with Jake, and saw a busty waitress leaning over his shoulder to fill his wineglass and strategically pushing up her cleavage with the inside of her upper arms.

Instant jealousy poured through Jodi, and that's when she knew she was in serious trouble.

Chapter 10

Jodi Carlyle's Wedding Crasher Rules:
Do not have sex in the coat closet.

Jake wished the busty waitress would stop blocking his view of Jodi. He couldn't get enough of looking at her. For the past two weeks, he'd been spinning sexual fantasies about the mysterious Gwendolyn and her secret identity. Alternately imagining that she was a spy or an undercover FBI agent, or the bored daughter of a Fortune 500 executive.

Strangely enough, discovering that Gwendolyn — aka Jodi Carlyle — was more girl next door than Mata Hari was not a turnoff. In fact, he was now completely intrigued and he ached to know more about her. What had driven an upstanding, rule-following woman like her to daringly crash the celebrity wedding of the season and spend one perfect night in his arms? She might look

212

buttoned-up, but underneath, she was pure firecracker, and he wanted nothing more than to light her fuse again.

Tonight she wore a simple navy blue skirt and a silky white blouse that rippled against her body whenever she moved. A heart-shaped gold necklace rested at the hollow of her throat and pearl earrings nestled in her earlobes. He remembered how those lobes had tasted and his mouth watered. Her scent wrapped seductively around him, whispering softly underneath the aroma of garlic, onions, and basil — *kiss me, touch me, hold me.* She smelled pretty damn good before, but now her smell was hypnotic. All he wanted to do was bury his face against her neck and inhale.

The conversation hummed around them, but Jake heard none of it. He was too focused on Jodi and the way the second button on her blouse stopped short of showing off cleavage. Over the sound system, Muse was singing "Madness." He took a long pull from the glass of cabernet the waitress had poured for him, felt the liquid slide down his throat warm and easy. All he wanted to do was lean across the table and whisper to Jodi, *Wanna get out of here?*

Why wasn't she married? She should be married — pretty, small-town woman, the right age. What was wrong with the men in Stardust that someone hadn't already put a ring on her finger?

Waitstaff moved in and out of the room, the draft caused the candle in the Chianti bottle sitting on the table in front of them to flicker. In the muted lighting Jodi's hair fell in loose curls to the top of her shoulders, her cheeks flushed, her eyes glowed, and her lips glistened, wet with wine.

"What is it?" she asked, looking wary, pulling her shoulders back and her chin up. The gesture caused the second button on her blouse to slip from the buttonhole, giving him a delicious peek at her creamy flesh. He thought of marshmallows, sweet and fluffy.

He managed to send his gaze back to her face instead of letting it stroll where it wanted to go — to those soft breasts jutting so provocatively beneath the folds of her white silk blouse.

"You look nice." He scooted his chair closer to her, as close to her as he could get. "That blouse . . ."

She glanced down at her open button, looked alarmed, and buttoned it up fast. "You're incorrigible."

"And you're gorgeous," he whispered, loving the way her hair brushed against her chin. He remembered how it had felt brushing over his skin.

"Shh." She frowned, quickly glancing up and down the table to see if anyone had overheard them.

"This is driving me crazy," he went on. "Being so close to you and not being able to touch you."

She gave him a look that said, *If you don't shut up I'm going to strangle you.* "I'll reserve you a straitjacket."

He smiled innocently.

She glared, her bosom heaving with a sharp inhale. The button popped open again.

He loved that button. "Great bra. I like lacy bras." His smile widened. He couldn't help it. "Although I will always have a fondness for you in black lace."

She rolled her eyes, and closed the button once more.

"You're mad at me because I like your lacy bra?"

She folded her arms over her chest. "Stop staring. Stop talking."

"C'mon," he murmured. "You can't expect me not to look at a wardrobe malfunction, especially when you've got such fantastic ti— breasts."

Her eyes could have blistered paint. "I

expect you to at least be a gentleman about my wardrobe malfunction and look the opposite way."

"What about me ever gave you the idea I was a gentleman?" he drawled.

"My mistake. Clearly."

"Why *are* you mad at me?"

"For being here."

"Sorry to ruin your playhouse, but I was invited."

On the other side of the table, Rowdy was telling the story of how he and Breeanne first met when a kid had accidentally beaned her with the baseball that Rowdy had autographed for the boy.

"But honestly," Breeanne said. "We met before that. When I was twelve in the children's hospital and Rowdy came on the floor to visit and he gave *me* an autographed baseball."

"Aww," said everyone at the table except Jake.

He leaned over to whisper in Jodi's ear. "We can beat that story."

"No we can't," she whispered back, and scooted to the far side of her chair. "We aren't a couple. Therefore we can't have a cute meet."

"Too late. We already did."

"I'm not going to talk to you anymore,"

she said, and purposefully leaned forward toward Breeanne, who was staring raptly at Rowdy and never saw Jodi trying to get her attention.

Jake laughed.

Undaunted, Jodi swung her gaze to the left, but her other sister was batting eyelashes at Talbot. Jodi tapped Suki on the shoulder. Her sister waved her away without glancing over.

Jake held out his palms. "All roads lead back to The Crown."

"What?" She scowled.

"Coronado. My last name," he said. "It means crowned."

"I see," she said. "Arrogant."

"Self-confident," he corrected.

"Delusional."

"Assured."

"Cocky."

"Are we talking dirty now?" He was having such fun pulling her leg, and while she seemed irritated on the surface, he could have sworn she was struggling not to grin. No matter how much she might want to deny it, she liked him.

Why did she want to deny it? Was she ashamed of him? Or embarrassed that her adventuresome one-night stand had shown up in her hometown, threatening her reputation and her equilibrium? That was not his intention.

Besides, she wasn't the only one feeling threatened. He felt like he was rappelling down the side of a muddy mountain in the rain with baby oil slicked over his palms. A smart man would come up with a good excuse and get out of here.

He wondered how much longer the party was going to last. How long was he obligated to stay? Could he get out of here after dessert?

Jake glanced back at Jodi. The button on her blouse had popped open once more, giving him a flash of lace. He was seriously starting to love that blouse. Hmm. Then again, he didn't want to seem rude. He was the best man, after all. He was probably expected to stick around at least as long as the maid of honor.

"Who is that older lady with the purple hair and tats talking to your mom?" he asked, hoping to make conversation that wouldn't irritate her.

Jodi bent over his arm to peer down the table, her breasts brushing lightly against his arm. Another plus for this new conversational direction. But sadly, she immediately jerked back. "That's Trudy, a close family friend. She's a Vegas stripper turned artist in her retirement. She's pretty good too. We sell her stuff in Timeless Treasures."

"Timeless Treasures?" he asked, more to hear her smooth voice than any real interest in what was going on down at the other end of the table.

"It's my parents' antique store. Although Timeless Treasures is much more than that. It's the hub of Stardust. Breeanne's bookstore is in it, and the Honeysuckle Café, and —"

"And apparently it's a haven for artists."

"That too. People come to hang out as much as to buy stuff. Most of them hoping for an invitation to one of my parents' backyard parties. They throw the best parties in Stardust," she said proudly.

"Maybe I'll get invited to one."

"No doubt, since you're Rowdy's best man." She didn't look particularly pleased about it, and he found himself scrambling to come up with a way to turn the tide in his favor.

"Trudy looks like she'd be the life of the party."

"What gave her away? The hair color, the tats, the piercings?"

"Her laugh. It's infectious." He chuckled.

"Well," Jodi said. "There is a downside to being the life of the party."

"Yeah? What's that?"

"Not having much restraint."

"Said the wedding crasher," he murmured.

"Shh," she said. "That wasn't me."

"No? I could have sworn —"

"Forget everything you saw."

"Can't. I've got exhibits A, B, C, and D." He patted his cell phone in his front shirt pocket. "Remember?"

Jodi looked down the long table again and mused, "I bet Trudy would switch places with me if I asked."

He looked into her blue-gray eyes and grinned like a shark. "I bet Trudy would love to see my camera roll."

"You are not a gentleman."

"I thought we already covered that."

"It needed saying again."

Back to the antagonistic position, huh? Another change of topic was needed. "So," he said. "Why did you make a B&B out of boxcars?"

She shrugged. "Why not?"

"No particular attachment to rail travel?"

"No."

"Hank Williams super fan?"

She quirked an eyebrow and her mouth. "What are you talking about?"

" 'Ramblin' Man.' Train whistle blowing —"

"You're reaching a long way for that one, Stretch. The Allman Brothers have a song called 'Ramblin' Man' too."

"I'm not talking about them."

"Honestly, I have no idea what you're talking about at all." She took a sip of wine. "When are they going to serve the food?"

Jake pointed out the platters of antipasto sitting on the table. He'd been so busy chatting her up he hadn't noticed when they'd arrived either. He reached for the plate the waitstaff had put in front of him and dished up a stuffed mushroom.

"I meant the main meal," Jodi said.

"You don't like appetizers?"

She gave him a pointed look.

"Oh yeah, that's right. You like for everything to come out even. Do you want me to put one or two aside for you so the waitstaff doesn't make off with it when the main dishes arrive?"

"Okay." She bobbed her head.

He reached for her plate and slid a stuffed mushroom on it. "Because I'm closer," he said. "Not because I don't think you can't get your own mushroom. I'm fully aware you can fend for yourself."

"Watch it, you're coming close to acting

like a gentleman."

"Thanks for the tip. Now . . ." he said, pushing his plate off to one side. "Where were we? You picked boxcars because they were —"

"Affordable."

"That's it? Just finances?"

"You sound disappointed."

"I was hoping for a romantic story."

"Jodi doesn't have a romantic bone in her body," Suki said, momentarily distracted when Talbot waved to get the waitress's attention.

"No kidding?" Jake eyed Jodi.

"She *hates* public displays of affection." Suki nodded. "Jo, do you remember that time when Ryan —"

"You can stop talking now." Jodi bumped her younger sister with her elbow.

"Ouch." Suki rubbed her arm, winced at Jake. "But clearly public displays of violence are just fine with her."

"I didn't hurt you." Jodi affectionately tousled her sister's hair.

"Hey!" Suki smoothed her stick-straight hair back in place. "It wasn't so much the nudge as the intention behind it." Suki turned her gaze back to Jake. "See what you're up against as best man? You have my sympathies."

"A little vinegar never hurt anyone," Jake said philosophically.

"So just because I take up for myself I'm sour?" Jodi glared, but he could see it was all a cover-up. She liked for people to think she was tough, but he knew better. "What? I'm supposed to roll over and let people walk on me just because I have a generous nature?"

Roll over. Oh yeah. He'd love for her to roll over him again.

Jodi lowered her lashes, took a sip of wine. A loose curl fell softly across her cheek and he gave up trying to hide his desire and was now seriously reconsidering sticking to their only-one-night agreement.

It wasn't just Jodi's sweet cleavage and the sight of that bra peeking through the open button of her white silk blouse and the sweet raspberry-colored bow of her mouth. When she canted her head the light glinted off the pearl earring and it made him light-headed. The urge to lean across the table and flick that gorgeous ear with his tongue was overwhelming. He wanted to dip the tip of his tongue inside the luscious seashell shape and whisper sweet, dirty nothings.

But then Breeanne said something and Jodi smiled and the softness in her eyes was so welcoming, he tumbled into those wide blue-gray pools and drowned. He must have made some kind of noise, because she shifted her gaze back to him.

"Are you sick?" she asked.

Oh yeah. Sick with desire. He held his breath and pushed his wineglass away. "Too much celebrating."

"Me too," she said, and pushed her own glass to the middle of the table.

She seemed nervous. Was she nervous? He hoped so, because he was damn nervous and didn't like being there alone.

Jodi licked her lips again and Jake's hands itched to touch her.

Control. Pretend you're at the plate. The bat is in your hand. Don't swing too soon.

If he wanted to convince her this chemistry between them deserved another shot, he had to take it easy. She was skittish. He wasn't going to make the first move. The next pitch was up to her.

But that didn't mean he couldn't send signals with his eyes.

Jodi couldn't hang on to Jake's inquisitive stare one second longer.

Thankfully, the waitstaff had finally brought out the main courses. The food was served family-style, everyone passing around platters of lasagna and spaghetti, veal

Marsala and eggplant Parmesan, and for a few minutes it provided a distraction from Jake. She took a small portion of each dish, focused on cutting her food into equal pieces so she could have a bite of everything at once, but her appetite had vanished. At least her appetite for food.

She hungered for something else entirely.

The waiter brought a fresh basket of bread and she and Jake reached for it at the same time, their fingers touching over the same slice of hot Italian bread. Simultaneously, they jerked back. The warmth of his hand short-circuited every rational thought in her head, leaving only two words imprinted inside her brain in bright red neon. *I want.*

She was inflamed.

For Jake.

"I was getting it for you," he said. "So you could divvy it up with the rest of your food."

"Thanks," she mumbled, and accepted the bread he offered and proceeded to tear it into small chunks.

All around her, family and friends were proposing more toasts. To the happy couple. To a long life together. To the future pitter-patter of little feet. Jodi smiled and raised her glass and did everything in her power to tamp down her lust for Jake. It was ridiculous, this excessive attraction, but it refused to be quelled. Every time she glanced his way she felt it — the leap of electricity, the memory of their scorching night together, the secret hope of what if?

No. Not what if. Something that burned this hot was bound to flame out and that's all there was to it. No what-if thinking allowed. Once was definitely enough. Once made it special. Anything more, and it would become a habit.

The waiter poured more wine. Between the toasts and her need to deny her feelings for Jake, Jodi drank more than she should have. Especially since she wasn't much of a drinker. Two glasses and her head buzzed sweetly. She felt smooth and mellow.

Alcohol lowered her resistance and she finally raised her eyes. How could she not look at him when he was seated right next to her? She had to look at him. He was *there* — big, commanding, oozing sexuality.

Play it cool.

Easily said, impossible to do when his look burned her up like a potato chip in a campfire. God, he was so sexy, and without the beard even more so. Her fingers itched to trace that smooth skin, to see what he felt like without the soft prickle of hair.

His eyes were transfixed on her. "What *is* the name of that cologne you're wearing?"

he whispered. "It's driving me crazy."

She shrugged casually past the rapid sprint of her pulse. There had been no name on the bottle. "Eau de hope chest?"

"What?"

"Never mind."

"Whatever it's called, the perfume is as intoxicating as you are." He growled so low she was hopeful that no one else heard.

"Stop it." She hissed as if she was angry, but really it was a seductive hiss that said, *Ignore what my lips say, listen to my eyes. I want you. I need you. Take me.*

Crazy. This was out-of-control crazy. A condition she'd spent her life striving to avoid.

But wasn't a wild sexual adventure the very thing she'd wished for when she opened the hope chest? She'd wanted excitement, something new and different from what she'd known, and Jake was certainly that.

"A secret toast," Jake whispered, and lifted his glass. "To a beautiful redhead."

"I'm not toasting that."

"Why not?"

"This is Breeanne and Rowdy's evening. Stop making it about us."

"You're right," he said, but kept his glass raised.

Just to get him to lower the glass since everyone else had finished toasting, Jodi clinked glasses with him and downed her last swallow of wine. Instantly her brain tingled dizzily. Oh wow. Okay. Time to back off the hooch.

Her father was telling a story about how he and Breeanne had been watching television together the very first time Rowdy took the mound as a pitcher in the major leagues. It was a romantic story that neither Jodi nor Jake was much listening to.

Jake's eyes held her fast, as if he knew every thought slipping through her head. He sent her a short, sly smile, and she felt as if she'd been lit on fire, her nerve endings blazing hot as she recalled the pressure of his lips on her skin. White-hot embers of yearning burned inside her, growing from the instant they'd first met.

She couldn't take it any longer.

"Excuse me," she said, putting down her napkin and hopping up. "Ladies' room."

Breathlessly, she escaped the banquet hall, rushed down the corridor to the lavatory, but in her altered state, took a wrong turn and ended up in the cloakroom. What if she just grabbed her coat and left? The thought tempted.

But she couldn't do that to Breeanne.

Knees shaking, she leaned her back against the wall of the roomy walk-in closet, took deep breaths, and tried to calm herself. How in the world was she going to make it through an entire month of events that put her in such close proximity to Jake? This simply wasn't going to work. She had to speak to Warwick about reclaiming his spot as best man. There were things he could do for his public-speaking phobia. See Dr. Jeanna. Take beta-blockers. Visit Toastmasters.

She came out of the closet and glanced back down the hall to the banquet room, saw Jake standing in the doorway watching her.

No. Go away.

He stepped into the corridor and shut the banquet room door behind him, his gaze drilling into her.

Her feet rooted into the floor. Around her she heard restaurant sounds — the clank of dishes, the soft whisper of romantic music, the hum of voices — but it was as if the sounds were an ocean away and it was just she and Jake on a desert island.

Nothing existed but the two of them.

He strode toward her and damn if she wasn't rushing toward him. He caught her up in his strong arms, whirled her around in the dimly lit hallway. "I need you."

"I need you too."

"We can't —"

"I know."

But he was planting a kiss against her neck and she was threading her fingers through his hair.

"This is crazy." She gasped.

"Insane."

"One more time?" she dared.

"Where?"

"Here?" she asked.

"In the restaurant?" There was shocked delight in his voice.

Yes, said her inner Gwendolyn. "Coat closet."

"Holy shit." He grinned.

She darted a glance up and down the hallway. The banquet room was closed off. No one from the dining area could see them from this angle. She grabbed his hand and pulled him inside the closet, her heart thumping like mad. She wasn't in her right mind. She was consumed with need for him and couldn't seem to fight it. Correction: Didn't want to fight it.

"Jodi." He groaned her name. "My sweet Jodi."

Why did he have to say it like that? Like

she was special. Like she meant something to him.

It was completely dark. She could be in the closet with anyone. The lack of sight served to push her lust into hyperdrive. Her palms spread over his broad chest and she felt the vibration of his low chuckle radiate through her fingers.

His mouth found hers. They kissed. Deeply, passionately.

"Hurry," she said, her fingers tugging at his zipper. "We have to hurry before they miss us."

"You really are serious?"

"Yes. Kiss me again."

"But you said —"

She grabbed him by the collar, pulled his face down to meet hers. "Forget what I said. Let's do this."

He groaned against her neck, lifted her up. She wrapped her legs around his waist. He lost his balance, crashed into the back of the closet.

"Shh, shh, shh, people will hear. We —"

He pressed his mouth to hers, cutting off the rest of her thought, but a second after she caught her breath the old panic flared and she thought, *This is not a good idea.* But he was charged up now and she didn't have the heart to keep yanking the poor man around. Plus she didn't want to look fickle. Besides, he smelled like her perfume and that turned her on even more.

Quit thinking.

That was her problem. She thought too much. But thinking was good, right? It kept her from doing reckless things and ending up like Vivian. Thinking —

Mmm . . .

Now his hot palm was sliding up the hem of her blouse to graze her bare belly, the buttons on the silky material surrendering of their own accord, gently popping open as his hand traveled higher to push underneath her bra and cup her breast, and the closet morphed into a rocket ship streaking toward the stars.

They groped each other, like horny people in an erotic movie. He bent to run his hand up her skirt, grab hold of the waistband of her panties, strip them from her legs. She kicked off her panties in the dark, yanked down his zipper without undoing the button, freed his shaft through the opening.

He lifted her up, she wrapped her legs around his waist, his stiff erection pressing against her bottom. If she wriggled just right, he would be inside her.

"Condom," they gasped at once.

"Hang on," he said, and moved in the

darkness, sending coats swinging and hangers clacking against one another. "Got one in my wallet."

She twined her legs tighter around his waist. He pressed her against the wall of the closet to hold her steady while he reached around for his wallet in his back pocket.

She slipped down the wall, and the nape of her neck rammed into hard metal.

"Ouch, ouch."

Jake's arms went back around her. "What is it?"

"Hook."

He pulled her upright. "Sorry, you okay?"

She put a hand to the dent gouged into her skin. "I'll live."

"Spontaneity isn't all it's cracked up to be," he said as she felt his erection drain away, along with their sense of urgency.

So much for wild adventuresome sex.

She unwrapped her legs, slid down the length of him to the floor. He put a hand to her shoulder to hold her steady. She heard him zip up his pants. She buttoned her blouse with shaky fingers, smoothed her skirt.

Thank heavens for that hook. It had taken a poke in the back of the neck to wake her up.

A knock sounded on the door.

Every part of Jodi froze, including the hairs on her head.

"Oh shit," Jake muttered.

The door cracked open, letting in a shaft of light and the sight of Axel Talbot's grinning face. "Um, I don't mean to interrupt, but Suki wants her coat if y'all are done rolling around on it."

CHAPTER 11

Jodi Carlyle's Wedding Crasher Rules:
Watch where you leave your panties.

Mortified didn't begin to describe the way she felt. Ashamed, degraded, horrified, embarrassed, chagrined. Check. Check. And triple check. All of the above.

Caught having sex in a public place. At her sister's engagement party. With her family and friends just yards away. But at the same time, the same glorious time, she felt electric. Like a switch had been flipped. A light turned on.

That she liked it made her feel even more ashamed.

They returned to the party as if nothing had happened. Jake went back first, while Jodi scurried to the ladies' room to splash cold water on her face and reapply her makeup.

When she returned to the banquet hall,

Jake was regaling the group with baseball stories and had them eating out of his hand. Hardly anyone looked her way when she slipped into her chair. It was only then that she realized she'd left her underwear somewhere on the floor of the closet, but she sure as heck wasn't going back to look for it. She pressed her knees together tightly and prayed no one knew or guessed what she and Jake had been up to.

But Suki knew. She grinned like an opossum when Jodi sat down. "You're my new hero."

"I thought you were leaving," Jodi said.

"Not after I heard you were having sex in the coat closet!"

"Shh!" Jodi whispered.

"Hey, hold your head up. Be proud. You're a sexual human being. Some of us were beginning to have our doubts."

"Doubts about what?" Breeanne asked from across the table.

Jodi cringed, waited for Suki to spill the beans and say something utterly outrageous. But surprisingly, her baby sister took pity.

"That you and Rowdy would ever work out your issues and get to happily-ever-after, but here you are," Suki said to Breeanne.

Breeanne slipped her arm through Rowdy's. "You'll find your own true love one day, I just know it."

"Thank you," Jodi mumbled to Suki.

"I got your back." Suki winked. "Us adventuresome sisters have to stick together."

It felt weird being compared to bubbly, impulsive Suki, but not bad. Not bad at all. A few minutes later Suki and Talbot left together, mentioned they were headed to the Swimmin' Hole for Trivia Night, and immediately the table started buzzing about that budding romance.

Whew. Off the hook.

The rest of the evening passed in a blur and somehow she managed to keep from looking at Jake, although her body was acutely aware of him beside her. Every time he moved, she felt it, his scent, combined with her own, rushed over her until it was the only thing she could smell. *Them.*

By ten o'clock many of the guests had already dispersed, and Jodi was stone-cold sober and seriously starting to regret her rash actions. Jake lingered. Why couldn't he just go? As Breeanne and Rowdy stood at the door saying good night to her parents, she and Jake got up from the table.

He leaned over and whispered, "I've got your underwear."

"Thank you," she said, relieved. She'd

237

been fretting over someone finding her panties before she could retrieve them.

He tugged the lacy teal from the front pocket of his pants, held it in a tight fist.

Jodi slipped her hand over his. "Give it to me."

"You have the hardest time holding on to your underwear." He chuckled and surreptitiously transferred the panties from his fist to hers.

"Because of you," she said, making sure no one was watching before quickly stuffing the panties in her purse.

"Oh, so this is my fault? As I recall you're the one who pulled me into the closet."

"It was a mistake. I lost my head."

"And your panties."

"It's time for you to go," she said.

"What?"

She nodded toward the door. "You go first. We shouldn't be seen leaving together."

"Why not? You're the maid of honor and I'm the best man. You have your car, I have mine."

"This is a small town. Do I have to spell it out for you? I don't need tongues wagging around here long after you're gone."

"Then why'd you pull me into the closet in the first place?"

"Just go," she begged. "Please."

"Well, since you asked so nicely. Have a good night, Jodi. I guess the next time I'll see you will be . . ."

"Rowdy and Breeanne's wedding shower on Super Bowl Sunday at Rowdy's house."

"I have to go to that?"

"It's a couples affair and as best man, yes, you need to attend."

"I'm guessing I also need to bring a gift?"

"It's a suggestion."

"What is the point of a couples' shower anyway? Guys don't give a rat's ass about tea finger sandwiches and housewares."

"Personally, I agree with you. I think showers should be a man-free zone —"

"Unless we're talking an actual shower," he teased. "In that case —"

"Pay attention," she said. "We're not talking actual showers."

"Because then you'd be open to a man being there, right?"

Jodi cleared her throat and shot him a pointed stare. "Breeanne and Rowdy wanted a couples' shower and it's my job to fulfill their every wish and make this their dream wedding. Hence the Super Bowl Sunday date. It will give the guys something to do so we women can sip tea and eat finger sandwiches and ooh and aah over housewares to our heart's delight. Except for the women who'd rather watch football."

"Good plan. If you gotta have a couples' shower at least make it fun for all."

"I thought so."

"Your idea?"

"Yes."

"Should have known."

Jodi sank her hands on her hips. "What does that mean?"

"It means you excel at making other people happy."

"On what are you basing this opinion?"

"For one thing you run a B&B, stocked with everything a person might need. I mean who stocks guest rooms with not only the obligatory toiletries, but toothbrushes, toothpaste, combs, complimentary water, snacks, cell phone chargers, and house slippers?"

"I want my guests to be comfortable," she said.

"My point exactly, but from a business standpoint, it's not cost-effective."

"Do you have any idea how much repeat business I get? It pays off in the end."

"For another thing," he said, lowering his voice, "while you were in the bathroom, Breeanne told me about the guy who stood you up at the altar and how you started seeing a therapist to deal with the fallout so you could serve as her maid of honor. You could have flaked out on her like Warwick did Rowdy."

"I would never do that."

"I know. You're willing to face your own demons in order to make Breeanne happy. That's pretty brave."

Sunshine burst in her heart at his compliment. *Watch yourself.* "It was nothing much."

"Thirdly," he said, taking his voice lower still into a super sexy baritone. "Because you certainly did your best to make *me* happy at the Grand Texan. Caring about others is a good thing. I promise."

"Yeah? Well, sometimes I'm so busy making things nice for everyone else, I neglect myself."

"I could help you with that." He wriggled his eyebrows. "If it's a flaw you want to work on."

Jodi shot a quick look around the room. The remaining guests were engaged in private conversations and no one was paying any attention to them. "Look," she said. "About that closet action —"

"I'm sorry about whacking you into a coat hook."

"That's not what I'm talking about. It was impulsive —"

"I know." His smile was so stunning she was starting to wonder if it was his secret superpower.

"It wasn't an invitation to start up a sexual relationship."

"What was it?"

"A momentarily lapse in judgment."

"Like at the Grand Texan?"

"No, that was me cutting loose for one night." She took a deep breath, inhaled his scent, and for a moment, she was so bamboozled she forgot what she was saying. She toyed with the necklace at her throat, noticed he was watching her intently. The attention was both flattering and unsettling. "Tonight I completely lost it. Loose is one thing, lost is another."

He nodded, but said nothing, his hot gaze on her face.

She shifted away from him, slid the pendant back and forth on the chain, fully aware she was moving it faster the longer she talked but seemingly unable to stop the nervous behavior. What would Dr. Jeanna say? Um . . . *stop.*

Jodi dropped her hands to her side. "We almost got caught in flagrante. We almost ruined the engagement party."

"We didn't."

"I know, but we were so carried away. Us,

together. It's not a safe thing. Or healthy."

"I'm afraid I'm going to have to disagree with you on that," he murmured. "Safety is overrated."

"You're a nice guy. I like you." *Way too much.* "But I won't be the cause of wedding distress for my sister. You're right. I love doing things for other people and making them happy."

"Even at the cost of your own happiness?"

"My happiness doesn't matter. Not now. I can't think of my needs until after the wedding."

"So where does that leave us?"

"Staying as far away from each other as possible."

When Jake got back to the orange boxcar at the B&B, the Great Dane was sitting on the steps waiting for him. "Don't you have a home?"

Skeeter looked at him as if to say, *Yeah, but it's more fun here with you.*

"Well come on in. It's cold out." Jake held the door open and the dog trotted inside like he owned the place.

Jake got a paper bowl from the stack on top of the mini fridge, filled it with water, and set it on the floor.

Skeeter canted his head in a that's-all-you-

243

got stare.

"I don't have any kibble or meat scraps."

Skeeter's ears pricked, rotated.

"We've got some peanut butter crackers. Those do?" Jake opened a package of the complimentary peanut butter crackers stocked on the shelf and fed them to Skeeter, who ate them from his fingers with surprising delicacy for such a massive dog.

Jake sank down on the edge of the mattress and peeled off his shoes. He paused before taking off his socks. "We have a spark," he said. "No denying it."

Skeeter sat at his feet.

"Not you and me," Jake clarified. "Although you're not half bad. I'm talking about Jodi and I. Or is it Jodi and me? I can never remember that grammar stuff."

Skeeter yawned.

"What? You don't care about grammar either? Shocking."

The Great Dane stretched long, taking up half the room with his extravagant Downward Dog.

"You know her better than I do. Throw me a bone. Am I barking up the wrong tree?"

Skeeter straightened, barked.

"Is that a yes or a no? Bark once for no, twice for yes."

Skeeter barked twice.

"Is that yes, I'm barking up the wrong tree, or yes, I have a chance with her?" Even as he said it, Jake thought, *What the hell am I doing talking to a dog?* "Or are you barking because I said 'bone.' "

Skeeter barked twice more.

"Shh, we don't want to wake the other guests."

The dog wagged his tail.

"Jodi makes a good point. Our priorities should be making sure Rowdy and Bree-anne's wedding goes smoothly. We're grown-ups. We can do this. She said she couldn't think about her own needs until after the wedding. That means there's hope there for later on, right?"

Skeeter looked skeptical.

"Yeah, that's what I thought. I'm blowing smoke."

Jake fell back on the bed, still dressed, feeling down in the dumps. He finally met a woman he could get serious about, a woman who lit his fire in a way no other woman ever had, and as startled as he was to realize it, that included Maura. He found somebody he wanted to know better but she was off limits.

"On the other hand, if there is a chance, now is the perfect time to deal with the house in Jefferson. Got to do it anyway. That way, after the wedding, I will be one-hundred-percent ready for her. Problem is, can I keep my hands off her until then?"

Skeeter whined.

"Yeah, I know. It's a lot harder than it sounds."

The dog looked at him sad-eyed.

"Well come on." Jake patted the mattress beside him. "I suppose any warm body on a cold night is better than nothing."

Skeeter hopped up beside him, and immediately Jake felt better.

Generally, he didn't have a lot of trouble looking on the bright side of life. Focus on what was working. Shift his attention off unpleasant things. Stick to the sunny side of life. That was his motto. His modus operandi. His natural optimism was the only thing that had gotten him through those dark days after Maura's murder. During the lowest of the low, he finally understood how grief could lead some people to do the unthinkable and take their own lives.

It had been his friends who'd parted the veil, reminding him of who he was buried down inside the sorrow. Without them . . . well . . . he might still be mired in depression.

Baseball, his teammates, had been the glue

that held him together.

Even before it became his career, baseball had played a major role in his life. The camaraderie of Little League, the comfort of watching baseball on TV and seeing his heroes take the mound, the satisfaction of memorizing statistics. Baseball had gotten him through the bumpy years of his parents' divorce. He had not grown up with a close-knit, meddlesome family like the Carlyles.

Maura had shaken her head over that, told him woefully that he'd missed out on so much. Her family had been close too. He'd thought of their meddling as interfering. She called it caring. They'd fought over the fact that whenever her family called, she felt compelled to answer the phone immediately, even if they were in the midst of making love. Or how she'd loan her shiftless cousins money without batting an eye. She said he was insensitive. He told her she was co-dependent. That made her look at him as if he was the saddest thing she'd ever seen, and she blamed his lack of a solid foundation as the reason he hadn't wanted children.

It wasn't that he hadn't wanted children. He just didn't think it was something people should rush into heedlessly. She thought love could solve any problem. But Jake knew better.

Jodi had the same all-up-in-your-business relationship with her folks that Maura had had with hers.

Just thinking about it made him claustrophobic, but it didn't stop him from wanting her, and that scared him too.

The lights were out in the orange boxcar when Jodi came home. She let out a long breath. Had she thought Jake was going to wait up for her? She was glad he wasn't waiting up for her. Didn't want him waiting up for her. He'd promised to stay away and that's what he was doing.

Good man.

She stopped by the office to make sure everything was in order for tomorrow. She stuck her key in the lock and was surprised to find the door already unlocked. *Dammit, Ham.* Yes, Stardust was a safe town, but locks were on doors for a reason. Ham had such a bad habit of forgetting to lock up.

Happy to have something to think about besides Jake, she pushed the door open and stepped inside.

"Where have you been?" Ham asked from behind the desk.

Jodi shrieked, threw her hands in the air.

Her purse went flying. "You scared the stuffing out of me." She fumbled for the light switch, turned it on. "What are you doing sitting there in the dark?"

"Saving electricity. What happened to you?"

"Nothing," she lied, yanking on the hem of her skirt, trying to make it look less wrinkled.

Ham narrowed his eyes. "It's almost midnight."

"So?" She picked up her purse, tried to calm the erratic pounding of her heart.

"You never stay out this late."

"It was Breeanne and Rowdy's engagement party."

"That was over at ten."

"How do you know?" She ironed a hand over her hair, smoothing it back into place.

"Because Vincente's closes at ten."

Oh yeah. Her cheeks burned. "Um . . . I hung around to help clean up."

Ham stood up, stared at her hard.

"What are *you* doing up so late?" she asked, attempting to turn the tables.

He wasn't falling for it. "One of your false eyelashes is missing."

"What?" She reached up both hands to check her eyelids. Sure enough, the right eyelash had fallen off. Most likely in the closet. Oh gosh, had everyone else noticed?

"Are you seeing someone?"

"No!" she said much too loudly. "Why would you think that?"

"You smell like men's cologne."

Did she? Jodi sniffed her arm.

"Were you having sex?" Ham interrogated.

He was protective of her, she knew that, downside of working with her best friend. And he was only concerned for her well-being, but she was a grown woman and didn't owe him an explanation.

A knock sounded on the office door and before either one of them could say, "Come in," it opened and Suki bounced in.

"Oh good," Suki said. "You're still up."

"What are you doing here?" Ham asked.

"I want to talk to Jodi about Talbot."

"Who's Talbot?" Ham shifted his gaze to Suki.

"He plays for the Gunslingers and is one of Rowdy's groomsman. And he's really hot."

Ham rolled his eyes. "You too?"

"Me too what?" Suki looked confused.

"Did all the Carlyle women get laid to-night?" Ham asked the ceiling.

Suki's eyebrow shot up and she grinned at Jodi. "Did you finally get laid tonight?"

Jodi hit the ball back into her sister's

court. "Did you?"

"Sluts." Ham threw his hands into the air. "Both of you."

They turned to him in unison and said, "I didn't have sex."

"I'll be glad when this wedding is over," Ham muttered. "Stardust is being overrun by baseball players. How are the rest of us supposed to compete?"

"What? You want to date us?" Suki asked.

"Eww!" Ham looked utterly alarmed. "You're like my sisters. Which is why I'm concerned about the company you're keeping. I'm speaking in generalities."

"I'm going to bed," Jodi said. "Some of us have to get up at five a.m. to make breakfast for their guests."

"But what about our heart-to-heart?" Suki asked.

"We'll talk tomorrow." Jodi went out the door. "And don't forget to lock up," she called over her shoulder to Ham.

She walked to her own sleeping car at the back of the property, leaving the van parked in front of the office, disturbed by how disheveled she'd looked and how easily Ham had discerned that something was going on with her. He did know her better than anyone else in the world, but still.

What was happening to her? What was

making her act so uncharacteristically? Crashing a wedding was one thing. She'd done it with intent and purpose. Even going to bed with Jake — while out of her ordinary realm of behavior — was still part of her design to move on after having been ditched at the altar.

But what she'd done tonight in the closet . . . well, that was beyond the pale.

Jodi walked into her boxcar, sagged down on the couch, and dropped her head in her hands. God, what she had done tonight, wildly pulling Jake into the closet with her, practically demanding he have sex with her, was completely out of control. It was the kind of thing Vivian would have done.

Feeling sick to her stomach, Jodi groaned and closed her eyes against that thought. That's really why she'd told Jake to back off — although to ensure Breeanne and Rowdy's wedding went smoothly was close to the top of her list — because being near him dismantled every bit of her self-control. Around him, she was shameless.

A secret part of her feared that if she didn't keep herself locked down tight, her DNA would take over and she'd become Vivian. And there was no scarier thing in the world to Jodi than ending up like her biological mother.

She had to ask herself some hard questions. Was it just Jake who stirred these impulses in her? Or was it her own genetics rising to the surface? Stardust was a small town and she'd heard through the grapevine that her mother was an ordinary girl until she hit her twenties and went off the deep end. Personality changes, wild behavior, partying into the wee hours, plowing through a string of men. No one seemed to know what had precipitated it. What if Vivian had some kind of mental illness that she'd passed on and Jodi was just a ticking time bomb? For the first time in a long time she wished she knew someone she could talk to about her mother.

What if Jake had been the fire that lit her fuse and now, once lit, she couldn't snuff it out?

Jodi raised her head, pressed a palm to her forehead, and spied the hope chest perfume sitting on the coffee table where she'd left it.

What if it was the perfume? What if the combination of Jake and perfume had caused her to go mad with lust?

Seriously? It was just perfume.

A perfume she'd found in a mysterious hope chest.

C'mon. You're not superstitious.

No, but why take the chance? She picked up the bottle of perfume, intending on dumping it down the sink, but then realized her house would reek of the stuff. Fine. She'd put it back in the hope chest and never wear it again. If the perfume was responsible for her behavior tonight — and yes, she was fully aware that she was grasping at straws — the problem was solved.

To be on the safe side, she'd leave the B&B early and give Jake plenty of time to clear out before she returned.

Decisions made, she locked up the perfume, left a text for Ham that she was going to be out of pocket after she put out the six a.m. breakfast service the next morning, and went to bed.

CHAPTER 12

Jodi Carlyle's Wedding Crasher Rules:
Having a good time is not an excuse for
losing control.

That night Jake dreamed hot dreams of Jodi, completing in slumber what they'd been unable to finish in the coat closet.

He woke feeling hot and achy and desperate. What on earth had that woman done to him? He was twisted inside out and didn't know how to bend himself back into the right shape. Worse, he didn't know if he even wanted to.

Caught in the sweet fire of his dreams, he got up later than he intended and only because Skeeter was at the door whining to be let out. It was almost eight and he'd already lost out on an early start.

Jefferson. He was going to Jefferson today.

He was ready for this, but it would take a certain mind-set to walk through that front door for the first time in three years. Just thinking about it tightened his jaw.

He'd much rather stay here and hang out with Jodi. But he'd promised to keep his distance, at least until after the wedding, and he didn't want to do anything to jeopardize his chances for afterward.

Different.

He felt different when he was with her. Different than he'd ever felt with anyone else. It was a good kind of different. He felt more solid, more alive, and yet at the same time, more peaceful.

It confused him because he didn't know why. Maybe it was because Jodi looked a bit like Maura, but if that were the case, wouldn't he feel for her the same things he'd felt for his wife? His relationship with Maura now seemed innocent, undeveloped, sweet. Like a rosebud that failed to bloom. Maybe it was why being with Jodi felt so comfortable. Or maybe it was because he just liked her. But he'd liked plenty of women before her. He fell "in like" quite regularly. Okay, so he liked Jodi a whole lot more than usual. More than he liked most people.

C'mon, you don't even know her. Until last night, you didn't even know her real name.

No? Then how about this? Whenever he

was with her, he liked himself more. He liked the way he was with Jodi. Being with her reminded him of how he'd been before fame set in. He was his old self again.

"Jodi." He said her name out loud as he shaved. "Jodi."

Was he making a mistake feeding this flickering flame? But c'mon, what was the worst that could happen? Even if he crashed and burned, he was feeling something again and even getting hurt was a damn sight better than the numbness he'd felt for so long. At least it meant he was alive. That he'd come up to the plate and swung, even if in the end, he struck out.

"Honor her wishes," he told himself as he tossed his suitcase in the trunk of his Corvette. "Smile, be nice, but don't press, don't push, don't make sexy remarks. Let things happen organically. If it's meant to be, great . . . if not, so be it."

He bounded up the steps to the office, a little unnerved at how fast his heart was beating. *No big deal. No pressure. Tell her you had a great stay and you'll see her in two weeks at the Super Bowl/wedding shower thingy.*

Sounded good. Why were his palms so sweaty?

He walked into the office, primed to flash

his batter-up-showtime smile, only to find the renovated train engine empty. Thrown off guard by the fact Jodi wasn't here to receive his quickly rehearsed, I've-got-no-problem-being-your-one-night-stand performance, he stood in the middle of the room feeling a little disappointed and disjointed. He was all ready to check out and be on his way, but there was no one to report to.

Jodi's coat was draped over the back of the chair parked behind the registration desk. He glanced over his shoulder, made sure no one else was in the room, and went behind the desk to smell her coat. Her intoxicating scent rose up from the garment and he took a deep breath. Instantly he was overwhelmed by the memory of the coat closet at the restaurant. He could feel Jodi's strong legs wrapped firmly around his waist, the tickle of her hair falling over his face, her soft moans egging him on.

The sweat that had slicked his palms migrated to his forehead. He put her coat back where he found it, swiped a hand over his brow. Christ almighty, what was this?

The door flung open.

He startled, jumped, unprepared now to face Jodi when he was behind her desk and dazzled from her fragrance.

Man up, Coronado. Face the music.

He spackled a smile on his face, desperate to hide the widening cracks spreading through him. Thanks to Jodi, his foundation was shaky.

But it wasn't Jodi who came through the door.

Instead, a young brunette, holding a kid who looked like the Gerber baby, burst into the room. A diaper bag dangled from her shoulder. Her sweatpants were on wrong side out, a side seam tag giving her away. Her hair was pulled back into a messy ponytail. Her lips twitched, her eyes anxious with excitement.

"Where's Jodi?" she asked.

"I don't know. I just got here myself."

"Oh shit." She covered the baby's ear with a palm. "Sorry, sweetie, Mama didn't just say a bad word."

"Is something wrong?"

"No. Yes. I need Jodi."

Clearly something was out of whack. But this woman's problems were none of his business. He should just keep his mouth shut but, damn, the knight in shining armor inside him pulled a sword, eager to slay dragons.

"Breathe. Calm down. Tell me what's wrong?" he said in a low, soothing voice. She was wound up tight.

259

"My sister . . ." She gasped. "She's in labor a month early with her first baby. I'm her birth coach. I need to get to the hospital and Jodi said if I needed her she could watch him when the time came."

"You're not breathing," Jake said, and ushered her over to a chair. Pressed her down. "Just take a deep breath."

The baby stared at him, a thin fuzz of hair sticking up from his head like a halo. He tried not to make eye contact with the kid. Babies made him antsy. He had no idea what to do with them.

"It's just the two of us," the young woman said. "Our parents died when I was twenty and my sister was fifteen. And when she got pregnant her boyfriend flaked on her. Luckily, I have a great husband, but he's out of town on business. Why do big things always happen when he's out of town? I'm so flustered."

"It's going to be okay," Jake assured her. "Your sister will be fine. You'll be fine."

"But she needs me and I don't have anyone to leave the baby with. Where is Jodi?"

"I'm sure she'll be back really soon."

"You're that baseball player, aren't you? Jake Coronado."

"Yes," he admitted.

"I heard about your wife. I'm sorry."

That made him uncomfortable. "I could try to find Jodi for you," he offered.

"No time," she muttered. "I have to get to the hospital."

"How can I help? Do you want me to drive you?"

"Here," she said, getting up from the chair and shoving the baby at Jake. "Can you watch him for me until you can find Jodi? Or Ham. Ham will do in a pinch. Find Ham."

"Um, okay." Jake grabbed for the baby, afraid that if he didn't, in her worried state the mom would drop him. He grasped the kid around his chubby waist and held him out gingerly. What did a guy do with one of these things?

The baby looked at him, gurgled happily, drool dripping from his bottom gum where one tooth half protruded.

"Thank you," the woman said. "You're a lifesaver."

Before he could ask the half-million questions revolving in his head, she spun on her heels and headed for the door, stopping long enough to drop the diaper bag from her shoulder to the floor, and then she was gone.

"Hey, hey." Jake tucked the kid in the

crook of his arm like a football and ran for the door. "What's the kid's name?" he called to her as she sprinted toward the minivan parked out front.

"Tobias," the mom yelled over his shoulder. "His name is Tobias." Then she was in her vehicle and peeling out of the parking lot.

Huh. That was an unexpected turn of events. Jake looked at the kid.

Tobias grinned. "Da!"

"Hell no, kid, I'm not your da. I'm not anybody's da." Yeah, but he almost was. Once upon a time. The shadow of the old ghost brushed up against him and he shivered, reminding Jake that he was outside in the January cold with a hatless baby. Right. Get back inside and figure this out. So much for a quick getaway.

He carried the baby back into the office. "So Tobias, huh? Too big a moniker for such a little tyke. How 'bout I call you Toby?"

The baby squealed happily.

"You like that, huh? That's good because we're stuck with each other for the time being."

Toby bobbed his head as if to say, *Fine by me.*

Jake blew out his breath through puffed cheeks. Now what? Did he keep holding the baby? Put him on the floor? Holding the baby felt weird. But putting him on the floor where the child could get into stuff felt weirder. What if Toby touched the potbelly stove? What if he poked his eyes out with the knitting needles sticking from the ball of yarn that rested on the arm of the couch? What if . . .

Suddenly, all Jake could see were baby booby traps everywhere — glass that the kid could break and cut himself with, small items he could pop into his mouth and choke on, electrical sockets he could stick a finger into.

"I better hold you. It seems safest."

The kid squirmed, bucked against Jake's chest.

Jake held on tight. "Sorry. Can't put you down. Your mom is under enough stress already."

Toby leaned over Jake's arm to rest his head against Jake's hand. Aw, that was kinda cute —

"Ow!"

The little rug rat raised his head, mouth open, eyes twinkling. A deep imprint of a single tooth dug into the base of Jake's thumb.

"You bit me!" Jake said, ignoring his throbbing thumb. "Dammit, Toby, I thought we were friends."

Toby grinned and opened his mouth wider to take another chunk out of Jake.

"No, no. I'm not a teething ring, kid." Quickly, he transferred the baby to his other arm. "You hungry? Is that the deal?"

Toby gurgled and drooled and patted his chubby palms together like that was the funniest thing he'd ever heard.

"Let's check out the diaper bag for some eats, you little cannibal." Jostling the kid in an attempt to keep his mind off sharpening his tooth on Jake's hide, he squatted to go through the diaper bag with his free hand — diapers, bibs, clean clothes. Grub? Where was the grub? Finally at the bottom of the diaper bag, he hit pay dirt.

Crackers.

The minute Toby spied the cracker package, he started rocking, grunting, and making grabbing motions.

Juggling the kid and the crackers as best he could, Jake got to his feet and tore open the package. The bag ripped right down the middle, sending crackers flying all over the room.

Toby let out a loud shriek of dismay.

Crap. Not a single cracker left in the torn bag. Now what?

A pair of tiny sneakers kicked him hard in

the solar plexus. *Ooph.* The air shot from his lungs as Toby struggled, trying to get out of his arms and onto the floor after the crackers. The kid had the makings of a cage fighter.

Jake eyed the floor, saw that it was pretty clean. "Five-second rule," he declared, scooped up a few crackers, blew on them to get rid of any germs, and held out a palmful to the baby.

Toby dove for them, grabbed crackers in both fists.

Yeah, granted, he wasn't going to win babysitter of the year award, but he'd been drafted. He hadn't volunteered for child-care duty. Besides, the kid was taking a bite out of something besides him. In Jake's book, that was a win-win.

Toby grinned, yellow buttery cracker crumbs clinging to his face.

"Ah, so we're friends again? Or are you just trying to lull me into a false sense of security so you can nibble on me some more?"

The kid's eyes turned wily, as if to say, *Stay on guard, hotshot, you never know what I'll do.* That was the scary thing about kids. They were so unpredictable.

The front door opened.

Jodi? His heart leaped and not just because

he needed rescuing from the baby. He wanted to see her again and he was already imagining her sympathetic smile when he showed her the one-toothed bite mark on his thumb.

Except it wasn't Jodi.

Instead, a blond, Nordic-looking man in coveralls tromped over the threshold, wiped his work boots on the welcome mat. He looked so comfortable in the place, like he belonged, Jake couldn't help wondering if the guy was Jodi's boyfriend.

Ah, a boyfriend. That would explain why she didn't want anything more than a one-night stand. No wonder she'd jumped into the laundry cart. She was ashamed of herself because she had a boyfriend.

Jealousy simmered like a kettle of hot soup low and hot in his stomach.

But if this guy was her boyfriend, why hadn't she taken him to the engagement party? And why hadn't she just been straight with him about it?

The guy stopped, and stared at Jake. "Can I help you?"

"Yes, please take this kid." Jake extended the baby toward the newcomer.

The guy held up his hands. "No way. Tobias is a biter."

"Tell me about it. Are you Ham?"

"Hamilton Gee at your service. You Orange Boxcar?"

"Yeah."

"Love the Vette."

"Thanks." Jake was still holding Toby toward Ham. "Are you Jodi's boyfriend?" Shit! He hadn't meant to ask that.

Ham looked like that was the most ridiculous question anyone had ever asked him. "She's my boss and my best friend."

"You two never . . . ?" Jake slowly shook his head, wanting the answer to be no.

"What business is that of yours?" Ham asked, his tone amiable enough on the backside of his blunt words.

"None," Jake said. "None whatsoever. Just making conversation."

Ham's eyes narrowed and he studied Jake for a couple of seconds before he shifted gears and said, "How'd you end up with Tobias?"

"His mom's sister went into labor a month earlier and she's the birth coach. She left the baby for Jodi to watch, but said you'd do."

"Jodi babysits for Kendra once in a while. She babysits for a lot of people. She can't seem to say no when folks ask." Ham nodded ruefully and grinned as if Jodi's generosity was something he adored about her.

"Sometimes this place looks like a nursery school. Whoever marries Jodi will have to love kids. She'll want a passel of them."

Jake hadn't thought about kids since . . . well . . . He tried not to think about them at all, easy enough to do when a guy focused on his career.

"If you'd just take the kid . . ." Jake tried to thrust Toby on Ham.

"Sorry," Ham said. "You've got him, you're stuck with him."

"I need to leave. I have places to be. Things to do." Yes, he was stretching the truth a bit with that. Nothing adverse would happen if he didn't make it to Jefferson today, but still.

"I'm busy too," Ham said. "I have to take care of the guests."

"So what do I do?"

"Take him to Jodi," Ham suggested.

"Where is she?"

"Most likely at Timeless Treasures."

"Her parents' antique store, right? Where's that?" Jake asked. Toby was wriggling something fierce, kicking his leg like an Olympic swimmer.

"Main Street."

"Good. Great. That's what I'll do." Jake stuck Toby in the crook of his arm, picked up the diaper bag, stopped. "Um, the kid isn't going to fit in my Corvette."

"No kidding."

"How am I supposed to take him to Jodi?"

"You can take the company van. Jodi keeps a car seat in the back for picking up guests with babies at the airport." Ham pulled a set of keys from his corduroys and tossed them to Jake, who caught them one-handed. "Nice catch."

"I am a ballplayer."

"So I heard," Ham said dryly.

"That bother you?"

"Men who don't treat women right bother me."

Huh? What was that about? "Did Jodi say something to you?" he asked. "Because the one-time thing was her idea."

Ham startled, scowled darkly, and looked like he was about to come across the room and punch Jake's lights out. "What?"

"Clearly I've said too much," Jake said. "Forget I mentioned it. Thanks for the van keys."

He hustled outside, baby in hand, wondering exactly what Jodi had told her best friend about him.

CHAPTER 13

Jodi Carlyle's Wedding Crasher Rules:
Don't get too attached to anyone you pick
up at a wedding.

Jodi brought a basket of the leftover home-made banana nut muffins that she put out for the B&B guests, and a brown earthenware crock of creamy butter from the Stardust Dairy, when she arrived at Timeless Treasures that morning.

The antique store didn't open until ten, but the Honeysuckle Café, located in the back of the building, opened for breakfast at six. The café, which was technically a tearoom despite the diner name, was famous in Marion County. It had even been written up with glowing reviews in *Texas Monthly*. The owner and operator, Atlanta Johnson, was her mother's best friend since grade school.

Going around to the side entrance where

270

customers were lined up to get into the café, the air rife with the aroma of breakfast tacos, Jodi paused to greet friends and acquaintances before heading into the antique store through the back way. The sloped old wooden floor creaked beneath her weight, and the familiar musty scent of antiques hugged her like an old friend. She skimmed down aisles crowded with furniture and knickknacks, objets d'art and collectibles, crafts and vintage clothing.

She caught sight of her family grouped around the checkout counter. Mom, Dad, Suki, and Breeanne, who, now that she had finished ghostwriting Rowdy's autobiography, had gone back to working at the upstairs bookstore, Bound to Please. But all that would change once she was Mrs. Rowdy Blanton and baseball season started. She'd be living in Dallas with her new husband and starting a new book. For a moment, Jodi felt a little sad about that, it was the end of an era. But she shook off the mood and waved with a happy smile.

"How are you this morning?" Suki asked, a sly grin on her face.

"Fine." Jodi shot her a hold-your-tongue look. "You?"

"No complaints."

"Are those banana nut muffins?" Dad asked.

"Yep." Jodi set the basket of muffins and the crock of butter on the counter.

"Are we being bribed?" Suki asked suspiciously.

"I can't bring my family muffins without an ulterior motive?" Jodi leaned against the counter and did her best to appear as if she didn't have an agenda.

"Hmph," Suki said, but plucked a muffin from the basket. "I don't trust Trojan muffins. If you know what I mean."

"I sense subtext here," Mom said. "What's going on with you two?"

From the corner of her eye, Jodi saw a shadow move from the second floor balcony. "Incoming," she warned.

Everyone took a collective jump back as Callie, the calico Suki had rescued during Hurricane Sandy when she was a student at NYU, dropped down from the balcony overhead to the checkout counter.

Callie glanced around, a displeased expression on her face that said, *Dammit, you people are catching on to my ways.* The calico loved pouncing on unsuspecting victims and was known to pout when she didn't pull off an ambush. The left half of Callie's face was solid black, the right half orange. Her chin and chest were fluffy white, while her left forearm was orange and her right forearm was black. The back of her body was a swirly blend of black, orange, and white, giving her an exotic, one-of-a-kind appearance.

"Come here, precious." Breeanne scooped the cat into her arms. Breeanne was arguably Callie's favorite.

Jodi leaned over to whisper to her sister, "Could I talk to you upstairs in the bookstore?"

"Sure," Breeanne said, stroking the calico's fur. "What's up?"

"Yeah," Suki said. "What's up? Jake Coronado?"

"Huh?" their father asked, looking unsettled.

"Have another muffin, Dad." Jodi held the basket out to him and gave her youngest sister a big-eyed, you're-bucking-for-a-strangling stare.

Breeanne had turned for the stairs and Jodi followed.

She studied Breeanne, who looked absolutely radiant as she sank down in a chair in front of the bookstore's computer. Seeing her looking so happy and healthy lifted Jodi's spirits to the ceiling. So many times the family had feared they were going to lose her. As a girl, Jodi had done her best to hold things together at home whenever her folks were at the Children's Hospital in Dallas at Breeanne's bedside during her numerous heart surgeries.

"You look beautiful," Jodi said, perching her butt against the corner of the desk. "I'm so happy for you and Rowdy."

"Thank you." Breeanne blushed, raised a self-conscious hand to her head. "I still can't believe I landed him."

"Rowdy should be the one who can't believe he got such an awesome woman as you."

"He tells me that every day." Breeanne's smile deepened, her eyes shining bright with love. "Jodi, I feel like the luckiest woman in the world." She reached across the desk to squeeze Jodi's hand. "You'll find your soul mate one day. I'm sure of it."

Jodi shook her head, but her pulse spiked strangely. "I'm not sure I buy into the whole soul mate concept."

"I didn't believe it either . . . until Rowdy." Breeanne took a deep breath. "Jodi, he's the most incredible guy in the world and he's perfect for me."

"I know. When I see you two together . . ." *I get lonely.* "I realize Ryan did me a huge favor leaving me at the altar."

"If only he hadn't done it in such a cruel and dramatic way." Breeanne's eyes brimmed with sympathy.

"It's okay," Jodi said, and meant it. "He toughened me up. I needed that."

"I hope he didn't make you hard." Breeanne's voice lightened, but her eyes saddened.

That alarmed her. "Do you think I've gotten hard?"

"No, not hard. Just . . ."

"What?"

Breeanne winced. "It's nothing. Forget I said anything."

"No, really. If Ryan has affected my behavior, I want to know. I don't want to become bitter."

"Not bitter," Breeanne said. "That's not what I mean. But maybe too tough? Don't let what happened close your heart off to love."

Jodi sank back on the desk. "Wow, is that the way I'm coming across?"

"I only mention it because I love you so much and want you to be happy." Breeanne patted Jodi's hand. "I know it took me a while to let go of my fears before I could fully commit to Rowdy."

"What fears?"

"Of not being good enough for him. Once

I let go of my fears, once I stopped being afraid, it was so easy to love. What are *you* afraid of, Jodi? What is holding you back from loving with an open heart?"

Breeanne's insight stunned her. She was right. One hundred percent. Yep. Letting go of past hurts. Putting yourself out there. Opening up. Good idea. But how did you let go of the values and beliefs and fears that made you who you were? What happened if she was able to let go of them? Who would she be then? Jodi had no idea.

"Listen," Jodi said. "You know that perfume I found in the hope chest?"

Breeanne nodded. The day after Jodi had found it, she'd asked Breeanne to smell the perfume, but like everyone else, her younger sister hadn't been able to detect the scent.

"It's alarming really," Jodi said. "Scary that I am able to smell this amazing fragrance that no one else can smell. It makes me wonder if I'm having hallucinations."

"I know," Breeanne said. "You're not. Initially, I felt the same way about the cheetah scarf."

"I don't believe in magical thinking or prophecies."

"What about a self-fulfilling prophecy?"

Jodi shrugged. "I guess anything is possible. It's a little overwhelming to go there."

276

"Jodi . . ." A knowing expression came over Breeanne's face. "Did someone else smell the scent too?"

Silently, she nodded.

"A guy."

"Uh-huh."

"A cute guy?"

"Yes." She hadn't been breathing and the word came out brittle and airless.

Breeanne's eyes caught fire and she gripped Jodi's arms with both hands. "Jodi, it's *him.*"

A shiver shook Jodi's bones. "Him who?"

"Your soul mate. Your one and only."

Jodi shook her head. "That's completely loony tunes. Cray-cray. Mad Hatter tea party nuts."

Breeanne clicked her tongue in a *tsk, tsk* noise, as if Jodi was the most unenlightened person on the planet. "It happened to me and Rowdy."

"I'm not like you," Jodi said. "I've got a deeply cynical side that just won't let me go to those airy-fairy places."

"You're not deeply cynical. You're just scared."

Um, yeah.

"What if I told you that smelling the perfume was all in your mind? Would that make you feel better?" Breeanne sounded like a wise old sage, as if she was a hundred and six instead of twenty-six.

"So I just imagined I smelled the scent and he caught a whiff of my delusion?"

Breeanne clasped Jodi's palm with both hands, peered earnestly into her eyes. "Something like that. I did some research after I found the scarf and discovered some really interesting things about how our brain can trick us."

"In what way?"

"As a survival mechanism, your brain looks for patterns even when there aren't any. It produces optical illusions, all kinds of things. Seeing — or in your case — smelling is believing, but reality can be subjective."

"Okay. And that doesn't make us nuts for even entertaining the idea that a scarf or a perfume could lead us to love?"

Breeanne laughed. "No, it makes us human. Everyone's brain deceives them in one way or another."

"So let me get this straight. According to your research, it's all in my mind? My nose doesn't really smell lavender or vanilla?"

"That's right."

"And you don't really feel soft material when you touch the cheetah scarf?"

"Well, I *do* feel the softness, but it's not

278

really soft. The sayings on the hope chest set up our expectations. Our brains are hardwired for myth. We *want* to believe, so we experience through our senses."

"All right. I'll bite." Jodi ironed her eyebrows with her fingers. She didn't know if she was buying this, but she preferred a more logical explanation to magical thinking.

"You smelled something because your brain set you up to smell something. It's psychosomatic."

"Key word being 'psycho'?"

"It's not psycho. It's brain chemistry."

"Okay, I can get into that, except now here's the tricky part. Why does this guy I've met smell the very same thing I do?"

"Ah." Breeanne raised an index finger. "But does he really? Has he told you specifically that the perfume smells like lavender and vanilla?"

"Well, he didn't get that detailed about it and I didn't think to ask. He just said I smelled so delicious that he wanted to lick me. Or something along those lines."

Breeanne giggled. "Oh my, that sounds nice. That is if you *want* him to lick you."

"I do, but I don't want anything more than that. I don't want a magical soul mate, twined-together-forever thing that you and

Rowdy have going on. At least not right now."

"Why not?"

"Because I wanted to be able to just have casual sex. You know. No strings. Simple. Fun. Have a good time and be on my way. I don't want our encounters to be fraught with meaning. Can't it just be for fun?"

"It can be, yes." Breeanne nodded. "But what if it's more? Do you really want to close that door?"

"Look, I just met this guy. I've only seen him three times. It can't possibly be love."

"But there's something there or you wouldn't be so panicky."

"I'm not panicky."

"Um . . ." Breeanne said. "You just tore a piece of paper to shreds as you talked about him."

"Huh? What?" Jodi glanced down. At some point she'd pick up a piece of copy paper from Breeanne's desk and had systemically torn it into pieces now littering her lap, and she'd been completely unaware of it. "Oh crap, I am panicking."

"No worries." Breeanne swept the pieces of paper that had fallen onto the desk into the trashcan with the side of her hand, while Jodi plucked at the paper fragments dusting her jeans.

"What do I do?" Jodi moaned.

"You want this guy for right now, but not for happily-ever-after."

"Yes."

"Why?"

"Why do I want him or why do I only want him for a fun fling?"

"The fling part. Why are you afraid of something more?"

"Because of Ryan," she admitted. "I was so wrong about him. I don't trust my judgment anymore, and I'm so attracted to Ja— this guy," she quickly corrected. "I don't want to set myself up for more heartbreak."

"You're not willing to take the chance that this guy could actually be the one."

"Right. And I'm certainly not trusting the predictions of hope chest perfume."

Breeanne giggled. "It does sound pretty far-fetched when you put it like that, but hope chest and perfume aside, there's a bigger issue here, isn't there?"

"Yeah, I'm not ready to get involved, and since I'm not really the casual-fling kind of woman, I should probably back off this relationship before I get in too deep."

"Or you could dive in headfirst and live in the moment and let whatever happens, happen."

Jodi decided not to comment on that.

"You were going to tell me why this guy smells the perfume too. If it's all in *my* head, how is it that he smells something too?"

"Because when you wear it, you exude confidence. You feel good when you're wearing it. That's what he's picking up on. Your pheromones. Not the perfume."

"More brain trickery?"

Breeanne nodded. "More brain trickery."

"Hmm. All right. That explanation might work for perfume, but what about your cheetah scarf? I can see how if I'm confident my body might give off an attractive scent, but how in the world did both you and Rowdy perceive the scarf as soft?"

"I'm no scientist or neurologist, but it's Rowdy's theory that when I wear the scarf he sees the world through my eyes — soft, gentle, kind."

"Ahh, that's so sweet I might just throw up," Jodi teased.

Breeanne laughed. "You're just jealous."

"Damn straight," Jodi said. "Damn straight."

Jodi hugged her sister and then sat back down. "I really am so happy for you."

"I know. Thank you."

"And I'm beyond touched that you asked me to be your maid of honor."

"It's a lot of work —"

"I'm loving every minute of it."

"So . . ." Breeanne canted her head. "What do you think about Jake taking over for Warwick?"

Jodi shrugged, trying to appear nonchalant. "Whatever works for you and Rowdy."

"Is Jake the one who can smell your perfume?" Breeanne asked coyly.

Jodi tried not to react, but goose bumps broke out over her skin. "What makes you ask that?"

"You seemed to be enjoying each other's company."

"He seems nice enough," Jodi said.

"Such a shame about his wife." Breeanne's eyes got sad and she clicked her tongue.

A chill rippled over her. His wife? Jake had a wife?

"What about his wife?" Jodi struggled to keep her tone of voice neutral. Why was she so bothered by the news that he'd had a wife? She barely knew the guy. And she was the one who'd refused to let him tell her anything personal about himself.

"You didn't hear about it?"

"Hear about what?"

"Of course, I admit that I didn't really pay that much attention either. I was in the midst of my final heart surgery and it happened in Chicago and I didn't know Rowdy then. But it was a big story in baseball circles."

"What happened?" Jodi asked, stabbing her fingernails into her palms.

"Three years ago, just before Jake's career really took off, his new bride was killed in a convenience store robbery. Jake was playing for the Cubs, but his wife was originally from East Texas. Jefferson, I believe and I think Rowdy mentioned they'd even bought a house together there."

"Oh wait, I vaguely remember hearing something about that," Jodi said. "It was about the time I started dating Ryan."

"It was so sad."

Jodi plastered a palm over her mouth. Sympathy for Jake and all he'd suffered pushed through her veins, rushed up to clog her heart, her throat, her tear ducts. "The poor guy."

"Jake was on the road when it happened," Breeanne continued. "And Rowdy helped him through those dark times. He was a real mess."

"Did they catch the guy who did it?"

"Yes. He's in prison serving a life sentence."

Jodi's stomach pitched, unable to imagine what that must have been like for Jake, but her whole body ached for him.

"Jake and Maura were only married six months," Breeanne went on. "But her murder just about destroyed him. Rowdy says Jake's still picking up the pieces of his life. That's why I was sort of hoping that Jake was the one who could smell your perfume. I know it's silly and it's the romantic in me wanting to play matchmaker. I wish you and Suki and Kasha could all find the same happiness I've found with Rowdy."

Jodi didn't know what to say. She sat there stunned by what Breeanne had told her. Jake's happy-go-lucky smile hid a lot of pain. How brave he was! Her admiration for him climbed into rarefied air.

"Here, let me look it up for you." Breeanne leaned over the computer keyboard to type something into Google and a second later an article about the murder of Maura Coronado popped up on the computer screen.

The picture of a smiling, auburn-haired young woman below the lurid headlines took Jodi's breath.

Breeanne gave a soft gasp, met her gaze, and said exactly what Jodi was thinking. "Oh my gosh, Jo, Maura looks enough like you to be your sister."

CHAPTER 14

Jodi Carlyle's Wedding Crasher Rules:
You just met him. Of course you don't
love him.

"Jodi," Mom's voice drifted up the stairway to the bookstore where Jodi and Breeanne sat staring at Jodi's look-alike, Maura Coronado. "There's someone down here to see you."

"Who is it?" she called down.

"Come and see for yourself."

Jodi went to the balcony, leaned over to look down on the first floor, and saw Jake Coronado standing there with a baby on his hip.

He wore a pair of faded button-fly Levi's, a white T-shirt, and a brown leather bomber jacket, looking hot as the Fourth of July. Her heart thumped crazily.

Jake glanced up at that moment. A slow, easy smile lit up his eyes as if she was the best news he'd had all day, and his sizzling gaze pinned her to the spot. The man looked even sexier with a baby on his hip. How was it possible?

A strange and wondrous flutter began at the base of her brain and slid slowly down her spine to lodge in her tailbone and unfurl graceful wings.

"Come on down, honey." Dad waved to her.

She was stuck. No sneaking out the back way and pretending she hadn't heard or seen any of this.

What was he doing here? And why now when she hadn't had time to process this new information about his dead wife and the fact she looked strikingly like Maura?

Keep up your guard. Don't go soft now because you feel sorry for him.

Squaring her shoulders, she went downstairs to see what he wanted and send him kindly on his way.

"Hey," he said as she approached, his eyes full of sunshine.

"What are you doing here?" she asked lightly.

He gestured at the baby in his arms. It was her neighbor Kendra's son, Tobias. "His mom left him with me because she couldn't find you. Her sister went into labor and she

287

took off to the hospital. Ham wouldn't watch him. So I took your van because it had a car seat in it and here I am."

"Krystal's in labor? She's a month early. I hope everything is okay," Jodi fretted.

"I just texted Kendra," Suki said. "Krystal is doing fine. They should have a new member of the family in a couple of hours. The doctors aren't expecting any complications with the baby. All is well."

"That's wonderful news." Jodi held out her hands to Tobias. The baby grinned widely and leaned toward her. She plucked him from Jake's arms, grateful to have something to hold on to, and sat down on a stool parked at the checkout counter.

"I've got him. You can go now," Jodi said a little more curtly than she intended because her pulse was pounding weirdly and she couldn't bring herself to meet Jake's eyes.

"Jodi," her mother scolded. "Don't be rude."

"There's no need to rush off," Dad said. "I'd like to hear about the Gunslingers' plans for you. Have a seat." Her father moved a gilded birdcage from an Art Deco bar stool right beside Jodi and waved for Jake to sit down.

Jake captured her gaze and Jodi felt a now-familiar flush of heat rise in her breast, expand to burn her throat and cheeks. He looked as mysterious as a trench coat–wearing detective in a smoky, shadow-shrouded film noir. There was something in his expression that both alarmed and stirred her. He was assessing her. Sensing that something had shifted between them? Jodi wondered.

She was pretty certain that most of the time he was a take-charge kind of guy. A man didn't get to the top of the heap by being a pushover. He rested his boot on the rung of the stool, but he didn't sit down.

He was waiting for her to okay it.

Suki plucked a tissue from a box on the desk, passed it to Jodi.

"What's this for?" she asked.

"You're sweating."

What? Oh. She was. Pearls of perspiration had broken out on her forehead. Urgently, she dabbed them away.

"Why are you sweating?" Mom asked, and wrapped herself tighter in her wooly sweater. "It's chilly in here. Are you coming down with something? Do you have a fever?"

Oh yeah, but not the kind of fever her mother was thinking about. "It was hot upstairs," she said.

"No, it's not," Breeanne called from the

balcony. "My toes are icicles. I just turned up the heat."

Gee thanks, family. She dabbed her forehead again as fresh sweat broke out.

"You're flushed too." Mom reached across the counter to splay a hand over Jodi's forehead. "No," she said, sounding surprised. "You're cool, but clammy."

"I'm fine," she insisted. She loved her family, but sometimes they were a little too close for comfort.

Tobias reached for the tissue.

"No, no," she said gently and tucked the tissue in the back pocket of her jeans.

Jake's eyes stayed latched on hers, a sly, slight smile barely curling the edges of his mouth. Why was he looking at her like that? Was it because she reminded him of Maura? Was that why he was so attracted to her? It explained a lot. If she had known she looked so much like his lost wife she would never have gone to bed with him in the first place.

Her mother glanced from Jake to Jodi, cocked her head, put an index finger to her chin, and looked pensive. Oh no. Mom was starting to put two and two together.

Go, she telegraphed him with her eyes. *Please just go.*

But he didn't leave. Instead, he sat down beside her, his knee bumping against hers.

Images of the previous night tumbled through her head. Jake's hot mouth on her neck as he braced her against the wall of the cloakroom, his hands spanning her waist, her legs wrapped tight around his waist, her skirt hiked up to her hips, her panties dropping to the floor, his burgeoning erection pressing against her buttocks. The sex they never got to finish . . .

It was a good thing too, a great thing. Having sex again would only further complicate things.

"Here, Jake," Mom invited. "Have a banana nut muffin. Jodi made them."

"Thank you, Mrs. Carlyle."

"Please," Mom said. "You must call me Maggie. We're practically family after all, Breeanne is marrying your good friend."

Jake reached into the basket, plucked out a muffin, bit into it.

Jodi's gaze latched on to his face, watched a dreamy smile touch his lips as he chewed.

"Mmm." He was eating her muffin.

And enjoying it.

She stared at him and thought, *How can I work this guy into my life?* And immediately squashed it. If she let such thoughts take root and grow she was opening herself up for dashed hopes and a broken heart. Because finding out she was his dead wife's doppelgänger slammed the brakes on any lingering hope she might foolishly have been clinging to.

Why had he stayed?

Jake had done his duty to Kendra. He'd delivered the baby to Timeless Treasures. He was free to go. Jodi had pointedly shot him a get-the-hell-out eye dart. Yet he'd sat down beside her and accepted a muffin.

A damn delicious muffin.

Everyone was smiling at him. Everyone except Jodi, and he felt . . .

Accepted.

In the same way as he felt accepted as part of a baseball team. As he had with Maura's family. Because of his parents' divorce when he was seven, he hadn't grown up in a close family. While both his folks had been loving parents, the cohesiveness hadn't been there. He and his sisters alternately lived with their mother or father, as circumstances and finances shifted and changed. And once stepfamilies got added to the mix, the dynamics shifted even more.

The Carlyles were a close family and had everything that entailed — meddling, teasing, and good-natured squabbling. He wished for that kind of close familial connection. It was fun to watch and he found himself longing to be part of it.

Uh-oh.

Jake shoved a hand through his hair. Christ, he was getting ahead of himself. He didn't know if he had a prayer of winning Jodi over. Not a smart idea to go falling in love with her family.

It terrified him that he was even thinking along those lines.

Jodi was bouncing the standing baby on her knee. She was pretending to focus solely on Toby's face, but he caught those quick sidelong glances she tossed over at him when she believed no one was looking. He saw drops of perspiration form a sheen on her forehead again and the pulse at the hollow of her throat pounding erratically.

Was she thinking about what he was thinking about? Last night in the closet? New Year's Eve at the Grand Texan? The possibility of more bedroom games?

Toby opened his mouth and leaned in toward Jodi's chin. Uh-oh, he recognized that I'm-gonna-bite-you look on the kid's face.

But just as he opened his mouth to warn Jodi, almost unconsciously, she stuck a hand in the side pocket of the diaper bag Jake had dropped onto the counter, pulled out a plastic teething ring, and popped it into the baby's mouth. Toby grinned, grabbed the teething ring with both hands, and went to town on it with that solo tooth.

"How did you do that?" he asked.

"What?" she asked, looking honestly perplexed.

"Anticipate what Toby was going to do and intercept him so easily before he did it."

Jodi laughed. "I'm the oldest out of four kids. I've got this mothering thing down pat."

"You were such a good second mama." Maggie Carlyle smiled at her daughter. "I don't know what I would have done without you, especially when Breeanne was so sick."

"Jodi was our little lifesaver." Carrying a cup of coffee, Dan moved to drop a kiss on the top of his eldest daughter's head.

"Another muffin, Jake?" Maggie urged, extending the wicker basket of baked goods toward him.

"Don't mind if I do." He took another muffin.

Jodi chuffed out an exaggerated breath.

"Problem?" he asked, taking a bite of the moist muffin.

"Why are you still here?" she muttered under her breath. "Muffins are completely portable. Feel free to take some and go."

"I'm pretty comfortable right here, thanks." He smirked, enjoying himself.

She shifted gears. "Give me the keys to the van. It's time for Toby's morning nap, so I better head back to Boxcars." She stood up. "Enjoy your muffins."

"Wait." He polished off the second muffin, dusted crumbs from his fingers, and got to his feet. "I need a ride back."

"You can take my car." She dug the keys out of her pocket and dropped them in his open hand. "Drive safe."

So much for getting a ride with her.

Jake followed Jodi back to the B&B. When they arrived, she jumped out of the van and rushed around to get Toby out of the car seat as if she was in a relay race. He got out of her Honda Civic, strolled over, reached for the diaper bag she was trying to hoist onto her shoulder while juggling Toby in her other arm.

"Here," he said. "Let me help."

"I got it," she said, and stepped back from him, the diaper bag banging against her hip, her lips pulled tight with distress.

"What's wrong?"

"You," she said so vehemently that *he* stepped back. Whoa. What had he done to set her off like this? "You're what's wrong."

"What'd I do?"

She stared at him as if he was as dumb as a box of rocks. "I thought we had an agreement."

He scratched his head. "About what?"

"Staying as far away from each other as possible."

"Oh," he said. "That."

"Yes, *that.*"

"Toby got thrust on me. What else was I supposed to do?"

"Tobias. His name is Tobias. His mother doesn't like for people to shorten it."

"Ookay." He pushed his palms down in a calming motion. He had no idea that she'd get so riled up.

Her chest was heaving, visibly rising and falling with each breath. "It wasn't so much that you brought Tobias to the store," she said, her voice softening. "It was that you stayed. You could have left right away. You should have left."

"Your parents invited me. What was I supposed to do? Say no?"

"Jake," she said, and shook her head. "Jake, Jake, Jake."

"Jodi?"

"I can't seem to keep my hands to myself and I hate that. I'm never out of control, but with you . . ."

"What?"

"I want to kiss you so much right now that I can't stand it."

"Me either," he said huskily, and closed the gap between them, moving decisively like a lawyer closing a plea deal. "So why are we resisting?"

"Breeanne just told me about Maura," she murmured, and lowered her eyelids. "I saw a picture of your wife, Jake. I know that I look like her."

Jake froze as a pump of emotions pushed ice down his spine. He shouldn't be surprised. He should have expected someone to tell her about his past. He wanted to be the one to tell her, but he'd waited too long, lost his window of opportunity, and now she'd found out from someone else. But he hadn't known how to bring up the topic of his deceased wife who bore an uncanny resemblance to Jodi. By waiting, had he completely blown his chances with her?

He opened his mouth. "I . . ." Shut it. He didn't know what to say.

"I'm sorry for all you've suffered," Jodi said quietly. "It's very sad and my heart aches for you, but I can't be Maura's stand-in. You can't replace her with me."

"I . . ." He swallowed hard. "I'm not try-ing to do that."

"No?" She gave a quick, brittle nod.

"No," he said firmly.

"You're going to stand there and tell me that the attraction you feel has nothing to do with the fact I look like the young wife you lost so tragically?"

"I admit that you initially caught my eye because you resemble Maura, yes, but you're wrong about me trying to replace her."

"Are you sure?"

Was he? Jake pulled a palm down his face. He didn't think so. Personality-wise, Jodi was nothing like Maura. But how could he know for sure there wasn't some truth to it? And if *he* didn't know for certain, how could he convince her?

"This is too complicated." Jodi shook her head.

"Are you trying to tell me we aren't worth exploring?" he asked. "I know I had the best sex of my life with you."

"Shh," Jodi darted her gaze over her shoulder as if checking to see that no one had sneaked up on them.

"I'm serious," he insisted.

Her cheeks reddened like vine-ripened tomatoes. "How was sex with Maura?"

Her question was a punch to the gut. She was right. Things were complicated. His lips tightened. "That's private."

"I see," she said softly. "Too many land mines. We're better off keeping our distance."

"All right," he said, not knowing why he couldn't just accept the fact she didn't want to continue their affair. "Sex with Maura was good. We were in love, but she was naïve, shy, hesitant. Not that I minded, but with you . . ." He shook his head. "Dynamite."

"Breeanne said you guys were only married six months, maybe Maura just didn't have time to get to dynamite."

His gut knocked against his spine. He took a step back, an uncomfortable feeling settling over him. Talking about his sex life with Maura felt disloyal. He felt like a boat with a broken rudder. Didn't know how to navigate these choppy waters. "You're right. Too many land mines."

Jodi exhaled audibly. "I was engaged before."

That stopped him. "When?"

"A year ago. He stood me up at the altar."

"Ah," he said. "The guy who soured you on relationships."

"The guy who burst my bubble about romantic fantasies. You, Jake Coronado, are a romantic fantasy."

"Sometimes dreams come true," he said.

"And sometimes, they're total bullshit."

"Wow, that guy really did a number on you."

She shrugged. "He ran off with a stripper to the Caymans after embezzling money from the savings and loan where he worked. I spent months convincing the feds I was not involved. The experience left me gun-shy."

The oddest sensation washed over him, the feeling that she didn't easily open up to people and she'd just gifted him with a pearl of personal information. She trusted him, at least enough to share that tidbit. It was a start.

"And you haven't been with a man since then," he said. "Until me."

She stared at him, pulled her bottom lip up between her teeth, and then slowly nodded.

"That's why you're so nervous about us."

She was brave and held her ground, but her eyes flickered warily. "I'm not ready for this. I'm not ready for you. I'm busy being a maid of honor and running a B&B and —"

"Running from your feelings."

"Yes," she admitted, and that stirred him more than he cared to admit. "It's ridiculous to feel this way."

"What way is that?"

"Uncontrollable. Overpowered. Overwhelmed. You're very overwhelming."

"So are you," he said sincerely. "But I'm willing to risk it."

"I don't overwhelm people. If anything I'm underwhelming."

"Why on earth would you believe that?"

"My ex-fiancé certainly thought so."

"Forget that guy. He had shit for brains."

"Not gonna argue with you there." She slanted him a glance that plucked at something in the center of his chest. "Do you ever wish life came with a giant eraser? A rubber do-over stick?"

Was she thinking about the night she'd spent with him and wishing she could expunge it from her life? The pull in his chest tightened.

"Regrets are useless," he said honestly. "You make mistakes and live with the consequences. It's how people learn."

"That's a healthy mental state," she said. "I doubt I'll ever get there."

"What? You think you have to be perfect all the time?"

She didn't answer and he realized that, yes, she thought she had to be perfect. "You're too hard on yourself," he said. "You're only human."

"You're going to tell me you don't beat yourself up for your wife's death?"

Jake gulped. She had him there. "I came to terms with it. Not saying it was easy, just saying it's possible."

"You're healed?" She sounded skeptical, looked surprised.

The muscle at his temple ticked. "It's taken a long time, and the scar will always be a part of who I am, but yeah."

"I'm happy for you," she said.

"But . . ."

"This is bad timing."

She looked so beautiful in the morning light with the sun glinting off her auburn hair, the baby cocked on her hip, her eyes filled with a grab bag of emotions. She wore a pink sweater and a cream-colored lamb's wool car coat with the collar turned up around her neck. She smelled of promise and hope and it was all too much for him. Looking into her eyes, he could hear his own heart beating and the sound was deafening. Sinking. He was sinking hard and fast. Good thing she was putting on the brakes.

Tobias fretted and squirmed in her arms.

"I better take him inside," she said, cupping Tobias's little head in her palm. "He probably needs a diaper change."

"Yeah," Jake croaked, swallowed hard. "Go take care of the baby."

Chapter 15

Jodi Carlyle's Wedding Crasher Rules:
Remember the past is gone, and the
future doesn't exist yet, live for today.

Well, she'd gotten what she wanted. She'd
sent Jake packing. Why did she feel so miserable?

Why? Because she wanted to have wild
monkey sex with him, that was why. She
wanted to be Gwendolyn all over again —
exotic, mysterious, sophisticated, urbane.

But she couldn't go back to that now.
He'd already seen her as the girl next door.
As the woman who made banana nut muffins and hung out with her family and knew
a seven-month old baby so well she could
anticipate when he was going to bite and
intercept him with a teething ring.

And what about the mad lust that had
driven them into the coat closet at Vincente's? That had certainly not been "Jodi"

inside that closet. That had been one-hundred-percent Gwendolyn.

Except it *had* been her.

Was that really the problem? She couldn't reconcile these two sides of herself?

After Jake left, Tobias kept her busy for a while. She'd changed, fed, and played with him until the tyke had fallen asleep on a pallet in the middle of the office floor. She called Kendra to check her sister's progress and reassure her that Tobias was doing fine. She learned Krystal had just given birth to a healthy baby girl, and Kendra promised to swing by soon to pick up Tobias.

While the baby slept, Jodi processed the online reservations that had come in since yesterday and sent out confirmations. She thought she was doing a splendid job of keeping her thoughts off Jake, until she started getting calls from customers telling her she'd made mistakes on their reservations.

Ham sauntered into the office and asked her why she'd left the door to the van hanging open with her car keys dangling in the ignition. He tossed her the keys.

Groaning, Jodi planted her elbows on the desk and dropped her head into her hands.

"You okay?" Ham asked, concern tingeing his voice. "You're usually so on top of

305

things. This isn't like you."

"The baby's a distraction," she fibbed. *Sorry, Tobias for using you as an excuse.* But it was easier that way.

Her mind was scrambled, muddled, scattered. She was making mistakes left and right, and for someone who prized order, discipline, and stability it was a difficult pill to swallow. Her feelings for Jake Coronado were the primary reasons for her confusion.

Big question. What was she going to do about it?

Did she hold the course, and keep her life on track just the way it had always been, knowing exactly what was in front of her? No surprises. No curveballs. But that meant no excitement either.

Seriously? She'd had enough of the wrong kind of excitement after Ryan's departure. Calm and quiet was perfect.

She nibbled her bottom lip and thought about the two sides of her. There was the dutiful daughter who desperately struggled to do the right thing, versus the secret vamp who thrilled to the idea of adventuresome sex with a stranger. Should she stay the course or embrace the unknown? Test herself or hold true to who she knew herself to be?

Both options scared her.

The logical part of her brain urged caution. The intuitive part whispered, *Come on, live a little. It's okay.*

What about the consequences? What if following her impulses led her to a whole new world of hurt? But what if, at the end of her life, she ended up feeling as if she'd stayed stuck in second gear while the world passed her by?

Jodi pulled her bottom lip up between her teeth, slowly released it, and blew out a pent-up breath. She couldn't make the decision on her own. She needed help sorting this out.

Determined to clear the mist fogging up her brain, she picked up the phone and called Dr. Jeanna to make an appointment.

By the time Jake pulled into the driveway of the frame house in Jefferson, he was feeling somewhat better. The yard was neat and well cared for, the landscaping company he hired had done their job. The curb appeal was spot-on. The one-story Craftsman would be an easy sell.

He walked up the steps, but didn't feel the flutter of butterflies he'd expected. In all honesty, he hadn't spent more than half a dozen nights in this house. They'd still been living in Chicago when they'd bought the place just a month before Maura's murder, and they had not even started the renovations they'd planned.

The key hung in the lock and it took him a second to jiggle the door open. Inside, the rooms were empty, dusty. "It's okay," he mumbled out loud. "You're here now."

The only room that had anything in it was the small room at the back of the house. Facing *that* room was going to be the toughest challenge of all.

He'd told Jodi he was healed. Now was the time to prove it. Not to her, but to himself.

In one way, part of what Breeanne had told Jodi was right. He wasn't one hundred percent over Maura's death. She'd died so traumatically, so tragically, so damn unexpectedly that he could never fully forget her. She was part of his past and she'd formed who he was. And he would always remember the ugly fight they'd had over his career just before she died. The apology gift he'd sent to her from the road that she never saw.

He'd told Jodi he didn't have any regrets, but it was all bravado. More than anything else, regret ate at him. Maura would never know how terribly sorry he was for that argument. She'd never know that he had changed his mind about everything.

While he had recovered from Maura's death, moved beyond his grief and his acting-out phase and into acceptance, he was still sketchy on forgiving himself. But he was working toward that.

And he was ready for that fresh start. His intense attraction to Jodi was enough proof of that. Except for the nagging question that he kept pushing to the back of his mind. Was he attracted to her because she looked so much like Maura?

Initially, yes, but the more he got to know her, the more he liked her for who she was. He saw her more for her differences than her similarities to Maura.

Jodi was generous, friendly, confident, determined, and involved. She had moxie. Maura had been a quiet, naïve, insecure, infinitely trusting, with a soul-stirring susceptibility. In personality, the two women were nothing alike.

Jake did a walk-through, seeing the place through the eyes of a potential buyer instead of the owner. He didn't feel numb, but neither were his emotions stirred. He felt . . . calm, and that surprised him a little.

Pulling his cell phone from his pocket, he started a to-do list. Replace stovetop in the kitchen. Replace carpet with high-quality laminate. Completely renovate master bath.

He was handy. Yes, he could pay to have the work done, but doing it himself would help him face his demons. But he would have to get on the stick if he hoped to have it done before spring training.

When he finished the plans, he felt resolved and hopeful for the future.

He didn't know where things were going to go between him and Jodi or if they could work out their differences. For now, it didn't matter. Until he dealt with the house, his last emotional tie to Maura, he wasn't free to embrace a new relationship.

Besides, Jodi had trust issues. The guy who dumped her at the altar had done a number on her self-esteem. But she had the spunk to get past it. He wanted to know Jodi better. Longed to explore their out-of-control chemistry. Yearned to find out more about her. Ached to sink his body into hers again.

But that wasn't what she wanted and if she wasn't all in, then he wasn't going to act on his impulses. He had a life to live and he was going to start living it. He'd give her some space until after the wedding. If at that point she wanted to come along for the ride, then great. If not, he was going to keep looking for someone who did.

Two days after her appointment with Dr. Jeanna, Jodi was still straddling the emotional fence. The therapist assured her that it was perfectly okay to explore her sexuality as long as she did so in a conscious, mature, and mentally healthy manner with parameters that made her feel comfortable. In fact, Dr. Jeanna considered it a positive sign of Jodi's emotional growth.

But she also cautioned Jodi that rebound affairs rarely progressed beyond physical attraction, and urged her to temper any expectations about a long-term relationship. She also warned her about carrying on a fling in Stardust where her life was under a microscope and family and friends felt entitled to weigh in on her love life.

Simple fact. Jodi shouldn't go fishing in her own pond. Jake's friendship with her sister's husband-to-be meant he was simply too close for comfort.

"Pick someone else to have a fling with," Dr. Jeanna advised.

Jodi stewed on it and decided there was nothing to decide. At least not until the wedding shower/Super Bowl party at Rowdy's house the following Sunday, where she'd be forced to see Jake again.

Who knew? By then the attraction might have blown over. In the meantime, she had maid of honor duties, and that's where she'd put her energies.

On the Tuesday afternoon before the wedding shower, she was meeting Kasha for a late lunch at the Honeysuckle Café to finalize plans for the bachelorette weekend. Suki and her mother had gone to an antique auction in Baton Rouge, leaving their dad in charge of the store.

Jodi arrived a few minutes early for her one-thirty lunch date with her sister, in order to spend a little time with her father. Things had been so busy that they didn't get to have much one-on-one time anymore. Her dad was at the checkout counter when she came in, gluing the leg back on a step-stool, reading glasses perched halfway down his nose. Callie lay on the overhead balcony railing, tail swishing, watching him with narrow-slit eyes.

"Callie is about to pounce," Jodi warned as she went behind the counter to give him a quick kiss on the cheek.

"I know," he said. "She's been up there for twenty minutes waiting for me to forget about her."

"Breeanne," Jodi called up to the bookstore. "Rein in Callie before she gives Dad a heart attack."

"On it," Breeanne called back.

"I'll be fine." Dad pushed his glasses up on his nose.

Breeanne whisked Callie into her arms. The calico meowed in protest. "How about some cream?" Breeanne asked the cat as she carried her off to the book stacks.

A customer strolled up to the counter with an antique lace tablecloth. "You know my favorite thing about this store, Dan?"

"What's that, Mrs. Q?" Dad asked of the sixty-something woman who used to teach third grade at Sam Houston Elementary. He set the mended stool upside down on the counter, capped the tube of superglue, and pushed his reading glasses up on his forehead.

"The wonderful relationship you Carlyles have. If more families were like yours, the world would be a happier place."

"Why, thank you for saying so, Mrs. Q. Are you ready to buy that tablecloth you've been circling for a month?"

"I think I am, Dan. I'm having my garden club to tea on Super Bowl Sunday while Ralph and his buddies are barricaded in his man cave, and this tablecloth will earn me high praise indeed."

"You'll be the talk of the garden club," he said, and checked out Mrs. Q and waved good-bye as she went out the door to the soft tinkle of wind chimes. Dad rubbed the back of his neck and grimaced.

"I'm meeting Kasha for a late lunch at the Honeysuckle," Jodi said. "What's the special?"

"Butternut squash casserole." He kneaded his neck harder. "At least I think. This confounded crick in my neck . . ."

"Sit," she said, moving behind the counter to direct him to the stool, and began massaging his neck.

"Honey, you don't have —" He lowered his head. "Damn that feels good."

Jodi increased the pressure.

"You were always so great at this," her father said. "From the time you were four years old."

"I liked taking care of you. Especially after all those long hours you and Mom spent nursing Breeanne back to health."

"I'm surprised that Kasha was the one who went into the medical field and not you," Dad said.

"I'm in hospitality. Same thing. Except my job is making people happy instead of healing them."

"You're fixing me right up." He waved a

hand. "So go on. You've got things to do."

"There's nothing more important than making you feel better."

"You've already worked wonders." He moved his neck from side to side to prove it. "Thank you."

"Put some mentholatum ointment on your neck and a heat pack."

"Kasha better be careful," he teased. "Next thing you know you'll be gunning for her job."

"No way." She laughed. "I love what I do for a living."

"Music to a father's ears. We're so lucky all you girls love your work." He lowered his voice. "But you're especially good at your job."

"Thanks, Dad." She kissed his cheek.

With her father's praise ringing her ears, she picked up her purse and tablet computer and followed her nose to the back of the building. She slipped in through the rear entrance of the café through Timeless Treasures. Most of the tourists came in through the outdoor entrance, ate at the tearoom, and then left the way Jodi had come in, stopping to browse antiques on their way out.

The lunch crowd had thinned, many of the occupied tables now populated with regulars who came later in the afternoon to avoid the tourists. The decor was eclectic country, decorated with finds from Timeless Treasures. Tall painted milk jugs served as table bottoms. None of the chairs matched. The tablecloths were different colors of gingham check. In the far booth, Jodi spied Kasha.

Her sister's face was alit, her head thrown back, and she was laughing at something the man sitting across from her had said.

Jake.

Air staggered up Jodi's throat. Rushed out of her mouth in a hurried swoosh. Instantly, her skin tingled and her heart floated in a warm bath of heated light.

Jake.

Seated with her sister. Looking very hot, handsome, flirty, and comfy.

The bottom of Jodi's stomach dropped out, dropped into her knees, dragged down to the floor.

What was Kasha doing with Jake?

She had no right to feel possessive. Had no idea where the intensity of her feelings was coming from. She was the one who told Jake to move on. That she wasn't in a place where she wanted a relationship, but seeing her sister with him changed *everything*.

Pulse thumping, she rushed over to the

booth. "Scoot," she told Kasha, and nudged her over with her hip.

Kasha scooted.

Jodi plopped down. *Be cool. Be calm.*

"What are you doing here?" she asked Jake brightly, desperately trying not to sound accusatory. The last thing she wanted was for him to think she was jealous. Even if she was.

"Jake was just —" Kasha blushed.

Blushing? Kasha? *Honestly?* Kasha was the unflappable one in the family. She didn't blush. She didn't simper. She didn't gush. But she was doing all those things now.

With Jake.

"Leaving." Jake got up and winked at Kasha. "I'll see you later."

Later? He was going to be seeing Kasha later? Jodi gulped, feared she was going to hyperventilate.

"Bye." Kasha wriggled her fingers and slanted Jake a sultry look beneath half-closed eyelids.

He passed by Jodi's chair without anything more than a pleasant "Good afternoon."

Oh snap. She couldn't handle this. When she'd told him he should move on, she hadn't meant for him to move on with her sister!

As soon as he was gone, Jodi swung

around to the other side of the booth. "What are you doing?"

"What do you mean?"

"What was that with Jake?"

Kasha looked taken aback. "Don't get your nose out of joint. He came by to ask my advice on what to give Breeanne and Rowdy for a wedding gift."

"And he came to you?" Why hadn't he come to *her*?

"Sure. Why not?"

"Why didn't he just call or text?"

Kasha shrugged like she truly didn't know why Jake had approached her in person. "You'd have to ask him."

"You blushed when you were talking to him. You don't ever blush." *Dear God, Jodi, hold your tongue.*

"Wait." Kasha leveled a long, appraising stare at her. "Are *you* attracted to Jake?"

"No," she said, too loudly, too forcefully.

Kasha held her stare without blinking. She wasn't the least bit shamefaced. But why should she be? Her sister had no idea about her relationship with Jake.

What relationship? They didn't have a relationship. They'd just had sex. That was it. Once. And almost in the closet. Mind-blowing, stupendous sex, but never mind that.

Kasha straightened. "So you wouldn't mind if I asked him out —"

"No."

"No, you don't mind or no, you'd prefer if I didn't explore a relationship with him?"

"Just . . ." Jodi took a deep breath, torn between her desire for Jake and her dread fear of that very desire. It was so strong. So overwhelming. "Don't."

"Is there something wrong with him?" Kasha asked.

"He's a widower."

"I know." Kasha lowered her voice. "All that angsty suffering makes him even sexier."

Jodi's heart did a frantic tap dance in her chest.

The waitress trotted over to them. "Whatcha havin' today, girls?"

"The special," Jodi said.

"Fruit plate." Kasha eyed Jodi suspiciously.

"And to drink?" the waitress asked.

"Sweet tea for me," Jodi said.

"Good choice." Kasha handed the waitress her menu. "You need something sweet to take the sour out of your mood."

"There's nothing wrong with my mood."

"Uh-huh." Kasha pressed her lips together in a you-are-the-Queen-of-Denial expression. "The last time you looked at me like that was in high school when Tad Farmer asked me to the prom."

"We were supposed to be going steady," Jodi said.

"Which is why I turned him down. I don't take things that don't belong to me. Does Jake belong to you, Jodi?"

"No, certainly not. Of course he doesn't."

"So no hard feelings if we go out?"

"Did he ask you out?" Jodi hated the anxiety in her voice.

"He didn't."

Jodi blew out a relieved breath. "I'm sorry," she apologized. "I didn't mean to come on so strong. Forgive me."

"Nothing to forgive," Kasha said. "If you've got designs on Jake, he's yours."

"I don't have designs on him."

"I see." Kasha looked hurt. "You just don't want him to date *me.*"

Ah, that old sibling rivalry. In some ways, she and Kasha were closest because they were almost the same age. Kasha was just ten months younger than Jodi. And both of them had first come to live with the Carlyles as foster children. They'd bonded over having known a harsh life before being adopted by Mom and Dad. But the situation had also made them more competitive with each other than either of them was with Suki or Breeanne, vying to prove who was worthiest of their adopted parents' love.

As they'd grown up, a lot of the competitiveness had fallen away naturally, but once in a while, it could raise its ugly head again.

Like now.

Not wanting to cause her sister pain, Jodi reached out to put a hand on Kasha's and came clean. "There's something I have to tell you."

Kasha straightened her regal spine. "What's that?"

"Jake can smell the perfume," Jodi whispered.

"What?" Kasha's eyes rounded. "The perfume you found in the hope chest?"

Jodi nodded.

"Oh wow." Kasha leaned forward, then back, put a palm to her cheek. "How do you feel about that?"

"Confused. Scared. Excited. Overwhelmed."

"You said you didn't believe in the hope chest prophecy."

"I don't. Of course it's silly . . ."

"But . . ."

"No one else can smell the perfume."

"Do you think Jake is The One?"

"That's a precarious limb and I'm not

dumb enough to climb out on it," Jodi said.

"So you're in limbo, and doing the classic Jodi thing."

"What classic Jodi thing?"

"Trying to control everything. Your emotions. Your reactions." Kasha paused a moment, murmured, "Your desires."

Jodi nodded mutely. She couldn't argue with that.

"Ultimately, sister, some things are just beyond our control and the heart wants what the heart wants whether it makes logical sense or not."

"What are you saying, Kasha?"

"Jake Coronado is a successful, sexy, handsome man. He's got money, a pleasant disposition, and a hot bod. If you don't make a play for him, you can bet your boxcar someone else will."

CHAPTER 16

Jodi Carlyle's Wedding Crasher Rules:
You can't save the wedding cake and eat
it too.

On Super Bowl Sunday, Jodi, Kasha, and
Suki spent the morning at Rowdy's sprawling ranch house high on the hill above
Stardust, decorating for the couple's wedding shower. Warwick was there to help with
the fetching and carrying, but Breeanne and
Rowdy had been banned from entering the
house until the four p.m. start time of the
party.

Jodi had left Ham, along with a temporary
employee she'd hired for the remaining two
weeks leading up to the wedding, in charge
of the B&B. She'd be too busy to spend
much time at Boxcars.

To separate the bridal shower from the
Super Bowl, they set up two party stations.
One in the dining room where the couple

would open presents before the game, the other in Rowdy's massive den.

They decorated the dining room with colors of the wedding. Red, white, and pink helium balloons, their strings taped to the floor at different heights at the back of the room, creating a festive wall of balloons. A white banner with pink and red lettering, stretched across the entryway, proclaimed: "HE PUT A RING ON IT." Framed pictures of Rowdy and Breeanne when they were both gap-toothed seven-year-olds sat on a side table, along with game cards for the personalized Mad Libs they would play later. Heart-shaped foil confetti was spread out across the tablecloths to create a glittery glow of romance. The food in this room leaned toward healthier fare — crudités and homemade dip, finger sandwiches, fruit bowls, pasta salads.

In the den, the party took on a Dallas Cowboys flavor, the colors of the decorations changing to silver and blue, even though the Cowboys weren't playing in the Super Bowl this year. Party favors were beer koozies imprinted with Rowdy and Breeanne's names, the date of their wedding, and the cutesy saying: "To Have and Hold and Keep Your Beer Cold." This spread would include chips and guacamole, colorful Fiestaware bowls of chili, buffalo wings, and pigs in a blanket.

Jodi had been so busy orchestrating the event that she hadn't spared a thought for anything else, and so she wasn't fully prepared for the sight of Jake coming up the walkway ten minutes early, a load of wrapped packages in his arms.

She caught a glimpse of him through the window as she buzzed from the kitchen to the dining room carrying a tray of banana pudding in miniature Mason jars.

He glanced up, met her gaze through the open blinds, and smiled that smile that never failed to turn her knees rubbery.

Oh glory. She'd better set the tray down before she dropped it.

He was with Axel Talbot, and she tried to school her features into a neutral expression, but wasn't sure she pulled it off. Ducking her head, she hurried into the dining room to set up the desserts, heard Warwick answer the door.

She felt the three men come into the room behind her, told herself she was not going to look around at Jake, but she did it anyway.

Mistake!

He was devastatingly gorgeous in crisp starched blue jeans with a sharp crease running down the front of his powerful legs and a white polo shirt. She kept remembering what Kasha had said: *If you don't make a play for him soon, someone else will.*

She fumbled the tray. The Mason jars slid, clanked into each other. Before she could cry, "Oh no," Jake dropped the packages in his arms, took two long-legged strides, and grabbed the tray like magic before it fell from her arms. Not a single jar broke.

"Perfect save," Talbot praised him.

"Great reflexes," she said, looking into Jake's eyes. He was so close, smelled so great.

"You have no idea," he murmured, and an instant jolt of electricity ran up and down her body like power line wires.

"You're handy to have around." A helpless smile overtook her. Why couldn't she stop smiling?

"You have no idea," he repeated, and winked. He helped her put out the pudding jars while Talbot and Warwick picked up the packages he'd dropped and set them on the gift table.

Jake sank his hands on his hips, the muscles of his arms cording beautifully with the stance, and surveyed the room. "You responsible for all this?"

"There's more in the den."

"You're handy to have around," he said.

She laughed, and the sound lifted all the way to the crown of her head. "You have no idea."

Jake looked at her like he'd found a fat nugget of gold in his mining pan. "You have a great laugh."

"What's going on here?" Talbot asked. "Something I should know about?"

"Know about what?" Suki asked, coming into the room with a pitcher of winter sangria. "You guys are early."

"Told you," Talbot said to Jake. To Jodi, he said, "He broke speed limits getting here. You'd think it was his wedding shower."

"I was eager for the game," Jake said, his gaze hooked on Jodi.

Lust and panic surged her pulse. Okay, no call to freak out just because he was looking at her like he wanted to lick her to death. That was good. She wanted to lick him too, from head to toe. Just not right now. She had work to do, guests arriving, a party to oversee, never mind that he was the most delicious thing on two legs, she —

"Jodi?" Suki said.

"Huh?"

"You're standing there with your mouth hanging open. Were you about to say something and stroked out?"

Yes. That was about the size of it. "Pigs in

a blanket," she said. "I've got to get them into the oven. Come with me." She grabbed Suki's hand just to keep from grabbing Jake, and pulled her sister from the dining room, unable to resist one last look over her shoulder.

He was staring at her as if he was thinking about her naked, which he probably was. She was certainly thinking about him naked. Too bad there was a houseful of people coming through the front door and they couldn't do anything about their mutual lusting.

Jodi sucked in a deep breath. She'd better pace herself. It was shaping up to be a long evening.

Forty minutes later, Jake slouched one shoulder against the dining room wall, a beer he didn't much want held loosely in his hand, watching as Rowdy and Breeanne opened shower presents. The room space was overflowing with family and friends. Jodi sat to one side on a stiff-backed chair, writing down who'd given what gifts. Maid of honor duties, he figured. She looked sexy as ever in black leggings that clung to her shapely thighs, black boots with stacked heels, a short green shirt, and a black and green plaid sweater.

Suki stood next to a gift-laden table picking out which presents to next pass over to the couple.

Jake had spent the past two weeks working on the house in Jefferson and the only projects he had left were renovating the bathroom, which was going to require knocking down a wall, and clearing out the small back bedroom. He still hadn't worked up the courage to walk in there. The jetted tub he'd ordered would be arriving tomorrow and if everything went according to plan, he should have the house ready to list after the wedding.

"Want another beer?" Talbot asked, and nodded at the ice chest that was underneath the table where Suki was standing.

Jake showed Talbot his almost-full bottle of beer, but he never took his eyes off Jodi. "You just want an excuse to go over there and try to look up Suki's skirt."

"Hell man, can you blame me? Look at her."

"Hot," he said, his gaze hooking on Jodi's mouth as she tucked one corner of her bottom lip up between her teeth.

"Not only that, she's a real live wire. Keeps me on my toes."

"And that's saying something," Jake said. Talbot was legendary for playing the field.

"Don't hurt her."

"Suki? Her skin is thick as an elephant hide." Talbot's voice lightened. "But soft. She has very soft skin."

"Do something to distract yourself."

"How? I'm hypnotized."

I know. Jake took a sip off his beer, watched Jodi pause in her recording to stretch her arms over her head. Her breasts rose. Jake hoped no one noticed his eyes were bugging out of his head.

Suki handed Breeanne a long slender box wrapped in gold foil paper that Jake had brought.

"From Jake," Breeanne read aloud from the tag. "Aww, thank you, Jake."

Jake tensed, pushed off from the wall, and cleared his throat. "Um . . ."

Breeanne glanced back at the label. "Ooh, it's not for us, Rowdy. This present is for Jodi."

Jodi's head shot up and her eyes met Jake's. "Why did you buy me a gift?" she asked curtly, but despite her cool tone, he could tell she was flattered.

"The best man is supposed to give the maid of honor a gift, right?" he said, knowing it was bullshit, but hoping he'd convince her that he was lovably incompetent in the art of wedding protocol.

330

"That's not a thing." Jodi shook her head.

"I think it's a new trend," Kasha piped up, glanced over her shoulder at Jake, and winked.

Thank heavens for Kasha. She was a great partner in crime. She'd been fully on board with his scheme when he'd met her for coffee at the Honeysuckle Café.

Jodi frowned. "I've never heard of the best man giving the maid of honor a gift and I've been on The Knot every day for weeks."

"Oh yes," Suki chimed in. "It's definitely the latest trend."

Hmm, had Kasha clued Suki in or was she just jumping on the bandwagon? Then again, who knew? Maybe the best man gifting the maid of honor with a present *was* a real thing.

"Is it?" Jodi's face colored and she looked embarrassed. "I had no idea." She held his gaze. "I didn't get you anything."

"Don't worry about it," he soothed, feeling sly, guilty, and a trifle worried. Could this backfire on him? "You didn't know it was a thing."

She looked at him as if she wanted to blow down his whole house of cards. He gave her a watertight grin. Solid. He was in it to win it. Self-confident bluster.

"Well don't just sit there," Maggie Carlyle

told her oldest daughter. "Open it."

Jodi shook her head. "Today is about Breeanne and Rowdy, not me. I'll open it later."

"No, no." Breeanne nudged Jodi with her elbow. "Go ahead and open it. I don't mind sharing the spotlight with my big sis."

Jodi looked uncomfortable and Jake shifted his weight, beginning to regret giving her the gift at the shower. Hell, he didn't know why he'd gotten her anything at all. He'd promised himself he was going to keep his distance.

Looking blindsided, she removed the tape with gentle care, unwrapped the box, and then folded the paper neatly after she'd removed it. And finally, she lifted the lid on the box. She looked down and her eyes lit up, and Jake knew he'd struck gold.

He blew out a long held breath. He'd pleased her.

She held up the charm bracelet for everyone to see. The charms were exact replicas of the boxcars at her B&B, including the engine office and caboose dining car. Kasha had recommended a local artist, who'd done the piece for him. He'd paid extra for a rush job. It was completely worth it.

Jodi's gaze met his again and although he was standing across the room, he could have sworn her eyes misted.

"Thank you, Jake," she said, her tone heartfelt. "It's one of the most thoughtful gifts anyone has ever given me. Thank you so much."

Jodi was doing her best not to notice Jake on the other side of the room, but that was like not noticing the sun. He was there, hot and omnipresent, eclipsing everyone and everything else.

What did the freaking gift mean? Yes, she loved it. Yes, it was sweet. But why had he given it to her at the party in front of everyone? Why had he pushed her into the spotlight like that? Why was he coming on strong when he promised to keep his distance? Why was she overanalyzing everything?

And here she'd planned on approaching him at the party to tell him she'd reconsidered, that she would like to have more than a one-night stand just as long as they laid down those conscious, mature, mentally healthy ground rules that Dr. Jeanna suggested.

But now that he'd pulled this stunt, and given her the bracelet in front of everyone, drawing attention to them, she was rethinking that plan. She fingered the hand-painted tiny boxcars on the sterling silver chain at her wrist and smiled. Okay, maybe not rethinking the plan entirely, but she was going to wait to talk to him about it when there weren't so many people around. In fact, maybe she would stay away from him for now and just call him later.

Best course of action? Play it cool.

Not all that hard to do since she had hostess duties to keep her busy, refilling glasses, cleaning up, making sure everyone was comfy and having a great time. Except there was Jake at her elbow as she wiped off paper plates and stacked them in a pile for the recycling bin.

"Need any help?" he asked.

"Nope," she said without looking at him. "Mom and I have it covered."

He cast a glance over his shoulder at her mother, who waved at them.

"That was such a charming bracelet you gave Jodi," Mom said to Jake, laughing at her own silly pun.

"Jodi deserves something special considering all the hard work she's doing," Jake said.

"Kiss ass," Jodi muttered, but she wasn't mad. In fact, she was secretly tickled that he found her so irresistible.

"Love to," Jake whispered. "Name the time and place."

"Hell, twelfth of never —"

"Never say never . . ."

"You are so right," Mom went on, blithely unaware of their private conversation. "Jodi does so much work behind the scenes that she never gets credit for and she does so with such an open heart and she never complains."

Well, she wouldn't say *never.*

"Your smell drives me crazy," he whispered, and pressed his nose so close to the back of her ear where she'd dabbed the hope chest perfume that he was almost touching her. "Promise me you'll wear that perfume for the rest of your life."

"Jake," her mother asked. "Could you help me set up an extra card table in the den for the food I brought?"

"Sure thing, Mrs. Carlyle." He straightened and turned, but not before barely brushing his knuckles along the curve of Jodi's butt.

Immediately, she closed her eyes against the blistering heat that rolled through her. God, she wished they were alone. She'd rip his clothes off his body so fast he wouldn't know what hit him.

"Please," her mother said. "I insist you call me Maggie."

"Maggie," he said obediently.

Then thankfully, before she broke all the rules Dr. Jeanna had laid down for a casual affair, plus a few basic rules of civil behavior to boot, Jake followed her mother out of the room.

At kickoff, more than forty people were crammed into Rowdy's den for the Super Bowl game. People sat where they could — on the floor, on the arms of chairs, on laps. Jake wished Jodi would sit on his.

But she barely sat at all. She moved around the room, making sure everyone had enough to eat and drink, perching momentarily wherever she could find a spot, but hopping up the second anyone needed anything. He wondered if she was always this keyed up at parties, or if he had something to do with her inability to stay in one spot.

Being in the same room with Jodi but unable to touch her was driving Jake out of his gourd. He sat on the floor near the window, Talbot next to him, and watched Jodi as everyone else's eyes were glued on the gigantic television mounted over the fireplace mantel, where a small fire crackled.

"I bet a hundred dollars Johnson makes a touchdown this quarter," Talbot said. "He's been coming in hot every game this season."

Several people took Talbot's bet and all talk focused on football. A group of the women had migrated to the kitchen, and Jodi kept shuttling back and forth between the two rooms checking on everyone.

Whenever she came into the den, Jake's spirits perked right up, along with various body parts.

Talbot yammered nonstop, predicting what plays the coaches would call, quoting players' stats before the announcers got to them. And politely, Jake tried to listen, but then Jodi bent over to pick up an empty beer bottle from the coffee table, giving him a terrific shot of her cleavage down the V-neck of her blouse and he didn't hear another word Talbot said. It was nonsensical white noise like the adults in the *Peanuts* cartoons — *wonk, wonk, wonk.*

He was hooked.

There was something about the way she moved, a determined fluidity that captured his attention. Smooth and steady like the power of water eroding stone.

"Ah," Talbot said. "I get it now. You never got to finish what you started with Suki's sister in the coat closet."

Jake stared as Jodi leaned in to say something to Warwick. *Hey, hey, come over here and talk to me.*

"Why aren't you tapping that?" Talbot said. "Because you should be. I'd be tapping that if I wasn't hooking up with her sister."

"You and Suki are —"

"Just having fun."

"You're pond scum. You know that?"

"Why? Suki doesn't want anything more and neither do I. And I'd rather be pond scum than moony."

"I'm not moony."

"Then why aren't you banging away?"

"Hush." Jake glowered and pointed at Talbot as if he was a wayward dog he couldn't teach how to sit, and swung his gaze back to Jodi, lingered on her full mouth. She flicked out a tongue to moisten her lips, tantalizing him, but he could tell the gesture was unintentional, guileless, and that uncalculated innocence made it ten times more erotic.

Talbot shook his head. "I've never seen you so worked up over any woman."

Not just any woman, but *Jodi.* "Seriously, Talbot, shut the hell up."

"Uh-oh." Talbot raised his palms and his eyes got big. "I get it. She's not just a base hit. Jodi is a line drive homer with bases loaded."

"What are you babbling about?"

"You've gone and fallen in love."

"I have not," Jake denied staunchly, but something ripped in the base of his throat. Two words. Two words wadded there, hard and tough to swallow. *You sure?*

"You haven't taken your eyes off her the entire time we've been here."

"So?"

"Just go get her."

"It's not that simple."

"Because you're not ready to settle down again?"

Actually, because *she* wasn't. "It's complicated."

"No it's not. Love is simple. You love someone. You want to be with them. You find a way to be with them. End of story." Talbot waved a hand. "Oh yeah, and that happily-ever-after part at the end."

If only Talbot were right. If only life — and love — were that simple.

But Talbot was right about going after Jodi. He'd never win her if he didn't try, so when she disappeared in the direction of the restroom, he followed, throwing "Bathroom," over his shoulder in case anyone was wondering where he was going.

"TMI, dude." Talbot waved him out of his field of vision.

Jake glanced over his shoulder, made sure

no one followed him, closed the door to the den, and went down the hall. He paused, considered knocking on the bathroom door, but decided that would be too intrusive, and instead pushed his palm against the nape of his neck and practiced what he was going to say.

Jodi opened the bathroom door, jumped back at seeing him there in the hallway.

"Sorry," he mumbled. "I didn't mean to startle you."

She ducked her head, stepped aside, the boxcar charms on her bracelet jangling together. "It's all yours."

"Wait." He put a hand to her shoulder.

She stopped.

That was encouraging. Right?

"I can't stop thinking about you," he blurted. "I know you told me to back off, but I don't think you really mean that."

Jodi darted a nervous glance down the hall. "This isn't the place for this conversation."

"All I can think about is touching you, kissing you, being with you."

She gulped, and goose bumps coated her arms. Momentarily, she closed her eyes, let out a soft sigh. "Me too."

His heart did a crazy cartwheel. "So what you told me in the B&B parking lot the other day —"

"My attempt at setting boundaries." She laughed a confused little laugh. "Didn't work apparently."

"You've changed your mind?" he asked hopefully.

"I might have been hasty before."

"Yeah?" His pulse skipped a beat, then two, then three.

"You're sort of hard to resist."

"So don't resist," he coaxed.

"There have to be parameters."

He had her! High frickin' five. *Don't blow it.* "What are we talking here?"

She darted another quick glance down the hall to make sure no one was there, lowered her voice. "A secret affair."

"Just sex?" he said, disappointment a rock in his gut.

"Just sex," she confirmed with a solid shake of her head. "If you can handle that, it's on."

Chapter 17

Jodi Carlyle's Wedding Crasher Rules:
Do bring a gift. It makes you look legit.

She'd gone there. Done it. Said it. Suggested it. Her heart pounded, and her mouth was so dry she couldn't even moisten her lips.

Suddenly, his arms slipped around her waist and Jake was kissing her. Her arms were pulling his head down and *kablooey!* His lips were pure dynamite, setting off all kinds of terrific explosions inside her.

Shades of Vincente's coat closet! And, um . . . oops, somehow her fingers splayed over his gorgeous butt, but seriously, what single woman in her right mind could resist?

With the tattered shreds of what composure she had left, Jodi stepped back into the bathroom, pulling him with her, closed and locked the door behind him.

His breath was hot on her cheek, his eyes

feverish.

She held up a shaky finger, dimly aware that she was breathing like a coal engine chugging up a steep grade. "Ground rules."

"Okay. Whatever you want. Anything. Name it."

Goodness, he sounded more unraveled than she was. She had him at her mercy. Jodi smiled. She did love being in control. It felt good knowing that a man wanted her so badly he would abide by whatever rules she set down. And not just any man, but Jake freaking Coronado.

"Anything." He was almost whimpering, she could see his pulse thundering at his neck.

Ah, this was the way to keep her heart from getting broken. Control. Something she hadn't had at Vincente's.

"Just sex," she repeated. "This is a rebound relationship for both of us and those rarely work out."

His mouth turned down like he was going to argue, but then he pressed his lips together and nodded.

Jodi took a deep, steadying breath and prayed he wouldn't guess how nervous this rule made her. She wasn't sure she could keep things strictly physical, was absolutely terrified she was going to end up with a broken heart, but she wanted him so badly, she was willing to take that risk.

His eyes roved over her, settled on her heaving breasts.

"Listen to me," she said, and his gaze snapped back to her face. "If either one of us starts to feel things are going beyond the boundaries of just sex, then we end the relationship."

"What about other parameters?" he asked. "Are we supposed to see other people? Do you intend to see other men while we're . . ." He swallowed so hard his Adam's apple bobbed.

The thought of him seeing other women at the same time he was having sex with her raised the hairs on her arms. "We'll be exclusive."

His eyebrows dipped in relief and he smiled. That made her smile too. "Good idea."

"Two, you can't give me any more gifts." She fingered the charm bracelet. "I love the bracelet, but gifts are too romantic."

"So 'just sex' means I can't romance you?"

She nodded. "Exactly. No flowers. No candy. No cute cards."

"Where's the dividing line?"

"I'm not sure. But if something starts feeling too romantic to either one of us, we talk about it."

"I'll try." His jaw tensed. "What else?"

"We have to take our affair outside of Stardust. You know how small towns are. I don't want people gossiping about us. I don't want my family to find out."

"Anything else?"

"That's all for now."

"Not quite," he said, his voice going low and gruff.

The sound of that voice, so confident and masculine, sent a spike of longing straight through her soul and even though she didn't mean to do it, not in the close confines of the bathroom, she took a step toward him, tipped her chin up to meet his gaze head-on.

"You have some ground rules of your own?" she asked.

Instead of answering, his big, calloused hands cupped her cheeks, holding her tenderly as if she belonged to him. His eyes searched her face for a moment and she slid her arms around his neck at the same moment he lowered his mouth to hers. She opened her mouth. Let him in again. Just for a heartbeat. Just for a taste to tide her over.

He bent her backward slightly, holding her safe in his arms, burning her with his kiss, ravishing her hard and sweet until she felt utterly branded. Then he pulled his mouth from hers, stepped back leaving her dazed and stunned and amazed. The man kissed like it was the end of the world.

"This is going to be a grand adventure," he said.

"A wild, sexy adventure."

"Oh yeah." He breathed and she thought — prayed, actually — that he'd kiss her again, but he didn't.

Jake wanted to disagree to Jodi's "just sex" rules, but he hadn't because it was the only way to get her into his arms. She was skittish. He understood that. It would take some coaxing, some tender loving care, some slow, sweet moves, but he was utterly confident he could win her over. Just as she'd already won him.

The key with Jodi was to let her feel like she was in control. He didn't know for sure why she needed it so strongly, but he realized letting her think she was in control was the only way to get her to open up and let down her guard to give him a chance to change her mind about him. About them.

Because he wanted her more than he'd ever wanted anything in his life, and that included his baseball career. Which, frankly, scared the living hell out of him.

Not just *wanted* her.

He wanted to be with her. He wanted to wake up in the morning and see that sweet smile. He wanted to go to bed at night and hold her close after making love to her. He wanted to travel with her and have adventures and build a future together.

Yes, maybe it was underhanded pretending to go along with her rules, and yes, he might upset her when she figured out he wasn't sticking to the bargain, but in the end she would forgive him. He'd make sure of it.

Ham normally had Mondays and Tuesdays off, so Jodi wasn't able to slip away to meet Jake and she wondered if it was possible to literally die from sexual need. On Wednesday morning, she drove to Tyler to buy sexy lingerie. She couldn't shop in Stardust and have word getting out that she had plans for sexing someone up.

When she arrived at Jake's house just before noon, she was wearing the silky lace things under jeans and a T-shirt. The contrast in the material — girl-next-door on the outside, sexy temptress underneath — stoked her desires to fever pitch, and by the time she reached his cute little cottage, she was so desperate for him that the second he opened the door, she flung herself into his arms, knocking him backward.

Jake took her down with him to the freshly laminated floor that smelled of wood and glue, his mouth gobbling her up as quickly as she gobbled him.

"Get me naked!" she exclaimed, shocking herself and kicking off her sneakers without bothering to untie them.

"Bossy," he said, and attacked her with glee, stripping off her jeans, yanking her T-shirt over her head, laughing out loud when he saw the G-string and pasties she wore. "Damn but you are one sexy woman!" he declared, and used his teeth to remove her G-string.

She giggled, and then giggled at the sound that was so unlike her. She sounded light, carefree. But ever since meeting Jake, she seemed to giggle a lot.

Heck, she would have had casual flings years and years ago if she'd known it would make her feel this good.

She dismantled his clothes as swiftly as he'd dismantled hers, and within a minute of stepping over the threshold, they were both on their knees facing each other in the entryway, naked and breathing hard.

He sat back and reached for her, pulled

her into his lap, his erection hard against her bottom. She folded her knees around his waist, and he did the same. They sat gazing into each other's eyes, enjoying the thrill of their rapidly pounding hearts.

Grinning, he leaned his head down to nibble the tasseled pasties from her nipples. She squirmed. He locked his legs around her tightly, holding her firmly in place. "Who's in charge now?"

Trapped.

Jodi stilled, felt a flash of momentary panic.

He must have seen the fear in her eyes, because immediately he released her. "I was teasing," he said. "I would never hold you against your will."

"I know," she said, but she heard the hesitancy in her voice.

The urgency had discharged, and the atmosphere changed into a slower, gentler rhythm. He cupped the back of her head in his palm, tenderly kissed her.

Softly, she kissed him back, tracing a finger over his face. They both kept their eyes open, watching each other with wonder.

He shifted her around until she was astride him. He leaned up to take one of her puckered nipples into his mouth, drawing a low moan from her throat.

She twitched her hips against his pelvis, clenched her inner thigh muscles against his belly. He rested his head all the way to the floor, reached for her breasts, but she grabbed his wrists and pinned them over his head.

"No hands," she said.

He made a guttural sound, a mix of despair and delight. "What are you up to?"

"Just wait and see." Honestly, she had no idea, she was just making this up as she went along, but he seemed to be enjoying the mystery.

Jake said a colorful word.

"Go ahead. Talk dirty to me. It turns me on," she teased.

She reached down and touched his erection and his entire body jerked. Still pinning his arms over his head with one hand — she was under no illusion that she could keep him there if he didn't want to play the no-hands game — she lowered her head and gently bit one of his nipples.

He chuffed out a groan and swore again.

Jodi licked her way up his body, to his neck, his chin, his jaw, and his earlobe. When she raised her head, he was staring at her with a look so blazingly hot she felt singed.

The pulse in his wrist leaped hard and fast and the pulse at her throat picked up the same tempo.

"Jake." She whispered his name like a prayer. "Jake."

"Jodi." He smiled soft, but his eyes held a wild gleam. Not tamed. No way. He was simply letting her take the lead in this game.

He would always be in charge. She knew that, even as the scared part of her bristled a little. It was okay.

She wasn't sure why, but she knew she could trust him. Maybe because he'd sensed her panic when he trapped her and instantly let her go. Maybe because he'd given her the charm bracelet that so matched who she was. Maybe because he'd been so patient with her while she'd flip-flopped about going to bed with him again. But most of all, because he could smell her perfume when no one else in the world could.

Maybe they were fated.

That scared her. But she trusted him, and that was big. And she was going to reward him for giving her this beautiful gift of trust.

She reached for the purse she'd dropped in the foyer when she tackled him, searched for a condom, found it. Using her teeth, she tore the foil packet open, extracted the rubber, and then shifted so she could roll it onto him.

"You are the most beautiful woman," he said.

She wasn't beautiful. She was average girl-next-door pretty and she wasn't just being modest. Okay, so maybe the red hair was striking, but she wasn't the kind of woman who drove men to their knees.

Ordinarily.

This man, however, seemed to feel otherwise. Oh damn. This was getting too romantic. Sex. This was supposed to be about sex.

"Still hands off?" he asked. "I want to touch you so bad, I can't stand it."

"Smell me instead," she said, and lowered her neck to his nose.

"God, you smell beautiful too." He worshipped each part of her body, kissing her as if she was a priceless treasure, stroking her skin and looking awed, whispering how much he loved her ears, her feet, her throat, her hair, her chin, her cheeks, her nose, her knees. She opened like a lotus flower to his touch, his words.

She was so wet for him, so ready. He was ready too, his erection so hard it was sticking straight up behind her. Sighing softly, she eased herself down on his shaft. He let out his breath long and slow. Whispered her name on a sigh. *Jodi.*

He was inside her and it felt like they were both in a great mysterious cave. "Ride me hard," he begged. "Give me everything, Jodi. Don't hold anything back."

She galloped, spurring herself on a wave of delight, taking him with her higher and higher, scaling the sweet mountain. She was giddy with passion. Filled with him.

They floated together in a vastness of sensation that rolled into infinity, and every blissful inch felt right and good and true. Jodi didn't know who was inside whom. They were both inside. There was no outside. They occupied the universe and spun in it together.

The delicious expanse of their joining spread and grew and swelled. A brilliant supernova twirling faster than the speed of light. They bathed in the white heat of their union until the last bit of energy drained from their bodies and they collapsed wide-eyed and panting back on earth.

They had gone so far together, had shared so much intimacy that when they came back into their separate selves, a soft melancholy sadness stole over her. The experience had been so ethereal that Jodi did not know where to go from here. From the look on his face, she could tell he felt just as befuddled as she.

They did not know each other well enough. That was the problem. They had no familiar ground, no safe place in which to retreat and reclaim their separate identities. They joined too swiftly, accelerated too rapidly to that cosmic place, and they were in uncharted territory.

A sense of loss set in. As though they'd stolen something from each other.

She was scared. More frightened than she'd been in a very long time. In an instant she was four years old again, all alone in the house, and there were people knocking at the door, coming to take her away.

Quickly, she turned her face from him, jumped up, pulled on her jeans, yanked on her shirt.

And then Jake got up, reached out a soothing hand, pulled her against his chest, tenderly kissed the top of her head. "Shh, shh, it's all right. I've got you. Nothing can hurt you now."

Nothing, she thought, *except you.*

What now?

Jake stood holding her.

After they'd come, he'd immediately sensed the shift in her from trusting lover to fearful stranger. That was okay. A waltz. He knew how to dance. He tightened his grip around her, just held her. He'd stand here all day and all night long if that was what she needed.

She was his only concern.

Her.

Jodi.

She stepped from his embrace, that independent tilt to her head again, a smile that said, *I'm okay, I've got this, didn't mean to flake out on you* tacked to her face. "I'm starved," she said. "You hungry?"

Part of him wanted to pin her to the spot and make her talk about the emotions she'd just been through, but hell, he didn't want to dig around in his own feelings right now, so he said, "I could eat."

In a regular relationship, he would take her to dinner. But she wanted to keep this all about sex. Wanted their affair to stay secret. They couldn't risk going out and being seen. Even though Stardust was thirty miles away, they could run into someone Jodi knew.

"What do you have in the fridge?" she asked. "I could whip us up some lunch."

"I've been eating out," he admitted.

"So no groceries?"

"Not much."

"Let's see what you've got. I'm pretty well a miracle worker in the kitchen."

"Honestly, all I have are Cheerios and milk. But if you want cereal for lunch, I'm game."

"Ugh, no." She gave a full body shudder. "I hate Cheerios. Call for pizza?"

"Sure. What do you like on yours?"

"Pepperoni and onions. Extra cheese."

"Hey." He grinned. "Me too."

"Thin crust?"

"Absolutely."

Thirty minutes later, they were sitting at the kitchen bar eating pizza. "Cute house," she said.

"Maura picked it out," he said, surprised at how easily he spoke of his dead wife. That was progress. For the longest time he didn't bring up her name because it hurt too much. But he was healing and it felt good to talk about her, especially when Jodi seemed interested. "She loved the Craftsman style."

"What about you?"

"I'm not picky."

"She'd be pleased with what you did with the place." Jodi inhaled deeply. "I love the smell of fresh paint. And the color you chose for the walls, Gray Owl, it's very popular right now. Should appeal to the widest number of buyers."

"How do you know the name of the

color?" he asked.

"I have Home Depot on speed dial. I renovate a boxcar a year."

"You still do all the work yourself?"

She nodded. "Me and Ham."

"I don't think Ham likes me."

"He doesn't dislike you," she said, although her tone of voice sounded if she didn't quite believe that. "He's just very protective of me."

"I like him for that."

"How much renno are you gonna do?"

"I want to knock out a wall in the bedroom and expand the master bathroom. Saved it for last. Soon as that's done the house goes on the market."

"Hey," she said. "I swing a mean sledgehammer if you need any help." She flexed her biceps. She was so damn cute.

"You mean it?"

"Sure."

"I'd love the help, but won't Ham miss you at the B&B?"

"I told him I'd be gone all day." She giggled and the sound lit up his heart. "Wedding-related stuff."

"That's a great excuse."

"Rest assured I'll be milking it dry." She winked.

"Do we really want to spend our time

working when we could be doing other things?" He wriggled his eyebrows.

"I can't distract you from your work. If I'm going to be hanging out over here, I might as well help. Wanna start now?"

He leaned over to brush his lips against hers. "Maybe in a little bit." He kissed her again. "After . . ."

CHAPTER 18

Jodi Carlyle's Wedding Crasher Rules:
Go for the gusto.

Three hours later, after they had sex on the kitchen counter, and started knocking down a wall in the master bedroom, they took a water break.

"Wow," he said, eyeing the rubble of sheetrock that was once a wall, and swiping his sweaty forehead with the hem of his T-shirt, guy-style. "You weren't kidding. You're impressive with a sledgehammer."

"Toldja. I've renovated eight boxcars, two cabooses, and an engine." She raised the sledgehammer over her head in a triumphant gesture. "Word to the wise. Don't ever tackle an engine renovation. It's a nightmare."

"Remind me never to make you mad." He stared at her in awe.

"I use my powers for good not evil," she joked.

He reached over and squeezed her biceps. "Popeye's got nothing on you."

His touch sent familiar heat wavering over her. She met his eyes and he met hers and she knew exactly what he was thinking. "No." She laughed. "No."

"Why not?" he coaxed, moving his hand up her biceps to her shoulder and then on to her collarbone.

Jodi stepped back. If he kept that up, she would pull him down on top of her and rip his clothes off. "Three times in one day?" she squeaked.

"Why not?"

"Um . . . it's painful to walk bowlegged."

Immediately, his smile evaporated. "Did I hurt you? Are you hurt?"

"Sore," she said. "But in a very good way."

"Rain check until tomorrow. Can you get away again? I'm installing the jetted tub and we can christen it."

"An offer I can't refuse."

"Until then, this will have to sustain us." He pulled her into his arms, dipped her.

She let out a whoop of surprise and he kissed her deep and long.

A fresh bolt of lightning illuminated her internal sky, the rising tide of tension. His mouth pushing them over the threshold of longing, into the fire of full sexual boil, but she tasted more in this kiss. It was sweeter, more solid, cementing her to him. A bond forming. A bridge being built. An invitation to go beyond the physical dance. *We could be so good together,* that kiss said. *Not just for now, but forever.*

Frightened of the unspoken offer, plagued by inner doubt, she drew back. "We better get this finished," she said in a quivery voice. "I need to get back to Stardust."

"Right." He nodded, and she could tell he was trying not to look disappointed that she'd pulled back.

"I just need some space," she said. "I'm feeling —"

"Overwhelmed again."

"Yes."

"No problem," he said lightly. "This is *just* sex."

Her words, when tossed back at her like that, didn't sound so appealing.

Jake picked up the sledgehammer she'd dropped, wrapped his hands around the handle where hers had just been. Firm hands. Strong hands. Tanned hands. Hands that just a short time ago had been — *Stop it, you'll never get any work done.*

He smashed the sheetrock, knocking the

whole wall away.

"Wow," she said. "What a sledge driver."

"You renovate train cars, I knock baseballs into the stands." He puffed out his chest, a little gloaty, yes, but he had every right to be. The man was a world-class hitter.

"We're a pair, huh? We can demo a bathroom in an hour."

"We could go into business together flipping houses," he said.

She laughed.

"I'm serious."

"Like you'd ever give up baseball."

"I can't bat forever."

Was he serious? Or talking pie-in-the-sky dreams? Ryan had made her lots of promises too.

He's not Ryan.

She met his eyes. "We'd make terrible partners."

"Why do you say that? I think we'd be great together."

They already *were* great together, but was she ready for him? She had her own business in Stardust. He was a ballplayer and on the road a lot. Women chased him. Hell, men chased him.

"Because we'd be constantly having sex."

"And that's bad because . . ."

"We'd never get any work done. Much like now."

"Yeah, right. Back to it." He knocked loose the last remnants of sheetrock. They could see into the master bedroom.

"French doors," they said in unison, and laughed.

"I like the way you think," he said.

"Taking the wall out really opens things up." She planted her palms low on her back and stretched out her spine. When she straightened, she saw him watching her, caught the hungry look in his eyes. "You have to stop looking at me like that."

"Like what?"

"Like you're the big bad wolf ready to eat me up."

"What is it they say? If the shoe fits."

"It's okay when we're alone, but it starts bad habits so that when we're around other people they're going to notice."

"Would that be so bad?"

"Yes."

"Why?"

"Because I don't want everyone knowing our business and weighing in on our affair. I don't want to take attention away from Breeanne and Rowdy. I don't —"

"You don't want to get publicly humiliated again like you did when you got stood up at the altar."

She fisted her hands. Nodded. "That was the worst part. Not Ryan blowing town with a stripper and embezzled funds. Not the federal investigation, although believe me *that* was no picnic. It was the scandal. Having everyone know. Having people comment on how dumb I was. Seeing it on social media. Feeling the stares. Hearing the whispers. Slogging through the pity and derision. I don't want to ever go through anything like that again."

"I would never put you through anything like that," he said staunchly.

"It's a promise you can't make. You're in the public eye. It's part of your job. Part of who you are. I'm not a limelight kind of woman, Jake. Believe it or not, I don't care for the spotlight. I like my quiet, simple life in a small town. At least, it was quiet until Ryan ran off. I'm still putting my life back together. Still trying to find my footing."

"You're searching for roadblocks to this relationship. Why?"

It was a good question and she didn't have a solid answer. All the objections she'd raised were justifiable, but couldn't love overcome any of those obstacles?

Love?

Where was that coming from? She was not

going to mistake powerful sexual attraction for love. Besides, it was far too soon to be thinking thoughts like that. She'd known him only a month.

You knew Ryan for two years and look how that turned out.

Exactly, if longevity couldn't assure you that you knew someone, then what could? Honestly, could one person ever really know what was in another person's heart?

"Let's just get through this wedding," she said, trying to buy time. "Keep things on an even keel."

"The wedding is only ten days away, Jodi."

"So keeping things just as they are for ten days shouldn't be a problem, right? Let's not push, Jake. Let's just enjoy the moment. Can we do that?"

"Sure. Whatever you want." He raked his gaze over her like she was the most gorgeous woman he'd ever seen.

Seriously? She was wearing ripped jeans and her hair was yanked up in a short ponytail and she had sheetrock dust all over her.

"Jodi . . ." He took a step toward her.

"Jake . . ." She backed up. Held her elbows out stiff and straight, keeping him at arm's length.

Her knees bobbled. Crap. If she was a

smart woman, she'd grab up her things and run.

He came closer.

"Please," she begged, laughing, dropping her stop-sign arms. "Please."

His arms were around her, his face buried against her neck. "God, you smell so good."

"Jake . . ." Her voice was so soft she wasn't even certain she'd spoken.

"I can't resist you. You drive me crazy." His mouth was at her throat, doing wicked things to her with his tongue.

She tossed back her head, let him burn hot kisses all over her skin. Weak. She was so weak.

"You're incorrigible," she said.

"C'mon, admit it. That's one of the qualities, you love most about me."

Love.

That word again. The one she did not want to face. Love. Was she ready for this? Honestly, no. But it was happening whether she wanted it to or not. Jake had gotten into her bloodstream and she was infected. Ridiculous that it felt so wonderful. Incredible.

Oh Lord, she was sunk.

Color her stupid, but Jodi returned to Jefferson the next morning at eight a.m. to help with the jetted tub installation.

Jake let her in the house. "I made breakfast," he said.

"Not Cheerios?"

"Not Cheerios. A real breakfast. I went to the grocery store and everything. Are you proud of me?"

"So proud," she said, because she was.

He ushered her into the kitchen where he had breakfast set out for two. One plate had toast points, each bite spread with a spoonful of scrambled egg and topped with a section of bacon.

"My plate?" She laughed.

"I made it come out even so you didn't have to."

She canted her head, interlaced her fingers, tucked her hands under her chin, and fluttered her eyelashes at him. "My hero."

They ate breakfast sitting side by side, chatting about their families for a few minutes, and then headed toward the master bedroom. All the doors in the house were open except the one at the end of the hall across from the master bedroom. Jodi had noticed it yesterday, but hadn't mentioned it.

"What room is this?" she asked, putting her hand on the doorknob.

"Don't!" He said it so vehemently, she

dropped her hand, jumped back. "Don't go in there." His face tightened.

Jane Eyre, she thought. *Rochester. Mad wife. Maura wasn't dead, but mad and locked in the bedroom.*

It was an outrageous thought, but his reaction to her question about the room was so over the top that something unpleasant had to be in there. What was it? Pornography? A kinky sex S&M chamber? Sex slaves held hostage? Or worse, a shrine to Maura's memory?

"Junk room," he said, moderating his voice and smearing on a weak smile. "It's a real mess."

Ookay. Odd since the rest of the house was empty, but she didn't say that. Instead, she pressed the palm she'd touched the door with to her hip pocket and was struck again by how little she really knew him.

And now not only was she dying to know what was beyond that door, but she was skittish again, wondering if she was being an idiot by trusting her instincts where Jake was concerned.

She pushed the thought out of her mind and followed him to the master bathroom, her gaze glued to the twitch of his delectable rump.

CHAPTER 19

Jodi Carlyle's Wedding Crasher Rules:
Enjoy the party while it lasts.

Thirty minutes later, the tub was in place and Jake was hooking up the pipes. He was on the floor, working in tight quarters, while Jodi leaned against a big cardboard box that contained a new bathroom vanity.

Her heart skipped extra fast, partly from the exertion of putting the tub in place, partly from the mystery of why he hadn't wanted her to open that door, and partly because his shirt had ridden up to reveal those amazing abs.

"Got it," he said, sitting up. He looked so triumphant, so pleased with his accomplishment that she could almost convince herself he hadn't gotten uptight and edgy when she'd touched that doorknob. "Let's test it out."

She walked over and turned the faucet on

wide open to fill the tub.

Jake got to his feet and they stood side by side watching the water swirl like it was the most fascinating thing they'd ever seen, the silence between them filled with unspoken thoughts.

"Listen," he said. "I'm sorry I barked at you when you tried to go into the other —"

"No apologies needed." She raised a palm to stop him. "This is your house. I overstepped my boundaries. We *are* just naked buddies. I'm certainly not your girlfriend. You don't owe me an explanation."

"I want to tell you —"

"*Shh.* I don't want to know." It was better this way, honestly. Let him keep his secrets. Boundaries. Walls. That's what they need to keep this relationship purely sexual. It was all good. She could do this.

He didn't push. Probably because he didn't really want to talk about what was in that room.

What *was* in that room?

"The tub is holding water. Plumbing looks right. Should we drain the tub now?" she asked.

"Let's take a bath," Jake suggested. "I've been fantasizing about getting you in there ever since I bought the thing."

Holy schmoe. The way he was looking at

her made her feel sexy and powerful, and that gave her the confidence to say, "Really? Where else do you fantasize about us doing it?"

"Everywhere," he said cheerfully. "In one of your boxcars, on a plane — I always wanted to join the Mile High Club — in the back of your van, on the hood of my Vette, on a sky lift, a monorail . . ."

"You have a thing for sex in modes of transportation."

"Motion, baby, motion. I like when things move."

Good to know. "It must have something to do with all that bat swinging," she teased.

He guided her down onto the vanity chair, and she did not resist. Slowly, he undressed her as carefully today as he'd been careless the day before. Once she was sitting naked in front of him, he took off his own clothes just as leisurely, peeling his T-shirt off over his head inch by inch, giving her a breath-stealing floor show.

Oh. My. God.

He was glorious, all perfect biceps and triceps and glutes and hamstrings. And his face! His jaw was square, his cheekbones prominent, his dark hair thick and lush, just begging for fingers to ruffle it.

She was woozy and tightly moist, mesmerized by the sight of his taut bare butt as he turned away from her to test the water with his big toe.

"Needs more heat," he said, and twisted the hot water faucet.

Leaving Jodi with her jaw hanging open, he sauntered into the bedroom, came back with lavender-scented bubble bath, a wash-cloth, candles, and an mp3 player.

He'd been a busy boy, planning this seduction. Had gone out of his way for her. Jake arranged the candles around the ledge on the far side of the tub, lit the wicks, dumped bubble bath into the water, turned on the music. "Kiss You."

Their song.

This wasn't just a seduction. He was romancing her.

She closed her eyes, bit her bottom lip. All her keep-it-sex-only plans were going straight down the drain.

"Jodi."

Slowly, she opened one eye. He was stand-ing next to her smiling tenderly, and she drowned in the pool of his luxe brown eyes.

See there. That smile. That smile was why she didn't believe him when he promised that he wasn't going to fall for her.

She must have looked like she was going to bolt, because he said in a very firm voice,

"Come here."

Reaching down, he took her hands, drew her to her feet. Kissed her. She kissed him back, kneaded her fingertips over his bare chest. He broke the kiss, took her hands in his, drew her closer to the tub.

He climbed in first, easing his big body into the oversized tub, turned off the hot water, turned on the jets, extended his hand to her.

She took his hand to steady herself and slipped into the tub with her back to the faucet so they would be facing each other.

Jake leaned back against the tub, bent his knees up, and planted his feet on either side of her hips. Her breasts floated on the water. Not too small, not too big. Perky and peeking through the bubbles.

He eyed them unabashedly, the blister of his gaze beading her nipples.

The scented white candles flickered, the smell of vanilla in the air mingled with the lavender bubble bath until the entire bathroom smelled like the perfume she'd found in the hope chest.

The song on the mp3 player shifted. "Crazy Love." Van Morrison. They'd played this song at the wedding she'd crashed as well. Jake had made a playlist of that night.

Her throat tightened and she could

scarcely swallow back her fears. Okay, this wasn't just sex. She couldn't keep kidding herself anymore. They were in a relationship. This was happening.

And she didn't mind.

Not in the least.

What if you get your heart broke? There's so many things that can go wrong. What if you're fooling yourself? What if —

What if she did get hurt? It wouldn't be the first time and it probably wouldn't be the last. Life hurt. That's how you knew you were alive. But life was also a beautiful adventure, and the bad things were what made the good things worth cherishing. She was here. He was here. It was now. She was going to open her heart and love and if she got hurt, then she'd deal with the pain.

For she'd come to realize that no matter what she'd told herself, she was not the kind of woman who could separate sex from her emotions. For better or worse, that's just not who she was. And now she was in this up to her neck.

He reached for a washcloth, soaped it up. "Turn around."

"What are you doing?"

"Just turn around."

"I'm —"

"Jodi, turn around," he said in a voice that

374

brooked no argument.

Slowly, she put her back to him.

"Thatta girl." He rubbed the nubby cotton cloth over her bare shoulders. It felt nice and odd. No lover had ever bathed her. She liked it, but it made her feel vulnerable in a way she was unsure of.

"Close your eyes," he whispered, "and tilt your head back, and don't make me get stern with you."

Part of her wanted to resist just to see what he would do, but the part of her that was loving being touched obeyed.

His warm lips kissed her eyelids, first one and then the other, while at the same time, his rough, masculine hands stroked the washcloth along her exposed throat.

Her senses absorbed it all. The aromas of lavender, vanilla, heat, soap, and man. The sound of Jake's low, deep voice humming "Crazy Love."

She bit her bottom lip, blinked away the tears pushing against the backs of her eyelids.

Nothing to be sad about.

She was alive and in the bath with a world-class major league professional baseball player, the most incredibly tender tough guy ever to crash her corner of the world. It was too unbelievable.

The washcloth dropped to her breasts and his fingers went to her neck muscles. "You are so tense, sweetheart." He breathed against her ear. "When was the last time you had a good massage?"

"I don't —" She swallowed. "Please, stop that."

"Stop this?" he asked, his voice husky, as he gently dug into a knot below her shoulder blade. "Or this?" He nibbled the nape of her neck with his nimble tongue until she puddled into mindlessness.

"Please," she whispered.

"Please what?"

"Please stop."

"Why, babe?" His voice was a velvet purr.

She tensed underneath his fingers. "It makes me uncomfortable."

"Why?"

"Massages are . . ." She couldn't put it into words. One, because his hand was so distracting she could barely knit two thoughts together. And two, she didn't know why having someone massage her made her uncomfortable, it just did.

"Relax. Let me take care of you."

See. That was just it. Helpless. Having someone take care of her made her feel helpless.

She wriggled away from him, scooted

toward the water faucet, surrounded by bubbles, and she managed to draw an orienting breath now that he was no longer touching her.

"There," she said, turned back around to face him to keep him from giving her a massage. "That's better."

He looked a little hurt. Guilt knotted up against her chest. He'd been trying to do something nice for her and she'd spoiled it.

"Let me give you a massage," she offered. "Doesn't that sound better?"

"What is it you don't like about massages? I know it's not the touching that bothers you. You are so damn responsive."

Yeah, she knew. That was kind of the problem. Every time he touched her, she lost control.

"Ah," he said. "You *always* have to be in charge."

She lifted a shoulder. Shrugged. Maybe.

He shifted, sat up straighter in the tub, soap bubbles clinging to his chest, looked at her with such pity he might as well have kicked her in the chest. "Don't you ever get tired?"

Up went her chin. *Go ahead. Give me the sad eyes. I can handle it.* "Tired of what?"

"Always having to take care of everyone. Never letting anyone take care of you."

"Who says I don't let people take care of me?"

"Kasha for one. Your mother for another."

"You've been talking to my mother?"

"At the wedding shower."

"Oh God." She drew up her legs, dropped her forehead to her knees.

"You don't have to hold on to life with a death grip." His voice was so soft, gentle. "You can't force things to be the way you want them to be. I know. I've tried."

"Why is being in control a bad thing? And don't you dare pity me."

He shook his head. "You're missing out on so much."

She was irritated now. Defensive. He had no idea the things she'd been through. The challenges she'd had to overcome to get where she was today. Who was he to tell her she led a sad life? "What the hell does that even mean?"

"No judgment, Jodi." He raised his palms. "We all have our strengths and weaknesses. But if you always have to be running things, you never get to sit back and enjoy the show."

"Relax, relax, relax. If I did things your way and I'd never get anything done. How do you think I renovated boxcars and had started my own B&B by the time I was twenty? I can tell you that it wasn't because I relaxed."

"Oh, sweetheart."

"I have a fine life!" Her cheeks burned. She knotted her hands in the water. Why was she getting so worked up?

"I never said you didn't. I just wanted to give you a massage. Do something nice for you. I never meant to start a firestorm."

She sat there feeling out of sorts and wondering why she'd made a big thing of this. Why couldn't she just let him massage her? What was wrong with her? Most women would fall over themselves to have Jake Coronado give them a rubdown.

"Jodi?" He stroked her forearm.

It felt so good to be touched. She didn't pull away, even though she probably should.

"Why are you so afraid to let go?"

She wrapped her arms around her knees, broke contact with him. Breathed. "Because if I let go, I could fall."

"That's right. What's wrong with falling? That's how babies learn how to walk. They pull up, fall, take a few steps, fall."

"Who are you to lecture me on letting go? You still own a house you bought with a woman who died three years ago. And you have a locked door in your house you won't let people look behind."

Boom! Dropped a bomb on you, baby.

And she could kick herself for it. The guy had lost his wife, for heaven's sake. Why was she lashing out at him when he was only trying to help? He was right too. Her obsessive need to control her environment *was* her biggest flaw.

He blinked, and took her retort like the man he was. His expression didn't change, nor did his calm tone of voice. "That's precisely why I'm talking to you about it. Because I've walked that road and I know how lonely it is when you won't let others help you. I'm here right now to let go of my past. I was hoping you'd want to join me."

They stared at each other, nothing breaking the silence except the gurgle of jetted bubbles.

She moistened her lips. Not knowing what to say. The water was growing cold and the skin on her fingers and toes was starting to shrivel. "I'm sorry," she apologized. "You didn't deserve that."

"Yes, I did. I was being hypocritical. Telling you to let go when I'm still hanging on too, but I'm working on it. I'm working really hard."

"I know," she said. "And I respect you for it."

From the mp3 player the instrumental

composition "Fate and Destiny" bled into the small room, rippled over the water. "I don't want to tell you how to live your life," he said, "but it seems to me you're going to eventually crash and burn if you don't learn how to take it easy once in a while."

"Don't you get it?" she cried, surprised at how anguished she sounded. "I can't take it easy! I don't know how!"

Her words broke, spun off into silence.

She could tell that he wanted to touch her again, comfort her in some way, but he did not.

Finally, he asked, "Why not?"

Her nose twitched and she pressed her eyes against her damp knees, saw brilliant yellow stars burst on the backs of her eyelids. "I'm afraid that if I take it easy," she mumbled, "the world will fall apart."

He tentatively stroked her hair.

Oh, how she wanted to bury her head against his shoulder and let the pleasure of sex take away all her pain.

"So, you're responsible for the whole world?"

It sounded stupid when he put it like that, but yeah, she felt as if it weren't for her efforts to keep things on track, *her* world would fall apart. "Yes."

"Wow," he said. "What's it like to have

that kind of power?"

She raised her head, shot him a dirty look. "You're poking fun at me."

"I'm not. I'm just impressed that the weight of the entire world rests on those two slender shoulders."

Her chin wobbled. No. She was not going to cry.

"It's okay, Jodi. It's okay to let go. No one is going to judge you for being human. *I'm* not going to judge you for being human."

"You don't get it," she said, puffing her cheeks out forcefully to keep from crying.

"So tell me. Help me to understand."

Dammit. She didn't want to cry. Her nose burned and her eyes burned and she blinked hard and fast.

"You asked me once why boxcars," she said, fiddling with the charm bracelet at her wrist. "But I wasn't ready to tell you then."

"I'm listening," he soothed. "I hear you. Talk to me."

She opened her mouth. Closed it. This was not easy for her. She paused. Moistened her lips.

He waited.

Okay. She could do this. "Until I was four I was raised in the worst part of Stardust near the train yard. I was literally from the wrong side of the tracks."

"Like Rowdy," he said.

"Yes. We were from the same neighborhood. Ham too. He was my next-door neighbor when were we kids. We were born in the same hospital on the same day. He's like my brother."

"The boxcars remind you of where you came from," he guessed.

"No," she said. "The boxcars remind me of who I am. When you grow up beside the train tracks the rumble is part of you. The tracks are security. They can take you away and bring you back home. But they don't move. They're always there. The tracks are something you can count on. They never let you down." She fingered the bracelet again. "That's why this gift meant so much to me. In essence, you gave me myself."

"Wow, that's deep. I had no idea boxcars carried that much symbolism for you."

She gave him a half smile. It was the best she could manage right now. "You get credit for it all the same."

"What happened when you were four?" he asked.

Jodi gulped and then slowly told him what it was like growing up with a drug addict mom and no close relatives she could count on. To never know her biological father's identity. To go into foster care. Even if it was with the best family in the world, it was still terrifying to be pulled from everything she'd ever known and plunked down with strangers. To be left alone in a house for days at a time with nothing to eat but Cheerios and orange juice.

"That's why you hate Cheerios."

She nodded, felt her lip tremble, felt herself losing control over her tears.

"Aww, sweetheart, that's terrible. No child should ever have to go through that." His voice was husky.

"At least I ended up with the Carlyles and they loved and adopted me. Things could have taken a really dark turn if they hadn't come into my life."

His thumb stroked the back of her hand, strong, reassuring. She thought she'd resent him for being witness to her breakdown, but instead, she was grateful for his touch. Loved the way he looked at her with strength and kindness.

Loved him for being here with her.

Even loved him for pushing her to let go. She resisted being pushed, but she felt as if she was perched high on a mountaintop and he was standing below her, ready to catch her when she fell.

And he would catch her. All she had to do was jump and he'd be there.

At least that's what his eyes promised.

But she'd heard promises like that before — from her biological mother, from Ryan. Even to a lesser degree from Maggie and Dan. Her adoptive parents promised her she would be safe and loved when they adopted her and she had been, but she'd also had a baby sister with a serious illness. A sister she loved with all her heart. A sister who could die as easily as not. Breeanne's illness caused Jodi to feel unstable too.

"I'm sorry for everything you went through as a little kid," he said. "I can't imagine it. The worst thing that happened to me as a kid was my parents' divorce, but they were both stable, loving, and tried to do what was best for us kids. Even though they weren't together, I always had support."

She wiped the back of her hand over her face wet with tears. Damn, damn, damn. She didn't want him feeling sorry for her. She was fine. Better than fine. She'd survived. Thrived. Made a good life for herself.

"Thank you for sharing that with me," he said, and leaned in to kiss her forehead. "Now let's get out of here before we turn into prunes."

He helped her from the tub, and gently toweled her off.

385

She didn't protest, just stood looking down at his dark head and strong back as he dried her legs. When he scooped her up into his arms and carried her to bed, Jodi surrendered, let go, gave herself up to him completely.

As he bent to lay her down on the mattress, he pressed his mouth to her ear and whispered so softly she wasn't even sure she heard him. "You're not going to fall, sweetheart. Never again, because I'm here now and I've got you."

CHAPTER 20

Jodi Carlyle's Wedding Crasher Rules:
You're from out of town, always.

Jake laid Jodi down on the bed, the towel falling just below the jutting peaks of her gorgeous pink nipples, and he salivated.

Did she have any earthly idea how freaking beautiful she was? From the innocent smile she was giving him, no. No, she did not.

Water dripped from his damp hair to his chin, dropped like beads to his chest. Watching her breasts rise and fall as she pulled in jerky breaths, her eyes fixed on him, made him feel like a randy bull in a pasture ready to knock down anything in his path to get to the object of his desire.

Everything about her was erotic. The curve of her cheek, the hollow of her throat, the fall of her hair against her skin.

Every whim of Jodi's body triggered the

hairs on his wrist to quiver. Every vagary of sunlight slanting in through the window across her sumptuous body registered colorful and vivid on his retina. Sensation after sensation washed over him like an ocean wave. Nothing was lost in translation.

She looked at him with an unusual light in her eyes. What was going on inside that head of hers? His body hardened and he took stock of the world, of this moment, like an intense and vigilant general manager building his team for a pennant race, searching for the configurations and subtext that would give meaning to each play.

He was riveted.

Jodi rose to her knees, reached out to touch his shoulder. His skin came alive underneath her fingers, tingled and ached.

"Make love to me, Jake," she whispered.

Make love. Not have sex. *Make love.*

He lay beside her, gathered her to his chest. Kissed her soft and slow. He threaded his fingers through her hair, held her close, and felt the steady beating of her heart.

She astonished him and he wanted her more than he wanted to breathe.

Their senses combined, mingled. He tasted the saltiness of their pooled flavors. Saw how the sun lit up her hair like fire. He smelled the sweet richness of her femininity.

He heard her raspy, excited breathing, realized his was just as fast, just as raspy.

He liked his body more when he was with her. His muscles seemed stronger, his nerves more alive. And he loved her body. Every inch of it. What it did. How she responded. He liked the way her back arched when he stroked her behind the knees. Loved the way she purred when he skimmed his hands over her buttocks. He thrilled to knead his fingertips along her scalp to her spine, loved to explore her bones, and make her tremble.

Again and again and again he kissed her, aiming for this body part or that. Her chin, her cheeks, her nose. Her navel. Her elbow. Her toes. He stroked the springy softness of the hair between her legs, took joy in her naturalness.

Jake felt powerless and exposed, shaking with emotion, desperate to be merged with her. He coiled around her body, tracing his quivering hands over her body, mapping every part of her that he could touch; her freckles, the little valley between her nose and her lips, the faint dusky network of veins beneath her pale softness. Luxuriant curves and elegant bones. Sturdy, agile muscles. She was a miracle of nature, holding him with all her potency, delighting him with her responsiveness.

She kissed his erection, then slowly drew the tip into her mouth, finally engulfed him fully with long, lazy, caressing strokes until he was harder than he had ever been in his life.

Hurriedly, he broke away to grab a condom, and when he got back Jodi had flipped over onto all fours on the mattress.

"Let's do it this way," she whispered.

Jake hissed in his breath. He'd rather stare into her eyes, but seeing her bare fanny wriggling in the air was more than he could withstand. He went onto his knees, gripped her waist with his hands, and gently eased into her.

She sucked in a sigh of pleasure.

He moved slowly, deliberately taking his time.

"More," she pleaded. "I need more of you."

On a groan, he sank deeper, connecting them to the full extent of their bodies. Vibrant impulses shot through him. He seemed to double in size. He was under her skin and she was under his. Literally and emotionally.

"Harder," she said. "Faster. Give me everything, Jake, hold nothing back."

He obeyed because he was helpless to do

anything else. He gave it all up. To her and for her.

Her body sheathed him. He disappeared from view and he was not scared. She opened to him. He added his body to hers and it was as if two jigsaw pieces had fallen into place. Meant to be together all along.

Jake and Jodi lay on their sides facing each other, hands stacked underneath their cheeks as they gazed into each other's eyes.

"I have to go," she said.

"I know." He stroked her chin with the back of his thumb. "I don't want you driving back to Stardust in the dark."

"I won't be able to meet you again until after the wedding," she said. "The B&B is booked solid this weekend and next. Tomorrow I have to double check the arrangements for the bachelorette spa weekend, then next week is the final push to the wedding. I have so much to do. I can't believe I'm here right now."

"Ditto with the best man stuff."

"That means we won't see each other again until the rehearsal dinner next Friday." She sighed.

"I hate that."

"Me too."

"You're so beautiful," he said.

She looked embarrassed at his compliment. "You're not half bad yourself."

He kissed her lightly, amazed once more at how soft and sweet her lips were. Raspberries in full bloom. Her tongue flicked out and traced the curve of his lips as if she couldn't believe her luck to find herself in bed with him. But *he* was the lucky one. Making love to her opened up a whole new facet of himself and she made him feel like an explorer ready to conquer new vistas.

She was changing him in ways he'd never considered.

He moved his hand down her arm to that slender wrist, fingered the boxcar charm bracelet, felt her pulse jump madly. "Before you go, I've got a confession to make."

"What's that?"

"Although I'd love to take the credit for the perfect gift, Kasha suggested it. And luckily the artist I used was able to devote all his time to getting it done in five days."

"That's what you were doing with her at the café?"

"Yes." He smiled at her just to see her answering smile that never failed to make him feel two inches taller. "Were you jealous?"

"Of my sister? You betcha. Kasha is gorgeous and she was interested in you before she knew you and I were . . ." She trailed off.

"What?" he prodded, wanting to hear how she would describe their relationship.

"You know." She gave a herky-jerky shrug.

Aww, she was going to cop out. "You've got nothing to worry about. While your sister is beautiful, she's got nothing on you."

"Are you kidding me? She's tall and stacked and hey, just look at her yoga body."

"I'd rather look at your body." He ogled her breasts and leered with a teasing wink.

"Nobody in my life has ever made me feel as good as you do," she whispered.

"Ditto," he said, and brushed a strand of auburn hair from her forehead.

"It's scary."

"I know."

"I'm glad it's just sex, because anything more would be —"

He scowled. "Are we still going with that?"

"Yes." She sat up, covered herself with a pillow. "Definitely."

He sat up too, but didn't bother trying to cover himself. "Why?"

"I'm not ready for anything more. After Ryan —"

"Stop using that guy as an excuse."

"But you don't get what he did —"

"I've heard the rumors. Rowdy and Breeanne filled me in. Ryan was a tool besides being a cheater, a liar and a thief. I'm sorry he treated you so badly, but it's still an excuse."

Her nostrils flared. He'd pissed her off.

Good. If he had to make her mad to get her to see what a good thing they were working on here, then that's what he'd do.

"I have to go," she said, scrambling off the bed and searching for her clothes.

"Yes, because running away is always such a great solution." He followed her into the bathroom, where she found her jeans and wriggled into them.

"You didn't really love Ryan," he said staunchly. "If you'd loved him you wouldn't have been able to shake yourself off and turn your wedding reception into a last-minute charity event."

"Because you know me *so* well." Steam practically rolled from her ears.

"Yes," he said. "We might have only known each other for a month, but I get you, Jodi Carlyle, and it freaks you out. You're not used to anyone getting you the way I do."

She pushed an index finger into the center of his breastbone, poked him hard enough to make him step back. "Listen, stud muffin —"

"Stud muffin?" He laughed.

"*Stud* muffin," she repeated, emphasis on the "stud." Her blue-gray eyes shot hot sparks. "You're great in bed, I'll grant you that. But that's all this is. Sex. Get it. S-E-X. Awesome sex, undeniably, but still just sex. Now, leave psychology to the professionals and get out of my way."

God, he loved a fiery redhead. She was just saying this stuff because she was too scared to admit the truth. That was fine. He was a patient man. He would wait for her.

She was tossing towels around looking for her shirt.

He found her shirt, passed it to her. "Here you go."

She snatched it from his hand, jammed it over her head.

"Bra," he said, pointing at her unharnessed breasts jiggling so beautifully.

"I know that," she snapped.

"You know why you're so mad, don't you?"

She turned her back to him, rummaging through the towels again in search of her bra. "Because every time I'm with you I lose clothing. I like order, dammit. I like things neat and tidy and folded up where I can find them. I like —"

"Control."

She snorted, spied the teal bra dangling from the back of the vanity chair, and grabbed it like it was a prize trophy. Put it on. She plunked down on the vanity chair to jam her feet into her sneakers.

"Admit it," he said. "You're just scared because you know this could be something spectacular and because when you're with me you lose control."

"Bingo," she said, and she was back at him with that index finger at his chest. Poke. Poke. Poke. "Now get out of my way. I have places to be, people to see."

Grinning, he stepped aside, watched her flee down the hall.

He followed her to the front door when she struggled into her jacket. She was doing her damnedest not to look at him.

"You're terrified that if you let yourself feel, you'll somehow manage to screw this up," he said.

But even as she slammed the door on her way out, he realized with that last jab that he was talking to himself as much as he was to her.

"You're pale as chalk," Ham said to Jodi when she walked into the office. "Did you see a ghost?"

"I'm fine."

"You don't look fine. You're pale and sweaty and breathing hard. Have you been running?"

Yeah, running away from Jake and the firestorm of emotions he stirred in her. Reluctant as she was to admit it, he was right. He did "get" her and she was freaked out about that. Jodi pressed a shaky palm to her forehead. That's why she kept insisting on sex only. That's why she kept pretending it was just physical between them. Because it was damn unsettling when someone could see right into your soul, and she was ill-equipped to deal with it.

"It's the baseball player, isn't it?" Ham said.

"What?" Jodi startled.

"You might have fooled your family, but you can't fool me, Jo-Jo. I've known you longer than anyone else in your life. You're head over heels for Jake Coronado."

Jodi slumped down onto the sofa. Damn. How had she managed to collect two very perceptive men in her life?

"I can't be," she said staunchly.

"Why not?"

"I'm still putting my life back together after Ryan —"

Ham waved a hand. "It's been a year, you're fine." He was right. She was. "Next objection."

"He's a famous ballplayer. Women throw themselves at him."

"Breeanne has the same issue with Rowdy, but if you're secure in your relationship, you don't have to fear other women taking him away from you."

"But that's just it. I'm not secure in this relationship."

"Why not? Has he ever given you a reason to distrust him?"

She thought of that night at the Grand Texan. How tender and gentlemanly he'd been with her. How fun and playful. She thought about that night at Vincente's when he only had eyes for her, and even when the waitress had tried to get him to stare at her cleavage, he hadn't even glanced at the woman. She thought of how nice he'd been to watch Tobias for Kendra. How at ease he was with her family. How much they liked him.

"No," she admitted.

"So what is it *really*?"

Jodi nibbled a thumbnail. "There's the issue of his wife who was murdered. He loved her a lot and losing her about killed him."

"How long ago was that?"

"Three years."

"If he's courting you, Jo-Jo and from that

bracelet on your wrist, I think that qualifies, he's ready to move on."

She shook her head, fingered the bracelet. "I don't think so. I look like her, Ham. Not just a little, but a lot. I think he's trying to re-create the love he lost."

"Have you discussed this with him?"

"Yes, and he swears that, yes, while my resemblance to his wife was what had initially attracted him to me, he says we have completely different personalities."

"So take the man at his word."

"Just because he claims he's not trying to recapture his past doesn't mean he's not trying to do it. How will I ever know if he's with me because of me or simply because I remind him of Maura?"

"Look at it this way." Ham plunked down on the sofa beside her and slung his arm over her shoulder. "If you really did remind him of Maura, wouldn't he be more likely to steer clear of you because of the emotional pain being with you would cause? You'd always just be a pale imitation of her anyway."

"My point exactly!" Jodi stared down at her interlaced hands in her lap. "That's why I can never let him know how I feel about him. It's too risky."

"Honey." Ham cupped her chin in his

palm and forced her to meet his gentle gaze. "Listen to me. He's seeing *you,* not his dead wife. If he wasn't he wouldn't be making such an effort to get past that wall of yours. It would be much easier just to move on."

"And then there's the hope chest prophecy."

Ham stared at her. "That silly perfume?"

"What if I'm imagining my feelings for him because I want it to be real? What if this is something I'm making up in my head because I truly want to believe in fate?"

"What if you are?"

"That's a pretty weak foundation on which to begin a relationship."

"On a hope chest prophecy, sure it is, but not on the belief that you're destined to be together. If you both believe that you're destined to be together, then it doesn't matter whether there's such a thing as destiny or not. If you believe it's true, then it's true for you. What could be more perfect than that?"

"That's a lot to wrap my head around, Ham."

"Give yourself some time and space. If he's the one, if this is right, then there's no rush. He'll still be there. The main thing is to open yourself up to the possibility that you could build a great life with him."

"I thought that once and look how it turned out."

"It wasn't the same with Ryan and you know it."

Jodi pressed her forehead to her knees and moaned. "I wasn't supposed to fall in love with him."

"Yeah, well, love isn't always logical. In fact, it's *never* logical. Get used to it."

Ham was right about all of it. She knew it in her heart. She was just scared of getting hurt.

"So what should I do now?" Jodi asked.

"Lay it all on the line. Tell him how you feel."

"That's damn scary."

"It is," Ham said. "But you're the bravest woman I know."

"What if this all blows up in my face?"

Ham patted his left upper arm. "Then this shoulder is all yours."

CHAPTER 21

Jodi Carlyle's Wedding Crasher Rules:
Don't get attached.

On Saturday morning, February seventh, a limousine deposited twelve women at the Lodge Spa and Hunting Resort, including the Carlyle sisters, Rowdy's two sisters, and six of Breeanne's friends. Jodi was in charge, making sure the limo driver got tipped, the luggage was accounted for, and everyone got checked in. After that, she was ready to cut loose and enjoy the weekend.

She'd decided to take Ham's advice and not to think about Jake until later. This weekend belonged to Breeanne, and her sister's happiness was her utmost priority.

The four-star resort was located on a sprawling ten-thousand-acre ranch halfway between Stardust and Jefferson, complete with a private airfield, full-service spa, nightclub, hunting lodge, and bowling alley.

Once everyone got settled in their rooms, the group reconvened for spa treatments.

They entered the darkened spa area, greeted by soothing music, gleaming marble, gurgling waterfalls, dispensers filled with cucumber water, and whisper-quiet attendants who whisked them into a communal changing area with lockers for their belongings. Just to prove Jake wrong, that she could indeed relax and let someone take care of her, Jodi had booked a massage.

Everyone was talking excitedly about the weekend and Jodi did her best to get into the spirit of things.

"Oh, Jodi." Breeanne hugged her as they waited in the fountain room, dressed in robes and slippers the spa provided. "This is awesome. Thank you so much for arranging the bachelorette weekend."

"You are so welcome." Heart swelling with love for her baby sister, she hugged Breeanne back.

A masseuse came in to escort Jodi to a treatment room for her massage. She told herself she was going to get lost in the massage. Let down her guard. Relax completely. But try as she might, now that she had no tasks to keep her occupied, her thoughts kept drifting back to Jake.

"Try to relax," said the masseuse. "You

are very stiff."

Jodi took a deep breath, let it out slowly.

"That's right," the masseuse encouraged. "Let go."

Letting go was scary. Sure, she'd done it as bold Gwendolyn, but that had been a persona. This was the real her. Uptight Jodi Carlyle. Letting go meant she was opening herself to the possibility of screwing up, making mistakes, getting hurt. What if she said the wrong thing? What if she said something she didn't really mean? What if she felt something she couldn't explain? What if she completely lost control? And what if, once the control was lost, she went completely off the rails and turned into her biological mother?

Control.

She was terrified of losing it because she feared losing everything and being that lost four-year-old again. Alone and helpless. That was the root of her fear.

At five that afternoon, all the bachelorette party attendees sat relaxing by the fire at the Lodge for happy hour cocktails. Jodi was sipping a peppermint toddy. They'd spent the day being pampered, massaged, exfoliated, trimmed, and manicured.

"Did anyone else have the hot stone massage?" Suki asked. "Heav-en-ly."

Everyone started talking about their experiences, but Jodi was only half listening. She couldn't get her mind off the simple massage Jake had given her in the bathtub. She could taste the salt of his skin on her tongue, feel the brush of his beard stubble against her cheek, smell lavender and vanilla and magic.

"Jo?" Kasha leaned over to snap her fingers in front of her face.

"What?" Jodi blinked as if a fog had parted and realized everyone was staring at her.

"You were daydreaming about Jake, weren't you?" Suki accused.

"No."

"You do realize you get a little quiver to your head when you lie," Kasha said.

"What?" Jodi reached up to touch her head. "I do not."

"But you checked to see if you do." Suki pointed at her. "She gotcha."

"That's okay." Breeanne leaned over the big hassock to pat Jodi's knee. "I know exactly how you feel. I wish Rowdy was here right now."

"I'm not pining for Jake. Jeez. Why would you even think that?" Jodi sat up straighter, the mild buzz she had going on from the toddy ebbing away.

"Because of the prophecy," Breeanne said. "He smelled your scent and he's smitten."

"That's just nuttiness," Jodi said.

"What prophecy?" one of Rowdy's sisters asked.

Breeanne was off. Telling the story about how she found the hope chest and the wish she'd made on it. The women who hadn't heard the story before listened enrapt.

"What did you wish for when you found the perfume?" Rowdy's sister asked.

A wild sexual adventure. And it had come true. But she wasn't about to tell them that.

"Look at the time." Jodi glanced at her cell phone. "Our dinner reservations are for six. Let's head that way."

But what the women didn't know was that the men had planned their bachelor party too . . . and at the same place. But instead of hitting the spa, they'd spent their day at a skeet-shooting tournament. Then they rode around the ranch on ATVs and finished off with a dinner of wild game. It was the wrong time of year for a real hunting party, so they hadn't done any more shooting, but Jake didn't care. He wasn't much for hunting anyway.

But by eight p.m. they were left with nothing much to do and Jake was starting to feel like a crappy best man, even though Warwick was the one who'd actually planned the weekend. Talbot wanted to drive to the nearest strip club, but Rowdy shut that down pronto.

"There's only one woman I want to see naked," Rowdy said.

"Good God, you are cracked in the head," Talbot exclaimed. "Breeanne is a nice-looking woman and all, but this is your last weekend as a free man. Cut loose!"

"Dude," Rowdy shook his head. "You just don't get it. You're clueless, man."

Talbot grunted. "You're whacked. With all the fish in the sea, why get stuck on just one?"

Jake got it.

"One of these days some woman is going to turn you inside out, Talbot," Rowdy said. "And you'll finally understand what love is all about. I don't *want* to be with anyone else but Breeanne."

"Pussy-whipped," Talbot said, and meowed.

And everyone pummeled him with soft fists just because he was asking for it.

"So what?" Talbot asked. "We gonna sit around and paint each other's toenails?"

"I'll have a beer or two at the Lodge

Nightclub," Rowdy said. "It is still early. Let me just text Breeanne good night."

"You text her one more time and I'm throwing your phone in the next toilet," Talbot threatened.

Reluctantly, Rowdy tucked the phone back in his jacket pocket.

The Lodge Nightclub was open to the public and the eight of them walked into a packed house. Music throbbed. Strobe lights flashed. People gyrated on the dance floor. It was going to be hard to find a place for all eight of them to sit.

"Catch you later," Talbot said. "I see Suki."

"What do you mean," Rowdy said. "Suki is supposed to be away with Breeanne for her bachelorette weekend."

"Don't look now," Talbot said. "But Breeanne is here too. Guess they booked the spa while we booked the hunting lodge."

"You didn't know they'd be here?" Jake asked Rowdy.

"No. The parties were supposed to be a surprise for Breeanne and me. You didn't know either? You're best man. I thought you and Jodi would have talked about it."

"Warwick had already made the arrangements," Jake reminded him. "I just made sure we all showed up on time."

"No worries." Rowdy's face lit up, and to Talbot he said, "Where is my Breezy?"

Talbot rolled his eyes. "This cutesy nickname stuff makes me want to hurl."

"You're just jealous," Rowdy said.

"Wait." Jake put a hand to Rowdy's shoulder. "Is it bad luck for you to see Breeanne tonight?"

"Quit being a buzz-kill, Coronado," Talbot accused. "If he's determined to see her, let him see her."

"Nah," Rowdy assured Jake. "The bad luck thing is for the day of the wedding. It doesn't apply to the bachelor party." He frowned, twisted his lips to one side, considering. "At least I don't think it does."

Jake glanced around the nightclub. If Breeanne and Suki were here, Jodi would be too.

He spied her immediately. Hair cut in that gorgeous auburn bob, wearing a hot green dress with a flared skirt that twirled when she moved. She was coming back from the bar with a tray of drinks in her hand as if she'd helped out the cocktail waitress by delivering them. He grinned. That sounded like his Jodi.

His Jodi.

Which was pretty damn presumptuous of him, especially since he had no idea where they stood after she ran out on him Thursday evening.

She glanced up and his eyes met hers, and a slow smile like the sun rising dawned across her face. And in his chest, he felt the same magical miracle stir.

Sweet Jesus, he'd missed her and it had been only forty-eight hours since he'd last had contact with her.

Still smiling, she ducked her head and started passing out drinks to the ladies around two tables. She tucked a strand of hair behind her ear and took the tray back to the bar. Jake's gaze trailed after her. More than anything in the world he wanted to go over, but he didn't know where they stood and they were both here with others and . . .

Hey!

A blond bodybuilder type standing at the bar leaned over and touched Jodi's shoulder. He said something. She leaned in closer. He spoke again. She laughed. And then the guy tilted his head back and cut his head sideways to ogle Jodi's butt.

Jake's fists clenched.

Then Jodi put her hand in his and the guy led her out onto the dance floor. What? Shit. No. She was dancing with the guy?

Hot, deep green jealousy rolled over him and he stalked across the room, almost running people over to get to her. He squeezed onto the dance floor, tapped the guy on the shoulder. "I'm cutting in."

The blond guy scowled. "Buzz off, buddy."

Jake tightened his muscles, set his best get-the-hell-out-of-Dodge-if-you-don't-want-a-bloodbath expression on his face, his hands knotted. "I'm cutting in," he repeated, slower, harder, louder.

The guy sized him up, then raised both palms and backed off. "Be my guest."

Jake turned to Jodi.

She gave him a look similar to the one his mother used to give him when she was displeased with his behavior. But when he held out his hand to her, she took it and gave a rueful shake of her head.

"Men," she muttered, and rolled her eyes, but he could tell she was trying not to smile. She *liked* that he'd chased off her potential suitor.

"Why didn't you tell me the bachelorette party was being held at the Lodge?" he asked as he twirled her around the dance floor, enjoying the way her skirt swirled against her legs as they moved.

"Why didn't you tell *me* the bachelor party was at the Lodge?"

"We had other things to talk about," he said.

"Like what a control freak I am?"

Uh-oh. Were they going to fight again? "Among others," he said.

"I want you to listen to me carefully," she said. "Because I don't very often admit something like this . . ."

"All ears." He leaned in closer.

"You're right."

"About what?"

"I'm a control freak and I was running away from you because I'm scared."

"What?" He acted shocked. "You're admitting you have a problem?"

"I didn't say it was a problem, I just realized that yes, maybe, sometimes I can be a bit stubborn."

"A bit?" He hooted.

She scowled as if she might enjoy yanking hard on his tie. "I thought you'd be a more gracious winner."

"Oh, I haven't won anything yet."

"What do you mean? I just copped to my biggest flaw."

"That wasn't my goal. I already knew your biggest flaw and wanted you anyway."

She cocked her head, slanted a glance up at him through half-lowered lashes. He tightened his arm around her waist, enjoying the feel of her in his arms as they danced. "What was your goal?"

"To get you to get serious about us."

"You're asking a lot," she said.

"I know. Agree anyway."

"Or else what?"

Jake laid it on the line. "You'll break my friggin' heart."

Jodi looked up into his handsome face, at the way his hair fell over his forehead, at the sad but sincere smile curling hesitantly at his lips and the I'm-not-kidding-expression in his eyes and she fell for it all, hook, line, and sinker.

"Let's get out of here," she said. "It's hard to talk and dance at the same time. Besides, the music's too loud."

She took him by the hand and led him from the nightclub. They claimed their coats on the way out and walked back hand in hand toward the Lodge. It was official. They were in a relationship no matter what fib she'd been telling herself.

"I'm afraid I'm a terrible best man," he said. "I've just abandoned Rowdy at his own bachelor party."

"He's with Breeanne," she said. "He doesn't mind."

"You're not going to beat yourself up for walking out on Breeanne's bachelorette party?" he asked.

"Are you not paying attention? I admitted I'm a control freak. I'm purposefully walking out to prove I can let go."

"Well done," he said, and squeezed her hand. "I know it's not easy for you."

"Look, I'm not even casting a backward glance to make sure the building isn't burning down without me there to keep watch."

"Progress." He raised a finger in the air.

"Now," she said. "What were you telling me?"

He stopped walking and drew her into his arms. It was a clear night and the moon was shining brightly, a silver beacon in the sky. She shivered. He pulled her closer, opened his coat, wrapped it around her. She slipped her arms around his waist, felt his warmth, heard the reassuring *lub-dub* of his heart.

"I tried doing it your way," he said. "Just sex. But it didn't work for me. After Maura . . ." He paused.

The pause was an arrow through her heart because she knew he was thinking about his dead wife. And she shouldn't be, couldn't be jealous of a woman who'd died so young and tragically. He had loved Maura. Jodi could see it on him, but it wasn't a desperate clinging. Rather it was a soft, wistful sadness for what might have been, but he wasn't wallowing in his loss. He was still living life. The fact he was capable of loving so deeply was a positive sign. Because of his loss, there was an appealing masculine sensitivity to him that a lot of men would never achieve. Some men would never let themselves love so hard, perceiving tenderness as a weakness. Some, like Ryan, were incapable of loving at all. Dr. Jeanna had declared, with the caveat that she couldn't diagnose Ryan because she'd never treated him, that Jodi's ex was a narcissist.

"What does that make me for loving a man like that?" Jodi had asked.

Dr. Jeanna had smiled gently and said, "Human."

"After Maura," Jake started again, "I went through a crazy phase. Lots of casual hookups to numb the pain."

Zing! Zing! More arrows implanted in her chest. *Please, don't tell me more.*

"Then I realized I was just using sex to cloak my emotions, so I stopped having sex and dealt with my grief and found acceptance and I was ready to move on. Days at a time would go by where I wouldn't think of her. I even started to forget what she looked like and . . ." He took a deep breath. "Then came you . . ."

Because I looked like her? Jodi wondered, but told herself to let it go.

"You made me feel fully alive again and I wanted more. Can you give me more, Jodi? Because if you can't, we have to stop having sex. It's not enough for me. Not where you're concerned."

"What . . ." She gulped, moistened her lips, felt the sting of cold air on her mouth. "What exactly are you suggesting?"

"I think we should start dating officially. Exclusively," he added. "Although we could wait until after the wedding to let people know were dating, so we don't detract from Rowdy and Breeanne's big day."

"Keeping our affair secret doesn't matter anymore. Everyone already knows we're seeing each other," she said. "Apparently, we weren't fooling anyone."

"How did they find out? We were really careful."

"It's my fault actually. I should never have told my sisters you could smell my perfume."

He wrinkled his nose, laughed, his eyes aglow in the moonlight. "You're so cute when you don't make sense."

"You can smell my perfume," she repeated, and explained about the hope chest and the perfume and the wish she'd made. He listened. She babbled. Then she thought, *Oh no, he's going to think that I think we're*

416

fated. "Of course, I don't believe in it," she rushed to add. "There's no such thing as fate or soul mates or —"

He cocked his head to one side, studied her for a long moment like he was contemplating the mysteries of life. "Why not?"

That took her aback. "You believe it?"

"I'm keeping an open mind. How else do you explain that only you and I can smell that great perfume that makes me want to tear the clothes right off your hot bod?"

She gave him the explanation Breeanne had given her, still surprised that he was weighing in on the side of the hope chest myth. Then again, he was a baseball player and they were notoriously superstitious.

"Your wish came true," he said. "That's kind of random if it's not related in some way to the hope chest, whether it's a self-fulfilling prophecy or something else."

"Actually, my wish didn't come true," she said. "I wished for a wild sexual adventure but, ta-da, I got a relationship instead. I did *not* wish for a relationship."

"But you got a relationship *with* a sexual adventure. Doesn't that mean it not only came true, but it came true in a much bigger way than you ever dreamed?"

Suddenly, Jodi realized there wasn't a molecule of oxygen in the air. That had to be it. Why else was she feeling so dizzy?

"True," she admitted, loving the fizzy feeling exploding inside her chest. "I'd invite you back to my room, but I'm sharing with Breeanne."

"I can wait."

"You're a patient man."

"When it's something worth waiting for." He kissed her and his lips tasted sweeter than ever. "Yes, I am."

"I don't have your strength of will."

"Sweetheart, you've got more strength of will in one strand of that gorgeous red hair than I have in my entire body. When can we get together again?"

"I'm slammed this next week," she said.

"Me too. I finished renovating the bathroom yesterday and a real estate agent is coming out Monday to list it."

"We're going to have to wait until after the wedding to get together again."

"Dammit," he said.

"I know," she whispered.

"But we will get to see each other at the rehearsal dinner."

"Maybe a quickie in the coat closet?" she teased.

"Behave," he said. "We can do this."

"Only because I'm a control freak."

"Probably." He laughed.

And then he kissed her again. For a long, long time.

CHAPTER 22

Jodi Carlyle's Wedding Crasher Rules:
At some point there's bound to be drama,
have an escape plan.

The following Friday, after the wedding rehearsal at the church, the wedding party reconvened for dinner at Vincente's. It was the best dinner place in Stardust, where else would they go? When Jodi passed by the coat closet, she blushed hotly, ducked her head, and grinned.

When Jake walked into the room with Rowdy and Talbot, her heart leapfrogged and she blushed even hotter. His gaze swept over the room, and when he spied her, a huge smile eclipsed his face. Jodi smiled back feeling like she'd been wandering in the darkness for a hundred years and the sun had finally shown up to light the way.

He came toward her, her pulse jumping with each step as he drew closer and closer.

"You're wearing it," he said, his nose twitching. "Our perfume."

"You can smell me from that far away?" She laughed.

"Sweetheart, I could pick you out in a roomful of a thousand women, blindfolded and with my hands tied behind my back."

"That would have to be a very big room."

"Outdoors then. In the Grand Canyon."

"Are you saying I should have taken a second shower today?"

"I'm saying no one on earth smells as good as you." He stepped closer, murmured, "You have no idea how bad I want to kiss you right now."

"As badly as the last time we were in this restaurant together?"

"Worse," he promised, his grin turning wicked.

Jodi fanned herself. Yep. She should have taken an ice-water shower.

"Listen, I know this is a crazy idea with everything we've got going on tomorrow, but what if you followed me back to my place after dinner? Just for a few hours. There's some things we need to talk about."

Jodi's heart jumped against her chest. "What things?"

"Just wait, my little control freak." He kissed the top of her head. "All will be revealed. Can you come?"

She should say no. There was so much on her to-do list. If she went with him, she wouldn't get a lick of sleep and she'd look terrible in the photographs tomorrow, but she couldn't resist. She was gone. So gone.

"Just for a little while," she said. "We both have a lot to do tomorrow. I'm leaving your place by midnight, no matter what."

"Thank God," he said. "I thought you were going to say no."

The rehearsal dinner went off without a hitch. Everyone got along, food and drink and conversation flowed. No one got soused or made a scene. It was a perfect evening, and by nine-thirty they were back at Jake's place. He took off his coat and suit jacket, loosened his tie. She removed her coat and started to carefully hang it up, along with his clothes, but stopped herself and dropped the coat to the floor to show she didn't always have to organize and control things.

"We've got two and a half hours," Jodi said. "I suggest you make the most of it, Coronado."

Instead of yanking her into the bedroom as she'd anticipated he would, Jake took her hand. "I didn't bring you here for sex."

"No? Why not?"

"Well, I did bring you here for sex." He

422

grinned. "But later. First there's something I have to tell you . . ." His eyes searched her face as if he was getting ahead of himself and trying to guess how she was going to react. That dinged Jodi's alarm meter.

"Um, you're scaring me a little."

"Don't be afraid." He took her hand. "I'm not."

"Okay, now I'm terrified. If you're secretly an axe murderer, kill me now and get it over with."

He laughed and kissed her cheek in a slightly different way than he'd kissed it before, as if he was prepared to kiss that spot every day for the next fifty or sixty years. "I love your sense of humor."

"Time." Jodi tapped the boxcar charm bracelet on her wrist like it was a watch. "Wasting."

He took a deep breath, his face going from happy to sad like a solar eclipse.

Uh-oh. She'd been teasing before, but now she was kind of frightened. "Jake?"

He was still holding her hand. Squeezed it. "Come with me." He led her down the hall toward his bedroom.

Okay. Good start. Not so scary.

But then he stopped outside The Door. The one he'd hollered at her not to open.

Oh no! Was he going to show her his porn

stash and admit to being an addict? Was he going to lead her into his S&M sex dungeon and show her fifty shades of Coronado? Was he going to handcuff her and stuff her into a closet and auction her off to the highest bidder as a long-in-the-tooth sex slave? Was he going to show her a candlelit altar shrine with numerous photographs of Maura wallpapering the room?

"You're shaking," she said, really alarmed now. "Are you all right?"

He nodded. Swallowed so hard his Adam's apple quivered.

"What's going on?"

"My past."

Jodi sucked in her breath, held it, tried not to freak out. This was good. He was opening up to her. But was she strong enough to hear whatever it was he had to tell her about his wife without feeling insecure or less than?

Squeezing his hands, she looked deeply into his eyes. "It's okay, Jake. Whatever you have to tell me, it's going to be all right."

"How can you be so sure?"

Because I love you. She couldn't say it. Not yet. Not until he said it to her first, but she put all the love in her heart into her eyes and simply smiled at him, softly, tenderly, acceptingly.

"I believe in you." She held her breath, heard her heart beating in her ears at the crazed tempo of jungle drums.

Did she really want to see what was inside that room? Did she really want to discover he was not the man she'd thought he was? Or that he might harbor dark secrets that could destroy them both? Did she —

"Shh," he said as if he could hear the anxious thoughts pelting her. "It's going to be okay. This is just something I have to move beyond before I can tell you the other thing I want to tell you. Do you trust me?"

Mutely, she nodded, bobbed her head like she was completely hunky-dory with what-ever freaky-deaky, porno-S&M-sex-slave-psycho-shrine thing he might be hiding behind that door.

She fished around inside her, rounded up every ounce of courage she could find, and braced herself. "Show me."

He gave her a smile of pure gratitude, turned the knob, pushed open the door, reached around, and flipped on the light switch. Because she had convinced herself there was some sort of strange sexual pec-cadillo he'd been keeping secret in this room it took a second for her brain to fully register what she was seeing.

Big boxes of unopened baby furniture,

labeled with what was inside. Crib. Changing table. Dresser. And on the floor, still wrapped in plastic, were a car seat, stroller, and diaper bag.

Confused, she looked from Jake to the items and back again and her heart just broke. "You had a baby?"

Jake pressed his lips together, and his eyes misted. He blinked hard, gulped. "Yes . . ." he said. "No. Almost."

"You're shaking," she said, really alarmed now. "Sit down." She pressed on his shoulder and he slid down the door frame, his knees bending up in the doorway as his butt touched the floor. Jodi knelt beside him. "Jake? Are you all right?"

"I wasn't there for her." He dropped his head into his open palms. "Maura needed me and I didn't protect her."

She reached out to hug him, but he looked so encapsulated in his anguish that she was uncertain if that was the right thing to do. Her hands hovered, but she backed off, interlaced her fingers.

Jake raised his head, met her gaze. "She was . . ." He trailed off, ran a hand over his mouth.

She didn't prompt or interrupt. This was his story to tell. He could do it on his own timetable. She sat next to him, pressed her back against the open door, stared at the baby things, felt sympathy pangs deep in the pit of her stomach.

"Maura had gone to a convenience store a block from our apartment in Chicago at ten o'clock at night to buy a pregnancy test kit when the store was robbed," he recited in a robotic tone.

"Oh Jake, I had no idea."

"My agent was able to keep that part out of the media," he said. "Maura had just bought the kit and tucked it into her purse when the robber came through the door."

"I'm so sorry."

He rubbed red-rimmed eyes. "They found out during the autopsy that she was six weeks pregnant."

Her heart broke. She couldn't hold back any longer. She wrapped her arms around him, held on tight. He leaned against her. "What a blow," she said. "I can't imagine. You lost not only your wife, but your entire future that night."

He tucked his lips around his teeth, shook his head.

"Do you know why she was buying a pregnancy test kit at a convenience store that late at night?"

"Yeah." His voice broke and he pulled from her arms, leaned his head against the wall. For the longest time there was no sound in the room except for their breathing. "It was because of me. I called her after the game, like I did every day when I was on the road . . ."

He paused, closed his eyes, clearly struggling with something. "We argued."

Jodi said nothing. What was there to say? She could offer no lifeline. No absolution. This was his sorrow. His story to tell. And she would listen. It was all she could do for him.

"She said we needed to talk and she sounded so serious it scared me. I thought she was going to tell me she'd been having an affair or something." He gave a shaky laugh, pulled a palm down his face. "I was scared she was going to tell me she wanted a divorce."

"Jake," she whispered. "Was your marriage that precarious?"

"No. Not at all. But I loved her so much. My greatest fear was losing her."

The man had so much love in him. So much to give. Jealousy lay in Jodi's lap like yeast dough, rising higher, expanding, growing. How could she be jealous of a dead woman? She wasn't petty. She wasn't that person. She punched down the jealousy, smashed it flat. This wasn't about her.

"I cracked a few jokes because I didn't want to take her mood seriously." He hunched his shoulders, shot a glance over at her.

Another long minute passed.

"What did she say?" Jodi whispered, unable to bear the suspense.

"She said she wanted to start a family. Hell, Jodi, I panicked. I wasn't ready to have kids. My career was just taking off and that's all I could focus on. And when we got married, well, I thought we were on the same page about kids. I told her I didn't know if I wanted kids. Ever. The sound she made . . ." He shook his head, regret and sorrow rolling off him in waves. "If you could have heard her. It was as if I'd punched her in the face."

"What did she say?"

"In a voice so quiet it strangled me, Maura said, 'You really don't want kids?' "

He hauled in a stuttering breath like he was standing on a thin precipice with hurricane winds at his back. "Selfish idiot that I was, my mind was on my career, and all I could think about was how I wouldn't be able to give a kid the kind of attention he deserved and I told her no, I didn't think so."

"Oh Jake, how were you to know she was

pregnant?" Jodi kept rubbing his arm, trying to dissipate the tension cording his muscles into knots. "You couldn't know that. Please stop beating yourself up."

"When I found out that she'd gone to the store *specifically* to buy a pregnancy test, that if she hadn't needed a pregnancy test she wouldn't be in that damn store in the first place, I knew it was all my fault. She must have suspected she was pregnant and couldn't wait until morning to find out if that was the case. I was the reason she was in that convenience store. I'm to blame."

Jodi touched his hand.

He flinched.

Quickly, she moved her hand away, tried not to feel hurt.

"If I'd have told her I wanted kids . . . that I was as eager and excited to have them as she was, then she would have waited to take the test when I was with her. She probably would have told me that night that she was pregnant instead of keeping quiet. If I'd only manned up." He buried his head in his hands.

"It's not your fault, Jake," she soothed. "Would you still be beating yourself up if Maura had gone there to buy a box of cereal?"

"But she *didn't* go there to buy cereal. She

went there because she was having my baby —" He choked off, his shoulders moving in silent torment. "When we first got together she was like me. Not sure she even wanted kids. That's why it was such a curveball when she told me she was ready to start a family. It was like a switch had been flipped and the bright light blinded me because I'd been enjoying the dark."

"You've got to let go of the guilt."

"But here's the thing," he said. "Here's the worst part of all. After I got off the phone with Maura, I called a couple of my teammates and asked them about their kids. Their voices lit up and they told me it was the best thing they ever did and becoming dads had made them *better* ballplayers and I realized I *was* ready to be a father. To let Maura know I'd changed my mind, I got online and ordered all this —" He waved at the baby stuff. "And had it shipped to Jefferson in care of Maura's parents, because this is where I wanted our baby to be raised . . ."

Another long pause swelled the room.

"I'd no sooner gotten off the computer when the police called to tell me what had happened. In the chaos, I forgot all about ordering this stuff until it was delivered here the day of Maura's funeral. Talk about crap timing."

She ran her palm up and down his spine, it was the only thing she knew to do. No wonder he'd thrown the baby stuff in this room and closed the door, unable to face dealing with it.

He sagged heavily against her shoulder and she cradled him, kissed the crown of his head. "Jake," she whispered. "You can't change the past. Maura wouldn't want you to suffer like this."

"Easy to say, a damn sight harder to do. My wife died thinking I didn't want our child. That's the stumbling block I can't push past."

"I didn't know Maura," she said. "But I know you. I know how kind and loving you are. I saw you with Tobias. You would have been a great dad and I bet you anything Maura knew that too. I'm sure she believed that you would come around once the pregnancy was a reality. I'm certain she knew that you would love a child as much as you loved her. You have so much love to give, Jake, how could you not?"

He sat up, met her gaze, looked hopeful. "Do you really think so?"

"I *know* so. I suspect she didn't tell you she was pregnant because she wanted to be absolutely sure before she told you. I bet she wanted to set the scene so the timing was just right."

"I wish I could believe that." He stared down.

Jodi grabbed his chin, forced his jaw up, put flint in her eyes and granite in her voice. "Choose to believe it, Jake. Choose to believe she knew you inside and out. Choose to believe she knew you had a good heart. That you are a good man who would always do the right thing, no matter what."

He stared at her as if she'd given him a great treasure. "You think it could be that easy?"

"Picture her in your mind," she said. "Imagine Maura standing here."

"Now?"

"Right now. Do it."

He closed his eyes.

"Do you see her?"

"Yes."

"She's smiling at you," Jodi coached.

He nodded, and a corresponding smile spread across his own face. The heaviness in Jodi's stomach deepened, but she put a lock on jealousy. It had no place here. She wanted only love in her heart. For Jake. For Maura. For herself. Because she loved him even more now than she had before he'd told her of his secret guilt, and she wanted to help him find the peace he so richly deserved.

"Maura is telling you it's okay. That she loves you and that there is nothing for her to forgive. Imagine it. See her, hear her."

A single tear slid down his face. He opened his eyes, reached for Jodi's hand, squeezed it. "Thank you," he said. "Thank you."

"You'll never forget her. She'll always be a part of you."

He pulled Jodi into his arms, kissed her hard and long. "What did I do to deserve you?"

"You loved with all your heart."

"I'm making progress," he said. "I opened the door. I showed you what was inside the room, inside of me."

"Thank you for that." She stroked his cheek, looked into those dear dark eyes she'd come to love so much in such a short time.

CHAPTER 23

Jodi Carlyle's Wedding Crasher Rules:
For God's sake do not fall in love.

Jake took her to the bedroom, and made love to her.

How different this time was from their previous couplings. There was a depth and breadth to their lovemaking that hadn't been there before. Was it a new sureness in their relationship? Was the difference trust? Or was it something more? Jodi had changed. Jake had changed her. And in those alterations, she'd become more her true self.

Jodi dug her fingers into his back, felt the thickness of his skin. Breathed in his scent so warm and male. This was love. Not just the joining of their bodies, although that was magnificent. No, this was far more than that. Their souls were entwined. Their hearts united. Because of everything they'd suffered they were bringing to their union a softness that a lot of couples did not have. An empathy and understanding that stretched them as people. They could overcome whatever obstacles life threw at them because they were stronger together than apart.

She looked into his eyes as he moved inside her. Their gazes locked. Their bodies one. On this exalted plane time did not exist.

They came together, collapsed panting against the sheets. They held each other for a moment, suspended in peace, and pleasure.

She dozed for a moment, knowing she couldn't allow herself to fall into full slumber. She had to get back to Stardust. Breeanne was counting on her. But for a sweet, short section of time, Jodi was the happiest she'd ever been in her life.

Something startled Jodi awake. She sat up. Disoriented for an instant, she blinked into the darkness and spied the man sleeping beside her and her heart smiled.

"No," Jake mumbled.

"Are you awake?" Jodi sat up.

"No." His eyes were closed, his brow furrowed. "Don't go."

"I have to," she whispered, easing back the covers.

He shook his head back and forth. "It's too late."

"That's exactly why I have to leave."

"Shumble frazzle msshh."

"What?" She leaned over to peer closely into his face. The man was sound asleep. Should she wake him and tell him she was leaving? Or just slip out? Neither option seemed right. He needed his sleep, but she knew he would be unhappy if she just took off without saying good-bye.

"Maura, no," he begged in a somnolent voice. "Please don't go."

Jodi froze. He was asleep and dreaming.

Of Maura.

She swallowed against the pain fisting in the center of her chest. He was dreaming of his dead wife. He wasn't over Maura. No matter how much he claimed to be. Not by a long shot. Trying hard not to be hurt or jealous — the man couldn't help what he dreamed about — she eased from the bed, searched for her clothes.

Shades of Gwendolyn. She'd been here before. Naked. Vulnerable. Sneaking out after a mistake. Deja-dumb.

She found her panties and bra — not exactly like before — slipped into her dress, and carrying her shoes, tiptoed for the door.

"Jodi?"

She cringed. Closed her eyes. She hadn't made it. Forcing a smile, she turned to face him.

Jake was sitting up in bed, sleepy-eyed and yawning.

"Go back to sleep," she murmured, her heart melting at the sight of him. She loved him so much!

"I've been thinking," he said.

"In your sleep?"

"I guess so." His endearing smile sucked the air from her lungs, wrecked her. He stretched his arms over his head, his chest muscles flexing gloriously with his movements. "I woke up with the idea in my head."

"What's the idea?"

"I've decided to keep the house."

Every muscle in her body twitched simultaneously. "Why?"

"I'm going to need a place to stay when I come back to East Texas to visit." His smile was so hopeful. He had no idea he'd just stabbed her through the gut with it. He'd been dreaming of Maura and now he was backtracking on selling the house he'd shared with her. Not only that, but he was trying to convince her it was a good thing.

"You can stay at the B&B," she said, trying to ignore a strange tickling in the back of her throat. Was it thrill that he was dancing around their future as a couple, or mounting fear that he was holding on to the house because he wasn't really ready to let go of Maura . . . and his guilt?

"You know I love your family, but we'd never get any privacy there," he said lightly, but underneath she heard a darker tone. A tone that said, *I'm scared. This is moving too fast. I'm not sure I'm ready for you after all.*

"Um . . . okay." She bobbed her head idiotically, as if she didn't care whether he sold the house or not.

Tell him, whispered the steely part of her that had been brave enough to crash a celebrity wedding and turn a botched wedding reception into a charity event. *Tell him that by holding on to the house it makes you feel as if he's holding on to Maura.*

But she had no right to tell him what to do with his house. They weren't a couple. Not officially. He hadn't told her he loved her, nor had she been able to say it to him. Being the first one to say it made her too vulnerable.

Like you're not vulnerable now?

"I really do have to go," she said. "I have to be up before dawn and so do you."

"I don't like you driving back alone at one in the morning." He threw back the covers, got to his feet, pulled on his slacks, not bothering with underwear. "I'll follow you."

"No. That's silly. If you follow me you won't get back into bed until after two. I'll be fine."

He gave an alpha man growl, sternly shook his head.

"Jake, I drive at night all the time. I'm an independent woman. I have a cell phone and pepper spray. I'm not going to let you make me feel like I'm incapable of taking care of myself."

He stood there bare-footed and bare-chested, looking like the answer to a prayer she'd not even thought to pray. "That's not the point, Jodi. You don't know who or what lurks out there in the dark."

For a moment, his eyes looked haunted and she knew he was thinking about Maura, who'd gone out alone at night and never come home.

"This isn't Chicago." She sank her hands on her hip. "And I'm *not* your wife."

"No," he murmured in a disappointed tone. "You're not."

For a fraction of a second, her heart stopped beating as if her chest had caved in. "I gotta go," she said, without meeting his gaze.

She grabbed her purse and got out of there as fast as she could.

Jake waited all of two minutes before he followed Jodi. He'd be damned if he'd let her drive that stretch of empty highway between Jefferson and Stardust alone in the wee morning hours.

After he and Jodi had made love, he had drifted off into a vivid dream where Maura came to him.

"She loves you, Jake," Maura said. "You could build a good life with her, but there's something you must do first."

"What's that?" he asked.

"Let go. Of me. Of the baby we never had. Of your guilt."

"But I failed you so badly."

"You didn't, but I forgive you if that's what you need."

"Tell me how to do it," he begged her.

"Just love her, Jake. Love her like you loved me. With all your heart and soul. Love until your love for her crowds out everything bad that happened in the past. Love her beyond all limits and then love her some more."

Love.

The word echoed through his brain, the

sound resonating like a tuning fork, sending golden vibrations steeping every cell in his body.

Love.

"Jodi needs you and you need her. Don't grieve for me and the baby any longer," Maura said. "We're safe now and happy. We want you to be happy too."

Maura was growing fainter, her face disappearing into a swirling mist.

"No," he said. "No, don't go." There was so much more he wanted to ask her. "It's too late," he murmured. It was too late for him and Maura, but not for him and Jodi. "No, Maura, please don't go." Not yet.

"Let go," Maura whispered. "Love."

A sensation unlike anything he'd ever felt before rushed over him. Peace. Tranquillity. Acceptance. His muscles relaxed as a gentle heat warmed his body. His eyes opened.

And that's when he saw Jodi sneaking out of the bedroom.

Jodi. His love.

Driving the lonely road, but not alone. He was driving it with her whether she knew it or not.

When he found her taillights in the darkness, his anxiety settled. He stayed as far behind her as he could without losing sight of her. He didn't want her to know he was following her. She was a tough cookie. His Jodi.

He'd upset her, but he wasn't quite sure why. He had dumped a lot of information on her tonight about Maura and the baby, and no doubt, she needed time and space to process it.

That's what he told himself anyway. But part of him was damn scared that he'd done something to ruin the good thing they were working on. Like the doofus guy he was, he'd unwittingly lumbered onto her hot button — independence. That need of hers to be in control.

And it hurt when she'd poked him that sharp barb and barked out, "I'm not your wife."

No. Not yet. But he wanted her to be.

He might have mucked everything up telling her about Maura and the baby the way he had. Maybe she was afraid he still didn't want kids. Or maybe — crap, why hadn't he thought about this before he opened his big mouth? — she didn't want kids.

Getting way ahead of yourself, Coronado. It could be she's afraid you've gone and fallen in love with her and she doesn't feel the same way about you.

That thought hit him like a wild foul ball upside the head.

She kept telling you she wanted to keep things casual, but you had to keep pushing for more, didn't you?

As Jodi's car drove past the Stardust city limits sign, Jake did a U-turn and headed back to Jefferson.

On the drive back to Stardust, emotions smashed into Jodi — hurt, fear, sadness, alarm, anger. Yes, anger. Not at Jake, but at herself. She was angry with herself for letting this happen.

But she refused to wallow in pity. She was not going to feel sorry for herself. She'd made a mistake. She'd let herself love again after she'd sworn to keep things casual. This hurt so much more than Ryan, whose betrayal had caused humiliation and exposed the crumbling facade of their relationship.

But this . . .

This was a shattered heart, sheer and sharp, brittle and broken.

No matter how much he claimed to be over Maura, Jake was still in love with his dead wife.

"Dumb, dumb, dumb," she muttered. "You knew better and you let yourself fall for him anyway."

It's better to have loved and lost . . .

444

People had said that to her after Ryan. She'd thought it was stupid. How could it be better to love and be hurt than to never have lost and never been hurt?

But now?

Now she understood the truth of it. Understood because this was the first time she had really, truly loved a man with an open heart.

Until Jake, she had not known what true love was. Ryan had gone through all the right motions. Said and done the things that people in love were supposed to do, but he'd never meant them. And some part of her had known that because she'd never allowed herself to fully let go. She'd held back, and when he'd left her at the altar, part of her had secretly been relieved.

This was so different.

This was aching and bittersweet and wretched. Because it *was* better to have loved Jake and let him go than to never have had the honor of falling in love with him in the first place. Better to play second fiddle to his ill-fated bride, and become the instrument of his healing, than to never have known him.

Loving Jake was worth the price, worth the pain, even though she was not going to be able to stay with him. How could she when he could not love her as much as he loved his dead wife? She loved him enough to let him go. And from the things he'd taught her, from the opening of her heart, maybe one day she would find love again with a man who could love her without reservations.

In the meantime, she was the maid of honor and she was not going to ruin Bree-anne and Rowdy's day with her personal drama. Later, when the wedding was over, she'd break up with Jake.

And her heart? What was she going to do about that?

Jodi raised her chin against the cold February wind as she got out of her car at the B&B. To take a page from Scarlett O'Hara, she'd worry about that tomorrow.

Jake didn't sleep, his thoughts going around in circles, trying to figure out when and where things had jumped the track. He finally got out of bed at five a.m. and knowing Jodi would be awake, he texted her.

GOOD MORNING. HOW DID U SLEEP?

She didn't answer.

"Busy," he told himself, and tried not to overthink it. He took a shower, got dressed, ate a bowl of cereal — not Cheerios, he'd banned them from the house — and texted her again.

GWENDOLYN, U OK?

She didn't reply to that one either.

He loaded his tuxedo in the car, made sure he had Breeanne's wedding band to give to Rowdy. Then he tried calling Jodi, but it went to voice mail.

No response.

He tried not to freak out. Why wasn't she returning his calls or text messages? Maybe her phone was off. Reliable Jodi turning her phone off on Breeanne's wedding day? Hardly.

He got scared then. He'd left her at the city limits last night. What if something had happened to her between there and the B&B?

It was still way too early to head to Stardust, but he went anyway, determined to see Jodi before she got submerged in the details of the wedding. He parked outside her boxcar, next to her sedan. Knocked on the door of her boxcar.

She didn't answer.

Maybe she was in the shower.

He whipped his cell phone from his pocket

and called her again. It rang and rang and rang and finally went to voice mail once more. Perturbed, he hung up. What if something had happened to her? What if she'd fallen getting out of the shower and hit her head? What if she lay bleeding on the floor? What if . . .

Screw that.

Jake tried the door of her boxcar. It wasn't locked and the door swung inward. He stepped inside, fear raising the hairs on the back of his neck. "Jodi!"

No answer.

He lumbered through the boxcar. "Jodi!"

"What is it?"

He whirled to find her standing in the doorway, dressed in a white terry-cloth robe, hair wet, a blow dryer in her hand, looking peeved.

Relief spilled through him, drew his shoulders into a sag. She was all right. Thank God. It was all he could do not to sprint across the room and pull her into his arms. "Hi."

"What are you doing here?" Her voice was cold, brittle.

"You didn't call me back. Didn't answer my texts. I was worried."

"I'm off schedule. I don't have time for you right now. Breeanne comes first."

"I know. I just . . ." He whipped out a grin, hoping to coax her into a smile. He felt like he'd missed something important. As if he'd walked into a theater during the middle of a movie, and had no idea what was taking place on screen.

She didn't smile back.

He upped the wattage, but it didn't sway her. What had he done wrong? Had he texted and called too much? Was he coming across as too needy? Shit. Okay. She needed space. And she was right. The wedding was upon them. Why was he pressuring her? He was acting like a lovesick teenager.

"I just wanted to make sure you were okay," he mumbled.

"I'm fine."

"You sure? You seem —"

She scowled, but he could have sworn her bottom lip was trembling. Something *was* wrong and it wasn't just the stress of the wedding. "I'm not at your beck and call, Jake."

"I know. I know." He bobbed his head, wishing like hell he hadn't panicked and come charging over here. "You're okay."

"Fine." Her tone so clipped he could have used it to give himself a haircut.

Staying here wouldn't help things. This wasn't the time to press her for answers.

Space. He had to get out of here. Give her space.

"So we're good?" He rested his hand on the door frame above her head.

Her mouth tightened. "Jake, I've got a lot to do . . ."

"Right. Right."

She hadn't answered his question, hadn't reassured him. Hadn't said, *We're good.*

She'd just stood there looking at him.

"Well, I guess I'll see you at the wedding." He tried a smile, but neither one of them bought it.

"Yes," she said. "See you at the wedding." That was what she said, but what he heard was, *We're in trouble.*

Just before four p.m., Jodi stood in the church vestibule with the rest of the bridal party, waiting for the wedding procession to start. This was going to be the hardest part of the day. Walking down the aisle on Jake's arm.

The groomsmen, Jake, Talbot, Warwick, and Rowdy's younger brother Zach, were still seating a few remaining guests before bringing Rowdy's mother and Maggie to the front of the church. Dan was prowling about, hands stuffed in his pockets. Jodi walked over to touch her father's shoulder.

"Dad, it's going to be fine. Rowdy's a great guy and he and Breeanne love each other so much."

"I know, I know." Her father bobbed his head. "I just keep having flashbacks to you and last year —"

"That's not going to happen." She kissed his cheek. "Everything is going to be okay. Breeanne needs you."

"Right. Got it. Thanks, honey." He hugged her. "Did I ever tell you that adopting you was one of the four best things your mother and I ever did?"

"You have, Dad. Many times."

"I love you," he said. "So much."

"I know that too, Dad." Tears misted her eyes. She looked up. "Don't make me cry, it'll smear my mascara."

The procession music started. She turned back to join the group while her father went to get Breeanne.

And there was Jake, looking at her with hot eyes.

She dropped her gaze, clutched her bouquet of red, white, and pink roses to her chest. *God, please let me get through this without breaking down.*

She loved him so much, but she deserved a man who loved her for who she was, not as a replacement for the woman he'd lost.

He squeezed her arm, kept his face turned forward, but whispered from the side of his mouth, "You okay?"

"Focus," she said. "Today is all about Breeanne."

"Not in my world."

"Maybe not, but she is in mine."

"We need to talk, Jodi."

"Shh. This is not the time," she mumbled.

The smell of roses filled her nose, but the fragrance of her perfume overrode it. Lavender and vanilla. So much for tricky brains and self-fulfilling prophecies. It didn't mean a thing.

"What did I do wrong?"

Nothing. Absolutely nothing. That was the sorrow of it.

"Are you mad at me?"

She didn't answer. She wasn't mad. Not at him anyway. She was mad at herself for giving in when she feared from the beginning that this relationship was going to go sideways. She was mad at herself for being weak and giving in.

But she wasn't mad at herself for loving him. How could she not love him? He'd taught her so much about herself. He'd been there for her. Held her hand when she told him about her messed-up childhood. He'd made love to her, sweet and tender.

He'd danced with her. He'd crashed weddings and walls with her and he'd done it all perfectly.

For the love of another woman.

When she reached the altar she told herself she was not going to look at him — how many times had she told herself she wasn't going to do something in regard to him and done it anyway?

Don't meet his gaze. Don't do it. She glanced up, peeped over the bouquet in her hand, saw his handsome face looking utterly confused.

He had no idea why she was giving him the cold shoulder.

She knew that when she told him why she had to break up with him, he would deny that he loved Maura more than he loved her. But last night, when he showed her the room full of baby things, when he'd told her he wasn't going to sell the house after all, the writing on the wall couldn't have been more clear. If she stayed with him, every time he looked at her, she would think, *It's Maura he's seeing.*

Her father came down the aisle with Breeanne on his arm.

Breeanne. The baby sister Jodi had devoted her life to caring for, looking radiantly healthy and so much in love. Tears burned the backs of Jodi's eyelids. No crying. This was a happy day. Breeanne's day.

Rowdy stood beside Jake, staring gob-smacked as his bride came toward him. They were going to make such a great couple.

As her father gave Breeanne's hand in marriage to Rowdy, and stepped back to sit with his wife, Jodi was forced to look in Jake's direction.

He caught her eye, softly mouthed, *I love you.*

Her heart somersaulted and it took everything Jodi had in her not to whisper it back.

CHAPTER 24

Jodi Carlyle's Wedding Crasher Rules:
Always have an exit plan.

The wedding of pitching legend Rowdy Blanton to Breeanne Carlyle went off like a no-hitter. A rare and beautiful success. No glitches. No mistakes. No one left at the altar. No embarrassing toasts. No overly drunken relatives.

It was a perfect affair except for one thing. Jodi.

She wouldn't look at Jake. Would only stand by him when forced by family members or photographers. Would only talk to him in mumbled monosyllables.

The party was winding down. The bride and groom had already caught a limo to a hotel at the DFW airport where they would catch a flight to Padre Island the following morning. Most of the guests were saying their good-byes. The DJ was packing things up.

And Jodi was helping the waitstaff clear tables in her bridesmaid dress. Anything, it seemed, to avoid him.

His heart contracted painfully. Over the course of the past few weeks, his longing for her had flourished like a farm team in a town without any other sports outlet — stretching, growing, expanding. His need for her burned hotter than his desire to be the best ballplayer he could be, and that was pretty damn strong.

He smiled, moved toward her. "Hey beautiful," he said when he got close enough for her to hear him.

They stood amid the remnants of the wedding celebration — confetti strewn on the floor, helium balloons floating across the ceiling, empty champagne bottles on the tables.

"I don't need any help," she said.

He took her elbow, pulled her up close even though she resisted. "What have I done wrong?"

"Nothing."

"Then tell me what's going on."

The expression on Jodi's face — understanding but incredibly sad — mixed him up. Why was she sad? He felt like he was slipping down an icy mountain on glass skis. All he wanted was to be with her.

"I told you from the beginning, Jake, this was a casual thing. Don't make a big deal of it."

He tightened his grip on her arm. "No way, lady. I'm not letting you give me the brush-off without a real explanation. Last night meant something for both of us. I saw it in your eyes. I felt it when you came in my arms."

"I don't know what else to tell you." Jodi's voice was so gentle, but he could see the hurt in her eyes. He didn't know what it was, but clearly he'd done something to cause her pain and she wasn't going to tell him what it was. "Please don't make a thing of it."

"Jodi," he said, but then stopped. What was the right thing to say? How could he erase that I'm-about-to-break-up-with-you look off her face? He didn't want to stick his foot in it and make things worse.

"Let it go, Jake."

"I don't want to let it go and I think, deep down, neither do you, although I can't figure out why you're still so scared. I thought we'd gotten past this." He reached out to take her hands in his.

She resisted at first, but he had backed

her into a corner, and finally, she relented and let him take her hands. She was so warm, so soft, but inside she was made of steel. He admired that about her, but was that steeliness the very thing that would keep her from listening to him?

"Talk to me," he said. "Whatever is eating at you, we can work through it if you just talk to me."

She pulled her hands from his, held his stare calmly, fully in control. Of course. That's what she did best. Stay in control.

"There's nothing to say."

"I love you, dammit. Doesn't that mean anything? Haven't I shown you over and over again how I feel? Aren't we good together both in bed and out of it?"

"I'm sorry, Jake," she said in a robotic voice that ran a saber through his soul. "I simply don't feel the same way."

Jodi couldn't stop sobbing. In the last four days, she'd gone through three boxes of Kleenex, five sad movies, and a whole package of family-sized Oreos. She'd never in her life hurt like this.

Her family were at their wits' end. Every day, they dropped by the B&B to check on her. She'd lied and said she had the flu. Mom brought her chicken soup. Dad brought her a little space heater to put beside her bed so she'd stay warm. Kasha brought a humidifier and some homeopathic ointment to put on her chest. She was well loved. She knew it. She had a wealth of family and friends, a thriving business she loved. She didn't need anything more.

At least that's what she told herself. But it was a lie. She needed Jake. Ached for him.

All you have to do is call him up. Ask him to come back.

Sure, she could do that, but nothing would have changed. He would still love Maura, while Jodi pined for him to love her the way he'd loved his dead wife.

No. She couldn't back down. She had to go through the pain. There was no other way through this. Eventually, the pain would ebb. Eventually, she would be okay. Eventually, she would stop thinking about him constantly.

Eventually.

For now, eventually seemed like forever.

On the Thursday after the wedding, Ham came storming into her boxcar with no more than a cursory knock on the door. "Get out of bed," he demanded.

"I'm sick."

"No, you're not." He tugged on her covers. "Get up."

"Go away."

"Not until you get up." He jerked the covers off her.

"You're fired."

"Nice try. You gotta quit moping around here," Ham said.

"You're not taking my threat seriously."

"I've worked for you for ten years. I'm your right-hand man. I've known you longer than anyone else in your life. You're not going to fire me."

"I already did." Jodi reached for her tenth Oreo of the day.

"Give me that." Ham snatched the cookie from her hand and tossed it in the trash.

"Hey! I was eating that."

"Oreos are not the answer."

"What is?" she asked glumly and then burst into tears.

"You threw him out, so get over it."

"It's not that easy."

"Woman, you got stood up at the altar last year, and you suffered a federal investigation. You lived through the scandal with your head held high. If you can survive that, you can survive a measly broken heart."

"It's not the same thing."

Ham snorted, sank his hands on his hips. "I can't believe this is Jodi Carlyle I'm talking to. The Jodi Carlyle I know doesn't whine and snivel when the going gets tough. She gets busy."

"I'm not sniveling."

"Hmph."

"I'm not."

He gave her a dirty look.

"Okay, maybe I am sniveling a little bit."

Ham snorted. "A little?"

"Okay, a lot."

"Thatta girl. It's time to fight back."

"How do you mean?"

"Woman up. Get out of that bed and get back to work. It's good for what ails you." Ham grabbed hold of her hand and tugged her from the bed.

He was right.

She had to get back to work. Work was the one thing that had always saved her.

"I screwed up big time," Jake told Talbot. It was Sunday the week after the wedding and he'd circled back to the bar across the street from the stadium after he'd taken LeShaun home from spending the afternoon at the batting cages with the boy. "And I don't know how to fix it."

Talbot took a tug off his beer. "You screwed around on Jodi, huh? Been there. Sucks to get caught."

"No." Jake bristled. "I did not screw

around on her. I love Jodi. You don't treat someone you love that way."

Talbot shrugged. "Then how bad can it be?"

Jake rolled his eyes. "Why do I even bother talking to you?"

"Because no one else is willing to listen to your sob story."

"You're only listening because I bought you a beer."

"True that." Talbot nodded. "But I'm not your therapist. So what did you do to make her so mad at you?"

"She thinks I'm only in love with her because she looks like Maura."

"Is that the case?"

"No."

Talbot leveled him a don't-lie-to-me-dude look.

"Maybe in the beginning her resemblance to Maura was why I was initially attracted to her. I like redheads. Is it wrong to have a type?"

"When you've got a dead wife you were crazy in love with, and she looks like your new girlfriend, um . . . yeah."

"But Jodi is throwing the game before the second inning. Giving up without even seeing if we've got what it takes for a pennant race."

"No one wants sloppy seconds."

"You have such a charming way with words."

"It's a gift."

"Jodi is second to no one."

"Go tell her that, not me."

"I tried to tell her that at the wedding. She doesn't believe me."

"Guess you'll just have to show her."

"How?"

"I find groveling usually works."

"She's not taking my phone calls."

"Better to have loved and lost, my man." Talbot clamped a hand on his shoulder, dug his fingers into Jake's skin. "Now could you move? I'm trying to watch the game and you're blocking the screen. I've got a C-note on the Mavs."

Jake got up, closed out his tab. "Later."

"Hey," Talbot said. "You could always go for the grand gesture. Women love that shit."

"Which is?"

"How do I know? She's your woman. You figure it out." Talbot waved a dismissive hand and went back to watching TV.

On Monday morning, Jodi stepped out of Old Blue. Skeeter was at her heels. She carried the sheets she'd stripped off the bed and headed for the laundry cart. Her jaw flopped open at the sight of a familiar red Corvette pulling into the parking lot.

Momentary panic had her glancing longingly at the laundry cart, but no she wasn't going there. She wasn't scared of Jake. She was brave enough to stand here and listen to what he had to say.

Jake got out of the car looking as devastatingly handsome as ever.

He smiled.

Her knees melted. *Do not fling yourself at him,* she told herself, struggling to breathe. *At least not until he gets a little closer.*

The wind blew against her, the February cold whipping against her skin, but his smile warmed her up inside as surely as a fire in her potbelly stove.

"Hey," he said, stopping a few feet away from her.

Skeeter trotted over to him, wagging his tail joyfully, and Jake leaned down to scratch the dog's nose.

When he straightened, Jodi tightened her grip on the sheets to keep from flinging them on the ground and jumping into his arms.

His eyes were soft, welcoming. "You're wearing it," he said. "Our perfume."

The way he said "our" sent her heart slamming into the wall of her chest. He took a step toward her. She stayed rooted, scarcely daring to hope that they could fix what had torn them apart.

"I sold the house in Jefferson," he said.

"Did you?" she whispered.

"Got a good price too."

"That's great."

"I realized belatedly that when I told you the last night we spent together that I was thinking about hanging on to the house, you thought it meant that I was still hanging on to Maura."

"You're not?"

"No."

"Are you sure?"

"Yes."

"You called Maura's name in your sleep," she said. "That's why I freaked out. Even though you told me you were ready to let go of her, clearly your subconscious was not and when you woke up and suggested keeping the house . . ." She gulped. "Well, I thought . . ."

"You were wrong," he murmured. "Yes, I did dream of Maura, but in the dream, she gave me her blessings and told me to let go of her. It wasn't until then I realized I was still hanging on to my grief. I suggested keeping the house because I wanted to have a place near you, not because it reminded me of Maura. But I understand now how insensitive that was. You aren't second fiddle to anyone, Jodi. I hope you know that."

"I overreacted. I admit it. I was just afraid you could never love me the way I love you."

Jake looked amused. "I wouldn't say *over-reacted*. But when you dig in your heels about something, you can be pretty stubborn," he said with the utmost admiration, like her stubbornness was a diamond-studded quality. "And I was afraid to take the risk that you would pull the plug on us."

"It happened anyway."

"I hate that I hurt you." Regret sharp and colorful as the Great Barrier Reef swam in his eyes.

"I was blindsided."

He nodded, his eyes graveyard somber. "I hope you can find it in your heart to forgive me."

"Forgiveness isn't the issue. I've already forgiven you everything. I will always forgive you, Jake."

"I can't lose you. I'll do anything you want to prove to you that you're the one I love." He took something from his pocket, sank down on one knee.

Twin fists of panic and elation hit her. "What are you doing!"

"Jodi Carlyle, will you —"

But he didn't get any further than that because Skeeter thought he was playing and hit him in the back and Jake went somersaulting down the hill toward the stream and Jodi burst out laughing.

And everything just felt impossibly right.

She trotted over to where Jake was laid out on the ground by the stream staring up at her, the ring box still in his hand. He flicked it open with his thumb. Showing off a big, fat diamond inside.

"Marry me?" he asked.

She burst out laughing, and reached down a hand to help him up, but he pulled her down on top of him. She tumbled against that hard chest and looked into his amazing eyes.

"Say yes," he prompted, and wrapped his arms around her.

"Or what?" she teased.

He tightened his grip. "Or I'll never let you go. No wait. Scratch that. I'm *never* letting you go regardless."

"Umm, I think that might be kidnapping."

"Not if you're a willing participant."

"I see your point."

He laughed and kissed the tip of her nose. "Have I told you lately that I'm crazy for you, Jodi Carlyle?"

"Not lately, no."

"Well, I intend on telling you every single day of your life," he said, and sealed his promise with the most heartfelt of kisses.

"I love you, Jake," she whispered. Telling him to his face for the very first time. "I love you."

"Jodi," he whispered, and squeezed her hard. "I love you so damn much."

It might not have been the most poetic of declarations, nothing flowery or pretentious, but it came from his heart, from the very core of who he was.

"I would do anything for you," he said. "Forever and always. I hope you know that."

"Jake." His name was a pearl that dropped from her lips. "Jake."

He kissed her, cradled her head in his hands, held her captive with his gaze. "You are mine and I am yours."

"Jake."

"I will spend the rest of my days looking after you. I won't let anything happen to you."

"Jake." Her hands were in his hair, her eyes full of him. She wanted more. She felt her pupils widen as she drank him in. She could never ever get enough of this man. "You have made me whole."

"No. It's you who saved me. Challenged me. Tested me." He dropped fresh kisses on her face — her eyelids, her cheeks, her chin. "Loved me. Forgave me."

She smiled at him. A smile filled with hope.

He kissed her again, and she could feel the passion rising in them both. She clung to his shoulders, arched her hips against him.

"More," she murmured. "I want more of you. Take me inside. Take *me.*"

His laugh purred over her ears. "God, I love you. How did I go so long without you?"

"I could ask the same question."

The joy in his kiss took her to places she'd never been before. Together they scaled the highest peak a man and woman could go together. One updraft after another took them higher and higher as pleasure drew soft moans from them both, as their bodies gave and received the ultimate treasure of the flesh.

He showed her just how much she meant to him in the most elemental way possible, through a joining that transcended time.

She had started this venture to prove she could have a casual affair and walk away unscathed and he'd shown her that she simply could not. She was a woman built for love. And he was a man built to give it.

His mouth devoured her. He flowed into her and she flowed into him and neither could tell where one started and the other began. They were complete.

In her joy, Jodi's heart rose like a phoenix shooting for the sun, brilliant in her flaming ascent, alive — fully alive — for the first time in her thirty years.

Alive and certain that she was free. Free of the past. Free of her childhood. Free of her mistakes. Free of the insecurity that had made her feel out of control.

Free to love.

This man.

Above all others.

Until the end of her days and beyond. For this was a love that breached time. Her wish had come true. He was her soul mate. Now and forever. The hope chest prophecy had been right. One whiff of a scent and they were whole.

And in the blissful moment when their eyes met again, Jodi Carlyle was reborn.

EPILOGUE

Jodi Carlyle's Wedding Crasher Rules:
When it's your wedding, reserve a spot
for the crashers.

On *her* wedding day, Jodi called her maid of honor to her boxcar.

She gifted Kasha with the hope chest. "It's yours now."

Kasha shook her head. "I don't need a hope chest. I'm perfectly happy with my life. I don't need a soul mate to make me complete."

"Everyone needs a soul mate," Jodi replied staunchly. "Even you."

"I'll take the chest off your hands," Kasha said. "Because I know you're not going to have a place for it in your new condo in Dallas, but I'm not looking for a key."

"You don't have to." Jodi winked. "The key will find you."

Kasha shrugged like she didn't care, but

471

that was only because she never got her hopes up in case they got dashed. "It's time."

"Not just yet. I've got one last thing to do."

"What's that?"

A knock sounded on the door and Ham popped his head inside. "I brought the van around."

Jodi crooked a finger at him.

"What is it?"

"C'mere."

Ham shot Kasha a what's-this-about gaze. Her sister shrugged. The best friend she'd had since childhood came over. "Getting cold feet?"

"No," Jodi said. "Never. I've waited all my life for Jake. This is the happiest day of my life, and the only thing that makes it even better is that you are here to share it with me."

"Shucks Jo-Jo, don't sap out on me."

Jodi opened her desk drawer and took out a manila envelope and passed it to Ham.

He lifted the flap, took out the documents inside, read them. His gaze jerked back to Jodi's face. "You're making me a partner?"

"I should have done it a long time ago," she said. "Boxcars wouldn't exist without you."

"But it's your land that your grandmother left you. Your money that paid for the box-cars."

"And your hard work and belief in me that made the B&B reality." She smiled, feeling her lip quiver, getting emotional on this, the happiest day of her life to date.

"Jodi." Ham gulped, clearly overcome.

"You'll be carrying the heavy load of the business now since I'll be living in Dallas with Jake. It's only fair to make you my equal partner."

"Thanks," he said, his voice clotted with unspoken emotions. "I'll do you proud."

"I know you will," she said, and kissed his cheek. Turning over the keys to her business to him was much easier than she thought it was going to be. She and Jake would visit often and she'd still run the financial side of things, but Ham was now officially in charge of day-to-day operations, and she'd hired a staff to take over the cooking, cleaning, and handyman activities.

Ham hugged her tight.

The door creaked open and Suki stuck her head in. "We're burning daylight, people. Let's get this show on the road."

"She's right," Ham said, holding out his arm to escort Jodi toward the door. "Your future is waiting."

■ ■ ■ ■

Jake stood at the altar watching his bride walk down the aisle.

The wedding pavilion at the Grand Texan was standing room only. It seemed almost the entire town of Stardust — and quite a few from Jefferson, including Maura's parents had made the drive to see them married.

She was radiant in white. Her smile touched him to the seat of his soul.

He was such a lucky man to have a second chance at love — to have found a woman like Jodi. A smart, strong woman who would keep him on his toes. A down-to-earth woman who challenged him. A woman he couldn't wait to wake up to every single day of his life.

Her father released her to him. A mixture of happiness and sadness on Dan Carlyle's face. "Take good care of her, son."

"I will, sir." Jake nodded solemnly. He knew just how precious life was.

Dan stepped back.

Jake took Jodi's hand. Together they turned to the minister. And in front of family and friends, they sealed their love and promised each other a lifetime of happiness.